PRAISE FOR
Kill All the Judges

"*Kill All the Judges* is replete with Stephen Leacock–like humour. . . . I have yet to find a writer who can capture the wit, whimsy and whirlwind pandemonium of her Majesty's Criminal Courts the way Deverell does."   – *Globe and Mail*

"*Kill All the Judges* finds [Deverell] at the top of his game."
 – *Toronto Star*

"A master of the laugh-out-loud crime novel." – *Vancouver Sun*

"This is one of the funniest books I've read in years. . . . Intelligent, perfectly plotted, cynical and fast moving. Like a runaway train that seems to be headed in all directions at the same time. . . . Preposterous, dramatic and hilarious. Highly recommended."   – Waterloo Region *Record*

"There is plenty of humour that threads its way through this novel. . . . *Kill All the Judges* provides a delightful, witty and satisfying read."   – *BC BookWorld*

"Deverell is a writer capable of generating a belly laugh with the turn of a phrase. . . . But keep your wits about you. *Kill All the Judges* is a tale within a story; a road map with no signs. . . . It's a testament to Deverell's skill with words, wonderful characters and a plot worth the journey."
 – *Hamilton Spectator*

"Amusing and witty."   – *Quill & Quire*

"Complex, fascinating, and fun. . . . *Kill All the Judges* is a classic crime work, from an author heralded as one of Canada's best, and with good reason."   – *Shelf Life*

BOOKS BY WILLIAM DEVERELL

FICTION

Needles
High Crimes
Mecca
The Dance of Shiva
Platinum Blues
Mindfield
Kill All the Lawyers
Street Legal: The Betrayal
Trial of Passion
Slander
The Laughing Falcon
Mind Games
April Fool
Kill All the Judges

NON-FICTION

A Life on Trial

KILL ALL THE JUDGES

William Deverell

McCLELLAND & STEWART

Copyright © 2008 by William Deverell

Cloth edition published 2008

Mass-market paperback edition published 2009

All rights reserved. The use of any part of this publication reproduced,
transmitted in any form or by any means, electronic, mechanical,
photocopying, recording, or otherwise, or stored in a retrieval system,
without the prior written consent of the publisher – or, in case of
photocopying or other reprographic copying, a licence from the
Canadian Copyright Licensing Agency – is an infringement
of the copyright law.

Library and Archives Canada Cataloguing in Publication

Deverell, William, 1937-
Kill all the judges / William Deverell.

ISBN 978-0-7710-2720-8 (pbk.)

I. Title.

PS8557.E8775K48 2009   C813'.54   C2008-904228-X

We acknowledge the financial support of the Government of Canada
through the Book Publishing Industry Development Program and that
of the Government of Ontario through the Ontario Media
Development Corporation's Ontario Book Initiative. We further
acknowledge the support of the Canada Council for the Arts and the
Ontario Arts Council for our publishing program.

Printed and bound in the United States of America

McClelland & Stewart Ltd.
75 Sherbourne Street
Toronto, Ontario
M5A 2P9
www.mcclelland.com

I   2   3   4   5   13   12   11   10   09

To the memory of David Gibbons, QC,
my former partner in law, whose generosity, good humour, and
largeness of spirit touched all who knew him,
and whose courtroom artistry was surpassed by none.

Kill All the Judges

PART ONE

THE LIFE OF BRIAN

"Neither fish, flesh, nor good red herring."
— John Heywood, 1546

1

THE MADNESS OF GILBERT GILBERT

There was no dispute about the facts. A hundred-pound weakling with the redundant name of Gilbert F. Gilbert had stepped into a crowded Vancouver courtroom and aimed a small-calibre revolver at Chief Justice Wilbur Kroop. A police officer leaped from the witness stand, and as he tackled Gilbert the gun fired. The officer stopped the bullet with his heart.

All these facts were admitted by the defence at Gilbert Gilbert's murder trial in January 2007. It was conceded, too, that the accused – forty-five, single, friendless – was a senior court clerk. Thus he had easy access to the courtroom from Kroop's chambers, where he'd been hiding.

They called Kroop the Badger, not just because of his squat, broad body but because of his claws. The defence portrayed him as a notorious bully who had taunted and shamed Gilbert, who made a fool of him in open court and sent him off in tears, who drove him to the precipice of madness and made him jump.

The defence argued that in his delusional state the accused had convinced himself Kroop was a former Nazi death camp commandant whom Gilbert had been ordered by God to eliminate. "God's will be done!" he shouted at his jailers, at the many doctors who examined him.

His counsel was Brian Pomeroy, of the feisty criminal law firm of Pomeroy, Macarthur, Brovak, and Sage, and he was assisted by young Wentworth Chance, who did most of the

3

work, burying himself in the law, interviewing specialists in post-traumatic stress disorder and schizophrenia. In comparison, the Crown's witnesses in rebuttal were a mediocre lot.

With Chance doing the heavy lifting, Pomeroy played to the jury, raising objections and cross-examining with his typical dry, manic wit. A celebrated neurotic, he'd won celebrated trials, most notably the recent defence of the assassin (alleged) of the president of Bhashyistan. But his life was in turmoil – he was drinking hard, tupping his secretary, and his marriage was heading for meltdown. Unable to face Caroline's cold silences and searing looks, he had taken to sleeping in the office on weekday nights.

In overcoming these handicaps, it helped that Pomeroy had drawn a dispassionate prosecutor and a judge with whom he used to smoke dope. The jury seemed interested and sympathetic – all except the sneering foreman, Harrison, a retired major from the Patricia's Light Infantry, a former combat training instructor. He would look at Pomeroy with a disdainful curl of a smile, as if to say, You lawyers will defend anybody, won't you? Even a hypersensitive worm like Gilbert.

Neither judge nor prosecutor interfered when Pomeroy portrayed Kroop, who, at seventy-four, was on the eve of retirement as a sadistic mountebank. However, the chief justice was spared the ignominy of having to testify, and thus spared the whip of cross-examination.

Meanwhile, Gilbert had got himself together while in custody, was functioning again, restored to his old rabbitlike persona but with total amnesia for the events of the previous June. Physically, however, he was deteriorating, stressed, complaining of dizzy spells and heart palpitations.

Pomeroy wondered what it would be like to take a holiday from reality. Was psychosis truly a haven from unbearable oppression, as the psychiatrists testified? Might it even be fun? Like tripping out on LSD. He'd tried nervous breakdowns a couple of times, but they weren't fun. More like tripping out on fumes from paint cans.

The prosecutor's summing-up was a concise, no-nonsense plea in which she urged her case for conviction but conceded that Wilbur Kroop had stretched the bounds of civility toward his beleaguered clerk. Kroop, during all this, was in his chambers on the next floor up, pretending lack of interest but in a tight-lipped, vengeance-seeking fury.

On the eve of his final address, Pomeroy was relaxing over a couple of drinks at the office – he felt he had it in the bag – when he got a distressing call from the oldest of his three adopted kids, fifteen-year-old Gabriela ("We miss you, Daddy, please love Mom, please come home . . .") The agony, the sleepless night, would have felled many lesser men, but Pomeroy gutted it out in a ninety-minute jury speech, covering all bases, thanks to Wentworth Chance's forensic *aide-mémoir*. Trauma-induced psychosis. Delusional ideation. Confabulation. Almost too much to take in one gulp.

At one point, however, he began to cry, and because he'd been going on about the tyrannies perpetrated by Wilbur Kroop on his client, the jury mistakenly believed he was crying for Gilbert Gilbert.

The jury went out on January 11 and stayed out for five increasingly tense days. They came back twice seeking clarifications, strain on every face, cold determination on the foreman's. Pomeroy feared that the wuss-despising major was winning the war in that barren, locked room. That he would miss the start of *Regina v. Reuben (Ruby) Morgan and Twenty-one Others*, a marathon drug conspiracy trial set for January 17, was the lesser of his worries.

But one day before, the jury finally trooped in after dinner, weary but ready. The clerk rose: "Mr. Foreman, what is your verdict? Do you find the accused guilty or do you find the accused not guilty by reason of insanity?"

Major Harrison stood at attention and hissed, "Guilty, by God."

A stunned silence while the other jurors looked at one another in confusion, finally remonstrating. "Excuse me, Major, but . . ." "No, no, we agreed . . ."

The judge asked if there was a problem.

Major Harrison did a quick shake of his head, as if coming out of a fog. "No, sir, I'm sorry, sir. Not guilty."

"And are you unanimous?" asked the judge.

"Yes, sir." Through gritted teeth.

Not many in the crowded court were focusing on Gilbert Gilbert during this exchange, but when the major misfired with his faulty verdict, Gilbert sat back as if punched in the face. Pomeroy turned to see him blanching, struggling to his feet, gasping and clutching his chest, and finally keeling over. He died almost instantly.

The fates had allowed Wilbur Kroop to exact revenge, but little did anyone suspect that more judges were about to be targeted . . .

As Brian reread that ghastly paragraph, he felt a Pavlovian shock, the kind administered to a rat making a wrong turn in the maze. Ever since he'd installed Horace Widgeon's program on his hard drive – *Secrets of the Whodunit*, $59.98, Version OS X – he'd been getting these little jolts, not painful but persistent. The sensible part of him believed there was a short-circuit somewhere in his ugly, glowing purple eMac. In his fantasies, he imagined Widgeon was pressing a zap-Pomeroy button on a supercomputer in his cottage in the Cotswolds.

Yes, Brian had mocked the legendary creator of the Inspector Grodgins series, his mentor from afar. In the section titled "The Author as Soothsayer," Widgeon instructs: *Do not predict! I find myself forever in despair that so many beginners subscribe to the "little-did-he-know" school of composition. Let this historic and holy injunction be your guiding light: "Just the facts, ma'am."*

Was Brian dealing in facts? Or was he making them up? Did he have any idea what the facts were? One obvious fact was that he was having the mother of all nervous breakdowns. (His shrink suspected it had gone beyond breakdown; she had a complex handle for it: stress disorder, disorganized type with delusional ideation. Ideas such as: *I can make a living being a writer.* And its corollary. *I won't have to practise law any more.*)

His collapse had been kindled by the pressure of work, the Gilbert Gilbert homicide, then the endless hell of *Regina v. Reuben (Ruby) Morgan and Twenty-one Others* – a conspiracy involving one ton of cocaine, eight hundred hours of wiretap, twenty-two traffickers, thirteen quarrelsome lawyers, and Justice Darrel Naught, an insufferable fat fascist who wouldn't know a reasonable doubt if it perched on his nose. Each evening after court, Brian and his cronies shared their woes, and he would often arrive home late – if he came home at all – smelling of pot and booze. Defensive and snappish, moody and uncommunicative, he had driven Caroline to file for divorce. This time, the grounds weren't adultery but cruelty. And this time she meant it.

He'd moved to a West End apartment but abandoned it after finding his twenty-fifth-floor balcony suicidally risky. Now he was in an artist's garret, or its pathetic facsimile: a third-floor room in a third-rate hotel, the Ritz, in Chinatown on the cusp of skid road. No one knew he was hiding here, not even his partners. Not even his secretary. Delete. He didn't *have* a secretary. Roseanne quit last month.

So here he was, armed with Merriam-Webster and Roget and Fowler and Widgeon and a wheezing computer and a full-monty breakdown, pouring another tequila, lighting another cigarette, staring gloomily out a dust-clouded window overlooking Main and Keefer, where the shops were closing for the evening and the grifters and hookers were taking over the streets. He thought of slipping out to one of the takeout joints, the Beautiful Sunrise Restaurant, the

Good Cheer Noodle House. Or maybe the Lucky Penny Pizza, for a change. These places depressed him. Everything depressed him. Especially his day job, the defence of Morgan and Twenty-one Others.

He was sick of law, sick of the whole system; he had broken under its pressure. Dr. Epstein had put him on tricyclics and told him to find some diversion, some favourite craft. Thus was born *Kill All the Judges*. Chapter One, "The Madness of Gilbert Gilbert," introducing said Gilbert Gilbert as tragic farceur and starring the author, the celebrated neurotic Brian Pomeroy, dazzling readers with his typical dry, manic wit.

He'll show Caroline. Such a literary snob, the academically hubristic Professor Pomeroy and her highfalutin graduate courses. Lit 403: Thackeray, Trollope, and Brontë: The English Novel in the Age of Vanity. And now *she* was published, having somehow persuaded a small press to put out her collected stories. He'd seen himself in some of them, the fucked-up boyfriend or husband. How dare she win a Best First Fiction Award for that?

He fully expects *Judges* to sell more than her paltry two thousand copies of *Sour Memories*. How might he pitch it to publishers? A memoir dressed up as fiction? Fiction disguised as memoir? Creative true crime? Creative untrue crime? A touch of Conrad? *I am able to write of these events only as I recollect them, and memory ever dims with age.* Truth, fiction, outright lies, who cares any more? Creative non-fiction, that's the general rubric, and that's what he's into, the hottest trend in literature; it gets you into the book pages, the literary blogs, *The Oprah Winfrey Show*. Eat your heart out, Caroline.

Yes, *Judges* will represent the cutting edge of creative non-fiction, stropped to razor sharpness. In the meantime, let's just call this lumpy stew of facts and fibs a mystery . . .

But was the Gilbert case merely an arrogant sidebar? The great Pomeroy! Poster boy of the Bhashyistan Democratic

Revolutionary Front, victorious defender of assassins and addled court clerks. He could hear Widgeon grumbling: Where is the meat of this story, the main dish? Does not the title promise a serving of dead judges?

Please forgive the delay in the kitchen . . .

2

NAUGHTY JUDGE

Brian Pomeroy had gone on an Easter weekend bender and only learned on returning to the Ruby Morgan trial in a bleary-eyed fog that on Good Friday a veteran family court judge had vanished after wandering from her cottage at Honeymoon Bay. She was well advanced in years, and her disappearance remained a baffling puzzle for family and friends.

Two months later, just as the bogged-down Morgan case was extended for another ninety days, there occurred a curious death at sea. A retired provincial court judge was spotted waving and shouting in the wake of the flagship of the B.C. Ferries fleet. He was swept away in the turbulent waters of Active Pass before a rescue team got to him, and he could not be resuscitated. Arguably, his eagerness to be saved ruled out a suicide attempt. But no one saw him go overboard — except, possibly, whoever might have hurled him over the railing. Father Time, he was called, with his 85 per cent conviction rate, a scourge of the criminal community and, it follows, their representatives.

An unease began to be felt among the judiciary, who shared nervous jokes about seeking danger pay for their job — inherently risky because the courts are crucibles of bitterness; every trial has its loser, some of whom are sociopathic or demented, and every loser has a lawyer, competent or otherwise, who shifts blame to those who sit in judgment.

Finally, on August 17, after the last objection was made and denied and the last plea for leniency ignored, the Morgan trial finally dragged to the finish line. Judge Naught had survived seven months of putting up with the defence counsels' whining, their insults, their spurious objections. He paid them back by sentencing each of their clients to twenty years. Except the ringleader, Ruby Morgan, who got life.

Though exhausted, Naught was in a mood to celebrate and began by sharing whiskies with the prosecution team. That was late in the afternoon, in chambers. Accounts are hazy as to where he went next. Not to the El Beau Room or any other watering hole favoured by bar and bench. Not home, to his dreary bachelor apartment.

A bland and forgettable face, a middle-aged paunch in a suit, Darrel Naught likely would have gone unnoticed in the city's better dining salons. Proof that he'd eaten was subsequently found in the remnants of lamb tenderloin in his stomach contents.

He was last seen alive at a quarter to midnight, at Fishermen's Wharf on the False Creek docks, heading for a boathouse owned by Minette Lefleur, whose cards advertised "personal, discreet escort and massage service" and who catered to the top tier, including several notables. One of her cards was found in Naught's wallet.

As Naught gained the boathouse ramp, Joe Johal – Honest Joe, as he's known in his commercials – was just leaving, shrugging into his coat in a light rain. They almost collided on the gangplank, a moment made more awkward because they recognized each other. Johal's Chevrolet-Pontiac dealership had lost a breach of contract case before Naught several years ago.

"Evening, Judge," said Johal, and he carried on briskly to the parking lot. His last view of Naught was of him standing uncertainly on the ramp. Or so Johal said at the inquest (to his credit, he'd come forward as a witness). Minette Lefleur testified that Naught failed to show for his midnight massage. She knew nothing further.

Judge Naught's body was found the day after his disappearance, floating in the scum of False Creek. Because there were no external injuries, the coroner's jury couldn't decide among accident, suicide, and foul play. There was scuttlebutt, not taken seriously, that the perpetrator was to be found among the many defence lawyers who'd been overheard calling down curses on his head.

The police couldn't connect anyone to his death. No one disliked him enough to kill him, nor were many going to miss him. In fact, however, he had not met his death by fair means but foul – committed, naturally, by the least likely . . .

Brian glared through a haze of cigarette smoke at that last ugly paragraph, its offensive foretelling, its runaway negatives, its blatant pandering to the reader. *Do not predict! Do not give the ending away!*

He was in a foul mood, felt he'd been sucked into the blackest hole of the galaxy. Two and a half pages had he written in the five weeks since he'd crawled from divorce court like a whipped dog. On September 4, that day of infamy, Caroline had won custody of the three kids, sole rights to the family home and to practically everything he ever owned, including his late mother's stemware, his Honda 350cc bike, and the bedsheets between which he and his wife of twenty years had loved and fought. Brian had the clothes on his back and this old Mac computer.

And here was the rub: Brian still . . . loved her. That was the tricky part, he loved her. Yes, he'd been unfaithful, somehow he'd never understood how to fight that; it was like . . . well, nicotine. Caroline had retaliated with her own lovers, insipid academics. Despite everything, he loved her, despite the competitiveness, the literary swordplay, the oh-so-clever duels over words. (Or maybe *because* of those things, he wasn't sure any more.)

The judge who presided over this carnival of marital injustice was Rafael Whynet-Moir, a rookie, newly appointed to the B.C. Supreme Court. He will also die – assuming Brian can think of a felicitous way of death, nicely worked but not too complex, fitting for one who had treated the author with such contempt. (*I'm sorry, Mr. Pomeroy, but this court isn't swayed to pity a defendant so bereft of the simple social skills required for the relationship of marriage.*) Poison à la Borgia? Too effete, too Dame Agatha. A gremlinized paraglider plummeting toward a hissing, spitting volcano into a boiling, sulphurous crater? Better.

These disasters inspired much black humour in barristers' hangouts like the El Beau Room and the law courts lounge. Judges became leery of going out in public. Security was tightened. Yet most thought the toll – two dead jurists, one unaccounted for, and one close call – was an unusual coincidence.

That consensus held until the second weekend of October, when Mr. Justice Rafael Whynet-Moir opened his waterfront manse at 2 Lighthouse Lane in West Vancouver to a fundraiser for the Literary Trust, which aids writers fallen on hard times. He had invited for dinner a dozen rich friends who paid handsomely for the pleasure of rubbing elbows with three published authors most of them had never read.

The evening seemed on its way to success. Whynet-Moir filled glasses with oleaginous charm. His partner, the capricious Florenza LeGrand, excessively wealthy heir to a shipping line empire, was at her effervescent best. At thirty-three, she was twenty years younger than Whynet-Moir, but he'd won her with his smooth good looks and false air of cultivation.

No one suspected that this posturing judge, this self-proclaimed connoisseur of the arts, this pander to performers, potters, and poets, would soon be crisping in hell . . .

—

Do not indulge in personal agendas, cries Horace Widgeon, Chapter Seven, "Creating the Credible Villain." *Avoid the temptation to put the black hat on your obnoxious boss or the civil servant who sniffily told you to come back after lunch. Otherwise, you may end up modelling your villain on a very dreary bloke. Likewise, subjecting those you abhor to cruel deaths may provide a fleeting thrill — but it's a self-indulgent, masturbatory thrill that's not shared with the reader.*

Presumably, Widgeon considered masturbation shameful. His amanuensis, the constantly complaining Inspector Grodgins, had a favourite adjective for the dreary blokes he had to put up with: "wanking bureaucrat" and "wanking judge" and "wanking bloody chief constable."

Obviously, Brian was in too much hurry to settle accounts with Rafael Whynet-Moir. But that might be the only way he could stop hearing his voice, which regularly percolated through the rumbling, the traffic in his mind. *This court is emphatically of the view that the children need to be with their mother, particularly since the respondent hardly seems able to care for himself.* All the time with an appraising eye on Caroline in the front row. While she looked right back at him, interested.

As a sidenote, Whynet-Moir's dinner was but one of several such literary benefits staged that night at fine residences in Vancouver. The prize-winning author of *Sour Memories* attended one that was far less dramatic. (*Too bad you weren't assigned to your admirer's house, Caroline, you'd have had raw material for a story in which something actually happens.*)

Brian had gone as far as he could to appease Widgeon: He'd made this cloying judge more attractive than he actually was. He lit another Craven A and knocked back a slug of tequila to sharpen the wit.

Of the three writers whom Whynet-Moir invited, the most exotic was Cudworth Brown, a roistering poet who was a surprise nominee for the Governor General's Award for Poetry for his second published collection, *Karmageddon*. A risky choice for any banquet table, this muscular ex-ironworker had a reputation for barroom brawls that was evidenced by a handsomely bent nose.

He was also a man of appetite who downed three martinis and a bottle of Bordeaux over hors d'oeuvres and dinner, and several cognacs afterwards.

By midnight, all guests had left but Cudworth Brown, who'd either imposed himself on the hosts, or, as the police surmised, hid somewhere in the house. A few hours later, neighbours on Lighthouse Lane were awakened by a metallic crash. They converged in a yard where a cypress tree had brought to a halt Judge Whynet-Moir's Aston Martin. Its sole occupant was Cudworth Brown, passed out behind the air bag.

West Vancouver Police were quickly on the scene but couldn't arouse anyone in the house. On the deck they spotted a metal patio chair, tipped over. They looked below the wraparound cedar deck and saw, thirty feet down, a nightrobe swirling in the waves and Whynet-Moir's broken body being gnawed by crabs in the tidal wash.

Cudworth Brown was arrested and charged with murder.

After stuffing the reader with appetizers, now comes the meat of the story – the prosecution of Cudworth Brown. But again his guru feels offended.

Set up as quickly as you can. Get your body to the morgue, create a taste of mystery or intrigue – and then you can afford the luxury of relaxing with your protagonist. Develop him or her. Humanize your hero with a charming quirk or pastime. And don't forget to describe him! (But be warned: it's no simple task for the rakish, square-chinned narrator to describe himself without sounding vain.)

Ah, the hero. Here is where Brian screwed up last time. A dozen years ago, during a sabbatical from practice, he had written his first and only Lance Valentine mystery – with

Caroline taunting him through the whole process. It never found a publisher but got encouraging responses. "Try again – this time with a credible protagonist." "Most of it works except your main character. He's a dud." Lance Valentine, private eye, was a snore; the dashing name failed to deliver.

But this Pomeroy character seems even less attractive, an overwrought lawyer whose life has gone to shit. Who buggered up his marriage of twenty years. Who has to seek permission to see his children. Who has been fucking up his practice. Who hates himself.

Maybe he should rework his creative non-fiction concept, revise it with a protagonist who won't disgust the book-buying public, recreate Lance Valentine, jazz him up, give him a vice or two. Look at the mileage Widgeon has got from his grumbling, rumpled, Meerschaum-pipe-smoking Inspector Grodgins. A grandfather, for Christ's sake. Drives a beat-up Ford Escort, for Christ's sake.

Brian has known only one hero. A grizzled, grass-chewing farmer who raises goats on a snoozy island in the Salish Sea.

3

THE ORANGE SUPERSKUNK OF
HAMISH MCCOY

Bundled against the wind-whipped rain, slogging up a rutted road, briefcase in hand, Arthur Beauchamp recited loudly, con brio, to no ears but his own. "'That time of year thou mayst in me behold, when yellow leaves, or none, or few, do hang upon those boughs which shake against the cold.'" He stalled, struggled with the next line. Something, something . . . then, "Where late the sweet birds sang." A sonnet half-remembered but fitting for this bleak mid-December Monday.

As he climbed, the rain became a slushy snow. Mists obscured the valleys. Usually he could see his farm, Blunder Bay, from here where he'd begun this trek with his grandson. Nick lasted half a mile, then announced, "This is crazy," and jumped into the first vehicle to stop. Arthur refused several more rides, defying the elements, keeping his vow, four miles a day.

He was in fine shape for sixty-nine, with all his healthy walks and farm chores. No recent messages from the heart. This tall, beak-nosed barrister was still an imposing figure, unbowed by the years, growing his annual winter beard – white with handsome streaks of brown.

He was content to be away from the house today, since it would be hosting the usual company of earthy feminists and aging hippies who made up Margaret's campaign committee. This was her latest adventure: politics, that despicable art.

Arthur had fled the city eight years ago, seeking rural peace on Garibaldi Island, then had astonished himself by falling in love with Margaret Blake, neighbour, organic farmer, former island trustee, inveterate letter writer to the weekly *Island Bleat*. He hadn't foreseen the consequences of marrying a relentless activist. Two years ago, she'd spent eighty days on a platform fifty feet up an old-growth fir, defying clearcutters and developers. Now, famed for her crusade to save Gwendolyn Valley, she was threatening to run for Parliament, refuge of the scheming, the slippery, the sly.

Puffing, he advanced toward the crown of Breadloaf Hill, his goal finally in sight, the community hall, which served as a courthouse on the occasional visits by the circuit judge. He hoped they had a warm fire going.

An RCMP van was parked at the back of the hall, and several smokers were on the steps in front of the wide doors, among them Cudworth Brown, whom Arthur was eager to avoid. He did so by steering a course for Robert Stonewell, locally known as Stoney, the self-proclaimed best mechanic on the island. It seemed he was always up on some misdemeanour, usually relating to the road worthiness of his vehicles.

"I thought this was a democracy, eh," Stoney said.

"What is it this time?"

"They want to take away my beauties."

Arthur presumed he meant the broken-down vehicles that cluttered his one and a half acres on Centre Road. The bylaw enforcement officer must have ticketed him.

"I'm a collector. Some people collect stamps. I collect cars. It's my hobby, man."

"I don't think that will wash, Stoney."

"Don't give him no advice." This was Ida Shewfelt, who'd circulated a petition to get rid of the rusting, property-devaluing eyesores.

Stoney glared at her. "Madam, I cannibalize them cars for spare parts. I'm a mechanic, they're trying to take away my home business . . ."

An imbroglio was brewing; Arthur should not have tarried here. And now Cud Brown was advancing with his smelly cigar. "Arthur, padrone, give me half a second."

Arthur pretended he hadn't heard, ducked behind the RCMP van, mounted the stairs. He had nothing to say to Cud, he didn't want to deal with the infamous fellow, with his bloated sense of self-regard. The island's resident poet had competent counsel: Brian Pomeroy, who had done well to get him out on bail.

He escaped into the hall, an old frame building that impersonated a courthouse poorly – even Her Majesty hung lopsided, partly obscured by a fifteen-foot fir crowned with an angel and laden with lights and glitter. Christmas banners and balloons hung from the ceiling. To the side, on tables, were unsold leftovers from a weekend craft fair.

About forty Garibaldians were here, a few standing but most sitting in folding chairs. A few reporters from the city were present too, on a bench behind a press table, feeling crowded by Garibaldi Island's resident news hawk, Nelson Forbish, editor of the *Bleat*, weighing in at three hundred pounds.

The offensively sweet smell in the room recalled to Arthur the time a skunk moved into his farmhouse's crawl space. It was likely the superskunk from Hamish McCoy's cannabis crop, in burlap sacks piled against the back wall: two hundred kilograms of a variety listed in Exhibit 5, the *Grow-Your-Own Seed Catalogue*, as "Orange Superskunk (Indica)." Standing guard was Constable Ernst Pound, not one of the brighter lights of the federal force, whose vacant look hinted he'd been in close contact with these exhibits for too long. He'd raided McCoy at harvest time, catching him bagging up his resin-laden pot in an underground grow room.

Arthur paused by the sacks, puzzled because he felt heat coming from them. They'd been stored in the rain, in the compound behind the RCMP detachment office, so it's likely the superskunk had started to compost, a process now aided by the nearby wood-fired barrel stove. Among those who'd jock-eyed their chairs close to the stove was gnomelike Hamish McCoy, bright eyes and stubby nose haloed by full white hair and beard. He was Arthur's age, a mischievous rascal but a talented sculptor whose case had attracted the off-island press.

He was up for sentencing today. That is why Arthur was here, even though he'd sworn to Jupiter, Juno, and Apollo he would never return to a courtroom. McCoy had leaned on him hard. He would have no other counsel, he mistrusted other lawyers, and if Arthur wasn't available, he would defend himself. Arthur caved in. His fee was to be *The Fall of Icarus*, a twelve-foot-high fusion of wings and tortured body of which Arthur had spoken admiringly. McCoy has promised to deliver it on a flatbed. Arthur had no idea what to do with it.

McCoy's pieces were large and expensive, and sold only sporadically. For the last two years the art market had been depressed. Many locals knew how he was augmenting his income, but there was an island tradition of *omertà*; it was considered dishonourable to rat on a neighbour.

Plump and amiable Mary something, a Sinhalese name Arthur couldn't begin to pronounce, was here representing the state. Last month she'd listened to his proposal, then said, incredibly, with barely a shrug, "Sure, let's do it." McCoy pleaded guilty to a reduced charge of simple possession, and she dropped the trafficking charge.

Arthur didn't believe she'd been afraid of going up against, as she put it, "the legendary Beauchamp." Maybe she was a pothead. Maybe she had an eye for art. Arthur had shown her a catalogue of McCoy's tall bronze figures, inspired by ancient legends, captured in exaggerated motion.

"Is that all the heat that stove's capable of putting out?" The querulous tone of Provincial Court Judge Tim Wilkie, seated behind a wooden table. A former small-town practi-tioner, he did the island circuit, showing up here every other month with a court reporter and a clerk.

Everyone was looking at island trustee Kurt Zoller, uncomfortable in suit and tie under a life jacket – he always wore one, to be ready, he insisted, for any emergency. This one was a bright fluorescent yellow. He finally rose. "Your Worship, the community hall committee never got round to insulate the roof after the snow collapsed it last year."

"And who chairs this committee?"

A hesitation. "Me."

Wilkie put on his coat. "Call the next case."

Arthur took a seat beside his grandson. He wanted to ask him if coming to court was as cool as he'd expected it would be, but Nick had headphones on and couldn't be reached. Fourteen years old. A scrawny, unfathomable kid, given to long silences, and phrases such as "Yeah, I guess so" and "Sure, whatever." The iPod generation, they'd lost the ability to communicate with humans.

Nick's parents were amicably divorced. Deborah, only child of Arthur's first marriage, was a school principal in Australia. The boy lived with her but was taking school holidays with his dad in Vancouver. When Nicholas Senior asked to deposit his son at Blunder Bay for a couple of weeks "to give him a healthy rural experience," Arthur had pretended to be overjoyed.

Mary Something called Kurt Zoller's name. "This is under the Water Taxi regs, Your Honour. Charge of failing to produce a safety gear certificate."

Arthur sensed something rancid behind him, like last night's beer. "I don't get it, Arthur." Cud Brown, at his left ear. "Of the two A-list creators on this island, one is busted for weed and gets the counsel of his choice. The other is wrongfully charged with murdering a fucking judge and gets Brian fucking Pomeroy . . ."

Arthur hadn't been answering Cud's calls. Now he was being stalked by him.

"What is it, man? I hope it's not because I spent two weeks up a tree with your lady."

Arthur turned, annoyed. "Of course not." He felt a flush of embarrassment at this lie. "We'll talk after court."

He wasn't going to take any more of this nonsense. Arthur had done his last murder trial. The previous year, coerced by the firm he'd supposedly retired from, he'd defended a wealthy financier, an adulterer who shot his wife on a hunting trip and pleaded accident. Arthur had to count it a victory when the jury compromised on manslaughter, but in his heart he believed his client deserved worse than seven years' jail time.

Arthur felt sick after that case. He was going to retire from unretiring. Since quitting practice eight years ago he'd been dragged back to the arena half a dozen times, always swearing this would be the last time.

Nick removed his headphones long enough to hear Zoller droning on in his own defence. The boy's expression said, I knew this was going to be bad, but not this bad. Back went the headphones. Arthur had insisted he come, to observe the consequences of illegal behaviour.

Having given up trying to follow Zoller's convoluted logic, Judge Wilkie sat impatiently to the end, then fined him three hundred dollars – the man responsible for the cold drafts was getting no breaks in this courtroom.

"I see Mr. Beauchamp is in the audience," the judge said.

"Oh, I didn't notice him hiding back there." Mary Something smiled at Arthur, who motioned his client to join him at the folding card table set out for defendants and their counsel.

"I note here," said the judge, "how your client told the probation officer he was growing this marijuana for his own use, four hundred and fifty pounds of it."

"I was gonna freeze it, Your Honour. Enough to last me a lifetime." McCoy got this out before Arthur could hush him, but no harm done. Wilkie was chuckling, maybe at the Newfoundland accent. Loif-toime.

"Mr. McCoy, you could grow as old as Methuselah and never smoke all that weed."

"Aye, but I was going to give it a mighty try, Your Honour."

Everyone was laughing, including the judge. "Stinks to high heaven, I guess that's why they call it skunkweed. Let me see some of it, while I hear counsel make their submissions."

Constable Pound, still in his own peculiar space, didn't budge. When Wilkie repeated himself, the officer snapped awake and began working at the knotted twine around the sacks. It was unclear why he'd hauled all that pot in here for a sentencing, unless out of vanity over the biggest bust of his career.

The hall's lights flickered three times then died.

"Now what?" Wilkie said.

Someone at the back explained. "When the lights sputter like that, it's usually a leaner falling on the line." A tree, he meant.

The windowless hall offered little ambient light. Flashlights came out. Emergency oil lamps were found, candles set on tables, a drill known to most who frequented the community hall in the windy winter.

Arthur carried on stoutly during all this, extolling his client's talent and virtues, urging that he be discharged after a period of community service. "Do not condemn this senior citizen, this celebrated artist, to live his sunset days with a criminal record." Reporters scribbled away by candlelight.

There came a ripping sound from the back. Frustrated by the knots, Pound had cut one sack open. Several flashlight beams converged on the great dollops of sticky, melting cannabis spilling from it. Pound found a discarded newspaper, deposited some of the gunk onto it, and showed it to Judge Wilkie under a flashlight beam. Wilkie squinted at it, making a disgusted face.

McCoy looked like a fierce, hairy elf in the glow from a stubby candle. He tugged at Arthur, whispered, "What's this blather about community service? I've a mind to do time instead."

"Ridiculous. You don't want a criminal record."

"I don't owe this community nothing. They let me down, b'y. They turned me in."

Wilkie turned to the prosecutor: "What do you think of Mr. Beauchamp's idea of community service?"

"I won't oppose." A glowing, candlelit smile for Arthur. Such an excellent prosecutor.

"So we just have to decide on some task . . . Who's the local government on this island?"

Once again Kurt Zoller rose. "I have the privilege of being our elected trustee."

"Okay, I want you to get together with other leading members of this community and recommend an appropriate project for Mr. McCoy to pay his debt to society."

"I'll speak to my advisers, Your Worship."

The matter was adjourned. McCoy nattered as he and Arthur walked toward the door. "That hypocritical shit. 'I have the privilege of being trustee.' He's the rat, b'y, count on it."

He suspected Zoller of squealing. The two of them were among a dozen property owners clustered around Potters Pond, all sharing the same power line. In the morning, when McCoy switched on his banks of grow lights, their kitchen lights would dim and their toasters lose their glow. Of the neighbours, only Zoller, an auxiliary coast guard, fit the usual profile of a snitch. Few other residents were particularly bothered: after all, marijuana was the number-two industry on Garibaldi after tourism but ahead of sheep and chickens and arts and crafts.

Arthur hoped to hustle home for lunch but wanted to dodge Cud Brown – who was no longer in the hall, maybe lurking outside. He would let McCoy leave first and then peek outside.

Nick was still looking as if he'd rather be somewhere else, on-line. He was at his laptop constantly, playing games or downloading stolen songs or looking at porno or whatever they do. Arthur didn't know what fourteen-year-olds did. If they were like Nick, their reading consisted solely of computer printouts and arcane texts with phrases such as "eighteen-bit recapture protocol." To give him credit, he seemed adept at computer arts, was rebuilding Margaret's broken-down machine, enhancing it.

"Bob Stonewell," Mary called out. "Unsightly Premises Bylaw."

Word was passed outside, and in a moment Stoney was peering in, holding the door open for McCoy, ushering in a cold wind that blew out some candles.

"Shut that damn door!" someone yelled.

Arthur could see his stalker out there, so he stayed inside. McCoy slammed the door behind him as he left.

Ill-adjusted to the dimness, Stoney stumbled into the cannabis sacks. "Yow, this stuff is really working." Constable Pound tried to pull him away, but Stoney resisted. "Hey, man, this hemp is heating up."

"What's the problem over there?" Judge Wilkie was standing.

"Mr. Stonewell is trying to interfere with the exhibits, sir."

Stoney spoke with urgency: "Your Honour, I have some experience in these matters, and this here skunk is dangerous, it's cooking . . ."

Pound gave his arm a tug. Stoney went off balance and their momentum carried them against a post, knocking a kerosene lamp off its hook. It fell on the sacks. There were loud gasps as the superskunk quietly ignited, giving off an otherworldly blue glow.

Stoney bolted up the aisle and past the judge to the front door. "That shit is going to explode!"

Arthur had known compost to smoulder but had never heard of it exploding. Despite this egregious case of shouting fire in a crowded theatre, only a handful of locals joined the court staff and visiting press in panicky flight out the two doors. Otherwise, evacuation was calm and orderly, children and seniors first.

He stayed put for a few moments, transfixed. A bubbling sound was coming from the oily sludge the cannabis had become. The flames had spread to other bags and were hotter now, yellow with orange tips, dancing in the gusts from the open doors. By the time the hall's extinguishers were finally located and brought into play, flames were licking up the cedar-shingled wall.

"Holy shit." Nick, beside him, finally excited about something. "This place is totally doomed, Grandpa, we got to split." He grabbed Arthur's arm, breaking him out of his rapture. Volunteers were running about, filling buckets, forming a brigade, as Arthur grabbed his briefcase and followed Nick out to the slushy lawn. Others hurried to move their vehicles out of harm's way.

A familiar voice. "I need to talk to you about this Pomeroy character."

"Cud, the community hall is burning down."

"I weep. I did my first reading here." He emerged from behind Arthur, a wet, hatless head poking from a Mexican poncho. "Meantime, another tragedy unfolds. Struggling poet Cudworth Brown is looking at doing life in the crossbar hotel for a murder he didn't commit. The evidence against him is flimsy, claims celebrity barrister Arthur Beauchamp, but he's too busy to take on his old chum's case, so he refers him to a lunatic."

A siren could be heard faintly; the volunteer fire department was on its way. But the pumper would be too late to save the hall – flames were leaping to the roof.

This would be a day to remember and mourn. A heritage building, a loss of history. Arthur felt depressed, weary. He wanted to go home, go back to bed, wake up again, start this day over. He wanted . . . a drink.

That was prompted by Cud pulling out a flask, having a nip. Brandy, by its scent. "The trial starts in two months. Pomeroy ain't nowhere near prepared, he wants to sell me out."

Arthur finally bit: "Why do you say that?"

"Last time I saw him he looked like a suicide bombing. Bedraggled, a week's growth, red, wacky eyes. Asked me if I'd be willing to cop to manslaughter. I almost punched him out." A pause to catch his breath, then he shouted frantically over the sound of the approaching siren: "*Manslaughter?* I didn't fucking chuck any fucking judge off a deck!"

4

THE VALENTINE AGENCY

Despairing of finding justice through normal channels, convinced that all lawyers were reactionary, mendacious, and corrupt, Cudworth Brown sought out a reliable private investigator. An arts reporter he'd seduced during his literary forays into Vancouver made inquiries, then recommended the enigmatic, urbane Lance Valentine, formerly of Scotland Yard. There were rumours of misbehaviour, she warned, rumours that the Yard had quietly let him go to avoid a scandal.

Cudworth called the Valentine agency, whose sultry-voiced secretary promised she could fit him in. And so it happened that late on a dreary, drizzling December day, Cud made his way to the tenderloin area, near Main and Keefer, which he thought an odd choice of location for this polished private eye . . .

The Widgeon icon was bouncing at the bottom of the screen. It did that once in a while; it meant Widgeon was trying to warn Brian. Trash this page, he was silently screaming. You are writing from the point of view of the wrong character.

A mouse-click took him to Widgeon's Chapter Eight. *We do not really care to know what lesser characters think — they have mouths to speak. See with your hero's eyes. Hear with her ears. Do not distance your hero from the reader, bring him close enough so the reader may sense his sweat, his prickles of fear, feel her hot breath as she closes in on the villainous cur who swindled dear Auntie Maude . . .*

"Who is this Horace Widgeon you're constantly on about?" Dr. Alison Epstein had asked a couple of days ago as he fidgeted on her couch.

She'd never heard of him? Brian was shocked. Thirty mysteries and three how-to's and five times nominated for the Dagger Award. "He writes escape fiction."

"I don't feel the need to escape," she said.

When piqued, this normally gracious woman occasionally gave in to an unprofessional snappishness. This happened when Brian was rambling and evasive. Which he usually was throughout his allotted three-quarters of an hour. She would peel and dig, trying to get down to the rotten core, but he wasn't going to let her find it. None of her business.

"I didn't fucking chuck any fucking judge off a deck!"

That is what this repulsive fellow claimed, of course. That, in Lance Valentine's experience, was what they all say: they're not guilty. Clients who protested the loudest, complaining they'd been falsely accused, were invariably guilty.

This one, this obscure backwoods poet, didn't strike Lance as being an exception to the rule. A rugged, cocky, broken-nosed look of a brawler. Unshaven. Tattoos were doubtless part of the package, but were hidden under his long-sleeved, tasselled deerskin jacket. He subscribed to some kind of conspiracy theory that he was being railroaded. The usual story.

"You want me to find the chucker?"

"Nobody else is trying."

Lance fiddled with a rose in a vase. He must always have a fresh rose on his desk in the morning. That's what he told the ravishing Rosy Chekoff when she applied to be his secretary. From the outer office, he could hear the tapping of her keyboard. If he twisted his head he could see her profile, a view that invariably caused him to breath rapidly. Rosy was also married to a detective, this one a civil servant, West Vancouver Serious Crimes.

"Let me ask you, Cudworth — is that what they call you? Or Cud?"

"Sometimes Cuddles. Sardonically."

"You got a lawyer, Cuddles?"

"Yeah, I got a lawyer. Mind if I smoke?"

"Have one of mine."

Cud bent over Lance's desk to get a light, then straightened with a wince. Chronic bad back, Lance reckoned. He'd been a high-rigger, an ironworker. Retired to Garibaldi Island, his childhood home, on a small disability pension. Ran the recycling depot there. Two books of poetry, one CD, muted acclaim.

Cud straightened, holding that back, and squinted out the dusty window at the little barrio of decrepitude that was the Downtown East Side. "Kinda pissy low-rent location, but I guess it's part of the private dick shtick. You keep a bottle of Johnny behind the books?"

Lance ignored the question. He wasn't going to let this smart aleck stereotype him. "Did you tell your lawyer you were coming to see me?"

"No."

"Why not?"

"Because he's an idiot. I don't trust him."

"Brian Pomeroy?"

"That's the one."

Delete, delete. What had been reborn with promise has evolved into self-flagellating mockery. A detour typical of the drooling nutter he had become, prompted by the mess he'd made of Cudworth's appointment on Friday.

Follow Brian, as he flashes back to his session with Cud, to restored Gastown, its cobblestone streets and tchotchke shops and failed chic, to Maple Tree Square, where the raw, rowdy Downtown East Side begins, where timorous tourists turn back.

The ground and second floors of his firm's building were occupied by Club d'Jazz, an exponential improvement over the last tenants and their nausea-inducing singalongs. Brian's third-floor digs offered views of pigeons strutting on the outer sill, whitewashing it with their excrement. He kept his windows closed, he feared those birds, was obsessed with images of them flying in and shitting all over. His partners had relegated him to this office because he wasn't showing up regularly. Macarthur, Brovak, and Sage: fickle friends who'd stopped expressing sympathy over his divorce, in fact had stopped talking to him. But they talked *about* him. He spied them once in a while gawking, whispering.

He wasn't taking many cases these days. A motor man-slaughter plea coming up. A couple of misdemeanours, a fraud. And this one, referred to him by the immortal Arthur Beauchamp, who hinted there was glory to be won by so enterprising a counsel as Brian Pomeroy.

Cudworth had done only one smart thing on the night he got busted. As Detective Sergeant Chekoff was pouring coffee into him, trying to sober him up for the third degree, he asked to make a call to Arthur, who advised him to shut up.

Brian had summoned Cud to the office because he'd lost his notes from his earlier interview. Nothing in the file but the bail papers. With surprising ease, during a lucid interval, Brian had got a judge to agree to a property bond.

Part of his problem in getting his ass in gear was that the Attorney General had appointed as special prosecutor a well-known feminist shit disturber named Abigail Hitchins, with whom, many years ago, Brian had a bizarre, disastrous affair. He didn't have the gumph to phone her – he couldn't seem to get drunk enough. As a result, he hadn't got around to getting her particulars of evidence. He should do that one of these days, especially since there'll be no preliminary inquiry – the A.-G. wanted a speedy end to this sensitive matter, so he'd indicted directly to trial.

No sooner had Cud Brown sat down when these words popped out of Brian's mouth: "Would you be willing to take a plea to manslaughter?"

What had possessed him to be so bold and obvious? Maybe a mental short-circuit, a disconnect, a fast rewind to his motor manslaughter file, an insurance agent who drove over a squeegee kid.

At any rate, Cud lost it. Went storming around, scaring the pigeons and the secretaries. Worse, he tattled to Arthur Beauchamp, who left a voice mail asking about this manslaughter nonsense. Brian's cellphone was off now, he didn't want to talk to Arthur, to anyone. He was disturbed, distressed, disordered, dysfunctional, the Latin prefix for *apart, to pieces*. At least the earlier panic had dissipated. He was learning how to get along with his breakdown, learning how to deal with people and not give himself away. It was an art.

He poured another tequila, got up to empty his ashtray. He'd have to make a run for more smokes. The bar downstairs never had his brand, and the waiters and the lowlifes who hung out there were always wanting legal advice. He was known here at the Ritz, he'd beat a gaming rap for the owner. Yeah, Cuddles, that's why Lance Valentine is in this pissy location; his creator gets cheap rent. Room 305, with its own sink, shitter, and shower. Furniture from about 1959. Prints on the walls by some unheralded Wild West artist. Brian identified with one of them: an unhorsed cowboy in a cattle stampede.

He played with his phone, stared out at the busy street, a squad car moving slowly, checking faces. A dealer fading into the shadows under the awning of Quick Loans, No References Required. Harry the Need, purveyor of quality off-the-shelf smack, flake, and meth. A whore shouted an endearment to the cops, and they joked with her, then moved on. Time for another Xanax. He took it with tequila.

It was just after ten. Abigail, like most witches, never slept. She answered on the first ring.

"It's Brian."

"For Christ's sake, I have friends over." A background babble.

"What kind of case have you got against Cud Brown?"

"Bry, are you drunk?"

"Yes, I am."

Abigail must have withdrawn to a quieter room because the noise lessened. "Take my advice, check yourself into a clinic for the fucked up."

"I forget, when's the trial?"

"Mid-February."

Things were starting to spin. He couldn't remember why he called her. The Crown evidence, the particulars, that's what he needed. He was having trouble pronouncing the word.

"Get back to me when you're normal. I couriered them a month ago."

"To my office?"

"Yeah, go there much? Get a pencil. I can now release the name of the eyewitness."

"Eyewitness?"

"Homicide, please, Detective Sergeant Chekoff... Yes, I'll hold, tell him it's Lance Valentine." He covered the receiver and swivelled back toward Cud, who was gazing at the silhouette of Rosy Chekoff. Pert nose, plumlike mouth, taut bosom, big hair.

"I know Pomeroy," Lance said. "He's one of the best."

"He ain't on top of it! He asked me to cop to manslaughter!"

"That's one of his tricks. He wanted to see your reaction, assess how strongly you believed in yourself."

"Bullshit." Cud plopped back into his chair. Lance wasn't sure if he wanted to help out this hayseed poet with his slightly rancid smell and sour attitude. He didn't seem to have unlimited funds – this would be a costly endeavour. Yet he was intrigued.

The first thing Hank Chekoff said when he finally came on the line was, "Is Rosy all right?" Possessive and distrustful was this porcine suburban copper. He often showed up at the end of the day to drive Rosy home. He wasn't happy about her working here.

"She's doing incredibly well, old boy, working her little, ah, head off. It's about his late Lordship Rafael Whynet-Moir."

"Why do you think I know anything about the file?"

"Because with your experience and skill you'd most likely have been assigned to it." Rosy had actually mentioned he had the file. "Give me your honest assessment, Hank, how tight is it?"

"What's your interest? Who do you represent?"

"Can't divulge, strict instructions. But . . . let's say a major underwriter is curious to know if it's homicide or suicide, in which latter case they don't have to make payment."

A hesitation. "You're talking big money?"

"Big."

"Tell your clients to pony up. A prominent lady of unblemished character saw the judge get shoved off by this Cud Brown creep."

"Good view?"

"Excellent. Deck to deck. The judge's neighbour. Hey, let me speak to Rosy after."

Lance got what he could from him, then switched him to Rosy and swivelled to watch her react. She turned and gave him a tired smile, as if to say, Thanks, but I didn't really want to talk to him.

He may have erred in hiring Rosy. She'd been as worthy as the dozen others he'd interviewed, with the bonus of being breathtakingly scenic, but he'd taken her on before learning her husband was a copper, and now there were complications. Hank may have heard exaggerated rumours about Lance's reputation with the fair, yet decidedly unfair, sex. The last thing Lance needed was a jealous cop tailing him around town.

He swivelled back to Cud. "It seems that the chair of the North Shore Arts Council saw you take care of her neighbour. Maybe you ought to go back to Mr. Pomeroy and apologize."

Brian clicked Widgeon open, hoping to find a help file for lost writers. Search for "mental."

Do not mentally exhaust yourself. Before chance (and whatever small talents I possess) favoured me with literary success, I, too, had a day job, as inspector for Her Majesty's Customs, and I would often arrive at work exhausted after scribbling till three in the morning. Many a smuggled item must have slipped through on my watch! So please, when you see nothing but rot on your page, take a deep breath, pack your pages away, and make a soothing cup of Earl Grey while you climb into your pyjamas.

Brian didn't have Earl Grey, and his pyjamas were in the Good-Luck Wash'n'Dry.

The tough-dame-assistant was rot on his page — if he couldn't rewrite Rosy Chekoff he'd have to scrap the hackneyed big-hair hoochie. There was no model to draw her from, he'd looked everywhere, all the bars up and down Main Street. Brian felt stymied in his effort to create credible female characters. He'd never given the concept of femaleness much thought. Generally, he was having trouble making people up, making things up.

Widgeon, Chapter Two. *The beginning author will be forgiven if he or she commits minor theft, stealing premise, plot, even characters from real life. But do not become wedded to reality; do not copy life. There is no point in writing fiction if you have no imagination.*

Fair enough, but it's so last year, as his older teen daughter might put it. Widgeon isn't hip to the trend. This is creative *non*-fiction, history pretending to be fiction. Write what you know, they say. But it was getting harder to cling to the remains of reality, especially when potted on cactus juice, harder to maintain a window to the world of sanity. It was a task just keeping the pigeons out, the shitting pigeons that haunted his imaginings . . .

After going through the pockets of his bomber jacket – two broken cigarettes in a crumpled pack – he went out the side window to the fire escape, clanging down it, avoiding the ground-floor saloon, avoiding the dopers in the lane, pretending he was sober, pretending he was normal, and in this way making it to the street and across it.

Harry the Need nodded, recognizing him, the mouthpiece gone bonkers at the Ritz. All the street people knew, his breakdown was all they talked about. They were waiting for him to do it finally. To self-destruct.

Walking carefully so as not to stagger, he made his way past the Golden Horizon Travel Agency, across the street, past the recessed staircase to the local bookies, upstairs from, appropriately, a second-hand bookstore that was open late, always busy. "Books! Books! Books!" Beside it, a honky-tonk bar, the Palace. "Girls! Girls! Girls!" A muscular black man out front, the doorman. He knew. The doorman knew.

At the corner was the New Consciousness Head and Smoke Shop. Brian bought two packs of A's there and was waiting for a walk sign when, right in front of him, a dish got out of a taxi, almost a Rosy, and went into the strip bar. He forgot what his plan was. The sign said, *Walk*, but he didn't. Then it said, *Wait*. A passenger door of the taxi was open, beckoning. Brian wasn't sure if he should go into the strip bar, take the cab, or wait. He got into the cab. He gave his previous address, on Mountain Highway in North Vancouver.

5

THE THREE-ELEVEN FERRY

"Would you care for more toast?" Arthur asked.

"Yeah, I guess, thanks." Young Nick made no motion to rise, though the toaster was five feet away. Perhaps he thought it operated by remote. The boy had slept till nine.

Arthur got up, slid two more slices in. It was Wednesday, December 19, a week after the hall burned down and three days before Nicholas Senior was to come by to fetch his son. Arthur and his grandson were strangers, that was part of their problem – the boy's parents had lived in Europe and Australia, there'd been no chance to bond.

He supposed the young man was still feeling the aftershock of his parents' split-up – one becomes thoughtless when angry. To add to that, he and Nick had got off on the worst possible footing – as Arthur was helping him unpack, he'd come upon a baggie of marijuana. Coals to Newcastle, but he couldn't pretend to ignore it. He'd delivered a lecture that made him sound, even to his own ears, like an old fart: sorry, son, there's a no-dope policy at Blunder Bay. Hey, he tried grass a few times himself, but at a mature age. Psychedelics can stunt emotional development. Be smart, alter your mind with learning. Nick stared at the floor, resentful.

Arthur was not equipped to handle adolescent trauma, cared not to remember the pain of his own growing up, his cold, indifferent, intellectual parents. He was getting only limited help from Margaret who, currently, was on Vancouver Island. Politics, schmoozing with Green Party members, lining up support for a nomination. Amazingly, Blunder Bay Farm was running smoothly despite its mistress's many disappearances. Thanks partly to the four resident woofers, hard-working kids from overseas. Willing Workers on Organic Farms. They travel the world on the cheap: a half-day of labour for room and board.

"Your father phoned, Nick. I didn't want to wake you. He said he's not able to make it over this weekend. Things have piled up, he said, a pre-Christmas rush in the markets." Nicholas managed two high-risk mutual funds. He was always on edge.

"Yeah, okay." An alarming catch in Nick's voice. Then he said, "I don't think I want any more toast, thanks." He got up and left the kitchen with troubling haste.

Disquieted now, Arthur jumped when the toaster popped. He'd relayed Nicholas's message with consummate ineptness. The boy's emotional barriers were breached, and Arthur was alarmed. Leave him alone a while if he's in turmoil? Seek advice?

He phoned Deborah's school in Melbourne. A machine responded, instructing him the school's hours were eight-thirty to three-thirty. He slapped his forehead. It was two in the morning in Melbourne.

Through the window he watched Nick go up the steps to the woofer veranda, sit on the swinging chair, plug a phone line into his laptop. He regularly dialed the Internet from there, to avoid tying up the house line. Arthur finished a third cup of coffee, poured a fourth, then walked over there, jittery.

"Your dad wants to clear the decks so he can take you skiing at Christmas."

"Cool. Thanks."

"Told me to give you his love, and he'll call later."

"Thanks."

"Okay, let's give that computer a rest. Why don't you give Lavinia a hand in the corral?"

Arthur had struck the right note. Nick closed his laptop. He'd taken a fancy to Lavinia, who teased him. Lavinia was twenty-three, a woofer from Estonia, a pretty blonde with an earthy directness. She and three agonizingly polite Japanese bunked in the former farmhouse of the former neighbour, Margaret Blake, just behind the apple orchard.

They found Lavinia carrying pails of feed for the cow and goats. She set them down, examined Nick critically. "You cute guy. How old you?"

"Almost fifteen."

That was varnish, he was born in July.

She squeezed his biceps. "We make you bigger muscles. Come. After, we will fixing fence."

Nick grabbed the heavy pails. Clearly, he preferred her company to that of old gramps. Arthur was grateful to leave him in her charge while he dealt with the headache of Cudworth Brown, who was clogging Arthur's answering machine. Brian Pomeroy was not returning calls, and no one, even his partners, seemed to know where he was.

Arthur had been too rash in flipping Cud off to Pomeroy. He wasn't Arthur's first choice, involved as he was in the aftermath of a devastating divorce, but several of the best had been unavailable, and he didn't dare deliver up Cud to an incompetent. Pomeroy had free time, and the case intrigued him. Arthur rationalized: there was nothing like a juicy murder to help a lawyer escape his marital troubles. He'd learned that during his own soul-destroying first marriage.

Brian had seemed fine the last time Arthur phoned, a few weeks ago. "I'm on top of it, maestro. Looks like a duck shoot."

Arthur went into the house to shower, shave, and put on a suit, pausing to try Brian's cell number again. This time he answered. "You have reached the Speech Defect Centre. Please garble your message after the tone."

"Why are you being impossible to reach, Brian?"

"I got into the worst shitstorm of my life last night. They just gave my Nokia back." A tired voice, hoarse, as if from shouting.

"Dare I ask where you are?"

"Under RCMP escort. I'm just out of the tank. I'm waiting for court."

Finally, here was the proof Arthur hadn't wanted to hear, proof that Brian wasn't holding it together. "What's the charge?"

"Causing a disturbance. Caroline wouldn't answer the door. I woke up the neighbours. Don't tell my partners, I'll deal with it. As to other matters of moment, yes, I did explore the matter of manslaughter with the loudmouth you foisted on me. If he hadn't made a theatrical show of indignation by stalking from my office, he might have learned that Astrid Leich, former stage performer, honourary patron of several worthy charities, and current chair of the North Shore Arts Council, having been awakened by a noise, slipped out to her balcony in time to see the accused pitch Justice Whynet-Moir onto the rocks of doom."

"You are not making this up?"

"If you chance upon Cuddles, tell him he might want to come back and grovel. Tell him I'm off the case if he acts up again. The only reason I'm taking this on is to show the world what a complete prick Whynet-Moir was. Got to go, my name is being called."

Arthur headed for the shower. This was another ticklish matter, Pomeroy's antipathy to Judge Whynet-Moir. Overeager to offload the file, Arthur hadn't borne in mind that Whynet-Moir had presided over the Pomeroy divorce. Pomeroy had run around afterwards calling curses down on the judge's head, alleging he'd been making eyes at Caroline all through the trial, that she was flirting back.

But despite last night's bizarre lapse, despite a doubtless majestic hangover, the fellow seemed sufficiently on his game. Arthur truly wanted to believe that.

Astrid Leich . . . he'd seen her a few times on stage. A touch overexpressive, some ham in her. There had been nothing in the press about her role as witness. She saw the deed in the dark, from across an inlet? Identification issues can be very tricky in court – this case was not the duck shoot Pomeroy boasted it would be. But if there was ever an expert on the identification defence it was Pomeroy, who famously defended a hothead charged with assassinating the visiting president of one of those gang-ridden Asian republics of the former U.S.S.R.

Arthur found it hard to see Cud Brown doing this. A ruffian, yes, and a scoundrel, true, but a murderer, doubtful. What motive could he have had? He'd been sitting pretty, enjoying his small fame, enjoying the literary life, library readings, CBC interviews, the circuit of writers' festivals.

Arthur had no firm idea why he so disliked the local literary luminary. It wasn't because he smoked cigars, or drank too much, or seduced countless women with his weary beatnik shtick. Maybe it was his undeserved success. His new collection, *Karmageddon*, was, impossibly, shortlisted for the Governor General's Award. The fellow was a sham, a poetaster, his verses self-indulgent and profane.

But was there a darker, hidden reason for his antipathy? *I hope it's not because I spent two weeks up a tree with your lady.* That comment rankled, and was the more hurtful for its taint of truth. Two years ago, in an anti-logging campaign, Cuddles and Margaret were chosen by lot to share a high platform on a fir tree. Cud lasted only thirteen days, but they were miserable days for Arthur. He embarrassed himself by being suspicious, flagellated himself with sordid, excessive, unworthy imaginings. He suspected he was neurotic that way, conditioned by his first wife, unfaithful Annabelle.

He had to smother his ire when Margaret joined the chorus urging him to take Cud's case. "Arthur, darling, I spent two weeks enduring his foul tongue and smelly cigars and smellier feet, and even *I* think you should defend him. Everyone on the island expects you to. Otherwise, it'll look like you're punishing him for some reason."

A reason she was too polite to define, or didn't understand. He didn't understand it himself, his pathetic jealousy. Call it a phobia, he was phobic about Cudworth Brown.

⚖️

The leftovers from last week's court docket – Hamish McCoy, *inter alia*, were being heard today in the legion hall. Because the sky was clear, the sun warm, and the hall reached as easily by sea as by land, Arthur had persuaded Nick to enjoy a trip on the *Blunderer*, his canopy-topped outboard.

He put Nick behind the wheel for a while, and they kept to a leisurely ten knots while dolphins followed. "This is brilliant," said Nick. He'd recovered from the disappointment of his father's cancelled visit, and, even better, was starting to tune in to country living. If all went well, maybe they could lollygag back, do a little fishing.

Nearing North Point, they could make out the charred stumps of posts on Breadloaf Hill, the remains of the community hall. Margaret had volunteered Arthur for a committee raising money for rebuilding. "It's not asking much, Arthur, it's something I'd normally do." Too busy seeking a nomination for a by-election soon to be called, in Cowichan and the Islands. Her clunky vehicle of ambition, the Green Party – aptly named for its unripe adherents – had never elected anyone to anything. Arthur had given up trying to persuade Margaret that hers was a quixotic quest.

He took over the controls, swung around the North Point beacon into the crooked-finger bay where sat the mildewed legion hall. Cuddles must have seen him coming, because he was on the small-craft dock, motioning for Arthur to toss him a line. Nick asked to stay on board with his laptop, so Arthur put on his jacket and tie, then went up the ramp, with Cud at his elbow, pestering him. "How can this Leich woman claim to see someone who wasn't there?"

"Cud, spare me the rhetoric. You've obviously talked to Brian Pomeroy. You know the worst. Be grateful he's still acting for you after you flounced out of his office."

"Okay, I prostrate myself, I'm abject. What cake did Astrid Leich pop out of? Why wasn't I told about her? Who's behind this attempt to job me? The system, the courts, the prosecutors, the police? They need a scapegoat, they got to look like they're doing something, too many judges are being offed. They hire a retired actress to identify prime suspect Cudworth Brown in a lineup."

"There was a lineup?" Arthur was startled.

"Yeah, I told Pomeroy. He said, don't worry, it's a formality, like fingerprinting."

Arthur made for the back door, paused, took a breath. "Cud, my advice to you is this: compose yourself, repair your rupture with Pomeroy, and help him plan your defence. Astrid Leich will be a key witness."

He entered, abandoning Cud. He was determined not to feel sorry for him. That was how wily defendants sucked you in, seduced you out of retirement. Here, in Branch 512 of the Canadian Legion, Arthur would sing his final swan song, the sentencing of Hamish McCoy.

Several regulars were there, looking miffed because the bar was roped off. Nelson Forbish again dominated the small press table, which tilted slightly every time he moved, causing the two young women at the other end to jiggle up and down as if on a teeter-totter. Absent was Constable Pound, licking his wounds, widely blamed for bringing combustibles into the community hall.

Hamish McCoy sat slouched, glaring at Kurt Zoller in his fetishistic life jacket. It would be a task reigning in the leprechaunish Newfie, who'd shown little appreciation after being merely slapped on the wrist for growing half a ton of potent pot. He'd called Zoller a "dorty, stinking Nazi squealer" when they bumped into each other yesterday at the general store.

It was a quarter past two when judge, prosecutor, and court staff finally got themselves organized at tables. "Okay, order in court," said Wilkie. "We're a little late starting, and we intend to catch the three-eleven ferry, so I want everyone apprised of that." A stern look at Arthur and ever-smiling Mary, the prosecutor. "Okay, where were we?"

"Unsightly Premises Bylaw," said Mary. "Robert Stonewell."

Stoney wasn't within the room, and emissaries couldn't find him outside, a search that consumed several minutes. Judge Wilkie spent the time staring at the glowing Bud Lite wall clock.

"Okay, hold that one down," he said. "Call the McCoy case." Arthur and his client came forward. "Mr. Zoller, you were to meet with some locals to come up with a program of community service for Mr. McCoy."

"Yes, sir. I have a list of recommendations." He flourished a sheaf of papers. "May I start by reading the minutes of the advisory planning committee?"

"You may not." His Honour hadn't reckoned on having to deal with a master of circumlocution.

"The problem is, Your Worship, this matter was debated last night with a lot of interesting views going back and forth —"

"Mr. Zoller, we have a ferry to catch. I just want your recommendation."

"Certainly, Your Worship, but I promised I would mention the minority report, which calls for defendant to do a hundred hours of beach cleanup —"

Wilkie interrupted again. "Thank you. What did your group finally decide?"

Zoller loosened his yellow life jacket, took a breath, began again. "Okay, well, there's one main project and a couple of things we'd like to add. Mrs. Hilda Kneaston, who lives across from the defendant on Potters Pond, wants you to order him to wear clothes in the summer while he's out in his yard, at least shorts or a swimsuit –"

Wilkie was battling to restrain himself. "Mr. Zoller, how long does it take to drive to the ferry?"

"Ten minutes."

"Okay. And it leaves in twenty-five minutes. When is the *next* ferry?"

"That would be the nine-forty-five tonight, but it's usually late."

"Understand this, Zoller, my wife and I have a dinner engagement tonight. Be it on your head."

"Yes, sir, I'll get right to the substance." Zoller began a rambling irrelevancy about how tourism was the mainstay of the island economy, and how the island's many cultural offerings should be on better display –"

"Get to the point!"

Before Zoller could do so, Stoney charged into the room. "Sorry, Your Honour, my car broke down."

Wilkie glanced anxiously at the clock, scrambled through his papers. "Stonewell. Unsightly premises. Do you want an adjournment?"

Stoney must have sensed profit in saying no. "Those cars are my babies. Most of them were there before there was even a bylaw. I'm ready for trial."

"Not guilty," Wilkie said.

"What?"

"Not guilty! I find you not guilty! And you, Zoller, sum up in no more than six words, because we have to get to the damn *ferry*!"

"That's what I'm leading up to, the ferry. The majority vote last night was for the idea of a statue at the ferry dock, maybe on the hill overlooking Ferryboat Bay, at least fifteen feet tall, like the ones in the front of the defendant's house with wings on them, and in time for tourist season this spring. And we could hang a sign on it to inform visitors of the island's many arts and crafts —"

Arthur had sensed McCoy simmering behind him, and now he erupted. "I ain't going to see my work compromised by a barnacle like Kurt Zoller! I don't do billboards! Nobody tells me what to create!" He aimed a stubby, muscular finger at Zoller. "Oi'll go to the clink first before I kowtow to you, you snout, you stool —"

The red-faced judge seemed ready to slap McCoy in irons — eighteen months for a missed ferry — so Arthur cupped his hand over McCoy's mouth and announced his terms. "Full artistic freedom, he's not to be policed in any way, or bothered when at work. Substantial compliance within six months. On that basis, my client informs me he will be pleased to place a sculpture at the ferry landing."

Wilkie was already sweeping papers into a briefcase. "So ordered! The accused is discharged! This court is adjourned!" He led the flight to the parking lot.

Arthur spent a few moments cooling McCoy down, talking sense to him: this could be to his advantage, could turn around a bad year. There would be publicity, it wouldn't hurt his fame or his pocketbook to be the creator of an island attraction, well photographed, sold as postcards. Moreover, Hamish needn't put in a wink of effort. Arthur would be proud to donate his fee, the twelve-foot-high Icarus, to a pedestal on Ferryboat Knoll.

McCoy reproved him for his offer. "You said you loiked it, b'y, and you'll keep it. The image is too tormented, it'll scare the tourists. Oi'll give them joy." As he wandered off with some friends, he was more relaxed; common sense had trumped anger.

As the editor of the *Bleat* rose from the media bench, it tilted, and one of the reporters slid off, landing rudely on her bottom. Nelson waddled up to Arthur with pen and pad.

"A lot of my readers are going to think he got off light. What do you say to that, Mr. Beauchamp?"

"I say to that, Nelson, that it would be most pleasant to drop a couple of fishing lines on a sunny, placid, winter's day." Contemplation of that prospect was put on hold as he stepped outside. Lying in wait, with tiresome predictability, was Cud Brown.

"Go check on Pomeroy, see for yourself. Come back and tell me if he don't belong in the cackle factory."

Progress to the docks was slow, Cud was walking backward, arms extended to prevent Arthur from darting past. Nick was watching from the *Blunderer* while playing with the ship-to-shore electronics.

"Maybe I have not been plain, Cud. I am not a conveyer of information about your trial, nor am I entitled ethically to advise you. Brian Pomeroy is a skilled counsel who, incidentally, a few years ago won a celebrated case involving wrongful identification."

Cud's voice lowered. "There's something about him that scares me. Something about his eyes . . ."

6

CAROLLING CAROLINE

Those wacky eyes, glinting like flints from the cheap meth they buff the coke with. Yes, stardust was what Brian was now abusing, blow was what he'd been tucking up his nose during the half-dozen shopping days before Christmas. It's got more oomph than Xanax, it brings security, a blast of self-esteem. He wasn't interested in going back to his couch doctor for more Xanax, he didn't even want to see Dr. Epstein, with her hints about "caring facilities." Institutions. Creepily smiling keepers, muscular warders.

Harry the Need makes home deliveries, just like the folks at Lucky Penny Pizza. Hell of a guy when you get to know him. He used to trade stocks, ran with a fast crowd, got hooked on meth, graduated to horse, sells to support his habit. He's against legalization; it would collapse the market.

Cud must have been seriously distressed on realizing he'd been bad-mouthing the winner of a famous case of failed identification. Maybe the lumpen poet now remembered seeing Brian's televised scrum, his sardonic bon mots after eyewitnesses failed to ID the assassin of the visiting Bhashyistan president. As a bonus, Brian was credited with causing Bhashyistan to break diplomatic relations with Canada.

Brian was grateful that Arthur took the trouble to wise Cuddles up. Brian wants this case. He wants to run an insanity defence. One in which the lawyer is insane.

No other counsel had the jam to take on the intemperate poet. Beauchamp had obviously fished widely in the lawyer pool before settling on a bottom feeder. Two of Brian's partners had been approached, they admitted it, Macarthur and Brovak. Brian taunted them – they were cowards, afraid to ruffle the bench by pleading the cause of a loudmouth who may have murdered a judge, maybe two or three. They claimed money was a factor: Cud had none. Brian wasn't proud, he would accept legal aid rates.

Morning coffee in hand, still in his underwear, he looked out the dusty window to see if any of his followers were out there. Last night it was a thin guy in a London Fog, watching him through the window of the Glad Times Noodle House.

Nine o'clock, and his room was already stuffy, sweaty, smoky. The Ritz's heat got trapped on this top floor, but you couldn't open a window without hearing Bing Crosby. Sleigh bells ring, are you listening? It was that abysmal time of year when the gluey, the garish, the mawkish rule. What happened to the beauty of it, the spiritual, the birth of hope? You rarely heard the great old carols any more.

That's actually what Brian had been doing Tuesday night, lustily carolling Caroline, "Good King Wenceslas," "Adeste Fideles." Standing below her window, reminding her through song of the coming celebration of the great Christian miracle – what could be wrong with that, he asked the judge, a young woman, unimpressed. She sought the view of Caroline in the gallery. "Just tell him to stay away from me. Especially when drunk."

Brian felt more rested today; he'd got four hours' sleep last night, the most in weeks, and four hours more than the night before, on a musty mattress in a barred room of the Redcoat Inn in North Vancouver. The disturbance charge has been bumped four weeks. Access rights are cancelled in the interim. Now he must confront Christmas on his own, without his three Costa Rican adoptees, Gabriela, Amelia, and Francisco, who always helped him survive the annual banality. He must show grit, suck it up.

He bent to the mirror, checked his eyes for wackiness. He did two more lines.

While his computer warmed up, he studied the wall prints. The unhorsed cowboy among the stampeding long-horns. A rider slouched over his galloping steed, two arrows sticking from his back. Four cowpokes sitting around a fire at night – a placid scene until one noticed the eyes glinting in the blackness. Ravenous wolves, maybe, scalp-hunting Apaches. The artist had captured the essential futility of trying to stay alive.

A pop-up screen, Widgeon's admonition-of-the-day. *Dialogue must sound natural to the ear, yet unembellished by the chaff of common parlance – the hideous "uh" and "um" and "er" – or by the repetitious four-letter obscenities of the ill-bred.*

Despite all his complaining and wanking, Inspector Grodgins doesn't say shit, piss, or fuck. In fact, none of Widgeon's characters commit such acts – especially Inspector Grodgins. His ungainly sidekick, Constable Marchmont, seems entirely asexual. So might be the author, whose manuals offer no aid for the sex scenes, let alone tips on how to write with a hard-on. Without Widgeon's guidance, Brian must walk alone into the valley of concupiscence.

Cudworth Brown, slouched in a chair, chewing on a toothpick, and staring with woeful eyes, conjured in Lance Valentine the image of a ruminating ox. What Cud was staring at was Rosy's bottom in a tight dress as she bent toward her printer.

"Let me get this straight. That centrefold, your secretary, is the wife of one of the crime-stoppers who busted me."

A tug at her blouse, a hand to her piled hair – she had a sixth sense, Rosy, knew when she was under scrutiny. Using this power, she often intercepted Lance's admiring looks, which she returned with knowing, teasing smiles. It had been a grave mistake to hire her. Too distracting. Too married. To a cop.

"That's right, old boy. Case officer, I would suspect."

"You bet he is. Detective Sergeant Henry 'Call-Me-Hank' Chekoff. I had a hangover like a spike through my head, and he cathauled me for two hours. Told him a thousand times I want to see my lawyer. Chekoff has a huge fucking interest in sticking it to me for the max."

"I shouldn't doubt that at all." Lance bent to the rose and sniffed it to mask the man's nervous sweat.

Cudworth bounded to his feet. "I'll take my chances with Pomeroy, you tin-star shamus." He stamped to the outer office, grabbed his poncho from the coat rack, slammed the door on his way out.

Rosy came in with the pages she'd transcribed, a divorcee rich already, seeking more in settlement. "What got *him* stoked?"

"He thinks you're a spy. You'd never disclose anything to do with my clients, would you, my love?"

"Of course not, Lance."

"Even to your husband."

"Especially him."

"He needn't know I'm working for Mr. Brown."

"You *were* working for Mr. Brown."

"He'll be back."

"You're awfully sure of yourself, aren't you, boss?"

Her hand lightly touched his shoulder as she leaned over him. L'Eau d'Hiver, complicated by breath mint. A braless breast brushed his shoulder while she guided his hand down the page. "This word, just before 'dirty whoring old goat.'"

"Scrofulous." He picked up yet another scent from her, an essence of something glandular. This dangerous woman was not just flirting with him. She was daring him.

"Here, line fifteen, she's describing how she caught her husband with the maid." Rosy's nipple scuffed his shoulder, hard as a pebble. The smell of her. She quoted the divorcee: "'I opened the door and they were on the floor.' It rhymes! Then . . . I'm not sure, I think I heard, 'with his hand between her thighs.'"

"His *head* between her thighs."

The beast below had begun stirring. He quickly swivelled to the window, and stood, trying to concentrate on Cud Brown jaywalking to the honky-tonk bar. *Girls! Girls! Girls!*

When he turned back, she was bent over the desk, displaying, offering her behind, heart-shaped in a tight skirt. He couldn't take much more. He reached behind the forensics texts and fumbled for his sixteen-year-old Laphroaig. Women didn't usually unsettle him this way. Maybe it was the L'Eau d'Hiver – how did she know he fancied that scent, with its subtle *sillage*? He poured an ounce and downed it.

Rosy turned, caught him staring. "Thanks, I'll have one." She hoisted herself onto his desk, her skirt riding up. "At first, with your little earring and your morning rose and all, I thought you were gay. But you're not, are you?"

He couldn't hide the proof of that as he passed her a drink. His breathing had become irregular. Lance couldn't bear not being in control. He was not in control now, the woman was exploiting his one great weakness – it was as if she'd known about it, the flaw that persuaded the Yard to quietly let him go.

She ignored the drink he sought to hand her, and without warning she grabbed his belt and pulled him on top of her, open wet mouth finding his, fingers sliding toward his groin.

In less than a minute her panties were dangling from her ankles, and Lance was between them. At the transcendent moment of merging, it came to him that he hadn't locked the outer office door. This ugly realization was confirmed when Hank Chekoff walked into the inner office, red-faced and spitting bile as he yanked out his police issue Smith 9 mm.

—

"It's *her* fault!" the coward screamed, and the burlesque queen died in a hail of bullets.

It had to be done. The author had lusted for Rosy but never loved her, and she must be buried in the graveyard of the stereotypical. The subtle essence of L'Eau d'Hiver was wasted on this femme pornographique, save it for a sidekick with cool, with class.

Widgeon, Chapter Nineteen, "The Credible Sidekick." *Ever since the pioneering Dr. Watson, the role of best supporting actor — the foil, the mirror against whom your hero humbly shines — has been crucial to the success of mystery series. If I may be allowed to drop the name of my own Constable Ed Marchmont, it was no easy task to create a totally humourless character and make him interesting!*

Brian remembered to back up, then put his weary old Mac to sleep. He must gird himself for the office, for Cudworth Brown and his ill-meant apologies for his ill-mannered accusations. He cut up some coke for the road, poured it into a little envelope torn from a Craven A packet.

He didn't feel especially bonkers now that he was off Xanax, which had done little, merely stabilized him. Cocaine seemed a more natural remedy, curative; he felt healthier after a snort or two, sharper, confident. And it helped cut down the drinking.

He shrugged into his coat and descended into the bowels of downtown, a gloomy day, a cold drizzle. An ATM on Georgia Street coughed up three hundred dollars. He was going through his account fast, that was the drawback of his mood enhancer of choice.

He had to buy presents for the kids, find a way to smuggle them in. The shops were busy, depressing. Dumbly smiling elves in tinselled windows, syrup from speakers, tunes for illiterate ears, Christmas lights everywhere, sputtering, blinking, inducing a new phobia, fear of epileptic seizure.

He tarried a while outside the Bay, listening to a pretty violin-playing busker play a stripped-down version of the *Four Seasons*. He gave her twenty dollars for trying out for Rosy. Then down to the pimped-up waterfront, right on

Cordova, then a ramble up Water Street, and you're at Maple Tree Square, and that's when you realize you're being followed again. It was the same thin guy in the overcoat, or his brother. Dark complexion, Brian hadn't noticed that last time. Who does he represent?

He hurried into an ugly so-called heritage building, avoided the elevator, took two flights of stairs, checking behind him at every landing. Yes, he'd shaken off the thin man. He entered through the portals of Pomeroy, Macarthur, Brovak, and Sage, whose freckled receptionist greeted him with a frozen cheery smile. "Good *afternoon*, Mr. Pomeroy." Loud, so everyone could be warned.

Cuddles wasn't here yet, just a couple of white-collar criminals in the waiting room. Brian had time to powder his nose. But stepping out of a doorway in a confrontational way – arms outstretched to hinder progress – was Maximilian Macarthur III, his dear friend, his woe-sharing buddy and partner of two decades.

"We need to talk."

"I agree, Max. I've got a client coming by, let's set a time." Brian couldn't get by, Max blocked all the holes. He was a little guy, bald and wiry, a runner, over-healthy. He pulled Brian into his office, closed the door.

"The divorce is over, Bry. It's time to get normal."

Brian stared grumpily out the window. Max had a pigeonless view, a choice view, over Burrard Inlet, a tableau of sea and mountains.

"Christ, you were coming around. Why did you relapse? For the last three months you've been like some ghoul who wanders in occasionally to spread gloom. Was it because your secretary quit? Roseanne got married. That happens. She's pregnant. That happens too."

Brian listened sullenly. Max doesn't understand. No one understands. They can't reach me, they can't get to where I am.

"We've got you another one. She's in your office now, restoring order from chaos. April Fan Wu, two weeks out of Hong Kong, she worked in a major law office there. Knows the lost art of shorthand."

"Appreciate it. I think my client's here." Brian edged to the door.

Max had to reach to put an arm around his shoulders. "We'll look after that disturbance charge, Bry, don't worry about it. But I want to know what's going on with you. Everyone's concerned . . ."

"Did they ask you to check me out?"

"Who?"

"Everyone. You used the word *everyone*. Who is that, I want to know. Who is everyone?"

"Your partners, Bry – Augie and the Animal and me. Wentworth too. The conspiracy doesn't go any higher. Where the hell have you been staying; why won't you tell us?" The tone was of a social worker admonishing an adolescent runaway.

"I'm in a cabin in the woods, Max. I'm centring. I'm a Buddhist now, I'm studying the ways of the ascended masters. Listen, Max, I love you for caring, but if I act a little crazy, I'm just putting you on. It's my sense of humour, Max, noir is in fashion. How's Ruth? How's little Jackie?"

"Jacqueline is not little any more, she's thirty-five, she's doing her Ph.D."

"I knew that." Brian made it out the door, waving goodbye, walking backward. "Later, right? We'll talk later."

"Let's hoist a beer at Happy Hour, okay?"

"Happy Hour, *claro*, excellent plan." Brian escaped down the hall, relieved he'd passed the test. Max hadn't guessed the full extent of the damage.

He locked his office door, withdrew his A's, fished out his bindle of blow, then turned to the sound of a soft "Hello?"

He'd forgotten about his new secretary, hadn't noticed this Modigliani masterpiece by the filing cabinet.

Brian tucked the bindle away, annoyed at himself, annoyed at her for smiling in such a knowing way. Why was this woman a legal secretary? Why wasn't she on a runway in Milan? Five-foot-eight, mostly leg, flat chest, catlike eyes, and that infuriating smile, as if she reads him, knows his addictions, his sicknesses. Poised, assured, masking her repugnance.

"I am pleased to meet you, I am April Fan Wu." The voice was musical, the accent British over a hint of Cantonese. "You *are* Mr. Pomeroy?"

"No, I'm the pigeon control officer. Mr. Pomeroy asked me to get rid of them; they're driving him mad." Preening on the sill outside, beady-eyed, occasionally taking a shit.

"It is bad chi to kill a pigeon."

"Who told you that?"

"My grandmother." Still studying him.

Brian looked about – his office didn't seem in its usual disarray.

"You have not opened your mail for two months." Matter-of-fact, patient, as with a child. "Almost two hundred e-mails, faxes, and telephone messages, some urgent, some not, demand answer. Dr. Epstein, your psychiatrist, is anxious that you call."

"Did she describe me as a menace to all of society or just to myself?"

"I do think you ought to see her. You are obviously unwell."

"Where did you get your medical training, Ms. Wu?"

"Sarcasm is a tool of the unimaginative."

"Your grandmother?"

She nodded. Her unforgiving smile.

"I'm under a court order not to see my children. I am an emotional mess, I'm having some kind of massive stress disorder. On top of that, I'm being followed. Dr. Epstein is part of it. Illegal drugs bring temporary relief. My preferred form of humour *is* sarcasm. I'm not sure, but I think I'm also suicidal. You will hate working with me."

"I expect it will be interesting."

Front desk was paging, Cudworth Brown was on the premises. Brian asked April Fan Wu to arm herself with several sharpened pencils. He wanted Cuddles's every uttered word, he had to find a solution to Astrid Leich, the surprise eyewitness.

Before greeting his client, he slipped into the washroom, locked the door, laid out a pair, inhaled, rubbed his nostrils, and quickly felt much better. Maybe he'll come to the office more often, get to know April Wu better. She's quick, she gave him tit for tat. Obviously likes him. Finds him charmingly eccentric. Handsome enough with his chiselled, strifeworn features, despite his cigarette-yellowed moustache. She's intrigued, here was someone different, the famed defender of an international assassin. The Abu Khazzam case, front-page news all through Asia. Ah, my love, did your heart skip a beat when you learned you'd be working for the great Bry Pomeroy?

He did a couple more rows, then peed, washed his hands, and went out to fetch Cudworth. A muttering of greetings, no apologies, no eye contact. He sat him on a sofa, well away from the Oriental goddess, who was cross-legged on a wooden chair, pencil poised.

"Okay, Cud, face this way, not at her. From the top."

Of the three writers Judge Whynet-Moir invited, the most exotic was Cudworth Brown, a poet of bawdy and muscular verse, and he was the first to arrive – eager to sup at the capitalist trough, to rub elbows with philanthropists and possible patrons.

As Cudworth's taxi pulled into the portico, Whynet-Moir came out to greet him. A thin, greying, straight-backed man, a soft city hand that went limp in Cudworth's gnarly grip. Waving off his ill-meant protests, Whynet-Moir paid the fifty dollars on the meter.

"Bless you, Judge. That fare would've wiped me out."

"My pleasure. Where are you staying?"

"I'll find a place, I'll get by."

Whynet-Moir saw that Cudworth had brought a backpack presumably stuffed with overnight gear, and he grappled with the implications for a moment. "Nonsense, you'll stay the night here. Plenty of empty beds. Self-contained suite above the garage if you prefer, the maid's room." Above-the-garage was what Whynet-Moir would prefer: this vulgarian had a suspect reputation.

He ushered Cudworth in, showed him where to hang his poncho. The brute had had a recent shave and haircut, at least, and the grace to use a deodorizer. Floppy boots, baggy black pants held up by red braces, the top buttons of a denim shirt opened to reveal a peace medallion nestled among chest curls. Poor Flo, she will be aghast. He wished she would quickly finish her makeup and rescue him. He would definitely check the seating assignments, to make sure he was at the other end of the table from this hulk-shouldered rural.

To kill time before the other guests arrived (the political essayist, Professor Chandra, would be His Lordship's preferred seatmate), he toured Cudworth through the main wing of the house. A catering chef and his assistant were in the kitchen, an atrium of stainless steel; servers were setting a long table in a dining salon whose sliding glass doors gave access to the wraparound cedar deck and views of rock faces towering over a narrow, frothy inlet.

A living room dominated by a two-sided fireplace. A glassed overlook to the heated pool, steaming and bubbling. Jade conveniences in each washroom. Elevator to the wine cellar. Just off the dining parlour, a well-stocked bar.

Whynet-Moir didn't know how to respond to Cudworth's

mantra, "Nice set-up," "Real nice set-up." With neither able to bridge the cultural gap, conversation was sparse, but Cudworth couldn't say no to a martini, and he lingered so longingly at the countertop humidor that Whynet-Moir gave him a Romeo y Julieta. "I'm afraid we prefer to smoke outdoors," he said, ushering Cudworth outside. With relief, the judge ran off to attend to new arrivals.

Cudworth twirled his cigar, playing with it, wanting to save it for the right mellow moment, with some of that Hennessy VSOP to go with it. He lit a cigarette, watched Whynet-Moir greet a couple in a high-end Porsche. Here coming up the driveway was a voluptuous car, a topless Lamborghini. Ever since he lost his virginity in a Jaguar, Cudworth had a thing about fine cars.

"Want to fire me up?"

He turned to see what looked like a frame from an early flick, Lauren Bacall in mid-career, maybe, or Greta Garbo, in what they call a little black thing, high black boots, a long set of pearls, an unlit cigarette proffered. There was something vaguely Oriental about her, in her eyes and colour, but he figured half the world had Genghis Khan's genes, sometimes they showed up more obviously.

He didn't skip a beat, had a match under her fag in an instant, his hand cupped to shelter the flame, her hand there too, touching, wine-red lips puckering, inhaling, smoke creeping from flared nostrils.

"You changed my life," she said.

Brian opened a window to let some of the heat escape. He hadn't been with a woman for months, was horny for Florenza LeGrand, what right had Cud to pucker with the transoceanic shipping line princess? She really say that, Cud? You changed her *life*? Sounds a little wheezy, falsely dramatic.

An image of Florenza and her little black thing and her wine-red lips came again, but his erection failed to last, submitting limply to an infernal chorus from a shop speaker about the coming of Santa Claus.

He should have had that beer with Max, should have gone with him to the Club d'Jazz at attitude adjustment hour. He shouldn't have sneaked out the back way, by the stairs of cowardice. He should have listened to Max diagnose him. *I'll be blunt, Bry. I don't think you're sick, you're just being an asshole.* He could have refuted that. Easy. But he *wants* them to think he's being an asshole. That's his cover.

At the same time he hadn't wanted a harangue from the scrawny long-distance runner, a drug abuse lecture. Brian took pride in his drug abuse, he was a gourmand of drug abuse, Max wouldn't understand that. Brian had hit on the perfect combination: a tequila on the hour, a line on the half-hour, and non-stop nicotine, a sustained creative high. Presumably most crime writers, from Dashiell Hammett on, composed while drunk or stoned, so Brian was maintaining a fine tradition. As Widgeon said, *I find a wee nip at the bottom of the day stirs the embers to one last spurt before the weary writer retires to the comfort of easy chair and telly.*

It had never occurred to Cudworth his verses might change a life; it was a wondrous concept to which he quickly warmed.

"I was living a lie," she said.

"How?"

"I'll tell you sometime."

She pulled two thin volumes from her bag. *Liquor Balls* and *Karmageddon.* "Write something scintillating." Then she had second thoughts, because she put them back. "Later, when you've got to know me better. Would you like to stay the night?"

"Thanks, I've already been asked. I'll be in the maid's room." Cud pointed to the room above the garage, in case she needed directions. She butted her smoke and went off to greet her guests.

—

You're asking me to buy this, Cud, this seduction scenario? I'll play along with it, but what's *her* version? There's the rub — she's made no statements and, on the advice of counsel, hasn't talked to the Crown. Brian had learned this from a letter from Abigail Hitchins he'd eventually found enclosed in a box with the particulars of evidence.

So Brian didn't know what Ms. LeGrand was going to say at the trial, he hadn't a clue. He'd read about her, seen photos of her, a favourite of the gossip columns, wild, eccentric, unclassifiable. Rumours abounded of dissolute early years, before her marriage two years ago to the handsome, allegedly suave, and utterly eligible bachelor judge.

Brian is going to dig up the dirt on her. If she's lying he'll cut her to pieces. Yes, Cud, your tireless advocate is going to get right on top of the case, you're in safer hands than Allstate. Bry is a late starter, slow off the blocks, but watch him skim over those hurdles.

He rose to the window, looked across Main Street. The thin man was still there — he'd traded in the London Fog for a windbreaker, but it was the same guy, the same scrawny build. Standing under the shouting sign, "Girls! Girls! Girls!" Talking to the doorman at the Palace. Pointing across the street. *That's his hotel, he's in 305, I want you to break his fingers so he can't use a keyboard — we have to stop him.*

The doorman nodded. He was a hulking fellow, a former Lions player, a tight end — Lance could only guess what that role involved; he'd never understood North American football, or why it was *called* football. Right now, the tight end was taking a pass from the thin man, several bills from his wallet. The thin man walked away.

Lance shrugged and turned from the window. He would rather look at his clever new secretary, who was doing the day's final filing. She smiled. "Is there anything else I can help you with?"

"Thank you, Ms. Wu. You've done splendidly for your first day."

"Good starts raise false hopes."

"Ah, the maxim of the day. You must write down your grandmother's sayings. Wisdom unrecorded is wisdom lost."

Finally a smile from her, a glint of interest. "Tomorrow I will remember the rose."

"The prettiest one the florist has. But you'll still put it to shame."

She smiled, but in a tired way, with a hint of scorn – she'd heard it all before. "Thank you. Now I must leave."

"I'm sorry, but that's not a good idea."

She paused while getting her coat. "Why?"

Lance pointed out the window. "See that bloke? The leviathan?"

She joined him, observed the tight end walking across the street toward their building.

"He means to do me harm."

Frightened, she went to the phone. "I'll call 911."

"Jolly good idea. Make sure they send an ambulance. He'll need one."

Widgeon: *The writer must endeavour to end each chapter with a gut-churning, page-turning moment of high suspense. Nudge your fickle reader into the next chapter before he escapes from your literary clutches, turns off the bedside lamp, rolls over, and enfolds himself in the arms of Morpheus.*

Despite the master's overblown prose, his advice, when stripped, is always on the mark. Yes, O Windy Sage, let's leave the reader hanging there for the moment, before kicking his butt right into Chapter Eight.

7

THE CONQUEST OF NORBERT

A dream held for a few seconds, then shredded, leaving hazy recall of a courtroom, a pitcher of gin, Arthur on trial for being drunk and disorderly – a typical alcoholic's dream that recurs in many guises. He blinked with relief: he wasn't hungover.

The dream signalled he was depressed and anxious, but in the fog of waking he didn't know why. Now last evening came back, a terrible evening, two long-distance calls featuring, first, the apologetic falseness of Nicholas Braid in Vancouver, followed by a detonation from Melbourne. Nick Junior had been abed when the calls came. How was Arthur to handle this, how to tell Nick that his father can't make it for Christmas at Blunder Bay?

Nicholas Braid's voice had been tight despite the few drinks he must have taken to brace himself. Something had come up. A group of VIJPs was in town for the holidays. Very Important Japanese People. The plan was to entertain them lavishly on Whistler Mountain, buy them choice seats for the World Figure Skating Trials.

"There's no way I can crawl out of this one, Arthur. But I'm going to make it up to Nick big-time. Tell him I've booked New Year's in Maui. Four days, five-star resort, first-class tickets."

He must not have felt able to tell Nick himself, that's why he called so late. Arthur could see no rational reason for his

ex-son-in-law's unpardonable behaviour and promptly
informed on him to Deborah's answering service.

Her return call woke Arthur at 3:00 a.m. She was spitting mad. Her lawyer was going to hire a detective to get
evidence on Nicholas and the floozy he was obviously shack-
ing up with. Then she was going to seek full custody.
Nicholas wasn't allowed on Garibaldi Island. He wasn't
allowed anywhere near his son. Nick was to stay on the island
until she could fetch him home.

Arthur, at a loss as to how he might enforce these dicta,
hadn't uttered a syllable before she said abruptly, "Never
mind, I'm going to tell him myself. Maui? *Maui? Forget it.*
That piece of shit."

What was Arthur to say to Nick?

Ten after seven. Through the window he could make out
pasture and sea covered in low, thick mist, strands of it spiral-
ling around the trunks of conifers. Apollo's chariot had yet to
wheel over the horizon, but there was a glow of his coming.

Margaret was in the kitchen, he could hear the blender,
a clattering of pans, her basic-training voice, Nick's responses.
Cool. Whatever. He'd been conscripted as sous-chef for a
spread planned for Christmas Day. A dozen carefully chosen
guests – major donors for the Greens – plus the woofers.

He rose from bed, showered, dressed, worrying and fussing
about Nick, about surviving tomorrow's dinner. Hosting a
houseful of ideologues was not Arthur's idea of a merry
Christmas. A humourless crowd, these Greens, with their
dispiriting news about the planet.

His walking shoes today – a hike to the general store, and
when the mists dissolved he might carry on up Mount
Norbert, the island's highest peak, more than a thousand feet.
Enjoy the view, find some peace.

In the kitchen, he poured a coffee, watched Margaret
demonstrate how to mash potatoes. "Got it?"

"Yeah, I think."

"Good. Run out to the root cellar and grab a few turnips."

"What do they look like?"

She explained. He slouched out. With flour-coated hands, Margaret gingerly reciprocated Arthur's hug. "Baking powder, silver wrap, and eight lemons, could you, please, Arthur? When you go to the store? Baking *powder*, not soda." A deep breath. "You're going to have to tell him his father's not coming."

"Yes, I must do that."

"Nicholas wouldn't have fitted in anyway. He's too straight-laced. He talks only about golf. Will you do the bar tomorrow, Arthur, can you handle that?"

"With steely determination."

"Otherwise, I want you to stay out of the kitchen. This is my affair. All I ask is that you attend. Be your usual courteous self. Don't scare people with obscure literary references. And, please, please, don't start arguing. You don't know anything about politics, dear. That's why you're a Conservative."

To Arthur, women were unfathomable, but after one failed marriage and seven loving but hectic years with this master of the indirect dig, he was learning. These guests were important to her and she didn't want him spouting off, damaging her chances at the nomination.

"I shall not make any speeches about corrupt, asinine politicians." He will stay out of the kitchen. Stay away from the heat.

"I don't want this to be a burden to you. I've heard your speech about politics a dozen times." A pause. "I won't ask you to support me in this."

He sought a satisfactory way to respond to that sledge-hammer line. Apologize? Repeat the speech? Fire back?

The phone rang, coitus interruptus to this prickly conversation. Before picking up, she said, "Have your talk with Nick. Look in on the woofers. It's milking time."

He went out into the mist feeling disloyal, misunderstood. Somehow he must get up the gumption to tell her he's afraid for her. The heartbreak, the humiliation and depression she will suffer. The Greens got trounced in this riding in the last election, ran a dismal fourth, just beat out the Marijuana Party.

The winner was the justice minister in the Conservative government, Jack Boynton, a large man with large appetites for food and drink who died of a stroke at a wedding banquet. Hence the by-election. The date for that had yet to be set, and the Greens' nomination meeting was just a few weeks off.

Arthur expected Margaret to be a shoo-in. Her main competitor, a charisma-deprived nursery operator, was the fellow who fared so poorly in the general election last year. Margaret Blake had been on the front pages and in the supper news for eighty straight days, guarding the gates to Gwendolyn Valley from fifty feet up an ancient fir. Now the valley was parkland, she had rescued Gwendolyn from a quick-buck developer.

After Margaret and Cudworth Brown were chosen by lot to do the sit-in, the regulars at the general store teased him cruelly about Cud's priapic prowess, recounting – or making up – stories of his conquests. *He's humped about half the island women, wouldn't you say, Barney? Well, he screwed my wife, and she ain't nowhere as good-looking as Arthur's.* Arthur joined in the merriment with a false grin and a palpitating heart.

Margaret's version, however, had been reassuringly credible. After two weeks, she'd decided she could no longer endure his company and had him replaced by an unthreatening female anarchist. Somewhere buried in this history was substantial reason for not getting involved in the murder trial of Cudworth Brown. There were many small, subtle ways in which Arthur didn't like the man, more reasons being discovered on each encounter.

He made out no sign of Nick outside, but he could barely see his own footfall in the heavy mist. Only the house and barn rose above it, and the milking shed up the hill. Arthur found his way to the root cellar – the door was closed, a bag of turnips set outside. When a breeze stirred the fog, he spotted Nick up at the milking shed.

A closer view, from the corral fence, might well have inspired Vermeer. In the glow of yellow rays slicing through the mist, Nick sat beside Lavinia, raptly watching her pull milk from Bess, their Jersey cow. Lavinia was sure-handed, in rhythm with Bess – but suddenly, a Chaplinesque moment, she gave Nick a squirt in the eye. He jumped, but Lavinia's infectious laughter made him grin. The kid was loosening up.

"I show you how." She extended him a teat.

Arthur would find another moment to talk to Nick, he had no desire to spoil this pastoral scene with its gentle touch of Eros. He retreated quietly, took the turnips to the house, slung his day pack over his shoulder, and headed briskly up the driveway.

He trod up Centre Road, where bungalows decked out in lights and tinsel glowed through the mist. Once again, as they had for time immemorial, Jack and Ida Shewfelt had celebrated the divine miracle of Christ's coming with the engineering miracle of hoisting Santa, his sleigh, and his entire team of reindeer onto their split-level roof.

Next door to them resided Bob Stonewell, target of their many complaints under the Unsightly Premises Bylaw. A sign advertising his car parts business was by Stoney's rusted gate, behind it a ramshackle house and an old barn converted to a garage. Everywhere, relics poking from the mist, a jungle of them, a whole hillside, Chevies and Fords, Datsuns and Skodas. Arthur's ailing 1969 Fargo pickup, his pet, his baby, was sitting by the garage on blocks, under a tarp.

There was the great mechanic himself, newly risen from bed, packing out yesterday's beer bottles, a cigarette aglow between his lips. He waved. "If it ain't the town tonsil, out getting his morning exercise. If you can't do it easy, do it hard, that's what I always say." The merry clink of empties going into boxes.

Arthur asked after the health of the Fargo.

"I got a line on a rebuilt transmission. I can get a real sweet deal for cash up front."

"What happened to the cash I already fronted?"

"Right. Well, it sort of got used on startup costs. I got a new business, limousine rental, I call it Loco Motion. Check out these beauties." Indicating a pair of shiny fin-tails from the 1970s, a Chrysler and a Buick. "I'm restricting operations to Garibaldi, so normal car rental laws don't apply, right?"

"Merry Christmas, Stoney." Arthur carried on down the road.

Baking powder, silver wrap, and . . . yes, lemons, eight lemons. He mustn't forget the mail. Above the fog was glorious sun, so despite his lack of sleep, he will adhere to his plan of huffing up Mount Norbert.

He found his way to Hopeless Bay, small-boat dock and a warehouse, century-old general store, a false-front structure with an enclosed porch serving as a coffee lounge. Here, several regulars were enjoying alcohol-enriched coffees. As a sideline, the proprietor, skeletal, dour Abraham Makepeace, sold brown-bagged bottles of rum or whisky to tippling locals. Hapless Constable Pound, wary of upsetting the community, turned a blind eye to the evils perpetrated here.

A couple of the lads were celebrating the season with Bacchus-like determination. Gomer Goulet, whose crab boat was tied up below, was standing, swaying as if in heavy seas, proclaiming his love of mankind. Gomer tended to get drunkenly soppy, especially at Christmas. Emily LeMay, the sultry ex-barmaid and untiring vamp, told him, "Sit down before you fall on your kazoo."

Lemons, silver foil, and . . . yes, baking powder. Or was it soda? He mined the lemon bin, excavated a dozen fat ones. At the next bin, bagging up oranges, was Al Noggins, a spry, short, bearded Welshman, Garibaldi's Anglican minister.

"Lemons? Fish for Christmas, Arthur?"

"Margaret has invited a dozen major contributors to the Granola Party, many of whom don't eat warm-blooded life forms. I am to be on my best behaviour."

"Firing up the troops, is she? Good luck to her; she's a fresh voice in politics. While I have your ear, old boy," Noggins moved close, "Cudworth came by for a spot of spiritual counselling. He's pretty messed up. Carried on about this lawyer fellow, Pomeroy. Couldn't understand why you recommended him, instead of . . . Well, he feels *abandoned*, Arthur."

"Reverend Al, I do not defend bad poets. It is a long-standing policy."

"Told him I'd speak to you. Merry Christmas." He walked stiffly off. An awkward moment regretted – Noggins was a close friend.

Lemons, foil, baking powder, and, just in case, baking soda. Arthur bought a packet of pipe tobacco as well, then waited patiently while Makepeace sorted through the Blunder Bay mail. "Mostly Christmas cards – this one came open, it's from that doctor you got off, the one who poisoned his wife. This here letter has no return address; I always get suspicious when I see that. Your *Literary Gazette*, your *Guardian*, and your *Island Bleat*, special holiday edition. And some stuff, I think from your accountant, about your retirement funds. Didn't know you were sixty-nine, Arthur."

"There's a lot about me you don't know, Abraham."

Arthur was about to go but couldn't pretend not to hear Emily LeMay calling him. "Hey, handsome, I got you something for Christmas."

It would be uncivil to run off without an exchange of yuletide greetings, so he made his way to the porch. "Merry Christmas," Gomer cried. "Very merry Christmas, it's a time of joy, the cup of love is brimming over. Hey, you look like Santa." That irked Arthur – he had the white beard and the pack on his back, but he didn't have the legendary hero's paunch.

"Santa, baby, you can come down my chimney any day."
Emily advanced, she was not to be denied her Christmas hug.

Nearly overcome by her perfume, its overlay of whisky,
by her bounteous breasts pooling against him, he had trouble
peeling himself free. "And a happy Christmas to you all."

"Arthur, you're gonna help out Cud Brown, aren't you?"
she said.

"You gotta defend him!" Gomer was gesturing wildly.
"Arthur, you gotta have heart; it's Christmas, the season of love,
and Cud's our buddy, he's one of *us*. We got to stick together
on this here rock." His voice rose theatrically. "Cud worships
you, man. Just like a father." He began staggering toward
Arthur. "He *loves* you, man, can't you see that? Oh, God, don't
let them nail him to the cross."

This last was blubbered to Arthur's retreating backside, and
then all he heard was sobbing. A few minutes later, as he crested
a rise, he turned to see Gomer, his legs so rubbery as to be
useless, being helped by friends down to his crab boat.

The episode was unsettling. The island was ganging up on
him. Cud had capable counsel, the successful defender of the
assassin of an Asian czar and, just last January, an addled court
clerk bent on shooting the chief justice. The locals didn't
understand, and Arthur was loathe to explain, but he was definitely the wrong lawyer for Cud. He began mumbling to
himself. "I wouldn't have my heart in it; I plain don't like him.
Doesn't have anything to do with Margaret, it's something else.
Not sure what it is."

A fleeting suspicion: had it to do with his own lack of
sexual prowess? He brushed off the thought like lint. Utter
nonsense. He may not be the world's most dynamic lover, but
he showed sparks of competency. With the aid of Viagra. It's
not the lack of gas, it's the engine. *Volo, non valeo*, I am willing
but unable. Oddly, however, he functioned with unusual facility after winning a trial. But then weeks would pass . . .

He hiked uphill to the Mount Norbert trail still talking to himself – a bad habit, especially for a lawyer – then paused to rest, folding open the *Bleat*. From the front page, Hamish McCoy grinned at the camera, brandishing a hammer at a scaffold on the rise known as Ferryboat Knoll. Below the photo: "Tourists to our lovely island will be welcomed soon by the *Goddess of Love*, the internationally acclaimed and world-renowned local sculptor Hamish McCoy told the *Bleat* in an exclusive interview."

A few days ago, Nelson Forbish was seen quaffing beers with McCoy in the Legion, and he must still have been drunk when this edition went to bed. Nowhere in the chaotic six-page special Christmas edition could Arthur find this exclusive interview. Even the image beside the Merry Christmas streamer was out of tune with the season – a turkey fanning its tail.

Here was Margaret, as he might have expected. Another letter to the editor. No strident calls to action today. Calmly urging a ban against deforesting steep slopes, a popular issue, nothing that would mire her in controversy just before the nomination.

Arthur was not looking forward to spending Christmas Day with a crew of eco-holics and their glum scenarios. He was depressed already. *I'm not asking you to support me in this.* He felt cornered. He'd never been so impolitic as to suggest Margaret's quest was quixotic or to openly oppose, though he had supportively urged her to think it over. Everyone hates politicians, why would a sane person want the job? Sitting in a raucous chamber with 308 preening narcissists. Giving up the great civil liberty called privacy. What Arthur most feared was that politics would corrupt Margaret, but of course he hadn't the courage to say that.

He lit his pipe, subsided onto a bench at the foot of Summit Trail, dug out the no-return-address envelope from his pack, and tore it open. Folded within was a note: "For your eyes only," and initials, "E.S." Who might that be? Stapled to it, a one-page report, obviously a photocopy, from the discipline committee of the B.C. Law Society. The date was September 8, 2006, it was stamped "classified," and had to do with unguarded remarks made by Provincial Judge J. Dalgleish Ebbe. It seemed unconnected with anything Arthur might be interested in, but he read on.

The matter was referred by a barrister who need not be named, who was among several counsel having cocktails with Judge Ebbe in a lounge after court. The judge was overheard to excoriate Mr. Justice Rafael Whynet-Moir, using foul language. He claimed His Lordship and his spouse were major contributors to the Conservative Party and accused him of bribing the justice minister, the late Hon. Jack Boynton, Q.C., to get the appointment.

As Arthur recalled, Boynton had named Whynet-Moir to the Supreme Court in late summer of 2006. Judge Ebbe often liked to entertain after court and was notorious for his acerbic tongue. The humourless tattler was doubtless a priggish and unseasoned counsel.

Judge Ebbe is alleged to have accused Mr. Justice Whynet-Moir of having been corrupt when in practice, and close to Boynton. He is reported to have said, "Someone would be doing a blow for justice if he'd drop him down a well." The committee is of the unanimous view that this matter need not be referred to the judicial council and that, because a fair amount of alcohol was likely consumed, no action need be taken.

Arthur gazed up at Chickadee Ridge, Mount Norbert's western wall looming through the mist. "Why me?" he asked the air. Why was this anonymously sent, and why to Arthur? That teased at him. He must fax it to Pomeroy.

He stared up at the switchback trail, seven hundred more feet to climb. The air was less hazy here, and Norbert faintly beckoned, double-humped like a Bactrian camel. *Let's see what you're made of, Beauchamp.*

⚖

It was mid-afternoon as he surmounted Chickadee Ridge, jutting out from Norbert's fir-crowned crest. Normally this mesa afforded a sweeping overlook of farm, field, and forest, but today all he could see, through fog gaps, were hilltops on the horizon and a stretch of shoreline, the *Queen of Prince George* nudging into the dock on Ferryboat Road, bearing a throng of Christmas visitors.

There was Hamish McCoy's community service project, and the energetic little fellow himself. Distantly came sounds of hammering and welding from his scaffold. Would it house a fifteen-foot-tall goddess of love and beauty? Would he put his own abstract stamp on the Venus de Milo? If one discounts the alleged exclusive to the *Bleat*, he has stayed tight-lipped about his vision.

McCoy had promised to haul the *Fall of Icarus* to Blunder Bay soon. Arthur regretted having spoken so glowingly of it. What was he to do with a bronze sculpture the height of two tall men? Put it up by the gate. The sight of doomed, horrified Icarus might deter unwanted visitors.

A couple of passing drivers honked, and McCoy waved back. The old scamp was in better emotional trim these days, with the tension of his trial over. He'd laid to rest his grievance against the suspect squealer, Zoller. "Oi've been given a rare break. There's a toime for anger, a toime for forgiveness." This was said in passing as Arthur was buying fencing wire and McCoy loading his truck with two-by-fours donated by the local lumberyard.

His watch said three o'clock, the shank of a rare December day, made warm as May by the sun reflecting off the whiteness below. The cheeky, cheery birds for which this ridge was named were calling "Dee-dee," flirting and flitting sideways and upside down on the cones of the tree he was leaning against, several feet from the lip of the void. Below: a sixty-foot wall, a few firs and spindly oaks rooted in the crevasses.

He backed away, looked about, and found a fine resting place in the crook of an arbutus tree. The base of its smooth, barkless trunk made an ideal chair-back, and the low-slung winter sun was directly on him. To the east, he could make out the Gwendolyn Cliffs, fractured by the Gap Trail. A mist hovered above Gwendolyn Pond, from which a pair of grebes took wing into the mist, raising wakes. He was thankful he couldn't see the carnage on the flatland by the beach, the twenty acres of spilled giants, firs, cedars, maples.

Parks Canada had decided to let those giants rest in peace, a graveyard with its sorrowful epitaphs about the depredations of man. Matters could have been immeasurably worse – the developer had proposed hundreds of lots and condos for these 580 acres. Arthur's case for an injunction had wound its way to Ottawa, to the Supreme Court. At the eleventh hour, as the court was about to throw him out on his ear, Parks Canada announced it had bought Gwendolyn Valley. This was Margaret Blake's triumph – after eighty days in a tree fort she'd won the Battle of the Gap, holding off the loggers, inspiring a campaign, winning over the public, the TV-watching masses, and, finally, the politicians.

He'd been proud of Margaret when she got that award from the International Wilderness Society. Now he felt hollow and cheap. *I've heard your speech about politics a dozen times.* With a steely stare at the stubborn old mule. *I'm not asking you to support me in this.* "Damn you, Beauchamp," he shouted, "nor should she have to ask." What a wretch you are, what an ingrate, you have devalued her before her comrades with your feigned, lukewarm show of support.

Yes, he will charm her dinner guests, he will be the prospective candidate's perfect husband, he will proclaim his support, extol her – a fresh voice, Reverend Al called her. *She's just what we need in Parliament.* (Of course, she has the merest hypothetical chance – a recent poll had the Greens at 11 per cent – so he'll not find himself spending his winters in a rented flat in the frozen hell of Ottawa.)

And with that resolved, pleased with his solution to a needless nuptial irritant, he sensed a burden lift, sensed it soaring off to join the three bald eagles drifting on updrafts from the Gwendolyn cliffs. He smiled and zipped up his jacket. He drifted off.

⚖

He awoke shivering, thinking he'd been blinded, then saw by the glow of his watch it was a quarter to six, already night, the early blackness of winter, hours after he was expected home. An owl whistling above him in the arbutus branches, that is what woke him, and the chill. Only starlight above, no lights below. As he scrambled to his feet, he sensed a whisper of wings, the owl abandoning him. Which way was down? How close was the precipice? He checked his pocket. Half a packet of penny matches.

8

EAT THE RICH

A heavy footfall up the stairs, the tight end making no secret of his coming. Lance supposed he could dispatch him with a well-timed scissor kick – his years of study under Master Dao should not be wasted – but just in case, he reached into his desk drawer for his insurance policy.

His 9 mm Beretta was gone!

April Wu spun toward him, smiling, the Beretta aimed low, horizontal with his testicles.

"So you're with them," Lance said.

"Loyalty is a delusion, trust but a false mirror."

The hallway door crashed open. It wasn't the tight end, it was . . . Cudworth Brown! Furious, stomping toward him, fists balled. "You sold me out!"

April Wu's bullet tore a hole through his bent nose. Cud gazed at her stupefied for a moment, then slumped to the floor.

"He had bad chi," she said. "So do you."

The pistol was aimed at Lance again!

"It was you all along," he said.

"I am but one of many." She barked. "Hand me the manuscript!"

Trash this page!

Flush this manic excursus, a digression from a plot barely coherent to start with. He was wandering off in every direction like a lunatic lost on the sanatorium grounds. Insanatorium grounds.

Point proved, however: When sober, as he was now, nauseated, shaking, skin prickling with the coca-Joneses, Brian wrote crap. If this is what abstinence wreaks on a single Christmas afternoon, what kind of hell would several days of it promise? But he'll soldier on, stay off the stuff a while, supplies were low.

He must start this chapter over, seek inspiration from the fountain of truth. April Wu will keep her day job at Pomeroy and company but will no longer moonlight at the Valentine Agency — it's gone out of business. Goodbye, Lance, you arrogant ponce. Live happily ever after, Cud Brown — for you, the rustic embattled poet, are the true hero of this tragedy, its true victim.

Suddenly I'm dining at the best tables, me, Cudworth Brown, scion of an unemployed miner, formerly of the working class myself, surviving on grants and a piddly-ass disability pension. So don't be surprised I never seen a dinner like that one.

It started off with jumbo shrimp on cracked ice with some wafers and what I guessed was real caviar, though I didn't want to be naive by asking. And those were only the starters, the whore doovers, as we say on Garibaldi.

I figured the sockeye salmon was the main course, I even took an extra offering, and I was sitting back, thinking about dessert, and suddenly the caterers were bringing out tenderloins and asparagus and baby carrots, new cutlery, the works; it was like the feast had just begun. Man, I was glad I smoked a doobie on the ferry — it gave me the appetite to pound the chow down. I didn't want it to go to waste; they weren't handing out doggie bags.

Before I forget, let me go back, there were drinks first, martinis or wine, you had a choice, they were coming around on trays. "Please mingle," Judge Whynet-Moir said. *Mingle*. Decoded, he was telling his friends to check out the hick in the red braces. One of these poshes, Shiny Shoes, I call him, some kind of downtown rainmaker, tried to fluff me off. "A peace medallion — I hadn't realized they were back in fashion." I told him I also got one tattooed on my ass.

I didn't mingle, I wasn't comfortable with all these pooh-bahs. Talked to the other two writers. One came dressed in a sari. She wrote right-wing political commentary, so she was right at home here. The other was Lynn Tinkerson, a dyke who is what they call an important writer, and I told her I intend to read one of her novels.

The table was set with little place cards, a practice I've never encountered in four and a half decades of hard living. Rafael Whynet-Moir had done the guy-girl-guy-girl thing and put himself at the far end of the table between the two lady guest writers.

Sitting on my right was a wrinkle-free woman with a ten-inch smile who'd obviously been in the shop for renovations once too often. She told me she'd never met a poet and wanted to know all about it. I was feeling rosy after a couple or three martinis washed down by a fine, crisp Bordeaux, and I told her how during misty shoreline walks my muse would rescue me from the heartsickness of wounded love.

Meanwhile, I am playing left-leg footsie with Florenza LeGrand, Flo she likes to be called. She'd kicked off her sandals, was casually running her toes up my leg. Judge Whynet-Moir would look our way occasionally, smiling, but I read a warning in his eyes.

Sometimes Flo also played handsie, squeezing mine under the big table spread, touching my thigh. I didn't know she had a rep, I didn't know anything about her — but I knew the type. Spoiled daughter of the rich, flirts with danger, likes to smoke, drink, and get laid, in no particular order. I was looking forward to tupping a member of the ruling class; she's rich beyond belief. She might be persuaded to set up a starving poets endowment fund.

You changed my life – that seemed like hoke. I figured she just wanted to bang me. There's an image in *Karmageddon* of me eating hair pie, maybe that got to her, but I wasn't sure it was me made her horny or if she was horny all the time. Her consort kind of answered that question when you saw him over there, tittering with the ladies in his overattentive way. You've got to figure Judge Whynet-Moir doesn't have hair on his ass.

The cosmetic surgery victim to my right asked, "And when did you first decide to become a poet?"

"Madam," I said, "I was born a poet. We are all born poets. Our first word is poetry. Ma-ma, da-da. Rhyme at its most basic but beautiful to a mother's ear." I was doing this mindless rap, with her hanging on every word. "You been there, eh, you got kids?"

"I have," she said in a kind of heart-fluttery way while, from the other direction, toes were wiggling up my pant-leg.

I went on about how we have to dig through the garbage of our lives to rediscover the poetic talent God gave us at birth. "It got buried in organized religion and spreadsheets and ads for SUVs and all the other shit capitalism throws at you."

She sat back; it was like I'd slapped her. As the waiter was topping up my Bordeaux, I was thinking I better pull in my ears, slow down. I'd promised my publisher I'd behave myself and not go around ticking off patrons of the arts.

I had to endure Mr. Sarcasm, Shiny Shoes, who was across from me, giving me this, "One of your claims to fame, I believe, involved some extended tree-sitting a couple of years ago."

Entertain me, clown. Tell me a rollicking story. I said something back to him, I can't remember. Before we got to the point of tangling asses, Whynet-Moir stood up to toast the celebrities. I drank along with everyone before remembering I wasn't supposed to.

I got to admit there was a certain class anger at work here. This is how the rich live. Cooked to, catered to, and coddled, while my folks spent their whole lives on the wrong side of the tracks in a depressed mining town and could barely afford pork and beans. And I felt even shittier because I'd been given the role of royal jester, I was being used, patronized, and the hostess planned to use me as her fuck-servant.

And I was *willing*.

Flo was getting bolder with each refill of her wine – her fingers were no longer grazing, they were sliding up my thigh. I whispered, "Is this cool? I hope your old man doesn't keep a loaded Magnum in a drawer."

She came close, her breath hot in my ear. "Don't worry, he's a lousy shot."

I don't think she saw Whynet-Moir looking at us just then, while her hand was making contact through the fabric with a stiff and unyielding object. Man, she was bold. You ever had a stiff one get caught in your pant-leg? I didn't want to wait until the book-signing, I wanted to fuck her right then, wanted to get down on the floor with her and fuck her while everybody else wiped gravy from their chins.

But as I was sitting there toughing it out, things got really awkward: Flo caught one of her rings in my zipper. She tugged, and it wouldn't come free.

Today's pop-up from Horace Widgeon: *Do not over-embellish your main suspect. The experienced mystery reader, aware that too many fingers of suspicion are pointed at some blackguard, will invariably dismiss him from contention, thus narrowing the field in the great battle of wits between writer and reader.*

What was the secret message? Did Widgeon suspect that Cuddles was innocent, that the real murderer lurked elsewhere? Brian can see why Widgeon feels sympathy for Cud. He's human, he has feelings, though he lets the little head do most of his thinking. Under a thin shell of braggadocio, he seems kind of scared. When you go over his story carefully, as Brian had, capturing the hidden essences, you start to wonder if Cud isn't telling the truth — maybe Florenza *was* coming on like a ballistic missile.

It wasn't right that Cud found himself in such a pickle. Brian would feel terrible if this working-class hero went down for killing Rafael Whynet-Moir, so he'll dry out, he'll pull out the stops.

He'd researched Florenza LeGrand, googled her: a teenaged delinquent, a runaway, her parents had to pull her out of an Oregon ashram and deprogram her. A few years later, she got busted in Guadalajara, shacked up with a Mexican dope dealer. It cost mucho dinero for her parents to repatriate her. They plunked her into an elite New England college that doubles as a finishing school. Marriage to the polished, worldly Rafael Whynet-Moir would straighten her out, everyone said.

Reminder: he must ask Special Prosecutor Abigail Hitchins if Florenza remains uncooperative. He must respond to Abigail, whose recorded messages have grown caustic and rude.

Enough of abstinence. He chopped up a snifter. It's just a party drug, an ice cream habit, coke light, a little fizz to perk him up when worries get him down. He should go out to score another gram, but the thin man was always there, the stalker. Was he to be feared? Were he an assassin, Brian would be dead by now. The man had some business with the author, but what?

Brian's neighbourhood ATM had turned against him, cancelled their friendship. He'd had to cash in his RRSPs to buy gifts for Caroline and the kids. Flowers for her, roses of love and repentance. Yesterday, Santa's sleigh — a rip-off artist's two-ton van — delivered to the backyard a three-thousand-dollar haunted playhouse.

Rubbing his nose, he studied the slumped rider with two arrows in his back. Funny how he looked just like Cud.

The Mormon Tabernacle Choir was coming through the wall, three ships a-sailing in from Room 303. From some nearby slum apartment, children being threatened in song, Santa's gonna see if they've been naughty or nice. In Cantonese. Add to this cacophony: a busker pounding bongos outside. "Books! Books! Books!" Christmas fucking morning at the Ritz.

He was disappointed in April Fan Wu. He'd asked her out for Christmas dinner.

"That might not be a good idea under the circumstances."

"My circumstances are that I am divorced."

"My circumstances are that I left Hong Kong to escape from a boss who wanted to have sex with me."

Brian felt aggrieved that she assumed he, too, was so inclined.

"I'm sorry, but I have plans to be with my partner."

"I didn't know you had a boyfriend."

"She isn't a boyfriend."

He'd have looked up one of his ex-illicit-lovers, but he'd lost touch with them. All but Abigail Hitchins, who had gone from promiscuous label whore to machisma-pumping ultra-feminist. She was probably a lesbian now too. That's what they do.

Brian hadn't been with a woman since Roseanne. Affairs didn't seem like fun any more, not since he got divorced; they lacked edge, the sense of illicit adventure. Were Caroline to have him back, he'd never stray, he's learned his lesson. He will congratulate her for her prize for *Sour Memories*. He'll even finish reading it.

It isn't much consolation, but life is even more difficult for Cuddles.

Not only was her ring snagged on my fly, she couldn't get it off her finger either – there wasn't wriggle room. And her old man was starting to look at us sideways, maybe wondering why his wife was eating her dessert left-handed. I was rattled – it's not like we could casually rise and say, Excuse us, we had a bizarre accident.

The ring, which was gold with an opal, by the way, on her middle finger, got snagged on that little deal you use to pull the zipper up. Its end had broken off. So she whispers, "Fuck, *do* something." I scoop a patty of butter and work it around her finger, which finally slides free, and by now I have a boner like the spire of St. Mary's.

There is a proper genre for the carnal, and it isn't crime, hectors Widgeon in a finger-wagging sermon about not making a disgusting exhibition of one's swollen libido to the gentle, mystery-devouring sweethearts who prefer blood-spattered bodies to hot buttered cock. Brian contemplated his cellphone, finally switched it on, dialed, connected with Abigail Hitchins's machine. "Pomeroy here, diligently returning your calls, and it's, I don't know, somewhere around three p.m. . . ."

She came on. "It's noon. Are you blasted already?"

"On Christmas Day you're screening your calls?"

"From my mother. In case you forgot, we have a one-week trial starting in February."

"I got it in my daybook."

"Did you see my e-mail? A list of facts we'd like admitted. Non-contentious shit, street maps, house plans, dates, times, places."

Brian vaguely remembered something like that.

"Without admissions this sucker's going to last two weeks." A pause. "What are you doing for Christmas dinner?"

"Hiding from the people watching me." Why does she laugh?

"Yeah, and I'm hiding from my damn mother. Want to get together? We can go over my non-contentious wish list."

"I'm too broke."

"I'll buy. Let's say seven-thirty, Il Giardino. I'll phone to confirm. Keep your fucking cell on. Capisce?"

"Capisce." She was too eager, which was disconcerting. She had, unfortunately, become enraptured with Brian lo those many years ago, and with lamentable intensity. But that was the 1990s, another century. She'd had relationships since, a failed marriage, then five years sleeping with her therapist.

Brian looked out, the bongo busker was still working the street, another at the Keefer corner, doing mime. He was probably in on it with the doorman. The thin man was the leader, but he wasn't around right now. There was Harry the Need, under Quick Loans, No References Required. He was the only one Brian could trust.

Abigail called right back. "We're on. You still allowed to drive?"

"Had to sell the Honda to make ends meet."

"I'll pick you up, how's that?"

"No, I'll get there."

"Where are you, Brian?"

They always want to know. "Ciao."

9

A BLUNDER BAY CHRISTMAS

He was scrambling down in inky darkness, going too fast, slipping on lemons. Suddenly, spread below him, were the lights of a throbbing city with a great cathedral . . . no, a colonnaded courthouse. He had taken the wrong trail, the one to the precipice. He was falling, falling . . .

Arthur awoke in fright, took his bearings. It was noon. It was Christmas Day. He was on a couch and the *Aeneid* was lying open on his stomach. He was in the woofers' house, with its youthful clutter of art film posters, electronic gizmos, compact disks, Japanese paperbacks. Arthur had proposed to Margaret in this very living room. Clearly she now regretted having signed on to the deal.

This morning, when he tried to make amends for last night's grand gaucherie by offering to be her kitchen slave, she snapped, "Just get out of here. Get out of the house." She *had* spoken to him, however, despite yesterday's vow never to do so again. That was after she checked his bruises and scratches, scolding all the while, after she drew him a hot bath.

His groping descent from the peak had been aided by the glow from a hotly burning pipe, but he'd lost the trail soon after his last match went out, and was hours working his way downhill. He'd been raked by thorns and low branches, and his clothes were in tatters. Finally, he'd come within shouting distance of the search party assigned to Mount Norbert. Other volunteers had been combing every nook and cranny of the island. Yes, all of Garibaldi had spent Christmas Eve looking for this lost soul. Arthur's humiliation was spectacular, immeasurable.

The troop that won bragging rights was commanded by Constable Ernst Pound, who loudly announced his triumph by radio phone. "Listen up, folks. Sorry to disappoint anyone, but Mr. Beauchamp has been found by lucky Team Seven. It's 21:51 hours, and we have him in our lights, he's coming down the service road near the west entrance of Mount Norbert District Park."

All this Arthur heard clearly in the cold, still night as he slogged toward those lights. "Someone better call his wife, she sounded real panicky . . . Yeah, he looks okay, he has a walking stick, he's waving."

Arthur accepted coffee from Pound's Thermos but refused all other aid, refused bandages, though some scratches were beaded with congealed blood. A dead branch had decorated his left cheek with a painful, cup-shaped smile. Another branch had brought him a thick ear.

He followed Team Seven to the turnoff where they'd parked. "We tracked you as far as the general store," Pound said. "I figured Mount Norbert, because it's near there. You got to give advance notice where you're hiking, Mr. Beauchamp. I have to file a report, a whole lot of people got inconvenienced, and I can't ignore it."

Arthur had sat slouched in Pound's cruiser, not wanting to be seen, ducking as he passed the church, ducking the worshippers leaving after evensong. But neighbours had gathered at his house. "I'm fine, I'm fine," he repeated as Pound escorted him past them, up the driveway of shame, toward Margaret in the doorway.

Thus was blind Oedipus delivered unto the Furies, to be punished for his unwitting crimes. Arthur had been stupid and thoughtless, and no apology, no explanation was acceptable. She'd been on the verge of cancelling the dinner she'd been four days preparing. "I see this as sabotage. You had better decide whether you're with me or against me, because I am going to run in this election, and I intend to win. With you or without you."

He tried to persuade Margaret that while watching eagles sail over the Gwendolyn cliffs, he'd been deeply moved by his love and admiration for her, a soul-cleansing epiphany that had resolved him to support her great democratic endeavour.

"Please don't patronize me with your bullshit," she said.

At night, feeling the whip of her silent fury, he'd again slept poorly, and he was glad for this short kip on the woofers' couch. He was still hurting, especially his right ear, which resembled a chanterelle mushroom. He stood and stretched. He had best rise, prepare himself for the gala dinner – it was to start early, at four o'clock, so everyone could make the late ferry. No point in trying to hide the scratches on his face. He'll make a joke of it, entertain these defenders of the wilderness with his tale of surviving it.

From the window, he saw that the mist was holding. Lavinia and the three Japanese woofers were warming themselves around a spit and its skewered lamb. No sign of Nick . . . Then he heard, softly, the tick-click of a computer keyboard from another room. Recall came suddenly of a duty not attended to. Nick. Good Christ, he'd forgotten to tell him his father had cancelled his Christmas visit.

Arthur saw the door to the den was ajar, a light within. He poked his head in and saw Nick studying the screen, speed-typing, studying the screen again.

"Ah, Nick, I've been meaning to talk to you." Nick looked up startled. "Don't mean to interrupt your, ah, research, but . . ."

"I was watching *The Simpsons*." He turned the screen to him: cartoon personae cavorted on it. Arthur was skeptical – the phone line was plugged into the computer – but he wasn't going to take issue. More important: how was he to say what must be said?

"This comes a little late from me, Nick, I'm sorry . . . Well, matters went awry – you heard about my, ah, goof-up last night."

"Yeah, you don't look that great, Grandpa."

"I meant to tell you yesterday that your father . . . he's not able to come today."

A painful few seconds. "He could have told me himself."

"An important business opportunity came up, it involves some visiting Asian investors. To make up, your dad has booked the two of you for a luxury resort in Hawaii over New Year's."

"Fuck him."

Arthur tried not to appear shocked but for a moment was without words. "It's not surprising you're upset. Your mother is unhappy about this too. Deborah will be phoning today, so you should probably stay in shouting distance. I . . . I'm sorry, Nick, I truly am."

"It's okay." His eyes were glistening. He turned his head away.

"The woofers are doing a lamb on a spit. Why don't you join them? Lavinia is there."

"Maybe later."

"And I thought we'd go out fishing again tomorrow. You can be at the helm."

"Sure. Thanks."

Arthur left him alone. As he pulled on his boots, he heard a sniffle, then tick-click-click from the keyboard. Outside, the mist swirled, and a distant foghorn moaned.

⚖

Dinner was served buffet-style because the drop-leaf table couldn't accommodate all the guests, who included two software millionaires and a distinguished business lawyer. The shy Japanese woofers were in a huddle on the rug, near the Christmas tree, but Lavinia bustled about, giving a hand.

Arthur did so too, with forced exuberance, knowing he was on probation, masking the distress he felt over his grandson, who filled his plate and quietly left, returning only briefly when summoned to the phone. Nicholas Senior, calling from Whistler, on a break from his business frolic with the VIJPs. All Arthur heard was, "Okay, cool. I don't mind. Merry Christmas too." His face showed no emotion.

Arthur ensured that wineglasses were filled, but this was not a drinking crowd – nor were they as dull as he'd anticipated. Mind you, they didn't have a chance to be boring. Arthur regaled them: picaresque tales about Garibaldi, recreating his role as the island's wandering jester, his epic journey to Mount Norbert, armed with a bag of lemons. "I didn't feel in real danger until I got home."

Margaret joined in the laughter, forgiving at last. She had graciously invited her competition, Malcolm Lewes, a skinny vegan who checked under every lettuce leaf as if he feared to find some grub, some form of animal protein. He spoke little, seemed ill at ease, as befitted a man so badly thumped in the last election.

In response to a toast to the chef, Margaret let it be known that all the food was locally grown, fished, or raised. "This is what sustainability is all about." Heads nodded as she decried the government's neglect of the small farmer, its support for the agro-industries. Then she laughed. "I'm sorry, this isn't a campaign meeting. Enjoy the food and the company. Merry Christmas."

Malcolm Lewes put his salad down, stood tall. "I guess this is a good time to make my announcement." He tried to smile, but the effect made him appear more forlorn. "I've decided we should all get behind Margaret Blake. I'm withdrawing my name."

The loud applause must have depressed him further, but he gamely shook hands with those who came by to commend him for his sacrifice.

Arthur suspected that Margaret had somehow set this up, had spoken to someone who spoke to someone else who spoke to Lewes – that's how he imagined such things were done in the shadowy world of politics. It bothered him that Margaret had been proving herself such a smooth operator. Was the corruption already setting in? Was a false face showing, was that an office-seeker's smile? Watch how she circulates, a word or two for every ear, watch how she laughs at nothing very funny. Watch as she frowns at the saboteur as he sneaks off for a second helping of pie.

Also bellying up to the table was rotund Eric Schultz, a partner in a major Vancouver law firm who was probably drawing half a million a year. Several months ago, he'd shocked his peers by abandoning the Conservative Party, in which he'd been an active insider, announcing his move to the Greens in a newspaper op-ed. Arthur knew him from Bar Association events.

"Arthur, I hope there's no house rule against trying another sliver of this delicious apple pie."

"It's highly addictive. I read your piece in the *Globe*, Eric. Admirable." *A Green Strategy for Business in a Finite World*.

"Lost some clients, picked up others, smart companies, they know they have to change to survive."

Arthur saw him fiddling with a pipe, so he led him out to the veranda for dessert and a smoke. It was dark now, after six, and the fog was thickening.

"You must be mighty proud, Arthur. Your wife has a great talent for this."

"Runs the finest kitchen on the Gulf Islands."

"I mean her political skills. Very persuasive woman. It seems I am to chair her campaign committee. Did it for the Tories, helped get a couple of duds elected." He spoke confidingly: "She could pull it off, depending on how the cards play."

Arthur sought a change of subject – their shared liking of pipes, the foggy weather, the sad state of the arts, anything – but for the moment he was too rattled to speak. Finally, he cleared his throat and said, "And how might the cards play?"

"The Libs, Tories, and New Democrats are all pretty even. With a good campaign, Margaret could win on a four-party split."

Arthur had trouble accepting this. Malcolm Lewes won 10 per cent of the vote last time. There he was, at a window, staring into the gloom. "Well, Eric, we can only keep our fingers crossed."

"Do you follow politics, Arthur?"

"The art is lost on me." Arthur's milieu had always been Conservative, his parents, his friends, law associates. He'd counted himself as an adherent without knowing why.

"By-elections favour the underdog. Voters aren't stupid, they know the government won't stand or fall on a single seat, so they'll gamble on a maverick to spice things up. Someone like Margaret."

Arthur coughed smoke. An image came of packing long johns for the flight to Ottawa. He'd never truly considered the dire prospect of her *winning*.

"Tell me, Arthur, you're involved, aren't you, in the case of this local fellow, the one alleged to have done in Whynet-Moir?"

"No, I am definitely not, but do not be surprised if Mr. Brown presently comes to the door begging me to *get* involved. He is the bane of my life. You knew Whynet-Moir?"

"He was once in my firm." Schultz, puffing his pipe, seemed to ponder his further response. "Stole several choice clients and set up on his own."

"I'd heard he was a bit of a slick fellow." Corrupt, said Provincial Judge Ebbe, though it may have been the cocktails talking. *Someone would be doing a blow for justice if he'd drop him down a well*. Arthur was about to say something more but faltered as illumination came. How had he been so slow to make the connection? *E.S.*

"Eric, did you serve last year on the discipline committee?"

"Good, you got my note. I knew I'd be seeing you, but mailing it felt more . . . anonymous."

"Your name will not be mentioned."

"It wouldn't do for poor Dalgleish Ebbe to have that catch up to him. Fine fellow, really, quite brilliant. His name keeps coming up for high court, but the Ministry of Justice keeps passing him over. Can't blame him for being bitter that Whynet-Moir got the job. He'll probably be buried forever in the bowels of the provincial court. Political correctness issues."

Ebbe, as Arthur recalled, was dogged by a long-ago unwise comment about a rape complainant's low-cut bodice.

"Rafael – Raffy, we used to call him – lobbied hard for his judgeship. You'd see him at federal Conservative functions, attaching himself to the justice minister, for whom, by the way, he served as a political aide in Ottawa several years ago, before the Conservatives took office. He made a substantial campaign contribution in 2006, the year he was appointed. I happen to know he wasn't the first choice of the PM or half the Cabinet, but the minister fought like a tiger and got him in."

Schultz was speaking carefully, but the insinuation was that money passed under the table – Judge Ebbe had made the accusation more boldly. There was a local angle here, an eerie convergence: appallingly, Margaret Blake could succeed that minister, the late Jack Boynton, as the Member for Cowichan and the Islands.

"Whynet-Moir's appointment came after he began squiring Florenza LeGrand about," Schultz said. "The romantic legend is that he then proposed. She probably decided it would be groovy to be a judge's wife."

"Groovy?" The word sounded old-fashioned even in Schultz's mouth.

"Florenza is still a hippie at thirty-three."

"If one assumes, Eric, that Whynet-Moir bought his judgeship, what motive might anyone have for doing him in?"

"A cover-up?" He shrugged. "Brown's counsel might want to check it out."

A good idea. Why was Arthur even blathering on about this case? "Brian Pomeroy. I'm in frequent contact with him." Was that so? He hadn't talked to him for a couple of weeks. He guessed Schultz knew more than he was letting on. He seemed uncommonly interested in the case, so Arthur asked him why.

"Well, this Cudworth Brown. Here's a fellow who was up a tree for two weeks with the Green Party candidate for Cowichan and the Islands. Wouldn't do to have him convicted of murder. Not at all."

Arthur puffed in grim silence. It bothered him that Margaret had joined the multitudes urging him to defend Cud. Why would she care?

He was about to suggest they retreat into the warmth of the house when they both jumped at what sounded like a shot. No, Arthur decided, a backfire. A lone headlight coming through the mist, a poorly muffled engine. A flatbed drew up to the house, Stoney grinning at the wheel. Beside him was Dog, a short, squat compatriot. Next to Dog was the even shorter Hamish McCoy. In the back was the legal fee, the twelve-foot Icarus, strapped down on a foamy, a red flag hanging from his toe.

"Where do you want it?" said Stoney, rolling down the window, letting out a cloud of cannabis-flowered air so thick that Schultz reared back.

"Sorry," Arthur mumbled, "this was unexpected."

McCoy left the cab, came to the steps, looking at the many parked cars. "Didn't know you was having a do tonight, but merry Christmas all the same."

"No, no, come in, meet some friends." Arthur realized too late that was a mistake.

"Hope we didn't miss dessert," said Stoney, advancing with a lit joint. "Anyone want a hit of this?" Schultz shied away again. Dog stumbled drunkenly from the truck, clutching a can of beer, and simultaneously drank from it while pissing on the lawn.

"Arthur, can I speak to you for a moment?" Margaret said, standing sternly at the door.

10

NEW LOVE BLOOMS AS THE OLD LIES DYING

Okay, I admit it, I was in hog heaven at the capitalist trough, quaffing wine and spooning up a third helping of crème brûlée. Crisis over, Flo was snickering, and the ring I'd butter-fingered off her was in my pocket. Incidentally, I still have it – did I mention that? The coppers released it to me after I got bail – I told them it was mine, to protect her.

Anyway, I figured if things went right, I could be Florenza's kept lover, her toy boy, no more living in a beach shack on Garibaldi. Maybe she'd set me up in a penthouse over English Bay. *You changed my life.* Okay, your turn, you change mine.

Little did I know that this romantic comedy was about to morph into high tragedy. But I was deaf to inner whispers Flo was going to cut me loose after I provided fast, fast relief for needs that weren't being met by the fuzz-nutted pucker-ass over there. He had nods and smiles for everyone but me, maybe because the last time he looked my way I was wiping globs of butter from my hand with a napkin.

Meantime, he was mewling over the important lesbian novelist, urging her to read from her new book. Not much opposition from her. She stood, smiled, said something self-deprecating, read a page or two about a woman on her fifth unhappy marriage.

I'd stopped drinking, mainly because my bladder had swelled to the size of Hudson Bay. I didn't want anyone to see my pants were slimed with butter, so I waited till the moment was ripe, when everyone was applauding her, to slip away, grab my pack because I've got a change of jeans in there. I can't find the nearest sandbox, though they've probably got a dozen of them, so I breeze outside and wee on the grass, the way you'd do at any function on Garibaldi.

I'm behind the Lamborghini, maybe getting a little spray on the back fender, and I don't know what attracts the curiosity of its owner, maybe my groans of relief, but here he comes, the insufferable snob in the shiny shoes, just in time to catch me shaking off behind his priceless ragtop.

He stops like he just walked into a wall when he sees I'm not zipping up, I'm lowering my gaunches, my balls and pecker dangling. Slowly, very slowly, he starts backing away, pointing a remote control, setting the car alarm, I figured, because I hear a little bleep. He disappears, I pull on fresh jeans.

Back inside, everyone was shuffling around with coffees and cognacs, except for Flo and a couple of other smokers, who were out on the deck. Shiny Shoes couldn't look me in the eye, and him and his wife left early. Last I saw of him he was checking to make sure I hadn't jacked off all over his backup lights.

Whynet-Moir was trying to get the other lady writer to read, but she declined, and I'm feeling affronted that he doesn't ask me. In case you didn't know, that's one of my fortes, doing readings; I get the crowd up at the coffee bars on Commercial Drive. Especially when I've had a few, like now.

I go out to the deck, bum one off Flo, a Gitanes, a prestige cigarette, I guess, but it smells like a burning tar pit. One of the tycoons and his spouse are out here too, him with a cigar. Mr. and Mrs. Bagley, he's CEO of a frozen food conglomerate. "When do we get a chance to hear *you* read?" he asks.

Exactly my thought, but I'm demure. "Aw, I don't know, it's getting late." I glance inside, and Whynet-Moir still has his back to me.

The spouse chimes in, "Oh, please, just one poem."

Florenza looks at her watch, as if to affirm it's getting late.

"We insist," Bagley says, and he dinches his cigar and runs in to fetch Whynet-Moir. Mrs. Bagley goes off to get another drink.

The hostess pats my right buttock in a sort of proprietary way, like it's something she owns and values. "The Bagleys will be the last to go, they tend to cling. I'll have to start yawning."

Then she pulls out my books again and asks if I know her well enough by now to sign them. I figured I had sufficient information on her, given I'd recently had my hand up her dress, but I didn't have any bon mots quick at hand. She told me "Never Regret" was one of her favourite poems, so I wrote that. And for the other book, *Karmageddon*, she wanted a line from its title track. It goes, "New love blooms as the old lies dying."

As I'm scribbling these out, she says, "How does a steam and a swim later sound?"

"Real sweet."

"After I send Rafael to bed."

"What if he doesn't go to bed?"

"We'll just have to find some way to get rid of him."

And here he comes, sort of slithering out onto the deck, a look of embarrassed relief. "Ah, here you are, Cudworth. I'd rather lost you, I thought you might have found our little event too staid and fled. But then I remembered with relief we're putting you up. Has he seen his room, dear?"

"Not yet, darling."

Whynet-Moir was smiling, but it wasn't real genuine. He must have suspected what's up, it's probably happened lots of times before. "A great hue and cry has gone up for you to read from *Karmageddon*. I beg you, please, grace us with a few lines."

I shrugged. "Okay, what the heck."

I followed him in, rummaging through my head for something raw enough to get the clinging Bagleys out the door.

I was also thinking about what Flo had said, it was causing me the willies. *We'll just have to find some way to get rid of him*. The way she said that, not tossed off but in a low, intimate voice. I wasn't totally hammered yet, but my defences were down. What a lamb in the woods I was.

It was after seven, nearly Hitchins time, as Brian slipped from the Ritz into the tinselled, foggy city, into the shimmer of storefront lights. He moved quickly, furtively, to Quick Loans, No References Required, the windows barred and dark. Its proprietor, a grizzled Iranian with a loaded .45 under the counter, was honouring the Lord Jesus, despite being Muslim, by not extorting repayments from the poor on Christmas Day. Soon Mr. Kharmazi might become more than a nodding acquaintance, given Brian's dire financial straits. Harry the Need has also taken Christmas off – Brian didn't blame him, but he's had to cut back, only a half gram left for the next emergency. Right now he was strung out like a taut clothesline, paranoid without that compensating muscular high. Possibly delusional, but there was no scientific way of testing that.

He didn't want to be too twisted tonight: Abigail Hitchins is a shifty stickhandler, she wants favours from him, admissions; he must not be tricked into signing away the family farm. What was on her wish list? His head maybe, to be mounted on her wall. She had detested the role she'd played in those distant times, mistress to an equivocating married man. How voracious she'd been in bed, selfish, demanding. Wanting to be on top. That's how she will prosecute, the dominatrix.

A cruiser went by, slowing as it passed Brian, getting a fix on him. Brian tightened his grip on his attaché case, headed to the corner, past the mime, who began following him, impersonating his long, hurried strides. The busker with the bongos commanded the next corner, and who knew what *his* game was. He had a big ugly dog. Brian was afraid of dogs. But Lance Valentine was with him, confident, in control. *It's only a busker and his mutt, old boy.*

Jaywalking Main, he encountered a seedy group outside the Palace – two dancers, two customers, the doorman, a smoke break between sets, between Candy Floss and Cherry Blossom, tonight's star grinders. He steered a course right at them, like he owned the street. The doorman smiled and said, "Merry Christmas, sir!" He respected Valentine, understood class.

He made it to the corner, looked behind. The mime had melted into the gloom, *You foiled him, old fellow.* Just to make sure, he slipped into the Eternal Happiness Café, went out the back way after buying a pack of A's.

Why couldn't he find Il Giardino? Was it on Homer, Hornby, or Howe? He'd been there a hundred times, why couldn't he remember? They may have doctored his orange juice at his hotel. Somebody had access to his room, not just the maid, somebody who wanted the information from his computer. He'd printed out his manuscript in case of theft, it was in the attaché case. Where had he left his backup disk? The usual place above the ceiling tile? Or had he changed hiding places again?

Responding to his Nazi salute, an empty taxi stopped, its turbaned driver looking at him suspiciously: a bum, a street thug?

"Il Giardino," Brian said. The driver locked the door, rolled up the window, and pointed across the street to where a man was hijacking a Mercedes, its owner standing by helplessly. The scene metamorphosed into a valet parking situation. Brian made out a sign in the gloom: Il Giardino.

He was too torn up, he needed a straightener before going in, a couple of rails to get his engine back on track. He had a murder trial to run. He had business with a prosecutor. Think business. Be clever, calculating, conniving. Be a lawyer.

He found privacy behind a Dumpster in the alley, booted up off the back of his hand, then entered the restaurant to a delicious wafting of garlic with its strange, power-enhancing properties. Now he felt on top of himself, in control, ready to face any situation, he was the legendary Brian Pomeroy, defender of assassins, hero of the Bhashyistan Democratic Revolutionary Front.

The maître d' greeted him with the effusiveness he deserved. "Ah, Mr. Pomeroy, I thought you'd deserted us forever. Ms. Hitchins is waiting for you."

Brian was led to a dark alcove, a table for two behind a gurgling fountain. While bending to take his chair he came to a sudden, paralytic stop. Not at the sight of Abigail Hitchins, in her long black witchy hair and witchy green eyes and witchy red puckered lips. Something else, something that had registered below awareness, caught from the corner of his eye.

Abigail's mouth tasted not of the Pinot she was drinking but of cinnamon, either from perfumed lip gloss or breath mint. An unromantic kiss, businesslike. "Can't afford a razor? You look like shit."

"It's the mujahedeen look. It's the rage." Somebody was staring at his back, he could feel it. He ordered a vodka martini.

"So, Bry, how's divorced life treating you?"

"I'm gutting it out."

"I heard you got busted for waking up the neighbourhood. Beating on a garbage can lid and singing 'Come All Ye Faithful' at the top of your lungs."

Brian didn't respond until his drink arrived. Just stared at her, fearing to turn around.

"How are the kids?"

"I'm *barred* from them! I can't even phone! Caroline delisted the number, even Gabby's cellphone. I haven't been sleeping, I get maybe three hours on a good night." He began rapping, speed-talking, discursive and repetitive, pouring it out. How Caroline sent him packing, allowing him meagre visiting rights, and now there were none. His sense of having been hijacked in divorce court, having his face rubbed in it by Mr. Justice Rafael Whynet-Moir, currently gratefully dead. *I reject the disingenuous testimony of the respondent husband, whom I regard as a kind of "fiddler on the truth"* (merriment in the courtroom) *and accept without reservation the candid, poignant version of his soon-to-be-ex-wife.*

Abigail stared at him, frowning but with an irritating lack of real concern. *Serves you right,* her face said. "You're having another breakdown, aren't you?"

He wondered how she could tell, he'd gone to great lengths to seem normal. "A little one, maybe."

"Maybe you shouldn't be taking on this trial."

"You're not getting rid of me that easy." At some point Brian must have ordered a seafood pasta, because a waiter slid it under his nose.

"Something obsessive going on here, Bry? Defending the killer of your *bête noire*?" No answer. "You going to dine that way? Chained to a briefcase? What's in it, gold?"

He released it from his wrist, opened it, showed her. *Kill All the Judges*, chapters one to ten. "Yes, gold. My masterwork."

"Thought you stopped pretending to be a writer after the last round of rejections."

"You'll be in it too. It's about dead judges. It's creative true fiction."

"I read Caroline's short stories. Heart-rending." She knew how to hurt. "You're in trouble, Bry. You're teetering on the edge."

He needed a smoke to help wash down the martini, that was his only trouble. But he was trapped in a smoke-free zone. Suck it up, focus, concentrate on business, he's not going to let Cud down, that's not his style.

Abigail handed him a printed sheet. "Let's do our admissions of fact before you totally wing out. The date, deceased's address, his identity, the list of dinner guests, catering staff, photos, prints . . ."

"What prints?"

"The defendant's. Plastered all over a cigar humidor, several on a cognac bottle outside the steam room. Okay? Next, the 911 calls —"

"What calls?"

"Astrid Leich at 3:11 a.m., possible homicide. A neighbour at 5 Lighthouse Lane at 3:15, Aston Martin in his front yard. It's in the material I sent. You're not on top of this, are you?"

"I'm idling. I'll get up to speed when I need to."

"Okay, I take it there's no contest over the gear Cud left behind in the suite over the garage. Backpack, toiletries, spare clothes. I'd appreciate admissions on the DNA —"

"What DNA?"

"Your guy's sweat. Learn to read. Take a remedial course. It was on a towel by the swimming pool's outdoor shower. We presume he went for a swim and a steam."

"With Florenza?"

"Maybe. No proof." She continued with her list: "Autopsy report, cause of death — blunt trauma consistent with a fall . . ."

"No, I want to hear about how he died." Every detail.

He finally turned around, saw no one staring, nothing untoward, nothing that would have caused that little jolt. He focused on a neatly bearded man in an expensive suit with an expensive bottle of red and an expensive redhead, her back to Brian, the guy's trophy wife or concubine. The way she bent to him, in intense conversation . . . He felt another shiver, another jolt, recognized her. Dr. Alison Epstein.

"Brian, you may want to back out of this trial, because the judge . . . Who are you staring at?"

"The redhead is my shrink."

"Well, she might come in handy."

Clearly, Dr. Epstein had known Brian would be at this very restaurant tonight, but how had she managed to secure a table ten feet away? Who was the man with her? Too well-dressed to be a cop. Maybe someone higher up. He'd been looking at Brian's feet. Why would he be interested . . . The attaché case, of course.

Concentrate, he hadn't caught what Abigail was saying. Something about the judge assigned to the Brown trial. "Sorry? The chief assigned whom?"

"Himself."

"Kroop?"

"Who loves you not."

The death camp commander, the Badger, who loves Brian as one loves a pit viper creeping into one's underwear. "A bullying, sadistic mountebank" – that was one of the lesser slurs against him that Brian had tossed off in defence of Gilbert Gilbert. Either the stars were out of alignment or the conspiracy ran deeper than he'd imagined.

"He pencilled himself in for one reason, Bry – he wants to eat you alive."

She only sees the surface. Kroop is at the centre of the whole thing, the mastermind. This had been a set-up from the beginning.

"Ready for him?"

"God's will be done."

"Hey, are you trying to send your guy down for the count? I have a better idea. Want to hear it?"

"*I* have a better idea. I'm moving for a stay of proceedings."

"You're not getting rid of Kroop that way."

"Fuck Kroop, it's because I haven't got notice of Florenza LeGrand's evidence."

"Get your head around this, Bry. She isn't talking to me, to the cops, to anyone but her mouthpiece, Silent Shawn Hamilton. And *he* ain't talking to me, the schemer. Call him. Good luck."

Silent Shawn will give him zip. A weird one, the mouthpiece who won't talk, you can't do a deal with him.

"I've subpoenaed Florenza, but we're flying blind."

"What's she hiding?" Her debauch with Cud, for sure. Maybe worse.

Abigail leaned toward him. "I know it's hard in your unbalanced state, but try to focus on what I'm saying. If Florenza LeGrand is complicit in her husband's death, she becomes a rich target. Of far more interest than some country Joe in red braces." She let it hang there, smiling.

"What would you want for that?"

"If he rolls all the way, manslaughter."

"No fank you. I'll cop him to drunk driving though."

Abigail looked pissed, but he wasn't going to explain how Cud stormed off when he mentioned manslaughter. He fumbled for his A's, he was having a nic fit. He looked back, Dr. Epstein was gone, presumably to the ladies. Her associate was waving a credit card at the waiter.

"I need some fresh air."

"Enjoy. I don't partake of the filthy habit any more."

"Anyway, I've got to run."

"Not interested in extending the evening? Dessert? One for the road? A hump for old times' sake? A visit to a mental health clinic?"

"I have a . . . an emergency." He wanted to get out of here before his shrink came back.

"I'll drive you."

He shook his head, rose. "Thanks for dinner. I'll call you."

He retrieved his case, clutched it to his chest, made his way out the back entrance, where the smokers gather, where one of the kitchen staff, chef-hatted, was taking a last drag before butting out. And here was Alison Epstein, staring at nothing, darkness. He was about to turn on his heels when she turned on hers, toward him, with a smiled "Hello."

"I didn't know you smoked," he said.

"I don't. I was hoping we could catch up. Briefly."

He lit up. Now she would want explanations, she'd want to know why he was hiding out, and where, why he'd quit Xanax. "Who's the man you're with?"

"My husband."

She could be lying, but he thought not. Maybe she hadn't lured him here after all. One of life's coincidences. They happen. Maybe he could trust her, maybe he could take that chance.

"Seems like a . . . nice fellow." His voice stilted. "I was with a friend. A prosecutor. A business date."

"I see. And how have you been coping?"

"No complaints." He struggled to invent a plausible lie. But Dr. Epstein had X-ray vision, she saw through him like glass. That was the problem, that's why he strived so hard to avoid her; she saw past his mask.

"Are you still hearing voices?" The voices of dead judges, he'd told her that. And Lance Valentine, his cut-glass accent. And Widgeon, telling him what to do, like God. Like God telling Gilbert F. Gilbert to kill the chief justice. Brian had gone back through that file, the psychiatric reports, seeking symptoms, clues, answers to his own problems.

He lied. "The voices don't bother me."

"Have you decided to terminate therapy?"

"I wasn't handling it very well. I needed a break."

A long pause, one of those significant pauses where she waits for elaboration, confession, expects to reel the truth out of him like a fish from the sea. He felt sudden, overwhelming defeat. He was imploding under the pressure, all the followers, the conspirators, the plots and subplots; he could no longer tell who was real, who fictitious, who was with him, who against him. He opened his case and thrust his manuscript at her.

"I want you to have this."

"Brian, I can help you."

"They're after me. I know too much. I know who killed the judges. All the clues are in here."

She took the manuscript, stared for a few moments at the title, then looked hard at him, penetratingly. "Brian, you've stopped the Xanax."

"Sort of."

"What are you on right now? Cocaine?"

Panic. "How can you tell?"

"It's the worst thing you can do in your present state."

He made for the alley. "I'll call you. I promise."

11

VALE OF TEARS

Arthur has soared too close to the sun, and his feathers are melting. Fire above, fire below, engulfing the hall, and he's falling toward those blue flames, totally doomed, totally doomed . . .

He opened his eyes before the impact and lay still, staring at the rough cedar ceiling, feeling no relief to have survived those flames. No interpreter of dreams needed. A telling metaphor for last night's disaster.

Margaret's side of the bed was distressingly unrumpled, denying him any flickering hopes she'd found a tiny corner of forgiveness in her heart. "Come in," he'd told Stoney, Dog, and McCoy, "meet some friends." This grossly negligent invitation was, to Margaret, further proof of his secret plot to abort her political career.

It may have taken a while for her Greens to realize that the tumultuous invasion of Bob Stonewell and the two dwarfs was not some picaresque after-dinner entertainment. Reactions ranged from puzzlement to barely suppressed dread.

McCoy sang bawdy songs, Dog threw up, and Stoney passed out business cards: *Loco Motion. Ride in style in our fleet of heritage limousines.* "One of them's a cherry 1970 Chrysler New Yorker," he announced proudly. "Gulps the gas, you only get eight to the gallon, but where you gonna go on a small island anyway? The fun is just laying some rubber on the roadways, man." The three of them polished off the leftovers, washing them down with the remaining organic wine and beer.

The champion worst episode involved a venerable, now broken, leaded-glass window in the parlour. The runner-up: a burning butt in a paper recycling bin. Third place went to Dog vomiting on shoes left by the veranda door.

The woofers, embarrassed, left early, though the noise was loud enough to draw Nick from his room, complete with iPod and headphones. Margaret skipped about with a fixed, ferocious smile until her friends and patrons sped off to the late ferry. Whereupon she wordlessly fetched her night gear and slammed the guest-room door behind her.

He'd slept poorly but late, Aurora had long ago rolled up the curtain of night. He dragged himself up, looked out the window – the family pickup was gone. He lashed himself with an ugly scenario, Margaret speeding off to the city to start a divorce. *Petitioner further alleges mental cruelty rendering intolerable the continued cohabitation of the spouses.*

The flatbed was still parked below, though Icarus had mysteriously disappeared. The driver's door was open, Stoney lying there under a dirty blanket. Somehow, despite having got awe-inspiringly drunk, he'd had the sense not to drive. Also in the driveway was the rust-scarred van of Mop'n'Chop ("We do it all, no task too small"), so Felicity Jones and Bobbi Rosekeeper must be downstairs, cleaning up.

There was Nick, standing by the pond, idly tossing pebbles, making ripples in the reeds. Looking down upon this sad, thin figure, Arthur felt devastated. He'd promised to take him fishing before breakfast. This skipped-generation relationship was being badly mishandled by the Baron of Blunder Bay. Lord Stumblebum.

He hurriedly washed, dressed, crept down to the living room. Beneath the staircase, the cat was sniffing at the stubby figure of Stoney's pal, Dog, who was face down on the cat's pillow. Where had Hamish McCoy disappeared to? Icarus had either been spirited away or regained the power of flight.

The girls had already done the living room, except for Dog's redoubt under the stairs, which they'd vacuumed around. They were in the kitchen now, dishwasher and washer-dryer going, the ninety-year-old house jiggling and rumbling.

He stepped out into a chill, dry morning. A wind had pursued the mists into the dales, and the sun was a pallid ghost behind the unbroken gloom of filmy cloud. A flutter in the bay, a school of fleeing herring, competition for his lures – pinks had been running, but now they'd be sated and lazy. As a backup, he could fetch his crab pots – he had put some bait aside in the freezer, salmon heads.

The Japanese kids were repairing fences. Lavinia was in the far distance, leading Barney, the overfed, farting horse, to a leaner pasture. Nick was staring forlornly after her.

Arthur called, "Come and join me in the barn, Nick, we're going to set a couple of crab traps while we go off in pursuit of the wily salmon." Why must he sound so pompous in front of the kid? Nick must see him as beyond square. Cuboid. Totally unhip.

He led Nick past the flatbed, past Stoney's prostrate form. Still life as object lesson: *This, young man, is where the loose life leads.* But who was Arthur to talk? He'd been no stellar example in his youth and worse in his prime. Arthur Ramsgate Beauchamp had descended to dizzying depths, a fool when drunk, bellowing threats at prosecutors, refuelling from a water pitcher spiked with Beefeaters. He ought to tell Nick about how he once lost his balance beside the jury box and fell into their laps. Or how he spouted the *Rubáiyát* at the top of his lungs in a crowded restaurant. The time he fell through a skylight while spying on faithless Annabelle. His years on skid road, defending street people for free out of a hole in the wall.

Seventeenth anniversary coming up next month. He and his fellow stalwarts of the Garibaldi AA will celebrate that. In their way.

"I gather you talked to your father." Arthur didn't want to open the wounds, but this had to be discussed. "How did that go?"

"Okay. I guess he felt pretty bad."

"He's still taking you to Hawaii for New Year's?"

"Naw, I told him I don't want to go. Mom phoned too."

It would be just like Deborah to fly in suddenly, scoop the boy back to Australia. Arthur would feel hollow saying goodbye, knowing he'd utterly failed to connect with his only male descendant.

"I told her I want to stay on here for another month. If it's okay with you."

That had Arthur blinking with surprise. Was Nick finally acclimatizing to Blunder Bay? Or was Lavinia holding him here? In any event, he was taking some control over his life.

"I'm delighted, Nick. By the way, did Margaret say where she was going?"

"I didn't ask. She wasn't in a good mood."

Arthur groaned. "What a debacle."

"Yeah, it was a ripper." Suddenly, Nick grinned. Arthur had provided some welcome comic relief. "You keep scoring own goals, Grandpa." He touched Arthur's shoulder. Contact. A gesture of commiseration.

The crab traps were hanging on hooks in the barn, but Arthur was more interested in Icarus, whose swaying, winged form was suspended from the rafters by ropes. Bronze eyes staring earthward, a look of agony as he fleetingly contemplated impending death. The creator of this noble work was asleep under a blanket of empty feed sacks.

He sent Nick to the *Blunderer* with the traps while he detoured to the house to get the fish heads. He was hoping to avoid the gossipy girls from Mop'n'Chop, not wanting to add to their store of anecdotes. He particularly didn't want to deal with Felicity Jones, the twenty-year-old, ever-forgiving sometime lover of Cuddles Brown and only child of Tabatha, a weaver, who fumed at the mere mention of Cud's name.

"Mr. Beauchamp, can I talk to you?"

Trapped at the open freezer door. "Yes, Felicity?"

"He cried last night." She was a poet herself, of sweet, runny verse that occasionally found its sticky way into the *Island Bleat*. Cud refused to stoop that low. *I don't throw pearls at swine, man.*

"You were with him."

"I was there *for* him. It was Christmas Day, and he was so alone . . . and he wrote a poem for me as a present. In return I had no gift to give but my love." Felicity had an uncommon speech defect: she talked like a greeting card. "We shared the night. I couldn't bear – and didn't dare – leave him alone."

"The matter must be very stressful for him."

"I'm not sure if you understand, Mr. Beauchamp, he's truly despondent, he talked about wanting to 'depart this vale of tears.' That's the expression he used, it's not mine."

"Yes, he does tend to romanticize his situation. Felicity, let me repeat, and I've told you dozens of times, Cudworth is competently represented. I have nothing but the highest esteem for Mr. Pomeroy."

"Cudworth can't find him. He's like, hiding from Cud, and his case is coming up in a month and a half!" Emotional now, tears building. "My Cuddlybear."

"I'll get in touch with Mr. Pomeroy later today. Now you go back to Cud and tell him to stop using expressions like vale of tears." He was about to race off with his fish heads but stalled. "Do you know where Margaret went?"

"I think she made an appointment with Reverend Al."

That was not what he wanted to hear. *You're his friend, Al, you'll have to break the news. I can't even look at him.*

He joined Nick on the *Blunderer* with a hearty, ill-felt, "Let's go fishing!"

⚖

A few hours later, their shiny offerings unanimously rejected by the wily salmon, their two undersized crabs returned to freedom, Arthur and Nick pulled into Hopeless Bay, to the general store, in search of more accessible prey. A frozen pizza must suffice for dinner tonight – but no, Arthur decided, pizza is poor contrition; he will offer Margaret the amends of a winter garden salad and his famous hearty pepper pot.

Nick helped Arthur tie up but stayed aboard with some electronic gizmo he'd brought. He hadn't talked much while fishing but listened politely to Arthur's grumblings about the disastrous Christmas of 2008. "You're letting things get to you, Grandpa," he'd said.

A hush as Arthur passed by the coffee lounge. Then a snort. A giggle. Emily LeMay's coo of sympathy: "There's always a spare bed at my place, you poor thing." Arthur decided not to invite further ridicule by asking if anyone had seen Margaret today.

"Heard things didn't go too smooth for Christmas up your way." Makepeace, the lugubrious storekeeper.

"A little bump in the flow chart of life." Maybe Arthur ought to move back to the city, where one's life is not a glaringly open book.

He found himself gazing down on a jar stuffed with small bills and labelled *Cud Brown Defence Fund*. Makepeace said, "I hear he's got a cheap legal aid lawyer you wouldn't hire for a parking ticket."

Even Makepeace was in on the conspiracy. The island was united in an unseemly campaign to shame Arthur into representing a duly certified permanent local, a title conferred on those who have survived Garibaldi for at least a decade.

Winnie Gillicuddy, Garibaldi's pugnacious centenarian, called from among shelves. "I'll ask again. Where's the goddamn oatmeal?"

"Winnie, set yourself down over a cup of tea, and I'll find what you need."

"Abraham Makepeace, you stop patronizing me. I'm not blind, just tell me . . . What is this poison? Honey-coated corn puffs. You should be ashamed of yourself." A whack of her stick, a sound of cascading boxes. Unfazed, she stepped over the spillage, kicking boxes from her path, triumphantly clutching her oatmeal. "And you, Arthur Beauchamp, you should be ashamed of yourself too."

⚖

Arthur let Nick be skipper on the long, smooth stretch by Clamshell Beach. "A little farther out, please, Nick." There were no reefs nearby, but Arthur didn't want to venture too close to the grassy knoll above the tideline where Cudworth Brown's beach shack stood. But the fates had it in for Arthur – there he was, Cud himself, on his porch, staring forlornly out at sea.

Arthur felt he had to wave. Cud didn't lift a hand, didn't deign to acknowledge him.

⚖

The Mop'n'Chop girls had gone, and the kitchen was gleaming clean, so Arthur set to work on his salad and stew and, carefully following the instruction booklet, mixed up a batch for the new bread machine. Four o'clock and she still hadn't come home. No answer at Reverend Al's.

Nor was there a response when he called Brian Pomeroy's cell number, just the machinelike civility of his answering service. He didn't expect anyone to be in his law office on Boxing Day but called anyway and was answered by a cordial, lightly accented female voice. "Good afternoon, law office."

"Hello, I'm trying to reach Brian Pomeroy."

"I have not seen him today, Mr. Beauchamp."

That gave Arthur a little turn. "Do I know you?"

It turned out she was Pomeroy's secretary, April Fan Wu, and her phone was equipped with caller ID, to Arthur's mind one of the more obnoxious novelties of modern times. By some manner of telepathy, she also knew he was inquiring as to why Pomeroy wasn't returning Cudworth's calls.

"Mr. Pomeroy has already had a long session with Mr. Brown. He is a client very demanding of a lawyer's time."

Arthur couldn't argue with that. He remembered how he, too, had gone into hiding, usually in his phoneless library, when preparing for a critical case. He wanted to ask about Pomeroy's emotional health, but it seemed indiscreet. Anyway, a good secretary will defend her boss, as Arthur's had, covering up for him, his debauches.

He dictated a memo about the alleged shady dealings between Whynet-Moir and the justice minister. She will draw it to Mr. Pomeroy's attention. She will tell him Arthur would like to speak to him.

"You are to be commended, Ms. Wu, for working on a holiday."

"It isn't easy to adapt to Mr. Pomeroy's style of practice."

With that ambiguous answer, their conversation ended. Arthur went to the garden to pick some of the season's late leavings and returned to a house silent but for the simmering stew and occasional indecipherable clunk from the bread machine. Five o'clock. Where *was* she?

Another call to Reverend Al's home finally brought his wife, Zoë, breathlessly to the phone.

"Were you calling earlier?" she asked.

"Earlier and often."

"Oh, you poor thing. They're in the hot tub."

"Who?"

"Margaret and Al."

"Together?"

"Why you old prude. If it makes you feel any better, I've been keeping them company and am now standing in the kitchen dripping wet."

Arthur mumbled an apology. He'd never been able to overcome his inhibitions about the Noggins' hot tub, their no-bathing-suit rule. As far as Arthur was concerned, being unclothed, *in puris naturalibus*, wasn't natural to the human species.

"And what, pray, prompted Margaret's visit?"

"I think she had to let off some steam."

She was home within the hour, entering the kitchen so quietly that Arthur, who was setting the table, started on noticing her. She looked at the oversized loaf billowing from the bread machine like some gigantic fungus. Hands on hips, she stared at Arthur, a comically helpless figure in an apron.

"What *am* I going to do with you?"

And suddenly she was smiling, laughing. She tossed her jacket onto a chair and came to him, and as they embraced he felt giddy, helpless, thick-headed.

12

THE WHISPERED ANSWER

So, okay, Whynet-Moir fetches me inside, makes a production of having prevailed on me to favour them with a few gems from my oeuvre, he called it. I give them something dense that I'm not sure even I understand; I was hammered when I wrote it. They pretend to like it, they applaud.

Then I let go with "Up Your Little Red Rosie, Rose," a bawdy ballad that had the desired effect of clearing the house. As guests made for the door, they gushed thanks for the "delightful" evening, it was so "interesting."

The judge and his wife were seeing people to their cars while the caterers bustled about, cleaning up. I topped up my cognac and went outside so I could savour my Romeo y Julieta while admiring their piss-elegant pool. It's down the staircase, tunnelled into the natural rock. Farther back is a three-stall garage.

This should feel like paradise, man. I have a five-star cognac in one hand, a fifty-dollar cigar in the other, and a pending hot date with a gorgeous, affluential fan. We're going to do a steam and a swim. Then she's going to show me to my room.

But it's paradise with a hitch. *After I send Rafael to bed.* Raffy, his pals call him, not Rafe, like a regular guy, but Raffy, and he'd been eyeing us slit-eyed across the table. He's going to sleep like a baby, suspecting nothing?

Maybe it's like they entered into an accommodation – she can't get no satisfaction, so she's got an unwritten licence to boff the occasional horny poet. Or maybe it's something else. *We'll just have to find some way to get rid of him . . .*

Raffy finally joins me on the deck, smiling, masking his irritation. I'd done what he asked, I read some gems from my oeuvre. He hadn't read the reviews? I write "muscular, bawdy verse."

"I've had your pack and your outerwear sent over to your room. Not too long a hike. Down to the pool level, then up those stairs beside the garage. The maid normally sleeps there, but she's off tonight."

This upper-class twit was banishing me to the servant's quarters. A garret over the garage. You stuffed shirt, I was thinking, I'm really going to enjoy your wife.

"Well, no rush, enjoy your cigar." Then calling: "Florenza, I think we should consider retiring."

She was at the door taking care of the caterers, handing them envelopes with tips. "On my way, Rafael."

He said to me, "It's been a long day for us, and no doubt for you as well. I truly want to thank you for coming."

"Hey, man, no problem." I asked a few irrelevant questions, like when is breakfast normally served. I figured he'll hang around longer if he worries I'll burn the house down, so I tapped a long ash over the railing and dinched the cigar out.

After he toodles off, I go back in and grab the Hennessy bottle, still half full. I've got time to check out my quarters while she puts Raffy to bed. Maybe she'll slip a sleeping pill into his glass of warm milk.

I investigated the pool, oval with a spring board at the deep end, vapour coming off it in the cold night air. Built into the rockface, like a cave, is what turned out to be the steam room, because when I fired up the timer by the glass door, I heard it burp and hiss.

My digs were neat as a pin but girlish, with fluffy animals. A firm mattress for which I was thankful — my back was aching – and an adjoining john, where I sat a long time, relieving my head more than anything else; it was spinning. I was pretty much in the bag by now, and I told myself to slow down, but I kept a grip on that cognac bottle.

I didn't want to underperform for Flo. However, and I'm not bragging, alcohol has never deprived me of the power of love, except when I pass out. Or because of penis exhaustion. I'm human.

I'm starting not to remember everything, but after I left I must've looked inside the garage, the side door wasn't locked. I saw an Aston Martin and a Land Rover. Pause here, because about a hundred witnesses are going to say I took that Aston Martin into a tree. I haven't the faintest fucking memory of being in that car, but I'm being honest here, I did see keys hanging on the garage wall.

Anyway, I returned to poolside, and in the dim light I could make out Flo skinning out of her little black thing. I'm almost choking on testosterone ogling her toned-up, drop-dead body, though, frankly, by now I'd have screwed a five-legged frog.

I sat on a bench, fumbling with my boot strings, and I can't remember the words, but I casually asked about Raffy. She said he's probably in bed. *Probably.*

She opened the steam-room door, and I watched her little apple-cheek fanny disappear into the mist. I smelled of lust and rancid butter, so I went under the outdoor shower before following her into that dark, hot cave. There was only a dim glow through the glass door. Everywhere, steam was hissing and belching. I expected Satan to emerge from the gloom.

"How hot do you like it?" came her voice.

I told her again I was more interested in knowing if this was cool. I wanted to ask if this went on a lot, her old man going to bed early while she fucks a stranger. I am reckless by nature, and tonight I was drunk, but her partner was a judge. You don't shag a judge's wife without dire consequences.

She goes, "Chill out." Rafael wasn't feeling well, she said, he doesn't hold his wine too good. I thought, if he's not well, he's probably awake. I remember her next line clear: "I gave him something to help him sleep."

I remember that because I had this premonition I'd be busted with a vial in my backpack that'll analyze for arsenic.

It's called paranoia, Cud. You're being portrayed by the master; no one knows paranoia like Brian Pomeroy. It gets worse when you're out of white lady, the paranoia lingers like a perpetual hangover. It's been a week since supplies ran out. Seven days, and the itches and tics and twinges continue, like rats biting. But he could feel it peaking, he might just be able to rout the devils, get clean. Good thing he wasn't addicted, the struggle would be hopeless.

The Need won't cuff him any more product, that's the snag. Brian's bank account was empty, his credit cards maxed, and his draw from the office wasn't due till mid-January, five days hence. He might have to rob a bank. He imagined himself in the clink, a family visit, Caroline and the kids crying.

Words reshaped themselves like crawling insects as he stared at his screen, page up, page up, finally locating Flo's opener. "You changed my life . . ." This stank of implausibility. A more alluring plot: she was conniving to suck a yokel into her orbit, to serve as a stooge in a homicide set-up. "We'll just have to find some way to get rid of him." Would his protagonist actually have got so drunk as to have done her bidding? Just to get laid?

Or would she have done the dirty herself? How? And with what motive? This was a brainbuster in his weakened state. *Toss it about*, Widgeon demands. Okay, he tossed it about. For public consumption, Whynet-Moir and the heiress pose as the happy couple, but Florenza can't get no satisfaction. She wants to dump her erotically challenged partner. (This collides with reality, of course, because in the confusing realm of non-fiction, Whynet-Moir had clearly shown himself a letch, making eyes at Caroline in court. And she looking boldly back.)

Back to the more comforting world of fiction. Flo lacks grounds for divorce. That's a risky route anyway – Whynet-Moir could walk off with half her fortune. So she decides to fast-track her way to widowhood. Though the carefree ex-flower child might seem an unlikely manslayer, in fact she will diagnose as one of those charming, guilt-free sociopaths that infest society.

That's the story line, that's the right plot for his creative non-fiction work. Which, unaccountably, he'd given to his shrink. What had he been thinking? She's been phoning again. Her diagnosis has been amended, drug-induced psychosis. She's looking for a care facility. Men in white are after him, men from the Clean Living Rehab Centre.

Chief Justice Wilbur Kroop is after him too. Little does he know that Brian *welcomes* his entry into this pot-boiling *roman à clef*. Finally he has a worthy villain. *That* was what this story lacked. Lex Luthor in a black robe with a crimson sash.

He butted out a cigarette into the soup dish he was using as an ashtray. He lit another, poised his shaking hands over the keyboard. Okay, so we have Cud being played by this psychopathic schemer, and she . . . What? Where does the author throw in his big twist? Pre-denouement? At the very end? It was exhausting thinking this through, especially when he was so antsy.

The Widgeon icon was jumping up and down, silently pleading, in its mind-reading way, to join the discussion. *As your tale unwinds, you must guide your reader down delightful one-way roads and detours. I must admit in all modesty that I have a facility with the twist and have turned around my poor Inspector Grodgins so often, he must get dizzy!* Ah, but Brian has devised a twist that will put his mentor to shame, a twist that might turn poor Grodgins's head backward.

How eager Abigail was to nail Florenza LeGrand. *Of far more interest than some country Joe in red braces.* Together, they might pin the whole thing on Florenza.

Cud hadn't told the cops – or anyone – that he'd shtupped the hostess. He was being honourable. He actually used that word. A part of his brain still believes she's keen on him, on supporting the arts. Why hadn't Brian insisted he hand over the opal ring? He'd better bring it to court. Does one confront Florenza with it? Or wear kid gloves? Should Brian even show his hand? Why hadn't Florenza reported the ring missing? So many questions . . .

So far, no one had linked Judge Whynet-Moir, who went off a deck, with Judge Naught, who went off a wharf. These deaths were more than superficially tied together, no question. Not the others, though: the old fellow who fell from the ferry, the family court judge who disappeared from her family cottage.

The memo Arthur Beauchamp dictated to April Wu, what was that about? Whynet-Moir bribing the justice minister – it smelled of red herring. Apparently a lawyer named Schultz may know more of the story. Brian didn't have the energy to deal with that right now, it was too confusing, too hard to prove, too unlikely.

He felt itchy all over, it was as if his skin were carpeted with tiny bugs. His quivering fingers hung uselessly above the keyboard, he was at an impasse. *Somewhere after your first hundred pages, a dead end must be reached, seemingly insurmountable. But your hero must plod on – until, often by chance or mishap, inspiration comes like a flash, a whispered answer.*

He got up, he paced, fidgeted, turned one of the prints to the wall. It was getting to him, the ravenous white eyes in the blackness, waiting for the cowboys to sleep. He rummaged about for his clunky old digital camera, went to the window, took a couple of pictures of the people he thought could be working for the other side. The Lucky Penny Pizza guy taking off on his bike. Guy in a ball cap crossing the street from the bookies, their runner. Harry the Need negotiating a sale under the awning of Quick Loans. Not Harry. Harry wouldn't turn him in.

I was still drunkenly groping around this sweaty, foggy cave, trying to figure where her voice was coming from. She wanted to talk – lots of married women do that before getting it on, to explain they don't do this all the time. She was hammered too, not as bad as me, going on about how she'd lived a lie for the two years they've been married.

"It's like somebody owns part of you." My poetry, *Liquor Balls*, *Karmageddon*, helped her "remember freedom," it "aroused buried passions." I believed her, how couldn't I? Cudworth Brown, ex-ironworker with a bad back, had changed a life; his words had inspired a passion for freedom. A passion for *me*, the "beautiful, lustful savage" she saw in my writing.

I can't bring it all back . . . Yeah, after I bumped into where she was sitting in a corner, I said something inane about soulmates. She said, "Fuck soulmates." Her hands slid up my thighs, her body following, slick and hot.

We ended up on the floor, writhing like pythons on those slippery tiles, pumping like our lives depended on it. What? Sorry, there's a lady present. I'll spare you the pornography, but we were both about a half-inch from coming, when, whoosh, we got this jolt of cold air.

You couldn't make him out at the door, you couldn't see through the pea soup. "It's after one o'clock, Flo," he said. "Are coming up?"

"Almost there, Rafael." In this choking voice. I'm growing small. The hissing vents drown out our heavy breathing.

"Why are you doing this to me, Flo?"

"Let's talk about it in the morning, okay?"

Another cold gust as he closes the door.

"Help me, Cudworth," she whispers. "Help me escape."

—

A motive for murder had just inflated like an airbag, Cud's lust for her body, his hankering to be her toy boy. Brian didn't like the way this scenario was going. Not at all, not if the next line was, *Help me get rid of him by throwing him off the deck.*

He shut his eMac down, stared at his cellphone for a while. He dialed the UBC English Department, turned over the phone to Lance. "Hello, I'm ringing from *The Times* of London about Professor Pomeroy's marvellous new book. I wonder if it would be possible to do a quickie interview."

"I'm sorry, she's away for the holidays, but if you'll leave your number —"

"Fank you." He hung up, went again to the window. The Need was still there. Widgeon was calling from somewhere, he could hear his voice, demanding, imperious. "Go away!" he shouted. He lurched out to the fire escape, down the rattling steps to the street, where the Need caught his eye and shook his head.

Brian walked past him into Quick Loans, into a waiting room with three wooden chairs, a travel poster, and a metal-grill window. A man in working clothes was standing at it, signing over his pay cheque. Some bills appeared on a tray beneath the grill. The borrower gathered them up and hurried out.

Brian studied the poster. The Cuban Instituto de Turismo. Palm trees draping a crescent of white sand, islands dotting the blue transparent sea. Maybe that was the solution. Get clean. Get healthy. Get ready for the trial next month.

But he'd need money for that too.

"Can I help you with something?" Kharmazi, behind the grill, his heavy accent. Square head, cold, ethnic-cleanser eyes.

Brian tried not to show he was in agony, stilled his shaking body. He begged. He needed two thousand dollars to go to Cuba. His wife had taken all his assets, but he was expecting a partnership draw soon. "I am a lawyer."

"I know who you are. The defender of Abu Khazzam. For you, three points over prime."

"That's fair."

"Per month. Sign here."

Stuffing his wallet with hundred-dollar bills, Brian returned to the street, pointing himself toward the Golden Horizon Travel Agency. He was deliberately not seeing Harry the Need, but couldn't help hear his invitation. "You looking, Mr. Pomeroy?"

A flash, a whispered answer. A couple of grams. That would get him on the plane. Then he'd stop.

⚖

Two hours later, in the waning daylight, he was studying a cypress tree, the one famously kissed by the Aston Martin, its trunk now swathed in a wide black bandage. Farther down twisting Lighthouse Lane he could see the château of Florenza LeGrand, high on the craggy cliffs of Burrard Inlet.

Brian had taxied to this wealthy waterfront barrio with a sudden surge of energy. He was on top of things again, Lance Valentine, suave and daring. He owed it to his client, to his art, to check out the scene of the crime before escaping to a palmy beach. That plan had also come like a whispered answer, as he snucked up his first toot in seven days.

With Lance-like urbanity and wit, he will charm the truth from the grieving widow. He will be blunt, candid, will announce himself not as Lance Valentine but as Cud Brown's lawyer – a gamble but a brilliant ploy. He will say, "They're trying to keep us apart, but it's vital that we speak." She will say, "I was hoping you would come."

He advanced with confident steps toward the low stone wall that guarded the house. Then he saw a closed steel gate, a dark-skinned man guarding it . . . the doorman from the Palace. He had a ferocious-looking dog on a leash, a Doberman, Brian thought, or some close cousin. He stepped behind the skirts of a cedar to reconnoitre. So the tight end *had* been watching him, it wasn't a delusion. His orders were to stop Pomeroy. They didn't want Florenza talking to him, she knew too much.

He got his courage up again. He had a right to be here, a right on behalf of his client to examine the crime scene. He trespassed over a lawn and hurried across the street while the doorman was folding open a newspaper. Brian stuck his head over the stone wall, had a closer look at him – he'd put on glasses, looked different, older, shorter, thinner. Maybe Brian should get glasses.

The dog was sleeping, it didn't look so dangerous that way. Brian's fear of dogs – not just guard dogs, all dogs, from Mastiffs to shin-biters – was a component, his shrink explained, of his extensive paranoid mosaic. The guard and the beast were likely there to keep away reporters. Still, they were obstacles best avoided.

On the other side of the wall were ornamental bushes, a neatly trimmed lawn, a garden shed. Staggered terraces cut into the natural rock, rising to a patio, then descending to a wide cedar deck with a four-foot railing. The deck seemed to cling precariously to the beams of a flat-roofed, heavily timbered house of many levels. View of a slender inlet, waves splintering against rocky promontories.

He found a spot where he could clamber over the wall unseen, then, glancing back – the guard was still at his newspaper, the dog not stirring – made swiftly for the terraces, for the deck, where he paused to catch his breath and ponder his next move. *Look around, old boy, before seeking an audience with the lady of the house.* But it seemed deserted – no lights within though it was early dusk. Here was an area of wide windows and French doors, all curtained, probably a grand salon or dining room. He tested a doorknob. Locked. He pressed on, ducking below the railing in case the guard glanced up.

He made a sharp turn toward the backyard, where he could see the three-car garage, the maid's suite overhead. (Where was *she* that night? Why was Cudworth offered her room?) This had to be where Whynet-Moir went over, the jagged rocks below, waves slapping them, sighing and hissing back to the sea. The deck furniture was heavy metal, chairs and occasional tables, rust-less, stainless steel or zinc. One of these chairs had been found tipped over at this spot.

Down a sturdy staircase, the pool – still steaming, the tiles wet, towels strewn about. He felt transported back in time, October 14, the early hours, when a similar scene had greeted police. They seized the towels, didn't they? Yes, they got DNA hits off Cud.

Someone must be in the house: flickering light through a ten-inch gap between the curtains of a bay window. Crouching close he heard muffled music, a film score from a wide-screen TV snug to the window.

It was too high to see over, so he brought one of the chairs to the window. Slowly, he raised himself up, peeked over the monitor. Caught within the screen's stark, spastic glow were two persons on a couch. A handsome male, swarthy or maybe just well tanned, handlebar moustache. Tucked beside him, a leggy brunette, Florenza LeGrand, in a bathrobe hanging open, her bosom exposed, two ripe peaches.

Some part of Brian knew he ought to duck out of view, but he was mesmerized by Florenza's bobbing breasts as she bent over a table to savour a ritual known only too well to the observer. She did two toots and raised her head, wiggling the residue into her nose with a finger. Brian withdrew too late from the window; he'd seen the shock as their eyes met.

Her yelp of fright was followed by an obscene torrent. "Get that fuckhead off the fucking deck! You *fucker!*"

Brian clambered from the chair but froze again, found himself gaping across the little inlet at the neighbour's house, at Astrid Leich, made up to go out, bangles and beads, again seeing something of interest going on across the inlet.

But now, Florenza and her boyfriend burst outside, she still raging, he with an open jackknife. "Cut his balls off, Carlos, it's the only way to deal with these media shits. Slit his fucking *throat!*"

"*Claro*, I weel carve heem up as a warning to these paparazzi." But Carlos looked nervous, his machismo failing him, and he stalled his advance until the guard scrambled around the bend with his barking dog. Brian put his hands up, terrified until he saw the dog was leashed.

"What kind of fucking security are you, Rashid? Get his camera, goddamnit!"

Brian was still riveted on the dog. But when it lay down on command, he lowered his hands. Rashid's pat-down brought forth only a cellphone and a wallet. "He does not have a camera, Miss."

Carlos slipped back into the house, presumably to stash the blow, but Florenza tightened her robe, advanced, grabbed the cellphone. "Back off, Rashid, I'll deal with this."

She examined the phone for a camera, then came nose to nose with Brian, looking hard at him with almond-shaped eyes. "If you write about this," she hissed, "I'll sue your fucking ass from here to Zanzibar."

"I have no intention of writing about the shocking scene I observed, Ms. LeGrand." Lance Valentine was cool in emergencies. "I'd really rather not mention it to anyone, in fact."

"Listen, jerk, I'm not offering you any money."

"I find that totally insulting, madam. I ask only that you agree to talk to Cudworth Brown's lawyer."

She stared at him, confused. "When?"

"Right now would be a jolly good time." A spectacular coup was in the making. He gave her Brian's card.

"Get this fucking asshole out of here," she called to Rashid.

The dog barked. Brian's hairs stood on end. "As a bonus, I'll agree not to tell the authorities about Carlos." Who hadn't reappeared, who hadn't wanted to tangle, who may be risking deportation.

"Just a minute, Rashid." Waving him off, she dialed Brian's office number. "I'd like to speak to Mr. Pomeroy . . . Then put me on to his secretary . . . Ms. Wu, there's a character here who claims to be your boss. Can you describe him? . . . Uh-huh. Rings under his eyes?"

Brian took the phone from her. "April, it's me."

April was cautious. "Say something else."

"I came here to scope out the scene of the crime, and there was a brouhaha. Tell her who I am."

After she did so, Florenza thanked her and switched off. "Come inside."

A tour de force, old boy.

13

RUNNING MATE

Arthur heard cheering outside, saw green balloons floating past his window. Why was Margaret throwing clothes into a bag? "Wake up," she cried. "we've won! We're going to Ottawa!"

Arthur heard his own voice, "No!" as he hovered in the netherworld between sleep and waking. Another nightmare, one of a series airing each morning around dawn, more intense as nomination day approached. January 19 was nine days away.

"Did you say something?" Margaret asked from the stairs.

"A loud yawn, my dear." He smelled fresh-brewed coffee. The lazy January sun was hiding, rain was beating on the roof. Too bad, he'd planned to work in the woods today. He might have to sit in his club chair instead and read Plutarch, with the Borodin quartet's sweet melodies caressing his ears.

But by the time he finished his last slice of toast, the thick clouds, finding little profit in wasting their juices on the Gulf Islands, had pushed north to the worthier target of Vancouver. There were even hints of sunshine, so at mid-morning he set out with chainsaw and gas for the west woodlot to buck a tall, windfallen fir. He sized up the job, sharpened his saw, and bent to his noisy task, begging forgiveness from Pan and his merry pantheon of wood nymphs.

Nick joined him at noon, with sandwiches and advice to "make sure Arthur keeps his helmet on and doesn't lose any fingers or toes." They shared a Thermos of coffee, not talking much though Arthur wanted to know Nick's thoughts. There hadn't been much reaction to his dad's visit on Sunday – four days past and he still hadn't said anything about it.

Nicholas Senior had brought Pamela along, shy Pamela of the twitchy nose and brittle smile. "We are serious about each other," Nicholas announced. Engaged, in fact. Father and son took walks in the woods while the shy fiancée ate homemade cookies and desperately tried to make conversation.

After they left, Arthur called Deborah, who wasn't as upset as he'd expected – Nicholas had forewarned her with a long, anguished e-mail about having "found someone," apologizing that his romantic circumstances had caused him to be a neglectful dad. Deborah seemed to relish Arthur's account of the strained day at Blunder Bay, his unflattering portrait of the blushing bride-to-be.

He put Nick to work piling branches and gave him a safety lesson. Know where your feet are at all times, snip the boughs from the point of stress, position hands and arms thus as you cut fireplace lengths. He illustrated his lecture with tales of his own close calls.

"The key is the sharpening, a chain should descend through wood as if through butter."

Nick patiently watched him file the links to razor sharpness. "Cool. Mind if I go now? It's milking time."

Deborah has let Nick stay through most of February, though he'd miss some school. Out of a quaint sense of delicacy Arthur didn't tell her of her son's fascination with an exotic Estonian milkmaid. He considered it harmless and rather charming. He remembered puppy love, he'd had a crush on his grade nine Latin teacher.

Nick raced off, and Arthur yanked the cord and the saw coughed to life. The sweet, dripping forest, the crisp clean smell of fresh-cut timber, the arcs of flying flakes, the sputter and roar of a manly weapon: all these made Arthur feel good. The outdoorsman. Happily engaged in the only profession he cared about, farming. Enjoying his retirement years. He should burn his gown, a public ritual, a proclamation to the Cudworths of the world that this lawyer is no longer in service.

The luckless fellow was dealt a joker when Wilbur Kroop nominated himself to do the trial – this made the paper the other day, with a sidebar account of Pomeroy's caustic portrayal of the chief at the Gilbert Gilbert trial. Surely, Pomeroy will move to have His Lordship stand down. Extreme apprehension of bias: a substantial ground of appeal.

"One more reason to stay away from that fiasco, Beauchamp. The Badger despises you even worse than Pomeroy." Twenty years ago, Arthur told Kroop his jury instructions were "a hopeless mishmash of error and speculation devoid of facts and biased to the point of low comedy." Arthur was then on a quart-a-day habit, and after three nights in jail couldn't take any more, so he apologized. "Grovelled. The unpitying old bugger." He must stop talking to himself this way.

He cut a last butt from the lower trunk, then bowed to the remains of a brave fallen warrior who will warm his house next winter. The task of splitting and hauling will wait until he has his Fargo back. "It will be gracing your driveway tomorrow," Stoney promised. That was ten days ago.

It was almost five-thirty, time for dinner. As he packed his tools away, he saw that Nick had left his day pack hanging on a bough. Retrieving it, he felt a budge in a side pocket and pulled out a clear plastic bag with half an ounce of crushed green leaves. Marijuana. This deeply saddened him – he'd already given the boy one lecture. It explained his detachment, his blank attitude to his father's visit and engagement.

He trudged to the house, hung up the day-pack, and pocketed the cannabis. He didn't want to bother Margaret with this problem right now, not before dinner, not as she was chopping peppers in the kitchen.

He asked, "How did it go with the old farts on Saltspring?" She'd been at a glad-handing session, the Pioneers Club.

"Arthur, I don't think it suits you, of all people, to use that expression. Old-timers are respected. They deliver votes."

"Is it fair to campaign when you're not yet nominated? What if someone decides at the last minute to contest?"

"I don't think it's in the cards."

"Not a healthy sign for your political party, this lack of choice. Undemocratic somehow. Odd there isn't some young crackerjack willing to test himself against the old guard."

"Old guard!" A scoffing laugh.

"My dear, your Green Party has an establishment. You are part of it."

"Oh, sure, the Green machine." She was enjoying politics, knew she excelled at it, her grin gave proof she was even vain about it. Had the infection begun? The creeping corruption? Sadly, her party still barely showed in the polls, a mere sixteen per cent.

Underfoot, the fat tabby, was on his lap, chewing his belt, some kind of rare leather deficiency. He pushed him off. "I hope we're to have a quiet evening together finally."

"I'm not going out, if that's what you mean. I'll be on the phone a lot." Somehow, Arthur didn't like the sound of that. "Wash up so we can watch the six o'clock news." He didn't like the sound of that either.

After showering, he transferred Nick's baggie into his fresh pants. The prospect of disciplining the boy repelled him, but there must be consequences. Confiscate the iPod. Cut off access to the Internet. Force him to read Dickens. Arthur ought not to delay the matter, he'd tackle him this evening. It was hard being a grandparent.

Rejoining Margaret, Arthur lowered himself into his club chair, face to face with the cyclopean monster. He'd resigned himself to it, a new thirty-inch TV, apparently an essential tool for the aspiring politician. Complete with the mysterious usages and workings of a DVD recorder.

He grumped loudly through the six o'clock commercials. A diabolical intrusion, this machine. Mind-numbing pap for the docile masses. He'd come to Garibaldi for peace and quiet.

"Then be quiet."

Underfoot was back on his lap, and his brother, Shiftless, was going up his pant leg. They may have sensed he needed love.

"Good evening. There'll be a by-election in Cowichan and the Islands on Tuesday, February 26. That word came down today from . . ."

That's all Arthur bothered to listen to. He looked up at Margaret, standing beside his chair, looking very intense and white in the television's glow. This is the news she wanted them to share, the starting pistol has fired. Arthur had visions of mindless sign-wavers covered in badges, staged photo ops, babies thrust at candidates. Worst would be the innuendos, the mudslinging, private lives stripped bare. But he shook off the cats, moved behind her, and encircled his arms about her waist. "In case there are lingering doubts, I'm behind you. All the way."

The phone was ringing. "Don't answer." She squeezed his hands and pressed him back into his chair. "Look."

A political analyst. "Well, Jim, all three major parties now have candidates in the field, and the Green Party, with its typically late start, is expected to go with former island trustee Margaret Blake —"

"Who is credited with bringing about a new national park in that riding."

"Yes, Jim, with her standoff against developers."

Fifteen seconds of free advertising for Margaret Blake. The other candidates didn't fare so well, a sentence each.

Both cats were on his lap, licking, getting his slacks wet with their saliva. But a graver matter was at hand: Nick had come in and was searching through his day pack, frowning. "Anyone seen the catnip I got for Underfoot and Shitless?"

"Shiftless, dear," Margaret said. "I suspect it's in Arthur's right pants pocket."

Arthur fished it out, tossed it over, wordless in his embarrassment – he had no idea what to say without seeming even more foolish. Margaret laughed quietly as she got up to a ringing phone.

⚖

On a hazy, rainless morning a few days later, Arthur found himself at the terminus of his health walk, the general store, getting the usual silent reception in the lounge – the latest tactic of the Cud Brown Defence Coalition.

That organization had started off as a small local body, but somehow it had taken a leap over the Salish Sea to the Mainland. Now there were chapters. Literary groups, artists, workers. Cud's old union, the Steelworkers. Bloggers (whatever they were) had taken up his cause, conspiracy theories were floating around the brave new world of the Internet. There was a sense that this working-class poet had been railroaded by the rich.

At least Cud had stopped pestering – he was on a reading tour of hinterland libraries.

Arthur strode guiltily past the school where he'd missed too many of AA's bi-weekly Tuesdays, past the turnoff to Breadloaf Hill, where lay the ashes of the community hall. Only fifty thousand pledged to date, the rebuilding drive was going slowly. Here was the Shewfelts' roof, still tenanted by Santa and his reindeer two weeks into the New Year. Rudolph had weathered last week's storm poorly, had buckled to his knees, his nose hanging by a wire.

Arthur had trained islanders not to offer him rides during his daily hike, and for a split second he wasn't bothered that Stoney drove out of his driveway and past him, eyes fixed ahead, as if deliberately not seeing him. It struck him there was something wrong with this picture, and he waved and hollered.

Stoney must have been watching his rear-view because he braked with a seemingly grudging effort and pulled over to the shoulder. The Fargo had been repainted a garish yellow as if in a clumsy effort to disguise it. Arthur took a minute to catch up – too long, time enough for the culprit to come up with a story.

"Hey, I was gonna call to say your truck is ready, but I been away. Pretty late for your daily walk, ain't it? You change your schedule? Yeah, I was just breaking in your new trannie. Not part of my regular service, but for my best customers, I go the extra mile."

"You have gone your last mile behind the wheel of this truck. Slide over."

Arthur pushed his way in, removed the view-blocking sign from the inner windshield. "Rent me," with the Loco Motion phone number. "How long has this truck been in service?"

"Just a brief little while, honest."

Arthur reached over to the glove compartment, fished out some recent ferry receipts. The Fargo had been on the Mainland for a week.

Confronted with the evidence, Stoney said, "I was gonna surprise you with it, but I may as well tell you the astounding news. This here pickup is going to be in a big Hollywood production they were doing in Vancouver, kind of set in the 1970s, a period piece. They put zero point three miles on it. I'm gonna give you your cut as soon as the cheque clears."

Stoney knew he could keep Arthur from erupting by rattling on, and did so until they pulled up at the general store. "Maybe I could take it out in trade. Dog and me, what do you say we come by and pour a base for that statue you got, Icterus."

"Icarus."

"Only charge you for materials. A bit of cement. Otherwise it's our thank-you for all you've done for our community.

By the way, ain't gonna see me joining them braying hyenas who think you let Cud down. That's your entire own decision. I'd be suspicious too if my wife was up in a treehouse with a guy like him, though I don't got a wife."

Arthur pocketed the ignition key before entering the store. The gang in the lounge greeted him with loud silence. Makepeace didn't look at him, handed over his letters without deigning to enlighten him as to their contents.

It seemed hypocritical of these locals to accord the status of persecuted hero to a reckless loudmouth who'd caused marriages to break up, who'd bedded a host of the island's wives and its every willing maiden. Felicity Jones was his main squeeze these days, the greeting card poet. Her mother, the only islander encouraging him *not* to represent Cud, was enraged that Felicity had joined him on his reading tour. According to oft-repeated rumour, Tabatha had had her own fling with Cud.

Here, finally, was someone willing to talk to him, Nelson Forbish, wedged between the new freezer and the junk food shelves. "I got a hot scoop, Mr. Beauchamp." Forbish secured the bag of Frito's he'd been fishing for. "I found out who killed that judge Cud is charged with. It's all in here, I got this long e-mail letter to the editor."

He showed Arthur several stapled pages. "It's from an old farmer named Vogel up at Hundred Mile House. He got his woodlot and half his land swindled off him by Clearihue Investments, and the case went before Judge Whynet-Moir."

That piqued Arthur's curiosity. Todd Clearihue was a familiar name – he was known locally as Todd Clearcut. He'd held Gwendolyn Valley hostage, profited handsomely when the federal government was forced to buy it for parkland.

"Except that Whynet-Moir got himself killed before he wrote the judgment." Forbish waved his printout. "So this farmer says Clearihue bumped him off so there'd have to be a new trial, and now he can't afford a lawyer for it. He tells the whole story, how he was defrauded by Clearihue, how he thought he was just selling an easement to a lake."

"This came to the *Island Bleat*?"

"He's reaching out to me for help."

"Mr. Vogel has obviously sent this to every paper in the province, and not one of them will dare use it."

"Then I'm his only voice."

"I shall not defend you on a libel action, Nelson."

"I didn't expect you would," he grumbled.

"Give me the letter." No harm will be done by passing it on to Pomeroy. It seemed unlikely that anyone, even Clearihue, would kill a judge to get a new trial, but the prospect of seeing him behind bars, however remote, brought a glow to the heart.

He stuffed a few purchases into his pack and before leaving made an elaborate point of sticking a fifty-dollar bill into the *Cud Brown Defence Fund* jar.

On his return home he called Pomeroy's office, and again was put on to April Fan Wu. "He has gone for two weeks to Cuba, Mr. Beauchamp." A holiday before the trial, not a bad idea. He will need to restore himself, gain strength for Wilbur Kroop.

⚖

On Saturday evening, he found himself in a meeting hall on Vancouver Island, awaiting Margaret's crowning as Green candidate for the election five weeks hence. Honouring his pledge to her, he mingled, shook hands, talked about the weather, avoided politics.

The crowd was sizeable, over three hundred, more than he had expected. Print media, TV cameras. Margaret was working the room, guiding Malcolm Lewes about, the fellow who dropped from the race, as if showing off a trophy. Something was changing in her. A false face showed, a too-wide smile, a too-loud laugh, rapt attention to the bon mots of bores.

Here was portly Eric Schultz, the corporate lawyer, motioning him to caucus in the corner. Three-piece suit, briefcase, a truly anomalous soul with his business connections, his long-distance jump from the right wing. "Not happy. Angus Reid has Chipper breaking out of the pack on top." This was gobbledygook to Arthur. "Forty-three per cent, margin of error three points plus or minus."

Arthur responded with a tentative "Hmm." He guessed Schultz was referring to a recent poll. Chipper would be Chip O'Malley, the Conservative candidate. He'd seen his TV ad, a chicken-farming mesomorph with sleeves rolled up, promising fewer laws, a leaner bureaucracy, expanded services.

"Got to push him under thirty to have a chance. Good scandal would help."

The meeting had got underway with announcements that cars may be towed from the medical-dental lot next door and that organic pastries and coffee were for sale at the back. Schultz led Arthur there, bought him a coffee.

"Your Mr. Pomeroy hasn't responded to my calls." Schultz pulled a thin computer from his case. "Too bad. A hint that Whynet-Moir paid millions for his judgeship would get the press digging. Would help if Pomeroy raised the issue in the privileged sanctum of the courtroom."

Here it was. Heavy-handed politics. "It would help whom?"

"Our candidate. Your wife."

A photo filled the screen, a guest table at a banquet. "That's Jack Boynton." The late justice minister. "At a wedding, just before he keeled over with a stroke. That's Chip O'Malley beside him."

"Ah, yes, Chipper, the candidate. He knew the minister well?"

Schultz seemed taken aback by Arthur's political illiteracy. "Served two decades as riding president, bum boy to Boynton, his impatient successor. And no stranger to Raffy Whynet-Moir. All members of the same cabal. Shit sticks."

Arthur excused himself.

"Nominations once," called the chairman. "Nominations twice."

"Yay, Margaret," someone yelled.

"Nominations three times. Hearing no further nominations, I declare Margaret Blake elected."

A great cheer went up. Someone raised Margaret's arm. She was held in a circle of clicking cameras, then led grinning to the podium. A chant: "Margaret! Margaret! Margaret!"

Arthur made himself small. Please, he prayed, don't drag me up to the stage.

"Arthur Beauchamp, where are you?" the chair shouted into a mike. "Don't be shy, come on up here."

14

TRIAL RUN

"Rafael likes to watch, that's how he gets off. Cudworth and I did it on the dining-room table so he could lick off the custard after. We had lots of leftover custard. Poor Rafael, he was dead in an instant."

Florenza smiled seductively as she recounted this merry tale. She and Lance were in her sitting room with Heathcliff, the Doberman. Carlos the Mexican had not shown his face since Lance felled him with a left hook. Rashid had returned to his guard post.

"I dosed the custard with this new product that stops your heart; they can't detect it. All Cudworth did was dump the body. Would you like another gingerbread cookie?"

"I prefer my facts straight, Ms. LeGrand, like a fine single malt." Lance rubbed Heathcliff's neck. Dogs loved Lance. "The prosecutor is wetting her knickers at the prospect of indicting you. They found his semen in the steam room, all over the towels, not to mention your skivvies."

"That's not true, I washed them."

He had her at his mercy. "This is the version I would prefer to hear: Distraught upon your return from your romp with Cuddles, Raffy waits until you're asleep, then, overcome with depression, he shuffles off into the night. After a few heart-rending moments contemplating the fickleness of love, he climbs on a chair, leaps, and joins the church triumphant. What we do not want to hear are the words 'Help me escape.'"

Brian was annoyed at himself, he'd just given away a dark secret of the criminal law, the crafty tactic of enticing a witness to alter testimony. No wonder the author had disguised himself as Lance Valentine for this shysterism. One ought not to add to the public loathing of lawyers. Select paragraph. Delete.

He's got to stop Valentine from oozing his way into these creatively non-fictional pages. The fellow has begun to wear, infuriating Brian with his snide advice and plummy accent. Brian can't get rid of him; alter egos cling. He'd fired the syrupy gumshoe but never properly killed him off, that's the problem.

Having persuaded himself he could coax his body back to health, clean out his system, Brian had spent two weeks in Cuba, swimming, hiking, but he'd got lost a few times and had to phone Dr. Epstein collect to ask directions. Then there was that scene at the Havana airport, after his return tickets went mysteriously missing. The matter had gone up to the highest level, resulting in a decree from the presidential palace that he be immediately deported to Canada.

Otherwise, he'd had two drug-free weeks – except for the excellent Ron Habana, only three bucks a quart. He felt tanned and fit but unwell in other, confusing ways.

Confusing because things didn't go good without Coke, things got worse. When not high, he got the full blast of a breakdown that seemed never to want to heal. Dismayingly, Harry the Need was no longer working Main and Keefer. He'd taken a fall, been detained, nicked, tumbled.

Dr. Epstein, who wants to put him away, finds his self-diagnosis – nervous breakdown – a fuzzy term, thinks he's paranoid or psychotic or something similarly off the wall. She's not supportive, doesn't believe his voices are real. Whynet-Moir's voice, for example: *Your feeble cause, Mr. Pomeroy, is hardly aided by these crude outbursts.*

He can't keep hiding much longer. He has to go public tomorrow. That's when the trial starts. Vancouver law courts, 10:00 a.m. A five-day endurance test with Wilbur Kroop, a weekend between. It's *good* that the Need got busted. Brian had to have his wits about him tomorrow, he must be straight.

He'd been holed up in 305 since his return from Cuba except for a couple of trips to his firm, everyone sidestepping him while he hid in his office resenting the pigeons, resenting April Wu because he had no work for her and now had to share her with Wentworth Chance. Bad chi.

His only other outings had been to Chinatown, to the Jolly Buddha, which serves an all-you-can-eat for twelve bucks, his only meal of the day. But today he waited too long; the smorgasbord ends at four. Also he was out of tequila, and the nearest liquor store was closed. He'd have to pay double to the mercenary bartender downstairs for a quart of Cortez. He didn't like the bar, too many former clients, some had gone down, served time. It's always the lawyer who's blamed by these complainers.

Brian hasn't been able to make contact with his wife (he can't bring himself to say ex-wife). Caroline had switched phone numbers, e-mail addresses. Two letters had been returned unopened. Little Amelia had tried to get through this blockade, calling his cell. But he had let it bleat away, discovering later that his thirteen-year-old had called to say, "Hi, Daddy, I love you. Thank you for the scary house." He'd wept an ocean. He's been doing a lot of that.

News less bleak: Max Macarthur got that disturbance charge dropped, the drunken carolling. Brian asked him how he did it. "I spoke to Caroline." That prompted another breakdown, though it was proof she cared.

He stared balefully at the Brown file, which he'd been avoiding because it caused panic symptoms, Kroop attacks. He's also been avoiding Cud, who calls incessantly, who haunts from the wall, two arrows sticking from his back, the same bent nose and pissed-off look. It's just your word against Astrid Leich's, Cud, so chill out. Brian will play it by ear, that's how he does best.

But first he had to get through the night. He took the fire escape, slipped in the back way to blasts of hot air and bad music, a bewigged, red-faced, top-heavy matron belting out "Your Cheatin' Heart," backed up by a slide guitar and a drum machine. It seemed real, like his voices, not one of Epstein's alleged delusions.

He mounted a barstool, showed the bartender a fifty-dollar bill, tried to hunch himself small, his jacket collar over his ears. But very quickly someone was beside him, a clean-cut yuppie, vaguely familiar but out of place in this joint. Gold earring, thousand-dollar watch. He took the stool next to Brian, and said, "Twenty years."

The only client Brian could remember who got twenty years was Tiny Stephenson, the double manslaughter, but he weighed three hundred pounds and half his teeth were missing.

"You don't remember me, do you, Mr. Pomeroy?"

"Sorry, but I'm expecting an urgent call and must hasten to my lodgings."

The bartender passed him a heavy paper bag and was about to pocket the fifty when the intruder waved him off, flipping a C-note from his money clip. "Mr. Pomeroy pays for nothing when I am here. Give him another bottle."

"Yes, Mr. Neff."

"Twenty years ago, almost to the day. Walking out of that courthouse, taking my first breath of free air in five months."

Search memory cells. Find Neff. Eureka, the Bolivian flake conspiracy, a big win in his early career.

"'Gaping holes,' you kept saying. 'Gaping holes.' You owned that judge, man." Neff looked around and his voice lowered. "Hey, if there's anything special you'd like, I just brought in some new lines."

Brian invited him to 305.

⚖

Zero degrees and slush falling from the sky. There were portents in the weather, messy twists had been written into this morning's script, the slush will turn to shit. An ugly growth outside the courthouse like a clump of monster mushrooms. He couldn't focus, something wrong with his eyes. As the taxi pulled up at the Nelson Street entrance he made them out: smokers under umbrellas.

He wiped his nose. His arm shook when he tried to read his watch. Twenty to ten. What day? Thursday. When had he got up? Had he even gone to bed? He couldn't remember waking.

He paid off the cab, grabbed his briefcase, hitched his raincoat over his head, got out and surveyed the scene. Among the smokers, against the wall, a two-headed poncho. One of the heads looked like Cud Brown but different. The other head smaller, some kind of fungal growth. No, a woman.

He felt confidence welling again, thanks to the line he snorted in the cab. This trial will be a snap. He is Brian Pomeroy, number three in the criminal lawyer survey of 1997, icon to the freedom fighters of Bhashyistan. Play this one loose, old boy, rely on instinct, throw away your notes. What notes? Did he have notes?

Reporters comprised a separate group of mushrooms, they were talking about him. He's going to blow it, they're saying. Others had talked about him today, the desk clerk at the Ritz and two cyborgs with religious tracts. A scene occurred, Brian had accused them of whispering lies about him, shoved the clerk. Keep your temper, old fellow. Keep your mouth shut.

Warning. Alert. Charles Loobie approaching, Loobie of the *Province*, pot-bellied habitué of the El Beau Room. No comment. Remember to say no comment.

"Hey, Bry, how you doing?"

"No comment."

Loobie laughed. "You may be onto this, I'd be surprised if you weren't, but I dug up an interesting case Whynet-Moir reserved on."

Brian put on his dark glasses, the light was hurting his eyes. He wasn't sure whose side the reporter was on. He seemed friendly but might be trying to set him up. A scandal monger, this guy.

"He was just about to go on reserve week when he got terminated by person unknown. I say unknown because Astrid Leich, as you know, is blind as a bat."

Brian couldn't get a flame to his cigarette, couldn't hold his hands steady.

"Whynet-Moir was supposed to write three judgments, which are now in limbo. A medical malpractice. An extradition hearing. The interesting one is a land deal . . . I'm probably telling you something you already know."

"No comment."

Loobie chuckled again. "A slippery developer, name of Clearihue, was going to make megabucks if he beat a misrepresentation suit. I saw some of it; Whynet-Moir was obviously in favour of the old geezer who sold the land, a rancher named Vogel. Now the case has to be retried."

This was flying past Brian. He'd lost attention after the tossed-off *blind as a bat*. Astrid Leich, linchpin of the Crown's case, was blind as a bat. Why didn't he know that?

"And Darrel Naught — how come everybody's forgot about a judge who drowned outside a floating whorehouse after nailing a bunch of hoods for twenty years to life?"

Cud was walking toward them. Loobie lowered his voice. "Naught was being investigated for consorting with hookers, one in particular. After he drowned, the matter was quietly dropped. Some people say suicide. I say maybe. Maybe something else."

Brian chain-lit another smoke, but the nicotine didn't help. Judge Naught. Floating whorehouse. Consorting. These word-scraps skidded about loosely. *Blind as a bat.* That stuck.

Cud was suddenly in Brian's space. "Any chance I could talk to you?" He'd had a haircut, lost weight, looked younger. He led Brian to the lee wall of the courthouse. "This is my girlfriend Felicity, from Garibaldi."

The fungal growth, a chubby little head poking from the poncho. "I'm going to see him through this with my dying breath, Mr. Pomeroy."

Brian wiped his nose. "I've got a cold. Don't get close."

"You able to function, counsellor?"

"I was up all night working."

"Working on what?"

"Be nice," Felicity said. "Mr. Beauchamp says you're awfully good, Mr. Pomeroy. You're the only hope we have." She pulled a ring from her finger, pressed it in his trembling hand. "Here is truth. Here is innocence. I give you the power of this ring."

Brian looked around for Hobbits. He took his glasses off, squinted, felt the ring's power. A fire opal, glinting orange and red, a spark of yellow, a blinking caution light, warning of betrayal. He rubbed the ring, made a wish. *Forgive me, Caroline.*

"Felicity wanted to wear it for a while, I said okay."

Brian pocketed it. "Blind as a bat," he said and led them into the law courts.

Rain slicked down the vast transparent ceiling above the great hall. People everywhere, cops, lawyers, curiosity-seekers, prospective jurors, the building was jammed, he felt suffocated. "Free Cud" buttons. A sheriff's deputy was seizing a sign from a bearded revolutionary. "Anarchist Poets for Justice." Later, Dr. Epstein will tell him this was yet another delusion.

As he stared at the posted docket, the lines blurred, went double. He made out *Regina v. Brown, court 67*. Sixth level, the big assize court, it was somewhere up there, behind the cascading, vine-draped tiers. He hurried Cud and Felicity to the escalator. He'll settle them in, then change into his gown.

Abigail Hitchins and the lead cop, Hank Chekoff, were conniving on the gallery overlooking the great hall. Alone by the wall, lanky Shawn Hamilton, Silent Shawn, Florenza's lawyer. She wasn't supposed to take the stand today, was she? Who was?

Astrid Leich . . . He braked, and Cud almost bumped into him. Cud shouldn't be here, shouldn't be in view, she might be anywhere. The courtroom, witnesses aren't allowed in there. He'd stash Cud on a back row. This intense thinking exhausted him. He needed another snifter just to stay awake.

Abigail and Chekoff broke off their scheming as he led his client and consort past them. He asked, "Where's Astrid Leich?"

"Witness room," said Chekoff with his porcine grin. "Snorting to go."

Brian glared at him. "Fank you."

Court 67 was packed, stifling. People had to squish over so he could seat his charges. Chief Justice Kroop wasn't here yet, some other judge passing sentence, a motor manslaughter, a drunk who blew a point one six. What did Cudworth blow? Did Florenza take a Breathalyzer? Was that in the particulars?

Abigail was waiting for him outside the door. "Where'd you go the other night?"

What night? He remembered a restaurant. "I was acting on orders."

"You were plastered then, and you look like you're plastered now. Are you ready for this?"

He wiped his nose and went off to see what Chekoff was up to. Just as he suspected, sidling toward the witness room.

*It's the guy with the poncho, Miss Leich, he's cut his hair since you
saw him in the lineup.*

While Chekoff exchanged jibes with the deputy sheriff
in charge of the witnesses, Brian peeked in. The room
smelled of expensive cologne. Men in fine suits and women
in fine dresses, standing, chatting. He'd stumbled upon some
kind of cocktail party. No, a secret society of the rich and
powerful. There was Leich, fumbling with her glasses, getting
another fix on him.

The deputy had him by the arm, tugging. "Sorry, sir, we
don't want no one disrupting the witnesses."

Brian hurried down to the barristers' changing room, but
stalled when he couldn't remember the combination for the
Pomeroy Macarthur locker. Flustered, knowing Kroop has
jailed lawyers for being late, he borrowed a gown from a
neighbouring locker, fought his way into a too-tight wing
collar shirt, tied on a dickey.

Then he headed for the can and an empty cubicle. While
lining up his rows he spilled powder onto the gown, a little
snowfall on black fabric. He tooted, wiped his nose, licked
what he could off the gown, flushed the toilet. At the sink
mirror, he saw he still had his sunglasses on. He removed
them, saw a pair of hot, bloodshot eyes. He replaced the
glasses. Saw a patch of white powder on his inner pant leg.
Attacked it with a paper towel. Heard a sheriff calling, "Mr.
Pomeroy, court 67."

He kept brushing at his gown as he hurried there. He
couldn't get rid of the white smear, he shouldn't have licked
it. He entered court, saw them all looking at him. He stumbled to a halt. They knew, the packed gallery, the press, the
glowering chief justice, they all knew that Brian was guilty.
"The Crown is ready to proceed," said Abigail Hitchins.

"Don't just stand there like a signpost." Coal-black eyes
gleaming from folds of face flab. "Get up here and let's go
to work."

Brian felt the earth giving way, like a cave-in. He steadied himself against a bench until everything went still, deathly silent, a grey zone. He was in the middle of a crowded room in a black gown, holding a briefcase, that's all he knew. What did all these people expect from him?

He swivelled. He bolted from court, scrambled through a swarm of press, fled down the cascading stairways, outside, down the street, the rain lashing his face, his gown flapping. He ran and ran . . .

15

THE NEWS AT SIX

Mid-February, the unrelenting wet season. After three weeks of rain, Arthur could no longer delay bringing in his wood, so he toiled in the muck with mall and splitters, making several trips to the woodshed in his trusty, mud-spattered Fargo. (Welcome, home, old friend!)

From time to time he fed a fire with bark and broken branches and took his breaks there, warming himself, smoking his pipe, trying to pretend he wasn't aware it was day one of Cud's trial. He was in denial, he supposed, *Regina v. Brown* denial. He'd cut off all contact with him, with his case, even with Brian Pomeroy – who'd been on holiday anyway, charging his batteries for court.

The profligate poet, on seeing Pomeroy in fighting trim, will finally stop hounding Arthur, who'll be shunned no longer at the general store. They were handing out "Free Cud" buttons there yesterday amid brave talk of going en masse to court on the morning ferry. Arthur doubted if any showed up for the six-twenty sailing.

He was having trouble leaving this warming fire, though he should finish up, get back to check on the roast he'd put in the oven. Margaret planned one of her rare visits this evening, to bone up for the all-candidates meeting tomorrow. With the election twelve days off, she'd been barnstorming by float plane, an environmentally unsound mode of transport. Her Conservative opponent had denounced this as eco-hypocrisy. Chipper O'Malley sees her as an emerging threat; he was down to thirty-five points on the last poll.

Yes, the tireless Margaret Blake had risen like Venus from the sea, was now tied with a New Democrat at twenty-seven, while the Liberals, their last corrupt government not forgotten, were fighting it out with the independents. Arthur has been learning about politics, attending Margaret's strategy sessions. The idea is to edge ahead of the New Democratic Party, collapse its left-wing vote, stampede its supporters into lining up behind her as the better hope of upsetting the candidate of the Right. All in the great tradition of Nicolò Machiavelli.

He threw more sticks on the fire. Only one more load to bring up. Nick, who wasn't much for physical work but had offered to help, seemed relieved when Arthur let him off the hook. The kid has finally settled in like a familiar piece of furniture but his tenure is up in ten days. He spends his mornings helping Lavinia and afternoons plugged in or studying programming codes. Occasionally he will hand Arthur a printout of local interest, ramblings from the World Wide Web claiming Cud Brown was framed to protect people in high places and that Whynet-Moir was eliminated to staunch political scandal.

⚖

The Syd-Air Beaver wheeled overhead, pointed its pontoons to Blunder Bay. Syd was a supporter, this was his donation. O'Malley had made something of that too. Despicable fellow, this chicken fattener – only by stretching a point could he be called a farmer, he imprisons his birds in cages for the fast-food market. He's been making none-too-subtle innuendos about Margaret's two weeks in a tree with an alleged killer. With pepper added, vile hints of wanton behaviour. As predicted, Cud Brown has become a political liability.

The fire was subsiding to a mat of woody coals. Arthur rose, stretched, shook the rain from his hat, and went off to split the last butts.

When he got to the house Margaret was on the phone, a press interview. She blew him a kiss, thanking him for putting the roast in. "No, I don't think eight points will be hard to make up, not at all. We have a lot of policies in common with the NDP. More and more of them see us as the most effective place to park their vote." Arthur had grown up distrusting these idealistic lefties. "A caboodle of soft-headed socialists," his father used to say. The NDP candidate was sharp, though, a labour lawyer.

Where had Margaret developed these political skills? She'd come to Garibaldi with the long-defunct Earthseed Commune as a sixteen-year-old flower child, but instead of dropping out, she dropped in. Home study courses in agrology. Twice elected island trustee. He could handle that, but not Ottawa. He was afraid of losing her to politics, the knives, the skulduggery. How could she prefer that to making goat cheese at Blunder Bay? How would they manage the farm from four thousand miles away?

When he finished his shower she was on the phone with her campaign organizer. "We rise above it, that's what we do." She hung up. "Bastards! They've got a picture of Cud and me on their campaign website. We're in the tree fort hugging and waving."

"This is on O'Malley's website?"

"No, the Liberals."

Politics served up raw, exactly as he'd anticipated. And bound to get worse. Cud's trial was likely to end just before election day, generating headlines that could hurt Margaret's chances. Thank God he wasn't defending him; that would be the cruellest irony.

Ignoring the ringing phone, they ate dinner in front of the television, waiting patiently through the accidents, assaults, and fires for a by-election update. That began with a mindless, depressing streeter. "Sorry, I don't actually know who's running." "None of them are going to reduce taxes, they're all the same." "I've voted NDP for the last forty years, and I'm not going to stop now."

A pundit: "That last gentleman may find himself a little lonely, Jim, if the NDP's numbers stay stagnant. The latest polls have the Greens moving up three points."

"Yahoo," Margaret cried.

"But Chip O'Malley's six-point lead may be insurmountable. A lot will depend on the first all-candidates tomorrow."

"Thank you, Floyd, next up, another mad cow scare . . ."

Arthur snapped to attention when he heard, "Also, strange developments at the trial of a poet accused of murdering a high court judge." Arthur sank into his chair. Cartoon characters tried to sell him toilet paper.

"Do you know what this is about?" he asked.

"I didn't have time for the news."

Feeling hollow, Arthur watched an athlete shilling for a lending institution. Finally, here was Pomeroy, in flapping gown and dark glasses, dashing from a courtroom, skidding to a stop, racing for the stairs. Another camera followed him out the door and halfway down the block.

"It's still not known where Mr. Pomeroy disappeared to," said a breathless correspondent standing outside the law courts. "His partner, Maximilian Macarthur, later appeared in court to say he didn't know where he went. The case has been adjourned until tomorrow. Back to you, Jim."

Arthur stayed in his club chair, sipping tea and drumming his fingers as Margaret checked the phone messages. He'd lost his appetite, left food on his plate. He wanted to go away someplace and hide.

"Okay, three calls from Cud, each time drunker. Tabatha, very teary . . ."

"Tabatha!"

"She's afraid Felicity will get pregnant, the baby will need a father, please defend him. Several calls from neighbours and nosy parkers. And Max Macarthur is anxious to talk to you."

She passed him the phone. He dialed Max at home.

"Arthur, thank God . . ."

"Good evening, Max, and before we waste any breath, no, I will not defend Mr. Brown."

"Did I ask that? Damn it, Arthur, give me a chance to ask how you are."

"Had a very good day, enjoying that most spiritual of rural pleasures, the sweet feel of axe cleaving wood. Split three cords. For the next week I will be framing an addition to the greenhouse. You and Ruth must visit some weekend, imbibe the bracing tonic of smog-free air. Now what about Pomeroy? He cracked up, is that what I'm to understand?"

"Some kind of panic attack, according to his therapist. I knew he was rough shape. I had no idea he'd gone over the edge."

"So he has been found?"

"He ran all the way to the West End, to his psychiatrist's office. She put him in a private facility for the behaviourally challenged that's costing us the equivalent of the national debt. There's a cocaine complication."

"Good lord. You've talked to Caroline?"

"Yeah. It'll be hard on the kids."

Post-marital stress. Brian's drunken carolling had cried out a warning wantonly ignored. Arthur remembered marital stress. It can drive you to drink, it can make you crazy.

"We're going to tell the press he suffered a nervous collapse, it'll gain the poor bugger some sympathy."

"One presumes Cud took the whole thing with his usual good spirits."

"He was berserk. Brian's name was taken in vain. Your name, ah, was also mentioned. As a possible solution to this mess."

Arthur remained silent, he could feel Max squirming. Let *him* defend Cud.

"Abigail Hitchins also asked about you. She has enormous respect for you, did you know that? Says you're the only male human being she *does* respect, in fact — the rest of us are overweening, patronizing, testosterone-pumping pigs. *Despises* Kroop. You won't get a fairer prosecutor, she's a civil libertarian. Anyway, she's got a crisis, eighty-five jury panellists twiddling their thumbs and about fourteen witnesses set to go, including six business tycoons, their wives, and two prominent writers. She complained about that to the chief."

Kroop. Whose snarling image came, causing a tremor. "Were God himself to command me on penalty of everlasting hellfire, I would tell him to light the kindling."

"Let me finish. Kroop is threatening to proceed without defence counsel unless I find someone . . ."

Arthur interrupted again. "Fortunately, your firm, though small in numbers, is deep in talent. Four of this nation's finest barristers, a reputation well deserved. Not least among them the brilliant Max Macarthur. Ah, I remember well how the young slugger pinch-hit for me in the Shiva trial." Arthur had injured himself in a drunken spree halfway through that notorious cult murder.

"I'm flying to The Hague on Sunday. I have a month to interview ninety-three witnesses for the International Criminal Tribunal. John Brovak is lead counsel on the Ruby Morgan appeal, which is set for a week. Augustina Sage is at a Buddhist retreat somewhere in the jungles of Thailand recovering from yet another failed relationship."

"You have that young fellow, what's his name?"

"Wentworth Chance. He's much too green, Arthur. But here's the deal — we'll give him to you; you couldn't get a brighter junior. You can have Brian's office, his amazing secretary —"

Arthur broke in once more. "What I suggest you do tomorrow, Maximilian, is insist that Kroop reset the trial for three or four months hence, at which time many skilled counsel will have lined up for such a headline-grabbing trial. Please keep me apprised of Brian's condition. Poor fellow. Overwrought. Well, big day tomorrow, I'll want to rise early."

"If I can get Kroop to put it off till Monday, that gives you and Wentworth tomorrow and the weekend to –"

"Max, I wouldn't dream of taking it on without months of preparation. I have already managed to make a fool of myself on Garibaldi several times, I'm not prepared to repeat the experience in a court of law. Must run. Ta-ta." He disconnected.

Into the silence that followed, he said, "Only a moron would expect a barrister to step into a major trial on three days' notice."

Margaret shifted uncomfortably in her chair, spoke softly. "He did make a pass, Arthur. I rebuffed him." More silence. "Maybe Cud can't help it. He suffers from an unregulated sex drive; I think you resent that." Arthur blushed, he felt shamed, a little queasy, he didn't like this conversation – so he answered the phone, which he'd sworn not to do.

"Arthur, so glad I got through." Abigail Hitchins. "Max told me you might be able to bail us out."

"Max told you –" He began fuming.

"I've *got* to get this trial in, my witnesses are raising a row, fat cats, friends of the Attorney General. I haven't got an airtight case, I'm in a weakened state, this is your chance, beat me up. It's in your client's best interest –"

"He's *not* my client." He subsided again into a funk. He wanted a drink. That innuendo by Margaret still smarted, like a slap in the face.

"Listen, Arthur, with all the fooferah, all the publicity, with Bry imploding like that in court, the Attorney General, the whole government, is pulling out the stops so justice is seen to be done. The case is so sensitive that the minister has bribed the Legal Services Society to pay you triple senior counsel rate. Complete disclosure, no hidden rabbits; I'll sit on my fanny while you cross-examine at will, and I'll produce any witnesses you want to have a go at, even if I have to subpoena them from Outer Mongolia. We can make a fresh start on Monday – Kroop has indicated he could bend that far. The episode shook him. He'll be easy meat for you."

As she carried on, offering the moon and the stars, he felt suffocated by the pressure: family, friends, neighbours, all of Garibaldi, various arms of the government, the entire free world was on his back. And now someone was arriving, doubtless another petitioner, maybe the Pope. "Just a minute, Abigail."

He joined Margaret at the front door. A tall, skinny young man was bending over a mountain bike, unhitching a pack and saddlebags. "I'm sorry if I've interrupted dinner or anything." A squeaky tenor, a bobbing Adam's apple. "I ate on the ferry, so don't worry about me. I'm not going to barge in; I brought a tent. If that's okay."

That was met with silence, which caused him to talk rapidly. "I brought Mr. Pomeroy's file, which is pretty thin, and some Internet printouts about the main witnesses. I thought you'd want to discuss strategy before I go further." He seemed to strangle on his words, had to clear his throat.

"Who are you?" Margaret asked.

He removed his goggles and gloves, put on wire-rimmed spectacles. A stringy fellow, late twenties. "I'm blowing it. I'm Wentworth Chance. I hope Max said I was coming; he was supposed to. Excuse me, but I'm a little nervous meeting you, Mr. Beauchamp. You wouldn't believe it, but I've got a whole drawer of clippings about you." He couldn't seem to look at Arthur directly, as if he were blinded by the sun.

"For God's sake, Arthur, just do it," Margaret said.

"Come inside," he said, still bruised by her insinuation he was a jealous and incapable lover. Well, the courtroom was one venue where he wasn't impotent. He'll show her.

He retrieved the phone. "Abigail?"

"Still here."

"I shall want your undertakings in writing."

16

HOTEL PARANOIA

Where was his damn manuscript? Obviously stolen, this rehab asylum was full of thieves. Brian will outsmart them yet, he has backup disks secreted back in 305 of the Ritz. This morning he'd demanded a Mac laptop and got a used PC. Who knew what diseases it had? He threw it at a nurse, who ducked, and it crashed and died against the wall.

They pumped clozapine into him, the house drug, and the headmaster – the Facilitator, they call him, his stage name – asked him to apologize to the nurse. Brian explained he wasn't aiming at her, that the computer was infected with deadly viruses.

Now he had nothing but a pen, a device he was unused to, and his hand was so shaky he couldn't read what he'd written. A scrawl. Something like, "Help me escape."

Hollyburn Hall, this infirmary was called. Hotel Paranoia. A rich benefactor must be paying for it. Overstuffed furnishings, balconies overlooking mountains and rushing creek, five-star food, staff always in your face. Downstairs, a big stone fireplace around which his fellow inmates gathered to confess to the Facilitator. Brian refused to partake. They're not getting any information from him.

He'd taken a leap of faith with Dr. Epstein, that's why he was here. She thought Brian had talent, his manuscript was eccentric but entertaining. To please her, he agreed to go to

Hollyburn. He's not crazy, but she doesn't know that. He's one step ahead of her.

He didn't tell her about the ring, the opal scintillating with the colours of flame and desire. He keeps it in a zippered pocket of his wallet. Occasionally he will take it out and hold it to the light to divine its secrets, its arcane messages. One day it will reveal them, one day it will tell all.

He gave a phony address when signing in, he didn't tell them about his safe house at Main and Keefer. He can make a run there anytime, slip out at night, flag a cab, fetch the zip-lock bag from his room and be back in two hours. Nearly an ounce, enough to get through a week of facilitation.

Florenza LeGrand, that's where he'd left off. He scribbled, "Raffy was prowling outside the maid's room as we were making love. Then he just . . . just disappeared." Bursting into tears on the witness stand, is that how it will be written? He hasn't told anyone about Lance Valentine's visit to Flo at her château. That's their secret. He's not going to say anything about Carlos, he promised.

Groggy with anti-psychotics, he was having difficulty decoding his writing, its hidden meanings. He rose, slid open the glass door to his balcony, stepped out into the drizzle, looked over the railing, two storeys down. If he aimed for those rocks he could smash his head open.

He decided not to do that yet. One of the custodians had just opened the door, lugging in a suitcase, a garment bag, and a large cardboard box. Custodians just come in, there are no locks. "Miss Wu is here to see you. Do you mind if I look at this stuff, Mr. Pomeroy?" Ms. Wu came in, grim, unsmiling.

As the custodian went through the bags, she drew Brian to a corner of the room. "The manager of the Ritz phoned to say you'd abused his clerk and he wanted you gone. I brought your clothes, toiletries, books, computer, printer, a box of manuscript, and five backup disks I found hidden in crevices."

She looked severely at him, then added, "Plus there was something else."

Brian drew close to her ear. "Did you bring it?"

"I flushed it." She continued to glare at him until the attendant left, then said, "Covering up for your sins is not part of my job, Mr. Pomeroy, and I don't intend to be deported because of them."

"You don't understand. They think I'm insane."

"Insanity is a state of mind."

Brian fell back on his bed. The cowboy paintings he'd grown to love had been replaced by impressionist landscapes. Soothing decorous slush.

"Mr. Beauchamp has taken on the trial."

That's something Brian hadn't written. He felt empty, as if something had been stolen, plagiarized.

"He wants to know where the ring is."

"Around a rosie."

"Cudworth says you have it. Florenza LeGrand's opal ring."

"You're not my type, you're gay. Don't expect me to give you a ring." He shuffled through the cardboard box. "Where are my reference materials? My Widgeon manuals?"

"I'll have them sent. You've received a number of personal messages from friends. Your former wife called to ask about your condition. What shall I tell her?"

"I'm burning up as I descend from outer space."

"What do you mean?"

"I love her."

"I shall be working for Mr. Beauchamp while you are treated for your illness. If that is what it is." Maybe she suspected he was faking it. Maybe he was. Maybe he wasn't. Keep them guessing.

He escorted her downstairs, past the fireplace, everyone watching, nudging, suspecting. At the door, he asked her to report back.

"About what?"

"About their plans. The people spying on me."

"Who's spying on you?"

"I think you know who. I think you know very well who your paymasters are." He had her dead to rights, he could tell by her startled reaction. "Is Caroline coming to see me?"

"She didn't indicate that." She turned and walked quickly to a waiting taxi.

He began to cry. They were staring at him again as he ran upstairs. Tears smudged the manuscript as he removed it from the box. The pages slipped and scattered across the floor. There was no point in finishing this book. He'd lost control over his story. Arthur Beauchamp had control over it now . . .

PART TWO

POETIC JUSTICE

"What is our innocence, what is our guilt?
All are naked, none is safe."
— Marianne Moore, 1941

17

THE THIRD FIDDLE THEORY

Arthur sat glumly on a porch chair on this miserable Saturday afternoon, his bags packed, waiting for the rental car. Wentworth Chance was prancing about the apple orchard like a nervous colt – the gangly fellow was ever in motion, stretching, fidgeting, twitching, as if afflicted by a strange muscle disorder.

Margaret had already said her goodbyes, was off to a rally in East Shipwreck, then the all-candidates debate in Duncan. Her slight of two evenings ago still rankled. He muttered, "As if I've an obsession with" – seeking the right phrase – "performance issues." Too many courtroom battles, he'd wasted all his juices, saving nothing for the bedroom.

Nick came running down from the milking shed, shrine of the teasing Estonian goddess. "Good luck, Grandpa, all the woofers are rooting for you too."

Arthur ruffled his hair. "You're in charge now. Show your dad a good time." Nicholas Senior was coming, sans Pamela, and would be staying for the week. He'd been on the phone to his son a few times, apologetic, making amends.

"I better get back to my chores." A hug – Nick actually hugged him! – and he hastened back to the shed.

Arthur resented having to forsake Blunder Bay to do the chores of court. He wasn't looking forward to a week in crowded, jarring Vancouver, already in a flag-waving fervour for the Winter Olympics two years hence. It had become foreign territory, this town where he'd been born, raised, enrolled in private schools, where he'd studied law, married, divorced, fought cases for forty hard years. Where he'd been an impotent, raging alcoholic.

His main libation was tea, and many pots of it had fuelled him over the last day and a half as he muscled through particulars and witness statements, as he planned courtroom strategy with his fussbudget junior. Three days was an obscenely short time to prepare for a murder trial, but in compensation Hitchins had promised him virtual rule of the courtroom. That will help keep Kroop on the sidelines – though doubtless the old boy will find excuses to nag and nettle him. His free reign, not Kroop's hollow threat to proceed without counsel (and definitely not Margaret's critique of his bedroom expertise), persuaded Arthur it was now or never, *carpe diem.* After a long delay, witnesses tend to reconstruct memories. Such changes cement. Eyesight improves.

Wentworth won marks by picking up on Arthur's antipathy toward the client and offering to be his handler. He even took an anxious call from Cud, arranging to spend time with him tomorrow. He was a willing mule for any task, sharp enough, but would occasionally fall into some manner of spell, daydreaming perhaps, or overcome by the radiance of the god he served. An annoying tendency to hiccups whenever Arthur lit his pipe.

They hadn't had much time to talk about Pomeroy's bizarre behaviour, though Arthur learned, gratifyingly, that Wentworth had experience in a murder case – he'd assisted Pomeroy in the defence of Gilbert Gilbert, Kroop's would-be assassin. "Ask me anything about legal insanity, Mr. Beauchamp." Sadly, that was not on the list of useful defences.

By peculiar coincidence, Wentworth's small stable of clients included Minette Lefleur, a sex worker known well to Justice Darrel Naught, who'd planned to enjoy her comforts before he drowned on a warm summer night six months ago. Several years earlier, as an articling student, he'd fought her case of keeping a common bawdy house. "I won on a technicality," he confided with pride. "The judge ruled a houseboat isn't a house."

Stoney honked a greeting as he came around the bend in his cherry 1970 Chrysler New Yorker – the gas-gulper. Arthur will feel guilty driving it. But aside from minor dents it was in decent shape. Stoney disembarked with a smile, seeming sober though it was already half past one. He saw Wentworth gawking at the car and gave him a card.

"This here is Loco Motion's finest model, a beauty, eh? Our stock also includes a splendid example of a Merc Cougar V8, from back in the days when they made cars instead of battery toys, and we expect to bring on line a superb '69 Fargo . . ."

Stoney wasn't sober after all, or so absorbed in his sales pitch that he forgot Arthur was present – his voice faded as he turned to see him hovering with his bags. "Of course that depends on, I gotta make, like, satisfactory arrangements with the, ah, registered owner."

"The Fargo is locked in the garage, Stoney."

"I won't touch it, I promise." He raised a hand. "I swear."

Arthur heaved his suitcase into the trunk. Lots of room for the disassembled bicycle too, which Wentworth carefully set inside.

"I had to fill the tank, set me back about sixty easy. Them vultures at the gas station are taking advantage of the world-wide fossil fuel crisis."

"Stoney, we have an arrangement. Three hundred dollars a week, a full tank at the end." He greased Stoney's palm and got behind the wheel, beckoning Wentworth to join him.

"You got me wrong." Stoney got in the back. "A deal's a deal, eh, I'm not gonna smirch my good name by reneging. It's just something to keep in mind when you're considering the tip."

The car lurched forward when Arthur nudged the accelerator.

"You got to use a gentle touch on this baby, Arthur. Pretend you're making love to her. The radio's broke. Probably could use new wiper blades, especially the right one, which don't work at all. Otherwise she's street legal." He got out at his driveway.

As they rounded a bend by the ferry dock, Wentworth said, "What's going on there?" He was pointing to a twenty-foot structure, the lower half hidden by draped black plastic, a complex armature above. A local sculptor, Arthur explained, was paying his debt to society.

"I got the creative spirit, b'y," Hamish McCoy had said when Arthur stopped to visit. He'd tried to peek at the plans, but McCoy rolled them up. "Artist at work," said his sign. "Keep out." He slept there at night, guarding his tools, his bags of plaster. A departure from his preferred métier of bronze or stainless steel.

From the ticket booth, where they had a better view, they made out that McCoy was welding: above the sheeting, a shower of sparks fizzed out between two thrusting arms of welded rebar. Wings? An angel? The *Goddess of Love*, he'd told the unreliable local news outlet. *Oi'll give them joy.*

The ticket seller wouldn't accept Arthur's money. "Lane two. You'll be first on, Mr. Beauchamp; I been asked to give you priority loading."

There came the sound of bagpipes, increasing in wheezy vigour as they headed to the ramp – the Garibaldi Highlanders' innovative version of "Amazing Grace." Near the Winnebagel, the ferry lunch wagon, were five kilted pipers, a drummer, and life-jacketed Kurt Zoller riffing on an accordion, along with four score festive islanders – Arthur was getting a send-off.

Here came Nelson Forbish, camera and burger in hand. "'Old warrior goes to battle for island ally.' It's the lead story, Mr. Beauchamp."

Zoller laid down his evil instrument. "I saw on the Internet that the judge was actually killed by a government hit man. We're counting on you to avert a terrible tragedy of justice." A cover-up, a hit man – these were the theories the blogs were wildly propounding, shadowy conjectures without a kernel of proof. *Nullius in verba*, Horace counselled – rely on the words of no one.

The howl of bagpipes had the compensating benefit of drowning further exchanges, but Arthur was forced to shake hands all around. "Free Cud Brown" signs and buttons everywhere. Defence counsel was finding himself under a disagreeable amount of pressure.

As the *Prince George* berthed, Cud's cheerleaders jumped into their cars, led away by Zoller in his jeep. Arthur craned up at McCoy's work-in-progress. There was the sculptor himself atop a ladder, pissing downwind, in the direction of the jeep.

From the aft lounge, upper deck, he watched his island slip away and bemoaned his lot. He'd planned to be with chickadees on this rare sunny day, and the other winter birds that hung around the feeder by the greenhouse. A ruined weekend now, to be spent in stuffy law offices and libraries. And in his equally stuffy club, the Confederation on West Hastings, where he'd reserved an honourary members' suite.

He frowned over Cud's account, ten typed pages transcribed from April Wu's shorthand notes. "Why do you suppose, Wentworth, that it ends abruptly in a steam room?"

"Maybe he blacked out."

Arthur's own experience attested to that possibility – he'd once awakened in the drunk tank with no memory for the previous forty-eight hours. "Extraordinary time to blank out. Whynet-Moir had just caught them fornicating in the steam room, their adrenaline must have been flowing." Arthur didn't want to hear that Cud was amnesic. If he couldn't firmly deny this homicide, his claims of innocence would sound hollow.

"'Help me escape.'" The three little words that concluded Cud's account. "What do you make of that, sir?"

"Please do not call me sir. Let us hope Cud wasn't so snockered that he blindly did her bidding. It doesn't help him a whit if he slew Raffy at her instigation – he's no less guilty for having been in mindless rut. Surely there was more conversation than this."

Wentworth made a note.

The Crown dossier included a photo of the lineup, eight men of similar build, of whom Astrid Leich had identified the most woebegone, number six, Cuddlybear. "That's the man," she'd said confidently, and wrote down a big curlicue 6. Astigmatic, according to several old interviews, short-sighted even thirty years ago, in her heyday on the stage. Wears contacts or glasses, but the latter never in public. Was she making use of either shortly after 3:00 a.m. on October 14?

That was when she claimed to have seen Cud pitch Whynet-Moir over the railing. Her call to 911 came in four minutes before the Aston Martin met the cypress tree.

Leich was a fitful sleeper, easily awakened – the noise that aroused her was "like something slamming, maybe a door." How that would persuade her to go out to her balcony was a puzzle. For reasons unclear, Whynet-Moir was standing on a chair by the railing when, according to her, number six rushed at him and sent him flailing onto the rocks below. She heard the victim's dying cry and the crunch of his body. The perpetrator stumbled off, down the outer staircase toward the pool and garage. She lost sight of him and hurried inside to phone.

Arthur will have to be extremely deft in his cross-examination of this appallingly observant eyewitness. If, as is likely, she fingers Cud in court, Arthur will have a fall-back position: in raptly following this case, Leich has surely seen him in the papers, the newscasts. It hasn't been Cud's style to hide under his poncho while running the media gauntlet – he has actually courted them – so Leich's evidence could well be tainted. Mind and memory are easily prey to such influences.

Much more intriguing was Florenza LeGrand's role in this grand *guignol*. Still a hippie at thirty-three, said Eric Schultz. Rebellious youth, stint in an ashram, affair with a Mexican drug dealer. Her blotter included, more recently, a hit-and-run and an assault. Shawn Hamilton, Q.C., had acted for her on both, had beat the latter.

Arthur expected to see him in court on Monday. Silent Shawn was an odd duck among counsel, one who thought long and carefully before he spoke, if at all. A competent defence counsel who also did prosecutions for federal Fisheries. A Tory with lucrative Ottawa connections.

Whynet-Moir's blood alcohol was point zero seven at time of death. Cud blew point two four, three times the threshold for impaired driving. At the very worst, a drunkenness defence was available. But that leads to manslaughter and a possible twenty-year residency as a guest of Her Majesty, hardly a clear win.

Arthur would prefer to prove someone else did it, though it might be easier to make a case for suicide. But Whynet-Moir didn't match the population most prone to it: depressives, alcoholics. The conspiracists didn't like suicide, they preferred the bizarre – payoffs, government hit men.

Wild theories about a corrupt payment to the justice minister from a wannabe judge didn't make much sense as a murder motive. "A cover-up," Eric Schultz had hinted, implying Whynet-Moir was eliminated to bottle up a scandal. He wondered whether he dared taint Whynet-Moir's reputation with hints he paid his way onto the bench. Maligning the dead is generally a bad practice, and when neither admissible nor provable can boomerang.

One of the calls Arthur hadn't answered was from Charles Loobie of the sensation-seeking tabloid the *Province*, with his, "I've got a couple of theories." The veteran reporter always had theories. "You should talk to an old guy name Vogel." The rancher from Hundred Mile House allegedly defrauded by Todd Clearihue – Loobie had obviously got the same e-mail that had so exercised Nelson Forbish. But a link to Whynet-Moir's death seemed tenuous.

There remained a possibility Raffy was somehow tied to other judges who mysteriously died. A demented serial killer wronged by the courts. One case has been solved, however: the provincial judge who wandered from her cottage at Honeymoon Bay was spotted two weeks ago, working as a waitress in a gas stop restaurant in Dawson Creek. Alzheimer's, though it didn't seem to affect her judicial duties.

"Was there no blood alcohol done on Ms. LeGrand?"

"I don't even know if she gave a sample."

"It would be interesting to know if Florenza was having an affair."

"What? Sorry." Wentworth had drifted off again. Where does he go?

"Let's assume Florenza had a lover."

"Well, she did, sort of. Cudworth."

"Assume he was playing third fiddle, duped into being stud for the night, set up as prime suspect. That neatly deflects suspicion from her real lover. Let's say her boyfriend was hiding, waiting for his chance."

"God, that's brilliant." Wentworth made a note.

⚖

Arthur found street parking on skid road, not far from the scene of his descent to the depths, a ramshackle street front where he'd swigged gin and defended bums for two years, living off legal aid. Though there'd be a substantial fee for this case, it will go to the community hall fund — he'll not profit from Cud's misfortune.

A five-minute walk took them to Gastown, Maple Tree Square, and to the old brick three-storey whose top floor long hosted Pomeroy, Macarthur, Brovak, and Sage. The cavernous space that occupied the balconied floors below was cursed, a graveyard of such failed businesses as a comedy club, a spiritual therapy centre, and an Irish sing-along pub. Its current tenant and likely next victim was a jazz club. A trio was rehearsing as they entered the elevator.

Through the locked glass doors of the office, Arthur could see a slender beauty, April Wu, running documents through a copier. When Wentworth inserted his key she jumped, then waved. Instead of coming to greet them, she quickly collected her papers and disappeared down the hall.

Wentworth proudly showed Arthur the firm's extensive criminal library, then his office, an overheated cubicle with a view of the fire escape. "In case you thought I was just trying to butter you up . . ." He unlocked a drawer, showed Arthur some expander files. "All your trials. Your life."

Arthur shuddered to see his entire career stuffed into expander files. "When I consider life, 'tis all a cheat."

Wentworth looked at him expectantly.

"Dryden."

"Wow."

Arthur didn't think he could take much more of this. He will seek ways to get the young man out of his hair. Keep him busy being Cud's interface. Busy in the library. Arthur needed time alone to think about the case, to hone his strategy. He liked the third fiddle theory, but who might Florenza's real lover be? The file yielded no clues.

Pomeroy's office was on the sunny south side, facing the lively square. Pigeons patrolled the outside window ledges. A depressing place, though the sprawling desk was tidy, thanks presumably to Ms. Wu, who entered and extended her hand.

"It's a pleasure to meet you finally. Wentworth has told me all about you."

"Then I am a man without secrets."

"No one is without secrets, Mr. Beauchamp."

She smiled. Her dark, intense eyes threatened to lay bare his secrets, his weaknesses. An emergency van bleated past the square and stopped on Alexandra Street, lights flashing. He swivelled to the window. Someone passed out on the street, that was all. Ah, the city, the frenetic, dismal city.

Wentworth was annoying him with his pacing. He told him to sit down while April recounted her adventures: visiting Pomeroy's room in a cut-rate hotel, flushing an ounce of cocaine down the toilet, her trip to Hollyburn Hall.

"Had you been aware of the extent of his disability, Ms. Wu?"

"He seemed deranged."

"In what way?"

"He was writing a novel."

"Ah."

She gave other examples, bursts of paranoia, festering conspiracies, a high-toned British accent coming out of nowhere. "Bad chi," she said in summary. "Very bad energy."

Poor chap. Suspicious, reclusive, self-medicated on drugs and alcohol, yet somehow able to cope. Brian had always been neurotic, and his friends may not have picked up that this was something worse.

"What did he say about the opal ring?"

"'Ring around a rosie.'"

"Good grief. His interview with Mr. Brown seems incomplete, Ms. Wu. It ends abruptly in a steam room."

"It is said that sometimes one must stop digging the well before water is reached."

Lao-tzu, he presumed. Again, that impenetrable smile. "I take it that means he shut the interview down."

"He didn't like the way the story was unfolding."

Arthur nodded. On reflection that seemed a wise decision, especially after Florenza's "Help me escape." This must have occurred during one of Brian's sensible moments – he hadn't wanted Cud to dig a deeper hole for himself. Self-incrimination tends to complicate things for a defence lawyer; the wiser course is to gather the facts before resuming such interviews.

"Wentworth?"

He came alert. "Yes, sir."

"Cud signed his two books for Florenza – are they among the evidence?"

"No, not that I'm aware."

Never regret, he wrote in one of them. *New love blooms as the old lies dying,* in the other. "Let us hope they don't turn up."

⚖

The Confederation Club was in the heart of the business district, a four-storey Ionic temple where Arthur had taken many wet lunches over the years. The rattle of the cocktail mixer brought memories and tremors as he settled into a deep chair in the lounge with his tea and the Saturday paper.

He regretted not being with Margaret tonight at the all-candidates. She had claimed he'd make her nervous. A businesslike kiss on parting. Shared good wishes for their respective campaigns. No apology for her crack about his low sexual appetite.

Shuffling through the newspaper, he paused at an item from Ottawa. In question period yesterday, an opposition MP asked about allegations that the former justice minister kept a secret, well-nourished bank account. The prime minister chided the member: in maligning the dead, he'd fallen to a new low.

This bribery business was showing growth potential. Arthur wondered how much there was to it. The Tory chicken farmer must be wondering too. *Shit sticks.* Margaret will have no trouble besting him tonight. But the New Democrat is crafty, a labour lawyer, she'll be tough in debate.

He heard snatches of conversation from the table behind him.

"He's staying here, is that right?"

"Yes, while he's defending that character who did in the judge, what's his name, Whynet-Moir."

"Ah, yes, the poet fellow who shared a nest with Beauchamp's wife."

"Tree huggers. They have different moral standards, I suppose."

18

SOMEONE ELSE IS GOING TO DIE

Wentworth Chance had not gained much courtroom confidence in his years with Pomeroy Macarthur, and his billings were low – too many hours in the library, grubbing for obscure precedent for the few cases entrusted to him, misdemeanours mostly. Worried about his future with the firm, resigned to being an academic nerd, he became indispensable, working nights and weekends, preparing briefs his bosses would recite in court as their own. When he wasn't working, he was dreaming.

Though almost thirty, he looked (and somehow felt) as if he was still in his troubled teens: skinny, awkward, and shy – especially with women. He'd grown up in a town on the Alaska Highway and hadn't learned the social graces. He wore thin ties and black horn-rimmed glasses that made him look like a refugee from a 1950s vocal group. The C-Notes, maybe, or the Mellotones. He would have been the tenor, with his high voice – though it was poorly oiled and needed frequent throat clearing.

He was fascinated by the courtroom, its theatre, its combat, its heroes. When told on Friday he was to junior the don of the West Coast bar, he'd had to lie down to slow his heart rate. He'd attended Mr. Beauchamp's every major trial for the last decade, skipping classes, shifting appointments. In the privacy of his threadbare two-room flat he'd imitated him, as best he could – the thunder of his voice, his jabs and gibes, his wit. He'd been dismayed when Mr. Beauchamp retired several years ago, delighted when he came back, however sporadically, to the arena.

Throwing himself into the Brown case, he was exasperated to find papers and records from the file scattered all over Pomeroy's office. Some of his scribblings didn't make sense, though that was to be expected, given his illness. Wentworth felt guilty; he should have alerted the partners to his last conversation with Brian. ("Do you know where I get my orders from?" "Where?" said Wentworth with a nervous laugh. "Hector Widgeon himself.")

His weekend visit to Garibaldi was a disaster. Mr. Beauchamp didn't recognize him, though they'd met four times: at a guest lecture at UBC, in an East End Bar dinner, in the hallway outside provincial court 10, and while serving documents at the great one's firm, Tragger, Inglis, Bullingham.

He'd been more comfortable with Margaret Blake – who'd fed him, despite his protestations – though he'd made the hugely embarrassing slip of calling her Mrs. Beauchamp. "He's just being crotchety," she said as he helped with the dishes. "He'll soon get over it."

But the icon seemed to be holding him at a distance. He was grumpy, saw this intriguing case (multiple suspects, political entanglements, hot sex in the boudoirs of the rich) as some kind of millstone. He flinched at the mere mention of the client's name.

Mr. Beauchamp had chided him in Pomeroy's office. ("Wentworth, I find myself wilting under your barrage of nervous energy. And stop calling me Mr. Beauchamp. I have a first name.") Further unsettling him was April Wu, whose alluring presence always left him sweaty and tongue-tied. If she weren't gay, he'd be in love.

When he sought advice about how to handle Cud Brown on Sunday, Mr. Beauchamp said, "Test him. See if his story holds up."

He'd come second in the footrace but fourth in the swim, and now, on this final day of the triathlon, he must win the bicycling to earn the gold. His lungs were raw, he didn't know if he had enough left in the tank, and the Nigerian and the Czech were still five metres ahead. The ultimate test was approaching, Heart Attack Hill. He dug deep . . .

Wentworth braked, swerved to avoid a car door swinging open in front of him. Had the exiting driver not yelled, "Sorry," he would have given her the finger – she had almost killed a lawyer involved in one of the biggest trials of the decade.

He powered up the hill to Eighth Avenue, pulled up in front of a tall, ramshackle wood-frame building, the Western Front, a theatre and artists' residence, an East End counter-culture shrine where Cudworth Brown was writer-in-residence for the next two weeks.

He found him in a two-room flat, swigging beer, bare-chested except for his peace medallion. His girlfriend was here too, Felicity Jones, sitting at a typewriter, puzzling over a dictionary.

Cud had a steely grip. "I forgot your name."

"Wentworth Chance. We met once at the office."

Cud didn't seem to recall that. "What's with the bicycle helmet?"

"It's a health thing." He didn't want to admit he couldn't afford a car on what they paid him.

"You're a lawyer?"

"Winner of the McKenzie Prize in Evidence."

"I hope Arthur ain't going to foist you on me like he did with Pomeroy."

"Be nice, Cuddlybear. He looks hungry, you could warm the lasagne."

"Thanks, I just ate. Mr. Beauchamp wants me to go over your story again."

"Okay, but I want to watch the game after."

"Game?"

"The Super Bowl, man. It's super Sunday."

"What rhymes with yonder?" Felicity asked.

"Launder," Wentworth said. "Fonder."

"Perfect."

"Tell me about the judge I got. This Kroop character. I hear he's an assmunch."

Wentworth had worked up a personality profile on Kroop for the Gilbert Gilbert trial. With his profound dislike of dissenters and radicals, the chief justice wouldn't like Cudworth's arrogance and hairy chest and peace medallion and views about proletarian revolution.

"Mr. Beauchamp will dance rings around him." No point mentioning the history of enmity. One old clipping recounted a trial at which the chief jailed Mr. Beauchamp three days for claiming his head was set in concrete. "He's just there to direct traffic. The jury decides."

When Wentworth declined a beer, Cud opened another for himself. They settled in a nook by a window. "Okay, Woodward, where do we start?"

"Wentworth. First of all, that medallion has to go; you can't wear it in court. Witnesses are going to be identifying you, there's no point in helping them. No suspenders either."

"Good thinking, man."

"Tell me how you got invited to Judge Whynet-Moir's house."

"I'd been nominated for the GG in poetry, as I guess everyone knows, and writers of a certain rank get asked to prostitute themselves for the Literary Trust – and believe me, I felt like a fucking whore in a Tijuana bordello."

"There were three other similar events going on that evening, right?" Wentworth had done his homework.

"Yeah, in fact I was originally supposed to go to a soiree in Point Grey, which was closer, but a few days before, they switched me to this one. I was kind of resentful, but it's all for the cause."

"Why did they switch you?"

"One of them inscrutable events of fate, man. Wish they hadn't."

Felicity asked, "Is there a word like nymphean?"

"Never heard if it," Cud said. "Anyway, I was all day getting there, ferry, bus, thumb, and taxi, and I was in a mood to tie on a good one and not worry about getting my ass back home. When Whynet-Moir greeted me I let the conversation drift to where I didn't have a bed for the night."

"How did he seem to you?"

"In what way?"

"Generally. His demeanour."

Cud looked hard at him. "You could see behind the jovial mask that this dude was tormented. I felt his vibrations right away. I got a nose for people."

"Okay, then what?"

"So he gave me this home and garden tour, and I'm thinking, there are people living in the street, and him and his wife have got eight baths and an elevator to the wine cellar."

"Did you express these views, or get in any kind of political argument?"

"He's not the kind of guy you can strike up an argument with. Too soft and squishy, if you get my meaning. There was this other heavy pockets, Shiny Shoes, who I took a dislike to for making cracks at my medallion. He had some kind of business with the judge, I saw them in a corner bending over some papers."

"You didn't mention this to Mr. Pomeroy."

"I remembered it later, thought it might be important. Shiny Shoes didn't look happy after that little discussion. He kind of rushed off with his wife. But maybe that's because I pissed on his Lamborghini."

Wentworth made a note. Cud's constant smoking was getting to him, bringing on hiccups.

"Anyway, a martooni or two later, I'm out on the deck and the judge is directing traffic and here comes the mink with her, 'Want to fire me up?' She had both my books, she's an appreciator of the arts."

"Those are the ones you signed?" Hic.

"Yeah . . ." A hesitant look at Felicity. "Maybe we should continue this over a beer."

"We are."

"Down at the Pig."

As Cud led him toward the Pigskin, a sports bar a few blocks away, he said, "I never told Felicity about how I got seduced by that dame. It's embarrassing."

"I ain't been beat in twenty-eight straight," said Two-Ton Tony, "and I ain't gonna let some rank amateur stop my run." He racked the balls as Wentworth tossed back his whisky. "What's your wager, four-eyes?" Wentworth pointed to his gorgeous girlfriend. "Her. For the night." He chalked his cue, broke the triangle, and the seven ball rolled into the right corner pocket. The rest would be easy . . .

The back end of a cue almost struck Wentworth's glass of ginger ale. "Hey, fat man," Cudworth growled, "you're bothering my friend; watch what you're doing with that thing."

Wentworth edged back in his chair, ready to bolt, while the hulk sized up Cud's try-me look, his biceps, his broken nose. Then the guy pretended nonchalance, as if this challenge to his manhood was beneath him, and retreated to the other side of the table.

Cud was into his fourth pint and becoming more garrulous, not to mention dangerous. Wentworth had seen his sheet, a minor record: two assaults, both in barrooms. Those, of course, were inadmissible evidence unless Cud took the stand, in which case the Crown could force them out of him. He was smiling and expansive now, celebrating, relieved that Mr. Beauchamp was on the case. "Like a grizzled gunfighter riding into town to take on the Cattleman's Association and the corrupt sheriff."

They'd been here an hour, and Wentworth was worried about his Outback 310, chained outside the Western Front. He would leave after the game started, but he still had a few minutes to venture into unexplored territory.

He was careful in his phrasing. "Cud, I'm going to leave it to Mr. Beauchamp to ask what happened after you left the steam room. But let's talk about some possible scenarios."

Cud leaned back, chewed on the matter a while, gave him a cagey look. "Okay, one logical theory has me passing out so I don't remember a fucking thing else. Another has Flo and me going up to the maid's room and screwing our tails off and not seeing anything. Or maybe we do see Whynet-Moir, hear him go, 'Goodbye, cruel world,' and jump." He put his finger up for another pint. "Game's starting."

"I've got some research to do." Wentworth rose.

Cud pulled him close. "Or how about this – maybe I stepped out to piss and witnessed some dude flip Raffy over the deck. There's a cold-blooded killer on the loose, I'm drunk and scared shitless, I race down to the garage to commandeer a car and run it into a tree 'cause I figure that'll bring the cops faster than a phone call." He grinned and turned his attention to the set.

⚖

Wentworth's desk was piled with files and notes, and he was seeing double. It was almost midnight, the city tucking in, sad jazz riffs from below, a drunk bellowing, "I wanna hear 'Temptation.'"

He tried to focus on his scribbled list of possible perps. A late addition to the cast: Terrence G. Whitson, a.k.a. Shiny Shoes, owner of the Lamborghini. Had some business deal going with Whynet-Moir. Specialist in offshore investments according to the Web. A file for him.

A file for the alleged scandal-silencing hit man from Ottawa. A file for Clearihue, the land-grabbing developer whose trial was aborted by Whynet-Moir's death. A file for Florenza. A file for her secret lover, if she has one. A file for suicide. A file for a serial killer specializing in judges. Seven possible perps if you include Cud.

The trial was only ten hours away, mind and body needed rest. He put his head on his desk, tried to summon the strength to rise, pack it in, get on his bike. He jumped when the phone rang next to his ear. An impaired driver, maybe – this was when they usually called, after midnight.

"Wentworth?" Brian Pomeroy's sad, haunted voice.

"Er, yes, it's me."

"Someone else is going to die."

19

THE BADGER

Arthur sipped a takeout coffee early on a chilly Monday morning as he waited at the locked door of Pomeroy, Macarthur. He would have preferred to work from his old firm, Tragger, Inglis, with its massive library and its coven of gnomic researchers, but the files were in Pomeroy's office, and as much as he'd like to escape the gluey ubiquity of Wentworth Chance, he felt obliged not to desert him.

He unfolded the *Sun* to a third-page item announcing the start of the Brown trial, with "veteran criminal lawyer A.R. Beauchamp, Q.C.," standing in for the stressed-out Pomeroy, under care at an unnamed facility.

Here was an account of the all-candidates debate. The NDP labour lawyer got top billing, her efforts applauded as vigorous and witty. That accorded fairly with what he'd seen on the late news. Margaret had been tentative, nervous, as if afraid of miscues.

But she'd been ready for Chipper O'Malley's low blow, a veiled reference to her acts of civil disobedience with a man charged with murder. "If it's Mr. Cudworth Brown you're referring to, he and I had drawn lots to be up that tree. We were fighting to save a beautiful wilderness area. What have you done to protect our natural heritage?" That televised quote didn't make it into the paper.

Finally the receptionist came, looking harried – the staff of this small, hectic firm was overworked. Arthur followed her inside. Passing by Wentworth's office, he glanced within and saw the young man slumped over his desk, asleep. Before rousing him, he scanned his list of suspects. The notes concluded with an underlined quote, "Someone else is going to die."

"Wentworth, we must be in court in an hour and a half."

He woke with a start, stared in horror at his watch. "Oh, my God. I have to shower and dress."

Arthur gave him the keys to the Chrysler. "I'll take a taxi. Meet me at court." Wentworth flung several files into his backpack and fled before Arthur could ask him about that curious quote.

In Pomeroy's office, he found April Wu settling into work – she was still collating the mess of Pomeroy's scribbles, snippets, and printouts, some of which had been found in his dismal lair in The Ritz, as well as a backup disk. Here was a collection of paperback mysteries, several penned by one Hector Widgeon, a CD-ROM, and a well-thumbed how-to manual by the same obscure writer. Arthur sifted through the manuscript pages.

"Who might this Lance Valentine character be?"

"Mr. Pomeroy's version of a private detective. An over-glamorized version, if you wish my opinion."

Any resemblance to others living or dead seemed not coincidental. Among the dead were Justices Naught and Whynet-Moir. Here was Detective Sergeant Chekoff. Cud Brown, and Flo LeGrand. Pomeroy himself. What an odd thing.

"April, please put me in touch with Brian's psychiatrist." Arthur should actually visit him, check on his condition – though he had ample proof of his mind's chaotic state. Recovery of that opal ring was essential, his possessions must be searched.

"Is this of interest, Mr. Beauchamp? It was crunched up in a bottom drawer of his desk." April handed him a crumpled page from the *Georgia Strait*, the entertainment weekly,

dated October 11 last year. Caroline Pomeroy staring from
the page, looking rather pleased with herself. An interviewer quoting this English professor's wry literary comments. Dr. Pomeroy being modest about *Sour Memories*, her
award-winning collection. A reference to a reading planned
for October 12 at the Vancouver Library. Then this: "Next
evening she'll be dining at the lush waterfront manse of
socialite Florenza LeGrand and Judge R. Whynet-Moir,
one of four Literary Trust fundraisers planned in Vancouver
that night."

How had they got that wrong? But then he recalled
Cudworth had been switched at the last moment from a
similar event in Point Grey. The Literary Trust had obviously
decided he and Caroline should trade places, and for good
reason: Whynet-Moir had presided over the Pomeroy divorce.

He had to rush away to his cab. First stop was the Bank
of Montreal tower – Tragger, Inglis occupied five upper
floors, but Arthur's destination was Roberto's hair salon in
the mezzanine. For three decades Arthur had entrusted his
hair to his fussy old barber – Arthur was one of few who
knew the secret of his baldness.

Roberto wasn't open yet, but on spotting Arthur behind
the glass, he let him in and hurried him to the chair.

"You look like a sea monster risen from the kelp. We can
only pray. The beard? Gone. I regret to say the geezer look
is out this year. We prefer something *très distingué*." Roberto,
who in his former life was simple Bob the barber, liked his
flowery French phrases, though otherwise knew little of the
language. "The distinguished barrister, a power look. I used
to do Whynet-Moir, did you know? Lovely hair. Silky. Met
Ms. LeGrand. *Très magnifique!*"

She was to be the final witness, probably Friday. A call
to the Crown confirmed she hadn't taken a Breathalyzer.
She remained the wild card, with her self-incriminating
silence. Arthur found no indication Pomeroy tried to contact

her – doubtless, in any event, she would have slammed the door in his face.

A swivel of the chair brought Roy Bullingham into view, staring at his lathered face from behind the glass. Bully, they called him, Tragger, Inglis's last surviving original, ninety-one, still at his office nine to five.

"Ah, it is you," he said, popping in. "Haven't seen you around much, Arthur. On holiday, were you?"

"Bully, I retired eight years ago."

"Evidently not so. Nasty case. A high court judge. A home of good repute."

"I shall not be using my old office."

"Just as well, I can't imagine we'd want to be associated with this dismal business. Your Rabelaisian poet and his drunken goings-on." He left.

"*Voilà*, a dapper statesman emerges from the ruins. I call this the British ambassador."

⚖️

Wentworth Chance was anxiously waiting for him at the curb, already gowned, looking confounded at the new, improved version of his idol. Arthur always felt more confident after his traditional pre-trial haircut. In his three-piece suit, he *felt* distinguished, ambassadorial. The transformation was setting in, from a doddering yokel to the lion of the courtroom. The process, vaguely magical but hinting of a dissociative disorder, tended to unsettle Arthur. It was if Stoney, say, had another life as a neurosurgeon.

He alighted from the cab, unfurled an umbrella. "What are you doing out here? It's starting to rain."

"I was worried you'd be late." Wentworth tried to take control of the umbrella, but Arthur wouldn't give it up.

"Where's Cud?"

"He's waiting in another courtroom. With Felicity and his mom."

Arthur didn't realize Cud had a mother. He herded the fusspot to the door. Reporters converged. A camera was thrust at him, microphones.

"Going to be any surprises for us today, Mr. Beauchamp?"

"The surprise is that this flimsy case is even going to trial."

Wentworth clapped with delight. They escaped into the male barristers' locker room, crowded with colleagues in underwear, deodorizing their armpits, buttoning wing collar shirts, gossiping, joshing. "Hey, Arthur, still enjoying retirement?" "You bring any goat cheese?" "It's Rocky Balboa, he's come back for his title."

Now came the final stage of the transformation, the robing, the costuming of Arthur Ramsgate Beauchamp, Q.C. He supposed it was similar for actors, dressing up, becoming another person. But here the drama was live, the players at risk, the consequences grave, the end unknown.

Down the aisle, John Brovak was also robing, about to launch a week-long appeal for Ruby Morgan and his gang of cocaineros. An obstreperous, broad-shouldered knave, a stud, Cud-like but with a law degree. "Hey, Arthur," he yelled, "make sure Kroop don't eat the kid alive. Watch your ass, kid, the Badger thinks you're shit." Referring, Arthur supposed, to the young man's role as Pomeroy's junior in the Gilbert Gilbert case. Brovak carried on, demanding Wentworth get some fees in, grumbling about the cost of keeping Pomeroy "in a high-end acorn factory."

As Arthur pulled on his striped pants, Wentworth looked away, embarrassed to see him in underwear.

"'Someone else is going to die.' What's that about?"

"Brian Pomeroy called in the middle of the night. That's all he said."

Brovak caught that as he came by lugging a mountain of files. "I got the same wiggy message. He better not be talking suicide."

"Just addled talk, I'm sure," Arthur said. "Wentworth, I'll

want you to visit him this evening. And while there, do a thorough search for Ms. LeGrand's ring."

The reporters were still scavenging in the hall but reluctantly allowed them access to the elevators. "How do you feel going into this with only three days' prep, Mr. Beauchamp?"

"Had no alternative. I couldn't stand by and watch an innocent man being railroaded."

Charles Loobie was waving his notepad, demanding Arthur's attention. "Hey, Artie, I got something for you."

"When I have a moment, Charles." Arthur didn't care for this gossipy newshound, a nuisance, a time-waster. He didn't like being called Artie.

Outside court 67, deputy sheriffs were denying entrance to those with "Free Cud Brown" buttons. They were having a particular problem with the frizzy blonde who had the words in lipstick on her bared shoulder. Silent Shawn was conspicuously absent; presumably he didn't want Arthur pestering him about his equally close-mouthed client.

He cracked open the door. The chief was finishing off a leftover from last week, a motion to exclude wiretap evidence. Lawyers won't be tasting his lash much longer – he was nearing seventy-five, retirement age. They might have to drag the old fellow out with a tow truck, he's up there for a third of a century, stubborn, unmoveable. Thickset, a broad fleshy face, a small, puckered, disbelieving smile as he rushed along a terrified young lawyer. "Get on with it, counsel."

Loobie came up from behind, a sneak attack. "Artie, I think you want to talk to this gent." He steered him to a wiry senior in scuffed boots who offered Arthur the dubious gift of a weighty file. "Mr. Loobie says I oughter talk to you about how that rattlesnake tried to bamboozle me."

Vogel, the rancher from Hundred Mile House. Arthur shook his knobby hand, then called Wentworth over. "Mr.

Chance will be pleased to look into it." Wentworth stuffed the file into his overflowing briefcase.

"I won that damn trial, and then Clearihue kilt the judge and stole victory away."

"Mr. Chance will also check his whereabouts on October 13."

"I can't afford a lawyer for a new trial without selling off my entire herd."

"Maybe Mr. Chance can help you out there too. He'll be pleased to take you for lunch today."

Clearcut Clearihue would be Arthur's preferred suspect, but a very unlikely one.

He popped into the next courtroom, where something complex about construction codes was underway. A dozen lawyers and an equal number of expert witnesses, and no one in the audience but Cud and his mother and girlfriend.

Irma Brown was introduced, here all the way from Northern Ontario, a portrait from *Hard Times Magazine*, thin and worn and tired, in a faded dress. "Cudworth says you're the man." He didn't know how to respond.

He led them out, took his first critical look at Cud. He'd had a haircut too, above the ears, no longer shaggy. Sans medallion, sans braces. Cleancut in sports jacket and turtleneck. With loving mother and rosy-cheeked girlfriend beside him, he would present as an upright citizen, unthreatening were it not for the broken nose.

Arthur felt obliged to pass pleasantries with Irma Brown. "Your husband couldn't make it?"

"He's in too much pain."

Arthur recalled something about a mining accident. "You have another son, right?"

"Jimmy, he's in Kingston."

"Ah, the university?"

"The penitentiary. Cud was the one we had hopes for."

"Yes, well, let's be off to court."

He asked a deputy sheriff to escort them because again he had to brave Charles Loobie, pest reporter. "You going to get to Whitson today?"

"I expect so." The owner of the Lamborghini, the investment counsellor.

"I got it on the q.t. from a reliable source he was in a scheme with Whynet-Moir that went off the rails. Raffy stiffed him for some big bucks, and Whitson was pissed."

Loobie seemed to have an inordinate interest in dredging up suspects. Arthur summoned Wentworth again. "When we break at noon, sit down with Charles here."

He led them into court 67, where Wilbur Kroop was bickering with counsel. "Your argument would put the police in handcuffs, not the culprits. Surely in these perilous times wiretap laws must be given a broad and liberal interpretation."

Impaled by his glare, the young counsel stammered incoherently.

"Well? Do you have more to say?"

"No, sir, that's my case."

"Appeal is denied, reasons reserved. I see, Madam Clerk, that the combatants in today's main event are present." Kroop acknowledged Arthur, advancing up the aisle, with a gracious smile belied by his pitiless eyes, black holes in a galaxy of wrinkles and skin folds. Abigail Hitchins was already at counsel table, with a couple of helpmates, arranging files. Her well-known animus toward Kroop – he'd made a couple of anti-abortion rulings – would help deflect some of his shots at the defence.

Arthur motioned Cud to enter the prisoner's box and introduced Wentworth as his junior.

"Ah yes, Chance, I believe you were involved with Mr. Pomeroy in that Gilbert matter." A menacing glint of a smile. "And for the Crown we have Miss Hitchins and a young lady I've not met."

Haley was the name of this freckled, Rubenesque redhead. *Young lady.* Arthur must refrain from echoing such expressions — for reasons he couldn't fathom, they were no longer in season.

Kroop studied Cud solemnly. "You're Cudworth Brown, the accused?"

"Last time I looked."

Arthur directed a harsh look at his client. This flipness was a bad start; Kroop had taken on colour and spoke sharply: "As is the usual practice in these courts, accused will be taken into custody and remain there until termination of these proceedings." Cud's mouth fell open.

"Before Your Lordship so directs, I wonder if I may be heard, if I may be so bold."

Abigail was quick to pitch in. "Milord, there's agreement between counsel to maintain the conditions of interim release during the trial."

A pause as Kroop digested this cozy deal, then sniffed. "Very well, but you might have considered alerting me. Let's bring the first batch in, Mr. Sheriff. We'll take about twenty."

And the first batch filed in, anonymous souls pulled from kitchen, office, and factory to serve their country. Names, addresses, occupations — that is all the information the sheriffs divulge. One must rely on a talent to read faces and body language. As they stepped up in turn, Arthur sought eye contact — long experience had taught him to read intelligence in eyes, empathy in smiles. He let go those with frown and worry lines, and a few who might lack strength to endure a fractious jury room.

He wanted a cheerful lot, and with no interference from Abigail, that's what he got. He picked a few plums from the second batch, a retired classics professor he'd once met; a Steelworkers organizer, Cud's old union; a restaurant hostess from hip Commercial Drive, Cud's milieu. ("I've been at poetry bashes at her joint," Cud whispered.) To Arthur's surprise, he ended up seating eight women, only four men. But his instinct in doing so seemed reliable. Men, with their petty sexual jealousies (*An unregulated sex drive; I think you resent that*), seemed less likely to side with the accused libertine.

"Well done, we're moving right along. Let's keep it up, stick to the timetable – I have to be in the nation's capital Monday for the Order of Canada ceremonies. We'll take five minutes."

Abigail came by. "I think he wants us to know he's getting the Order of Canada. You okay with those admissions of fact? Same ones Pomeroy approved in his brief lucid state."

"I'm fine with them. I'd like to mull over Astrid Leich, if you can put her off for a few days."

"Your word is my command."

"I assume she has been breathlessly following the news coverage of this titillating case."

Abigail raised a hand: "I swear. She hasn't seen your guy's face since the lineup. Hank Chekoff, who has been babysitting her, insisted she cancel cable and morning paper in favour of a line of credit at Blockbuster's. She's actually a very honest woman."

Arthur doubted that, doubted she could be so incurious, but said nothing.

"Gag me, but I'm going to suck up to Kroop by dispensing with an opening. I don't know what to say anyway, and I've got impatient witnesses."

⚖

It was almost noon when jury and judge returned. Arthur was pleased to note the thin, bespectacled classics professor, Jane Glass, was foreperson. Sitting beside her was the Steelworkers organizer, Tom Altieri, a robust man with an air of confidence, probably a good tongue on him, an experienced persuader. The jury, Kroop directed, could spend their nights in their own beds but were admonished to ignore news reports of the trial – though everyone in the court system knew such directives were ineffectual.

The registry had cleverly assigned as clerk a stout woman whom Kroop rarely badgered, possibly because of their reputed affair many years ago. She rose and bawled out an indictment charging that on the fourteenth of October, in the year of our Lord 2007, in the Municipality of West Vancouver, Province of British Columbia, Cudworth Brown did commit the murder in the first degree of Rafael Whynet-Moir against the peace of our lady the Queen, her Crown and dignity.

Cud entered his plea with a modicum of theatrics, a firm "Not guilty" and a slight nod for emphasis.

"Identification issues are in play, milord." Arthur wanted the jury to know this early. "So may the accused be seated in the body of the court."

"Mr. Beauchamp, in nearly four decades on the bench, I have yet to countenance that kind of arrangement . . . Yes, Ms. Hitchins?"

"The Crown has no objection, milord."

Kroop was taken aback. "Well, I do."

"In fact, the Crown consents, milord."

A long pause. Kroop wasn't bound by her consent, but he regularly sided with the Crown, he was infamous for it, and now looked confused as he worked through his dilemma. He tried to salvage the moment by turning to the jury with a mock helpless look. "There doesn't seem much role for a judge here. Those two agree on everything." He got a ripple of laughter as compensation for having been shown up.

Cud joined mother and girlfriend in the third row. Too close to the front for Arthur's comfort – he must meld him with the hoi polloi in the back when Astrid Leich takes the stage.

"You may open to the jury, Ms. Hitchins."

"I'll forgo it, milord. We want to get you on that plane to Ottawa."

A grunt of satisfaction, the old boy mollified by the blatant pandering. "We'll break now. Fourteen hundred hours, Madam Clerk; let's be on time."

Arthur packed his files, roused Wentworth from a trance.

20

SEE NO EVIL

*H*is cry for justice still echoed through the courtroom. Then silence, except for sobs from the jury. Suddenly the gallery erupted in applause. Mr. Beauchamp looked up at him with newfound respect. "Exceptional piece of work, Wentworth, absolutely brilliant . . ."

Wentworth returned to this world: a sub shop. He was on a stool, the old rancher beside him was bitching about the rotten justice system. He riffled through the mammoth transcript of *Vogel v. Clearihue*, wondering when he'd have time to read its eight hundred pages. He was besieged. Consult with Vogel, help him out. Handle Cud. Talk to Loobie. Look up the law. Mr. Beauchamp was testing him, putting him through boot camp; he'd better not buckle. Arthur, he must learn to call him Arthur. The boss, that felt more natural.

A visit to Pomeroy tonight – he wasn't looking forward to that. *Someone else is going to die.*

"Mr. Vogel, why didn't you see a lawyer before you signed this deal?"

"I figured it was simple, I didn't need no lawyers. The one I hired for the trial cost me a year's receipts and didn't know his arse from his elbow."

"Have you even got a scrap of proof Clearihue murdered this judge? Any idea where he even *was* that night?"

Vogel scratched his head. "Maybe at home. He lives up there with all them moneybags in West Vancouver."

"How far from Whynet-Moir?"

"Twenty-minute walk downhill, I did it mesself."

Mr. Chance will also check his whereabouts on October 13. How was he going to do that? Call him up? Was it even worthwhile pursuing this? But he must, for Mr. Beauchamp, for Arthur, whose wife spent two and a half months up a tree because of this jerk. Wentworth will provide pro bono services to the rancher. Justice must be done. Beauchamp's enemy is his enemy.

He repacked his briefcase, paid the bill, got a receipt, two $7.99 specials with Big Gulp colas, then checked the time. "Oh my God, I'm due in court."

"I'm down here for only a few days, then I got to get back to the range. I got two hundred head and only my three granddaughters there to help. If you're able to come up when it ain't winter, we got a pretty swimming lake."

Wentworth thanked him and hurried up Granville Street.

"We're so happy you're here to save Granddad's farm," said the prettiest one as she pulled her jeans off. *"We usually go in with no clothes on."*

⚖

The first witness was already on the stand as Wentworth rolled in, two minutes late. Kroop examined him like a buzzard circling roadkill, hungry for this defender of Gilbert Gilbert. His legs buckled a little as he bowed to the court and sat. The judge scared him, the Darth Vader of the courts.

Abigail Hitchins was examining a stout miner of Arctic diamonds, who gave the impression he'd rather have attended a street riot than a literary salon at Whynet-Moir's. Wentworth would bet his wife had to drag him there.

He hadn't had any dealings with Cud except to shake his hand, so Wentworth wasn't sure why they'd bothered to subpoena him. No damage done until Abigail steered him to Cud's reading of "Up Your Little Red Rosie, Rose."

"Do you remember what that poem was about?"

"Well, as the title suggests, an unconventional sexual practice." He seemed to be trying not to smile. Wentworth was scribbling madly, recording all this, but he couldn't resist an urge to turn to Cud, looking sheepish beside his stern mother. Mr. Beauchamp nudged him: pay attention. Not Mr. Beauchamp. Arthur. He has to learn to think of him that way.

"Could you be more explicit?"

"An act of buggery."

"And what was the reaction?"

Wentworth couldn't understand why the boss wasn't objecting; this evidence was irrelevant, highly prejudicial.

"Some people were shocked, the ladies especially. It was fairly . . . vivid."

Arthur rose, strolled over to Abigail, offered a slim volume. "It's all in here, Ms. Hitchins, funded by the Canada Council for the Endowment of the Arts. Why don't you read the whole thing?"

"Order."

Arthur ignored Kroop and turned to the witness, who'd given up trying not to smile. "I'll bet you had a good laugh over it afterwards."

"I was in stitches."

"We will have order!" Kroop bawled, quieting the rumble of laughter in the room. "Counsel, await your turn. Ms. Hitchins has the floor."

The boss gave Wentworth a friendly nudge as he sat. That's how it's done, he was saying. Turn the tables on them.

Abigail was obviously expecting a suicide defence, so she asked about Whynet-Moir's mood and demeanour. "Happy, attentive, entertaining, charming to the ladies. Very gracious host. He seemed pleased the way his literary evening was going."

The hostess was, ditto, very pleasant, spirited, happy, said the mining mogul. He'd been seated several chairs from Cud and Flo, saw no unusual interaction, but wasn't really looking.

It went on like that with the next witness, and the next. Whynet-Moir the perfect host, Cud knocking them back like there's no tomorrow, no one picking up on the under-table grope session. Abigail asked each to identify Cud in the gallery, and no one had trouble, despite Cud's cleaned-up act, his neat haircut, though the bent nose was a kind of give-away. Arthur didn't ask many questions and looked sour. "We need that blasted ring," he grumbled.

The judge didn't say much, except for some apple polishing, lauding these big shots for doing their civic duty, regretting they'd been inconvenienced.

Thesalie Smithers was Cud's left-hand table companion — the facelift victim, thirty going on sixty-five, and sugary sweet.

"Mr. Brown was so interesting. We talked about poetry. I asked him where his inspiration came from and he said, 'from the heartsickness of wounded love.' I remember that, it was so poetic. I have to say he was a little . . . frank with some of his language."

Abigail pursued that with gusto, had her describe how Cud cussed out capitalism and organized religion. This didn't get marks from Kroop, who was looking so malevolent that Wentworth shuddered. The boss again gave him the point of his elbow: Settle down.

"What can you say about his state of sobriety?"

"I'd say he was feeling it. His glass never seemed empty."

Whynet-Moir, though, was sober throughout. "Such a lovely host," Wentworth scribbled. "So attentive. So charming and witty. Never a sour expression."

Arthur rose in cross-examination. "You found Mr. Brown interesting and entertaining?"

"He was, yes, quite different from my experience."

"He used a little rough language, but he was otherwise pleasant and polite?"

"He was . . . yes."

"Charming in a kind of rugged way."

"Yes, interesting. Charming."

Arthur teased from her Cud's spiel about how poets are born not made, babies with their rhyming "ma-ma" and "da-da." Wentworth had heard him use the same line on daytime CBC, it got several moms phoning in for a giveaway copy of *Karmageddon*. He saw only one cynical expression in the jury, the restaurant hostess from Commercial Drive. Maybe she'd heard Cud deliver that line at a poetry bash.

"Florenza LeGrand also seemed to find him charming and entertaining?"

Thesalie Smithers hesitated. "All I can say is they seemed to be having a very nice conversation."

"They were smiling, laughing."

"Yes, but others were too." A change of tone, defensive.

"They would get close, whisper in each other's ear."

"They might have."

"Mrs. Smithers, let's speak boldly. They were getting on like a house on fire, were they not?"

She took her time framing an answer. "Florenza is a high-spirited young woman. A bit of a tease." It must have griped her, Wentworth figured, that Cud had focused his attention on Florenza.

"A flirt."

"You could put it that way."

"Indeed, the flirting had extended to playing footsie."

"Footsie? That's a new one on me." Kroop made a sound like "Hmf, hmf." A kind of chuckle.

"I think it might have been called foot snuggling in your time, milord."

A ripple of laughter. Kroop's smile stiffened. "Mr. Beauchamp, nothing has been heard that even remotely supports this, this . . . footsying."

"The trial is young, milord." Wentworth was perplexed by the extreme lack of deference Arthur was paying to the fearsome judge – it was as if he *wanted* to get up his nose. "Madam,

I doubt that you are such a poor observer not to have noticed the intimate play of feet and hands next to you."

"I had no such idea." Mrs. Smithers spoke boldly under the judge's protection, but if her blush meant anything, she was hedging.

"Would you like to think about that answer?"

"No, I . . . I wasn't really interested in knowing what they were doing."

The blush broadened. The boss sat with a loud, lugubrious sigh.

"We'll take the mid-afternoon break."

Wentworth heard this with relief; he needed to pee badly. As the gallery cleared, Abigail huddled with her junior. Wentworth wanted to go over there and say, "Nice try. We're way ahead of you." He knew Haley, he'd gone out with her once, sort of, she'd invited him to a party. It didn't go well, he spilled a glass of red wine on her yellow blouse and it turned orange.

Arthur blocked his escape. "How many more of these unobservant diners do we have?"

"The two women writers and the Whitsons. And the catering staff."

"Did you speak to Loobie about Whitson?"

"He didn't have much to add except he has reliable information that Whitson was pissed purple at Whynet-Moir over a deal that went south. He wouldn't say who told him."

"You need to consult with me, Arthur?" Cud said behind the counsel railing, looking unhappy he was out of the loop.

"In good time."

Wentworth could tell he wasn't satisfied with that, he wanted reassurance, an opinion on how it was going. Finally Cud led away Felicity, who was in a pout over him making out with Florenza. Worse was coming, Cud should have been up front with her.

Arthur muttered something Wentworth didn't catch, something about an unregulated sex drive.

"That was great how you handled the obscene poem. Most lawyers would just have objected."

"Signals the jury there's something to hide. We're going to stick with what we've got, and what we've got is a rammy, scatological anti-establishment poet. Let the jury see him in the raw. He'll come off worse if we pretend he's anything else."

Wentworth noticed Haley smiling, mouthing a hello. She couldn't have been that upset about the wine spill; in fact, now that he thought about it, she'd written her cell number on the dry cleaning bill. Maybe he should buy her a drink or something . . . *When their lips finally drew apart, she said hoarsely, "I was desperate to see you again."* He couldn't take it any longer, he had to decant the Big Gulp.

⚖

As court resumed, juror Tom Altieri caught Wentworth's eye and smiled broadly. He wondered if it was a message. Don't worry, pal, I'm on your side, a union brother is in trouble.

Cud's fan club occupied a back section of the gallery, bearded bohemians and braless girls in flouncy dresses. Wentworth had seen some of them talking to old farmer Vogel, who was back there with them, a kind of mascot.

Taking the stand was Shiny Shoe's wife, a sour little apple of a woman. Abigail went through the litany about Whynet-Moir being the affable host and Cud juicing it up. The Whitsons said their goodbyes early "because Terrence had a headache." Abigail took all of four minutes with her.

Arthur contemplated her a while as if figuring out his approach, then asked, "You drove right home?"

"Yes."

"What brought on your husband's headache? Was there a distressing event?"

"Not that I'm aware."

"Before you left, he had an exchange with Judge Whynet-Moir. Did you see that?"

"I'm not sure . . ." She reflected. "Yes, they did have a discussion. Terrence had brought some papers to show him."

"Did you pick up any ill feeling between them?"

Kroop had been clearing his throat, a sign he was going to jump in. "Where is this going, Mr. Beauchamp?"

"With respect, milord, I do not ask questions idly."

Kroop looked sternly at the prosecutors. "I don't hear anyone objecting. Carry on."

"Shall I repeat the question?"

"I remember Terrence wagging his finger at Judge Whynet-Moir, but he wasn't angry."

"Was Mr. Whitson complaining about him on the way home?"

"I don't think he said anything."

"Did you go directly to bed?"

"I did."

"What about your husband?"

"I don't know."

"Why?"

"We sleep in separate rooms."

"Again, I don't see the prosecutor objecting as she ought to. This is a bit much, Mr. Beauchamp, prying into private lives."

For the first time, Wentworth noticed flecks of impatience on Arthur's face, red spots. "Thank you, Mrs. Whitson." He sat.

"We're grateful to you, madam. It's a trying experience, but alas the law requires that all present at the scene of a crime must be heard."

"Alleged crime, milord. It could have been suicide."

"Please do not interrupt me, Mr. Beauchamp. Alleged crime."

Wentworth decided Arthur was baiting Kroop to force him into error. He'd won a lot of appeals doing that. At least thirteen, if you counted three for the Cape Mudge triple killing.

Terrence Whitson carried himself well as he entered court. Dapper, silver-haired, robust, works out maybe, or plays handball at lunch. His marriage didn't seem real blissful, maybe he had a mistress. An investment counsellor – why would he have let Whynet-Moir engineer a deal that went sour?

Abigail had him identify Cud, who returned his look with a scowl. As she took him through drinks and hors d'oeuvre and dinner, he responded crisply, recalling a couple of exchanges with Cud. "I made a joke about his peace medallion, and he said he had one tattooed on his rear. I assumed he was being droll."

As to their table talk: "Well, there wasn't much. I'd heard about his stint on a tree platform, one of those save-the-forest demonstrations, and I asked him about it, and he said, 'You had to be there, pal.' I assume he'd had a little too much by then."

"Any dealings with him after that?"

"After dinner, I went out for some air and saw him urinating on the lawn. He was behind a car – my car, actually – and he looked at me and lowered his pants. When he took off his under shorts, I turned and walked back in."

Wentworth was horrified at how bad this sounded, Cud came across like a pervert. No one was finding it funny.

"We thanked the hosts and left soon after."

"Your witness."

Arthur didn't like this guy, Wentworth could tell from the way he rose, slow and controlled, adjusted his bifocals, snapped his suspenders. He'd seen that lots, Arthur going on the hunt. According to the police interview, Astrid Leich had heard "something slamming, maybe a door." Like the door of a returning Lamborghini?

"You remember Mr. Brown rushing off from the table, don't you? I think there was a reading by Ms. Tinkerson from her latest novel, and he went outside during the applause."

"I can't say . . ."

"You were seated across from him; surely you *can* say."

He frowned. "Yes . . . Yes, I think I remember that."

"Ever felt the need to relieve yourself in a hurry, Mr. Whitson?"

"Of course."

"Mr. Brown lives in a rural area. So do I. We pee outside. You've done that yourself, I'd imagine."

"Not in the city."

"He had his backpack with him, did you see that?"

"It may have been behind the car."

"And what he was doing was changing his pants."

"I didn't see that part of it."

"But later you saw he was wearing different pants. Jeans."

"I'm not sure if I noticed."

"You've had that happen too, haven't you? Stained your clothes at the dinner table and been forced to change them. It's embarrassing, but we've all done it, yes?"

"I . . . sure, it happens."

"Mustard. Gravy. Tomato sauce. Mr. Sheriff, would you produce Exhibit 18, please." The deputy unbagged and unfolded a pair of blue jeans. "It is an admitted fact that the accused had these on when arrested. It's also admitted that his backpack was found in the guest suite above the garage. I'd like a couple of items from it, Mr. Sheriff, first a pair of black slacks, number forty."

All circuits were go. The boss was breezing along like nobody's business. Wentworth had worried that in working with him, riding saddle with him, his Tonto, he'd get let down, that Arthur wouldn't have the old quick draw. Not so.

"Show him the black pants." The deputy brought them to the witness stand. "Quite an extensive stain in the crotch area — do you observe that?"

Whitson nodded. "Yes."

"Now the underpants." The sheriff borrowed a ruler from the clerk and picked up the underwear with it, white briefs discoloured a sickly yellow. Wentworth imagined they smelled rancid, because the witness curled his nose.

"Looks like something quite messy was going on, doesn't it?"

"I would hesitate to say." He reared back from the exhibit.

Kroop chided the deputy. "You don't have to hold it right at his nose."

"Madam prosecutor, I take it this substance has been analyzed."

"Yes, it's butter."

"Butter." A long pause to let the jury absorb this. A few were stifling smiles. Someone in the gallery gave a snort, the sound made when you suppress laughter.

"Mr. Whitson, how long had you been the deceased's investment counsellor?"

"Oh, for seven or eight years."

"So I take it you were fully conversant with his net worth during that time?"

"Of course."

"Before and after his elevation to the bench?"

"Yes."

"And prior to his appointment in 2006, what was his worth, in round figures?"

"Mr. Beauchamp, is this really necessary?"

"For every question, there is a reason, milord."

"I'll be the judge of that. You're on a leash, counsel. Proceed at your own risk."

Wentworth saw where Arthur was going: the alleged bribe to the justice minister. Whitson replied that his client's net worth was just under two million dollars in 2006, and when Arthur asked if there'd been a substantial shrinkage shortly before he was named to the court, Whitson said, "Not at all."

Nor was Arthur able to show that a major sum moved from Whynet-Moir's accounts after his appointment. His assets actually grew after his marriage to Florenza, "in the form of a beneficial interest in the house at 2 Lighthouse Lane."

Arthur wasn't getting very far with this, but when he snapped his braces again, Wentworth felt prickles – the boss was about to move in for the kill. "Mr. Whitson, I understand you and the deceased were jointly engaged in a business venture."

The witness seemed taken off balance. "I wouldn't put it in those terms."

"A venture that cost you a substantial loss."

Whitson looked astonished. "Not at all." Wentworth didn't like this. He glanced at the press table, at Loobie, who wouldn't meet his eye. "I'm an investment counsellor, Mr. Beauchamp, I don't enter into joint deals with clients. I don't take advice from them, I give them advice. And I don't suffer substantial losses."

Kroop was getting off on seeing Arthur take one on the chin. "Counsel, exactly where is this going?"

"Nowhere," he muttered to Wentworth, who was distraught. He thought Arthur might drop this like a hot potato, but maybe he was into it too much. "You were observed having a spirited conversation with the deceased just before you left. You were showing him a document, wagging a finger."

"I was reprimanding him, but . . . no, it wasn't anything like that."

"Why were you reprimanding him?"

"For making such a large donation to the Red Cross from his bond holdings when he was overweighted in equities."

You could tell this was like a hammer blow, at least you could tell if you were Wentworth Chance. The way Arthur's face went dark. A fierce look at Loobie, whose head was down, like a dog who'd been bad. Kroop did a soft "Hmf, hmf."

There was time for one more witness, Professor Chandra, a political writer often seen on TV, a tall older woman, in a business suit this time, not a sari. She was composed, well spoken, but didn't have much to add – she'd been corralled all evening by guests, admirers of her opinion pieces.

"Did you talk to the accused?" Abigail asked.

"For thirty seconds. I asked him if he was enjoying himself, and he said, 'Pretty good' – he gestured at the elegant surroundings – 'considering all the famine and disease and poverty in the world.' I told him I'd be interested in hearing his solution to those problems. A waiter came by with shrimp dip, diverting him, and I was drawn into another conversation."

She wasn't so acerbic when describing Whynet-Moir, who was engaging, charming, and witty. Wentworth could picture him fawning over her at dinner, pelting her with praise for her new collected pieces, listening spellbound to her views on current events.

She recalled that Cud's bawdy recital was followed by embarrassed silence, guests scuttling about for their coats. "Judge Whynet-Moir seemed in a very sombre mood indeed as he led us out. I imagine he felt his party was spoiled."

Wentworth whispered, "Is that admissible, what she imagines?" But there was no life from Arthur, who was morose, not paying much attention. That zinger from Whitson still stung; the boss had asked one question too many. Maybe not a historic first but a rare event. A sign the great man might be over the hill.

Chandra was one of the last to leave. On her way to her car she smelled cigar smoke and turned and saw Whynet-Moir on the deck talking to Cud in low tones. She thought of pausing to watch. "My sense of propriety, I suppose, held my curiosity in check, and I carried on to my car until they were out of view."

"No more questions," Abigail said.

"Professor Chandra, this court and all who serve here are forever in your debt. I deeply regret you waited so long . . ." Kroop finally noticed Arthur standing. "Ah, a moment, madam, I think Mr. Beauchamp may have a few questions."

"Your Lordship is very kind. But may I suggest we break for the day? I'd like to complete my cross-examination in one fell swoop."

"Are we on time?" Kroop asked.

"At least fifteen minutes early," Abigail said.

"Then you've earned your reward. But we shall be doing shopkeeper's hours starting tomorrow. Nine-thirty. On the dot."

21

THE SNAKE PIT

Arthur left Wentworth to park the Chrysler in a lot near the Pomeroy, Macarthur offices, and as he entered, April Wu was at the copy machine. She removed a bundle of papers, handed them to him. "Mr. Pomeroy's collected works. It's five o'clock, so if you don't mind, I'll end my work day."

"Yes, of course. I hope we haven't overburdened you."

"There's no greater burden than having nothing to do." She left with some homework in a file folder, nearly bumping into Wentworth on his way in.

"Intriguing young lady," Arthur said.

In Pomeroy's office, he eased himself into the big swivel chair, put on his bifocals. He needed a new prescription, his eyes were aging. All his systems were aging. Why had he been so foolish as to have enlisted in this opéra bouffe? He'd just been getting into the trial, a little bit, when he pulled that gaffe, the nadir of a taxing day pulling teeth from the West Coast patriciate. He sighed. *Quod incepimus conficiemus;* what we have begun we shall finish.

He flipped through the pages April had assembled. Some were marked up with edits. Here was Detective Sergeant Hank Chekoff making Swiss cheese of Rosy, whoever she was. Cud Brown was woven prominently into the story. The hero seemed to be snooty Lance Valentine, surely the *nom de guerre* of Pomeroy himself.

Arthur spun his chair to the window. A late afternoon deluge was washing pigeon excreta from the statue of Gassy Jack, Gastown's guzzling founder. Scaffolding rising around Maple Tree Square, the quarter getting a facial for the Olympics. Cars clogging the five streets that joined here, fleeing the inner city, honking and braking, reminding him of where he'd rather be.

He must call home, check on Nick. Try to get through to Margaret on her cell, wherever she is, in Shelter Bay or Oyster Beach or Gypsy's Landing. But he was in too black a mood to talk to anyone.

"I'll *kill* Loobie!" A bellow that elicited a startled yelp from behind him, Wentworth, who'd just walked in. "That idiot and his harebrained theories."

"Actually, on the whole you did a masterful —"

"I blew it!" That was accompanied by a trumpet blast from below, a quintet warming up. It galled the more that Arthur had goofed in front of this groupie, who demanded a consistent level of genius from the old wheezer.

The opening bars of a Bach fugue from his briefcase. His cellphone, another of the devil's devices — he'd taken it out of mothballs for the trial. It was his ex-son-in-law, ensconced in Blunder Bay until Arthur's return. "I'm doing some quality time with Nick. Everything's moving along slick at the old homestead; those woofers are right on the beam. By the way, Nick likes to hang around one of them, Lavinia. Should I worry?"

"Teenage crush. He enjoys her kidding."

"You sure she's not loose? A lot of these East European women are. Anyway, we're getting along hooper-dooper. Nick is helping with Margaret's campaign, handling the computer traffic or something." He hadn't much more to say, but Arthur was relieved his worries weren't compounded by disasters at home.

He pressed the off button, fiddled with the phone. "How do you get your messages on this thing?" He flipped it to Wentworth, who pressed a button, listened, handed it back. "I'd like you to study the autopsy report, absorb it." Wentworth fled.

Bob Stonewell. "Wondering about my jitney. Just checking, no reason to be concerned. Part of the service." Presumably that meant there was indeed reason to be concerned. Arthur will check the tires, the brake fluid.

Dr. Alison Epstein, who seemed agreeable to discussing her patient – with a lawyer, in confidence. "The matter has gone beyond doctor-patient privilege, Mr. Beauchamp."

He called back immediately, found her at her office. After pleasantries, she turned grave. "I'm extremely concerned about him; he isn't adjusting to treatment."

"For what exactly is he being treated?"

"Let's call it a severe substance-induced delirium."

The etiology of his near-psychotic state had to do with an intense feeling of being wronged, by his wife, by the divorce court, cheated out of his children. He loved them, but was morbidly fixated on Caroline, an obsession Epstein found troubling.

"It was a very intense two decades of marriage. They're both highly intellectual, and rather arrogant about it. They competed about everything, argued each other to a standstill over philosophy, art, literature; they played word games, competed at tennis, even birding. They competed at sex – Caroline wasn't without lovers. And latterly they competed about writing. And Caroline won that competition."

Thus the latest obsession, starring Lance Valentine.

"I don't claim to have some vast, penetrating insight into him, Mr. Beauchamp. He's the most enigmatic patient I've ever encountered."

They promised to keep in touch.

A final recorded message was patiently waiting. "Sorry, I missed you, darling. I'll call again." She sounded down, not her effervescent self.

He shut the door. It was already dark outside, rain sheeting against the window, a lone pigeon flapping off for cover, souvenir shops closing up, restaurants opening. Another blare from beneath the floorboards.

Margaret answered right away, to background chatter and music. "Where are you?" he asked.

"At the grand opening of the Duncan Doughnuts Diner. Free coffee and twizzlers. There's a hundred people here. In two minutes I'm off to Cowslip to have more coffee and nibbles, with the United Church minister, very important guy there, then I'm speaking to the Save Our Estuary dinner in Floodwater. I'm getting fat."

"Nonsense, you looked gorgeous on TV."

"A new poll gets released tonight. I'm sure I lost points after the all-candidates. I blew it."

An echo of Arthur's own plight. "I saw a clip and thought you were masterful."

"I botched the offshore fishing quota and added a billion to defence spending." It pained him that she was so strained, so stiff upper lip. "How was your day, Arthur? Sec."

A pause to shake a hand or two, affording him a chance to devise an answer. He shouldn't burden her with his own foot shot, shouldn't depress her further, not with the election only a week away. "How good to meet you both," he overheard. "And isn't that a sweet dress. Three and a half? What a big girl." How does she manage not to go batty?

"Sorry, Arthur, I've got to scoot. You're bearing up?"

"No complaints, my love."

Cellular kisses. He pocketed the phone and opened the door to find Wentworth like a lonesome dog waiting to be let in. "What do I do after I absorb the pathologist's report?"

"I want you to do the autopsy. Some of the other forensics while you're at it, the substance analyses."

Wentworth's Adam's apple became active in his struggle to find words. "You want me to *do* them."

"I need to concentrate on getting Cud into that steam room with Florenza."

"Excuse me, I'm to actually cross-examine them?"

"No, you're to take them to the playground and climb the monkey bars. When are we hearing from them?"

"The pathologist is tomorrow afternoon," he said faintly. "Ah, Mr. Beauchamp . . . Arthur . . . you mentioned that you wanted me to visit Pomeroy this evening, and, ah . . ."

"I'll see Pomeroy." It was long overdue.

Wentworth declined a dinner invitation and instead phoned for a pizza and got busy. Raincoat, briefcase, car keys, Arthur made sure he had everything. He was almost outside when Wentworth raced up with his umbrella.

"Wait, I'll make a copy of tomorrow's witness list." Before doing so, Wentworth removed a page still in the copier, glanced at it, frowned. "First I've seen of this."

Arthur read it over his shoulder, a scene featuring Lance Valentine, a Doberman named Heathcliff, a guard named Rashid, and Florenza LeGrand – a sitting room tête-à-tête missing from the material April had handed him. *I had dosed the custard with this new product that stops your heart; they can't detect it. All Cudworth did was dump the body.* This seemed the author's attempt at drollery. More interesting was a reference to Carlos the Mexican.

"Run off another copy. Let's find out if there's a Carlos in her past." Florenza's drug-dealing Mexican lover of many years ago?

Wentworth made a note.

⚖

At his club, Arthur took tea in the lounge so he could make some calls and catch the news. He first tried Stoney, who was either not home or not answering. Arthur's worries might be for nothing, he'd had a garage man look under the hood, everything was topped up. He left a message on Dr. Epstein's service inquiring whether Pomeroy had ever mentioned a visit to Château LeGrand, then connected with Hollyburn Hall to announce his coming. He turned his attention to the big wall TV and the six o'clock news.

On a sofa nearer the set, two bald heads, old gaffers into the brandy, one hard of hearing but loud of voice, the other shouting into his ear. "Send more troops, that's the answer." An item on Afghanistan. "You wouldn't get me near that place." AIDS in Uganda. "By-election coming up." Cowichan and the Islands.

"What?"

"By-election!"

"Where?"

"Jack Boynton's old seat!"

"Who?"

"Jack Boynton!"

"Thought he died."

As a result of this cannonade, Arthur missed the latest poll numbers. When the shouter paused for breath, a talking head was finally audible. ". . . perhaps lacks the right cachet for this rural riding, a Vancouver labour lawyer who only recently moved to Cowichan."

The interviewer: "So it does appear the Left is coalescing around the Greens."

"Yes, Jim, around Margaret Blake, who has run a strong rookie campaign." A shot of Margaret shaking hands on a fishing dock.

"Nice legs!" The shouter.

"Extremist. Wants to turn off the gas pumps."

"World's changing! You got the hippie generation running things now!"

"Women's libbers."

Jim and the pundit were drowned out, but Arthur saw a graphic of the poll: Margaret was now seven points ahead of the parachuting labour lawyer, four points behind O'Malley, almost within the margin of error. He didn't know whether to be glad or appalled. Glad for Margaret, ecstatic for her, sorry for himself. The last time he argued a case in Ottawa it had been forty below . . .

"Next up, the opening day of a murder trial at which a top Vancouver investment analyst was accused of being a party to a failed business deal . . ."

Arthur was out the door.

⚖

Dreading that the clutch, gears, or drive shaft might go at any moment, he clung to the right lane of narrow Lions Gate, conquered the span's summit, tested the brakes on the decline. All systems seemed go, and ultimately he was spat out onto the North Shore.

On the Upper Levels Highway, as he neared the exit to Hollyburn Ridge, it struck him that he wasn't far from Château LeGrand, so he descended into the maze of curling hillside streets above Lighthouse Park, finally coming upon Lighthouse Lane.

That was it, from the photos, a many-winged manse that seemed ready to take flight from a rocky promontory. The rain had not let up, and it was difficult to see through the one-wiper windshield, so he stopped and rolled down his window. He was on a narrow street that curled around a tiny inlet, perhaps sixty metres wide – Astrid Leich's home was on the other side. A low stone wall circled the LeGrand property, its driveway protected by a forbidding steel gate. A uniformed guard, a dog on a chain.

Arthur went cautiously ahead and pulled up by the gate-keeper, who unfurled an umbrella as he left the protection of a portico.

"Can I help you, sir?" A booming voice.

"Just stopped to admire your handsome dog. What's his name?"

"Heathcliff, sir."

On hearing his name, the Doberman perked up, but not in a threatening way. "And you must be Rashid."

"I am Rashid, sir."

"Splendid," Arthur said. "Splendid." He drove off.

⚖

The rain came in cascades under the shadow of the mountains, obliging Arthur to sprint from the parking lot to Hollyburn Hall, three storeys of post and beam and cedar shakes overlooking a frothy creek.

"Beastly weather," said an attendant who met him at the door. "Mr. Beauchamp, isn't it? You're here to see Mr. Pomeroy?"

"Please." He was led past a reception area to a baronial hall with a fireplace so wide-mouthed as to be a threat to the forests. Fifteen or so inmates of either sex, some reading, some playing cards, a woman at a baby grand performing a nimble-fingered polonaise. All were alert enough yet slightly robotic, as if being kept at maintenance level.

He spied Brian on the lip of that vilest of architectural conceits, a conversation pit, staring into the roaring, spitting fire. With him was a balding, bearded man with a therapist's attentive air.

Brian's voice rose over the ambient tinkling and shuffling. "To be alone is the fate of all great minds." He glared at his companion. "Schopenhauer."

"He's so very insightful, isn't he?"

"I want to be *alone*! Leave me to my fate!" Brian's shout echoed in the vast hall. The pianist paused mid-bar, then carried on gamely.

"Here's Schopenhauer now," Brian said.

"Schopenhauer?"

"Yeah, you idiot, Arthur Schopenhauer, my guru." Brian didn't rise but grasped Arthur's hand. "Thank God you're here. I'm being facilitated. They're driving me bonkers."

Arthur sat by the pit's carpeted steps and introduced himself, as did Dr. Oswald Schlegg, who said, "Brian has a flair for the dramatic. Delightfully challenging. I enjoy our little tussles."

"Tell this dick he's not getting anything from me. He's working for them. He funnels everything to them." Brian was shaking. His eyes darted about. Though Arthur couldn't put a finger on what kind of madness this was, he could read the obvious withdrawal symptoms.

As Schlegg continued on his rounds, Pomeroy eyed him disdainfully. "The elevator doesn't go all the way to the top. He hasn't a clue I'm faking it."

"I see. Well, how are you, Brian?"

"Boss. The fun never stops. I'm trying to figure out their game. Did Caroline ask you to come?"

"No."

"I have to get word to her. She got sucked in."

"How, Brian?"

"It happened because of her." He closed his eyes, swayed to a Chopin étude. "Everything."

Arthur couldn't make sense of this. "I'll try to speak to her."

His eyes snapped open. "What happened to my trial? Why am I off the case?"

"I'm taking it on. I'm using your office. I hope you don't mind."

"You haven't let the pigeons in?"

"No, everything's fine."

"I hope you can finish it."

"The trial?"

"Yeah, I had a block, I couldn't get it past Chapter Fifteen. How far have you got into it?"

"The book?"

"The trial. I can help. I can do some edits."

Arthur twisted uncomfortably. He had no back support. He eased himself down to a cushioned ledge. Brian followed.

"We call it the snake pit. I'm fine, don't be fooled, I'm playing along with them." A waiter came by with a tray of drinks; Arthur took an orange juice. "It's safe, I checked, everything is fresh-squeezed here. You're in the Buckingham Palace of recovery centres, they specialize in drug psychosis, the joint's full of cocainiacs. You get traders, speculators, lawyers. Hard not to feel sorry for them."

A burst of sparks and a hiss from a cedar log. Despite the fire, Arthur felt clammy. As advertised, Brian was crackers. Arthur wasn't sure how to relate to him.

"What's the latest? I have to keep on track." Brian produced a pocket pad, and made notes as Arthur described his day in court, his lacklustre performance.

"I should have warned you," Brian said. "I didn't make Shiny Shoes a suspect. I had to pare down the list."

"Loobie set me on the wrong path."

"Loobie doesn't know the path. Only I know the path. Anyway, he isn't a suspect either."

"Who?"

"Loobie. But I may make him one."

Arthur played with the concept of Loobie as suspect. All his misdirections . . . Nonsense. "Brian, were you ever in Ms. LeGrand's house? Did you talk to her?"

That provoked a startle response. Brian cast a wary eye at Arthur. "That wasn't me. Ask April. She'll confirm."

"April? Was she there?"

A pause. He seemed rattled. "Lance called her."

"Florenza has a guard named Rashid out front. With a dog named Heathcliff."

Brian began twitching. "Don't talk to me about dogs."

"You remember Heathcliff? A Doberman pinscher."

"It wasn't me. It was Lance. He likes dogs."

"Who's Carlos the Mexican?"

"Her pretty boy. Lance wasn't explicit."

"Help me, Brian. Tell me what Florenza had to say."

"Lance wouldn't tell me. He was sworn to silence." He looked around as if for rescue. "When you call Caroline, tell her to bring the kids. I want them to know I'm okay."

This was going nowhere. Something in Brian's disordered mind was blocking transmission.

"Let's discuss the opal ring. I'd like to help you look for it."

Brian hollered at the pianist. "Do you know any Bartók?" In a lower voice: "Chopin, for God's sake, mush for the masses."

"Let's go to your room and look for it."

"For what?"

"The ring. What did you do with it, Brian?"

"It's not there. It . . . it was filched. This place is a den of pilfering thieves." Suddenly he rose, hurried away, the pianist glaring at him. Arthur followed him up a carpeted staircase, arrived at the landing in time to see a door close. Arthur found it unlocked and Brian within, scuttling about in his madness, searching drawers, shelves. "You see, it's gone!" He slumped into his desk chair, stared at the ceiling. "The power must not be used for evil, and now it's too late."

Arthur guessed Brian had hidden the ring and forgotten where. He did his own desultory search, room to room. These quarters were far grander and more tasteful than the spare, cell-like rooms at the Alcohol Addiction Centre, in which he'd gone fairly mad himself. A balcony view of dark forest, pelting rain. Camera, cellphone, computer, printer, a few paragraphs of foolscap in the tray, proof of some productivity.

Here were the bound transcripts of *Regina v. Gilbert F. Gilbert*, presumably research material. Encouragingly, there was evidence of rehabilitative effort: an addiction manual lying open on the desk, a fifteen-step course book. Even some psychiatric texts. The Diagnostic Manual of the American Psychiatric Association. He was seeking answers – an interesting task given his delusional state.

"They're connected, you know."

"Who?"

"Those two pricks. Darrel Naught and Whynet-Moir. Everything is connected, but they're especially connected. Not the way you think, not in an obvious way. You have to dig deep for this one."

Arthur quit the hunt. "Brian, we found a seemingly errant page from your manuscript." He read from it: "'He and Florenza were in her sitting room with Heathcliff, the Doberman.'"

"That was Lance. You're too late, you're not going to get anything from him. He's dead." He pulled a page from his printer. "His secret died with him."

Arthur perused a long paragraph in which Lance Valentine met his bloody end, torn apart by a junkyard pit bull.

"I warned Wentworth this was going to happen."

Someone else is going to die.

"I'm finally free of him."

22

APRIL FOOL

"*Surely, doctor, the presence of trace amounts of diometa micro-bials in the bloodstream, despite the Category Three oxidation rate, proves that deceased had inhaled a lethal dicyanogen at least ninety minutes prior to his body being discovered. I take it you've read Clark and Tree's definitive study, 'Parameters of Cyanogen Oxidation Rates.'" As the so-called expert bowed his head in defeat, Wentworth turned to see his leader smiling with pride . . .*

How unlikely that scenario seemed in the cold light of dawn as, on a drizzly Tuesday, Wentworth Chance wearily pedalled his aluminum-frame click-transmission Outback 310 past CN's sprawling railway yards, past the train station, up into the old city, Chinatown, skid road, Gastown. He had dug all night into forensics manuals, autopsy procedures, bodily fluids analyses, studied with morbid fascination the police close-ups, the body in the tidal wash, naked on a morgue slab, awaiting the knife. He'd slept only three hours, a sleep disturbed by gory dreams.

He'd compiled sixty legal-size pages of notes for his cross of the pathologist and serologist. He'll prove . . . well, he's not sure what he wants to prove. Maybe that because Whynet-Moir landed on his head, he must have intended suicide. He has a list of poisons, he'll ask if they tested for them.

He locked his bike in the rack outside Club d'Jazz. Or what was Club d'Jazz – workers were dismantling the sign. Pasted inside the door was a notice: "The Gastown Riot – Opening

223

Soon." What kind of deal was this? "Heavy metal is BACK! Opening Wednesday, Blood'n'Guts!" He assumed these new tenants would be even louder than the brass sextet that was going all hours last night, probably their eviction party.

In the waiting room, the frazzled receptionist was fending off a pair of sports-jacketed thugs demanding to see "a goddamn lawyer, any lawyer." Macarthur was in Holland; Sage in Thailand; Brovak in a week-long appeal; Pomeroy in a ding ward; and Wentworth, still in helmet and rain gear, looked like a courier, so they paid him no attention.

He escaped to his office, changed into his suit, twisted the cap from a bottle of Zap energy juice, and began a final read-through of his cross-exam notes. He hasn't even started ploughing through the eight hundred pages of transcript the old rancher gave him. He hasn't had a chance to track down Carlos the Mexican. Now the boss wants him to interview a guy named Rashid, the guard at 2 Lighthouse Lane. He's also supposed to spend time with the client, prepping him for the stand. Junioring his god has not become the glorious lifetime experience he'd anticipated.

Arthur came to his door looking dead serious.

"I am going to have Hank Chekoff busted from the force. Come with me."

He joined him in Pomeroy's office, where April Wu was seated stiffly on a chair. Brian's cellphone records were on the desk, a January 9 call circled with a marker.

"Let's go over this again. Brian called you from Ms. LeGrand's house." She didn't respond. "You spoke to her, to confirm Brian's identity."

"Very well, yes, I remember." Wentworth was blown away, this sounded grave.

"Bad chi, Ms. Wu. You might not have been caught had you not left this behind in the copy machine." Flourishing the page of manuscript, the unfinished scene with Pomeroy, Florenza, and Heathcliff the Doberman. "A little carelessness can make for great undoing." That fetched a resentful look; she'd been out-maxim-ized.

"I had no intention of stealing it. I was simply making a copy."

"For whom?" Met again with silence. "Whom do you report to? Sergeant Chekoff?"

She looked at Wentworth as if for help. He shuffled uncomfortably, embarrassed for her. She picked up her handbag, made as if to leave. "I presume you won't be wanting my services any longer."

"Ms. Wu, you have committed a criminal offence. Close the door, Wentworth." He stood against it with arms folded, feeling foolish. April gave him a look he'd never seen before, cold, as if measuring him for a karate kick to the groin.

Arthur read from the Criminal Code: " 'Anyone who wilfully attempts to obstruct, pervert, or defeat the course of justice is liable to imprisonment for a term not exceeding ten years.' I can't imagine you want to do penitentiary time, Ms. Wu." The boss softened his tone, that's how he does it, tough, then cool and confiding. "I suspect you'd rather come clean with us."

She whirled to say something to him, thought better of it, sat again, and muttered something in Cantonese. "You will allow me to walk out of here if I . . ."

"If you're truthful about what you've been up to. You can walk out of this office with a head start but I intend to raise the matter in court. Wentworth, make notes. Oh, first call the Registry and let them know we may be late."

He connected with Kroop's clerk, explained something had come up, something he couldn't discuss. Which was that the firm had been infiltrated by an enemy agent. She'd been hired just before Christmas, after phoning to ask if there was an opening. Wentworth began to pace. Despite his exhaustion, he was thrilled, this was scandalous, heads will roll in the West Van cop shop, it could even abort the trial.

"Please settle down, Wentworth."

"I'm not a police agent." April drew a wallet from her bag, and a card from that. Ace Private Investigation Services, an address in Kowloon. "I've been with them only a few months. Before that I *was* a legal secretary. I was retained by Florenza's parents to find out if Mr. Pomeroy knew anything incriminating about her."

Arthur raised his eyebrows. "I should like proof of that."

"There's nothing in writing."

"There's always something. How do they pay you?"

"Cash in advance."

"In thousand-dollar bills, I suppose."

"They pay very handsomely."

"How was your ticket from Hong Kong paid?"

"In U.S. dollars."

"How do you deliver your reports, the documents you copy?"

"To a lawyer's office."

"Shawn Hamilton's?"

"I believe so. I know it as Viglio, Hamilton, and Prescott."

"Is anyone there privy to this?"

"I don't know. I drop them off with the receptionist." This was coming rapid-fire. Wentworth wished he had April's shorthand skills.

"The LeGrands have *all* the relevant files?"

"Only as they relate to their daughter."

"I take it you haven't kept from them, as you did from us, the fact that Brian met with Florenza, presumably to get her side of the story."

"They know that."

"And they have Cudworth Brown's entire statement. Such as it is."

"Yes." She was probably desperate to grab the next flight home.

"Well, it seems they haven't got good value for their money, Ms. Wu."

"It was not for want of trying, Mr. Beauchamp."

"Florenza's parents still have no idea what she might say at the trial — is that what it comes down to?"

"She has refused to communicate with them."

"Do *you* have any idea?"

"I have no more idea than you."

He turned to Wentworth. "What about your last interview with Cud?"

Wentworth patted his briefcase. "I haven't had a chance to dictate it."

"Minimal damage. Please read Wentworth's notes, Ms. Wu, clarify anything you need to, and initial each page. Then you may leave, but I can't say this won't come back to haunt you." The process took several more minutes, and by now it was a quarter to ten. Nine-thirty on the dot, the chief had said.

⚖

Sure enough, Kroop was doing a slow burn when court finally convened at ten-fifteen. He flexed his fingers and scowled, took a bead on Arthur, a schoolmaster ready to administer five on each hand. "I take it you have something to say?"

"Regrettably, a matter of great urgency came up about which I intend to alert Crown counsel. In the meantime, milord, full speed ahead."

Kroop was not expecting such a confident little speech and didn't have a good counter. "It had better be good, Mr. Beauchamp." Abigail and her crew were whispering, exchanging shrugs. The jury also seemed confused, and you could tell the press was thirsting for more. Cud was gaping, silently mouthing "matter of great urgency," it looked like. All the way from the third row, Wentworth could feel his vibrations, dying to be in the loop.

Professor Chandra returned to the stand. Wentworth had almost forgotten about her. So had Arthur, who murmured, "I'm a blank." He looked over Wentworth's shoulder as he flipped through his notes.

"Ah, yes." Arthur straightened, turned to the witness. "Yesterday, madam, you described seeing my client in conversation with the host."

"As I walked to my car."

"In low tones, you said, while enjoying a cigar. This was hardly an excited or passionate conversation?"

"No."

"They could have been talking about the price of tea in China."

"I suppose."

"It would be quite uncivil, wouldn't it, for the host not to pass time with his remaining guest and wish him a good night?"

"I wasn't suggesting there was anything sinister about it."

"Of course not. Now let's go back to your dinner conversations with Judge Whynet-Moir."

"I trust we'll not get into a lot of hearsay here," Kroop said. Arthur studied the wall clock. "Shall I proceed?"

"Yes, move it along."

"Thank you. What did you and the judge talk about?"

"Well, politics."

"Help us out. Politics in what sense?"

"The shakeup in the federal cabinet." Chandra reflected. "He asked my opinion of the new justice minister. His predecessor, Jack Boynton, had died recently; we talked about that." A sharp look at Arthur, a sly smile. "Had we known your wife would be running to replace him, we might have talked about that too."

A whispered buzz from the back. Arthur smiled broadly. "Indeed she is, and putting on a vigorous campaign, I think you'll agree."

"Tuesday will tell the tale."

"A day that will not come too soon for me."

That brought chuckles, but not from Kroop, who looked impatient.

"I take it you knew Jack Boynton, Ms. Chandra?"

"I'd met him several times, interviewed him."

"And did Whynet-Moir know him?"

"*Mr. Justice* Whynet-Moir," said Kroop.

"Did Mr. Justice Whynet-Moir mention that he had an old association with the minister?"

"There we are, hearsay."

"Milord, if you intend to make your plane to Ottawa, fewer interruptions will help speed you on your way. This is not hearsay, it is part of the *res gestae*, as are all the deceased's conversations that night."

The chief could barely still his fury. "What do you say about this?" he asked Abigail.

"I tend to agree with my learned friend."

The judge went redder still, embarrassed now, you could hear the clacking of his false teeth. "Continue." He barely got the word out.

Arthur went on amiably. "Thank you. Did the deceased indicate he knew Jack Boynton?"

"As I recall, Justice Whynet-Moir worked for a while in the nineties as Jack's parliamentary aide, before he entered cabinet."

"Ah, close friends."

"Presumably."

"And did he have anything further to say about the late minister?"

"Oh, a story or two about his addiction to junk food. Couldn't pass by a hot dog stand without stopping. He said, 'Good old Jack,' laughed, and then said he'd rather discuss my book."

"Changed the subject, did he?"

"I suppose, yes."

The press table was busy. It wasn't that Chandra looked smug or anything, but Wentworth had the sense she was sneakily pleased, she'll be in the news, it won't hurt book sales.

"So how long did Whynet-Moir work in Boynton's parliamentary office?"

"Barely a year and a half, then he returned to his Vancouver practice. I believe he had enough of Ottawa."

"I don't blame him."

The boss was playing to the crowd, getting his laughs. Cud was finally looking more relaxed, here was the grizzled gunfighter in action, taking on the Cattleman's Association.

"Counsel, I *beg* your indulgence – where is this going?"

"I'm as eager to find out as you, milord. No more questions."

Wentworth turned to see a tall, lanky, and dour gentleman, dressed like a banker, approach the counsel bench with a burglar's soft walk: Silent Shawn Hamilton, here on a watching brief for Flo LeGrand. Or maybe for her parents. Wentworth found it hard to believe such an experienced lawyer would have hired April Wu as a spy; he'd be in serious breach of ethics.

"Call Lynn Tinkerson."

She walked in, an older woman, smallish and trim in a pant suit, no decorations, little makeup. An important novelist, Cud had called her. Wentworth had looked her up: her novels were mostly about heroines in emotional crises. "A keen observer of human foibles," said one critic on the Web. "Strips bare all pretension, leaving her characters naked and shivering in the cold glare of authorial appraisal." Prompting recall of an embarrassing checkup Wentworth had for a groin itch several years ago.

Tinkerson had a direct manner on the stand. "I went up to Mr. Brown, introduced myself, and we had a brief chat. He asked me which of my books I'd recommend that he read. I suggested he'd find *The Fishmonger's Daughter* the most accessible. I congratulated him on his shortlisting for the

Governor General's, and he said it gave him the courage to go on. He said it was a hard life being a professional poet, and that he had to play all the angles."

"Any further discussion?"

"I asked him where he was staying, and he said, 'I'm bunking right here; they made me an offer I couldn't refuse.'"

Wentworth was relieved that finally came out, the jury may have thought Cud stayed on as an unwelcome guest. The keen observer of human foibles wasn't much help with the all the petting and footsying under the table, though she noticed Cud and Flo were relating "in a very cordial manner."

Whynet-Moir was engaging and affable, and complimentary about her writing. "He'd bought several of my books and said he was 'delightedly speeding through them.'"

Arthur took his turn. "While you were at the table, madam, with the unstoppably affable host, did you note that his attention was often drawn to his wife?"

"Occasionally."

"No slippage in his engaging manner when he did so?"

"What do you mean?"

"No frowns of discontent?"

A long pause. "Perhaps once."

"Did you not get the impression, Ms. Tinkerson, that the hostess was making other offers to Mr. Brown that he couldn't refuse?"

"You needn't answer that question," Kroop said.

"Then I have no more."

At the morning break, Arthur drew up a chair beside Abigail, and they began an intense conversation. Wentworth assumed it was about April Wu, but didn't feel invited to attend. Another smile from Haley as she left the room. She was pretty, sexy in a plump sort of way. It looked like those freckles extended down her bosom.

Again he studied his cross-examination notes. Three hours' sleep, he had to suck it up, this could be his breakthrough, his chance to find favour with Arthur, who'd been stand-offish. Not unfriendly. Sort of indifferent. Cud was on his feet, staring at Arthur, waiting to be noticed. Finally he tamped out a cigarette and walked out with it dangling unlit from his lips.

Haley led in Sergeant Chekoff, an iron-pumper if those chest muscles meant anything, a square head with worry lines. He joined the huddle, and as he got filled in, he looked shocked, and put his hand to his heart as if swearing to the truth. Wentworth didn't think it was a put-on act.

The boss was beckoning Wentworth . . . no, Shawn Hamilton behind him, who got up and conferred with Abigail. She retreated with her cellphone. Wentworth couldn't stand it any longer. He joined the scrum, Arthur and Shawn and Chekoff and Haley.

"I have no knowledge of this," Shawn said calmly, "and I have no other comment."

"Shawn, you were hired by Florenza's parents."

"Can't say. Solicitor-client privilege."

"Your office was used as a drop-off."

"Solicitor-client privilege."

"It doesn't apply to criminal agreements, Shawn."

Shawn excused himself, strolled back to his seat as if he hadn't a qualm in the world. Haley looked at Wentworth. He smiled. She smiled.

Abigail finished her call. "Sorry, Arthur, the police weren't involved, so the Attorney won't agree to a mistrial."

Cud was back, the gallery filling, and the clerk was urgently beckoning counsel – the judge was antsy.

"I can't see Shawn involved in this," Abigail said, "his career would be in the toilet. Let it go, Arthur; the chief won't order a mistrial and he won't give you a directed verdict. Anyway, what does a mistrial get you? A retrial. You'd have to do it all over again."

That seemed to curb Arthur's enthusiasm. The jury were filing in, the judge lumbering to the bench.

"Abigail, you've undertaken to call any witness I want."

"Well, yes . . . within reason."

"Then call Florenza's parents. I will hold my guns for a while."

He shepherded Wentworth back to their side of the table. "This could actually rebound in our favour."

Whynet-Moir's caterers were next up, four of them, but none had much to add but a young server – she was nervous but soon proved to have been more sharp-eyed than any of the dinner guests. At one point, as she was tending table, she saw Florenza's hand in Cud's lap. "When I leaned over next to her, she kind of pulled it away fast."

"And where in his lap was her hand?" Arthur asked.

"Well, ah, sort of between his legs, actually, and, ah . . ."

"Yes?"

A rosy blush. "When she withdrew it, he had . . . I think he had a . . ."

She couldn't say it, so Arthur did, "An erection."

"I would say, yes."

"You didn't assume he'd stashed a cucumber in his underwear?"

Kroop quelled the laughter with a grunt of displeasure. "Mr. Beauchamp, *please.*"

"What did you next observe?"

"I returned to the kitchen, and when I came back a while later, I saw Mr. Brown's, ah, crotch area was kind of . . . all greasy, and he was zipping his fly and then he wiped his hands with a serviette."

"Thank you, miss, you've been most forthright and helpful."

Abigail said her next witness would be Dr. Rosa Sanchez, the pathologist. Wentworth sat upright, aquiver with anticipation. He was about to take the stage, his name would be in the papers. He ordered himself to be calm as he dove into his briefcase for his notes. If he pulled this off, he could win the award for best supporting lawyer.

"How long will this witness be?" Kroop said.

"'He weighs time even to the utmost grain.'" That was Arthur, *sotto voce*. Wentworth must check where that came from, probably Shakespeare.

"A little over an hour," Abigail said.

"It's almost noon break. Can we pick up the pace? I'd like to recess at four o'clock today; I've been conscripted to attend a rather special event this evening." Wentworth had seen the notice, a bar dinner to honour the chief for his upcoming Order of Canada. Only a hundred dollars a plate.

"Bear with me a moment, milord," said Abigail. She leaned on Wentworth's shoulder to talk to Arthur. "You going to this dinner?"

"Fortunately, I have other things to do."

"I'm on the menu, have to give a sucky speech. Listen, for some stupid reason, Brian wanted the jury to hear the whole post-mortem. Do you really need Dr. Sanchez?"

"What I don't need, my dear, is to have the jury looking at all those grisly photos."

Wentworth knew those photos too well. Whynet-Moir's broken skull, his death mask.

"Okay, no post-mortem pics, and you'll let the autopsy report go in?"

"I can't see a problem."

"And what about the other stuff, serum analysis, the DNA guy?"

"I don't really suppose we're much interested in that either, are we, Wentworth?" Without waiting for a reply, Arthur rose and said, somewhat grandly, "Mindful of the pressing demands on Your Lordship's time, the defence will admit all forensic evidence."

"Thank you. Adjourned till two o'clock."

Wentworth continued for a while to look dully at his sixty pages of cross-examination notes, then swept them back into his briefcase.

23

THE CARNIVAL COMES TO LIGHTHOUSE LANE

On his way out of court Arthur was almost knocked over by Felicity, barrelling up the aisle in tears. He turned to see Mrs. Brown looking censoriously at her wastrel son. Arthur couldn't find much sympathy for Cuddles, who'd reaped what his hyperactive libido sowed. Better to be a tepid lover than suffer an unregulated sex drive.

Margaret's remark still bothered him. *He did make a pass, Arthur.* A *pass* – the word encompassed all manner of repugnant undertakings. *I rebuffed him.* Of course Margaret would say that. Then he abruptly rejected his imaginings as unworthy and false.

Arthur was no sooner out the door when he saw Charles Loobie aiming for him like a torpedo. He tried evasion tactics, pulling Wentworth into an alcove as if they had critical business to discuss.

That didn't deter the bad news bear, who cornered them. Resistance was futile. "I got my headline, 'Bawdy Poet's Banana Peeled and Buttered at Banquet.' Juicy stuff about Boynton and Raffy, keep it coming. Hey, Artie, I'm real sorry about Whitson; my source turned out not to be as informed as he claimed. But I got another theory."

"Charles, I'm hungry, and I already have indigestion from one of your theories."

"Okay, but I ask you, why do two Supreme Court justices get dumped two months apart? I think we're looking for a guy who had a motive to kill both. Maybe you should key on Judge Naught. Maybe he had some corrupt dealings with Whynet-Moir."

Arthur was minded to brush aside this latest speculation, but Pomeroy's words came back: *They're connected, you know, Whynet-Moir and Naught . . . Everything is connected, but they're especially connected.*

"I found out they knew each other since law school," Loobie said. "There's a pattern, both those guys were flung into the drink. No weapons, same MO."

"Interesting, Charles, but that and a dill pickle don't make a sandwich."

"This is off record, you guys, but when I was covering the Naught trial, one of the cops told me off record Naught was being investigated for frequenting high-end pros like Minette Lefleur."

"All the more reason why he may have taken his own life."

"When he died, so did the file."

"And how does all this relate to Whynet-Moir?"

"I got a deep gut sense those two deaths mesh. Maybe Whynet-Moir was blackmailing him, or maybe the reverse; maybe they each put out a contract on the other." A lowered voice: "Try this on for size, Artie — maybe Raffy personally rubbed him out."

Arthur would prefer proof over gut sense, but no harm exploring this latest dubious theory. Again he wondered at Loobie's persistence in directing traffic for the defence. Time and again he'd sent them down blind trails.

"Order a transcript of Naught's inquest, would you, Wentworth, then brief me on it. And take Charles to lunch at the El Beau Room."

Loobie agreed to meet him there. Wentworth went off to change, paused in his tracks, returned to Arthur. "I'm in pretty solid with Minette Lefleur."

Arthur recalled him mentioning he'd won her bawdy-house case, his first trial. "Of course, I'd almost forgotten. Excellent. When you have a moment, you might go over her account with her."

"When I have a *moment* . . ."

"How about this evening if you have nothing on?"

Wentworth looked woefully at his heavy briefcase but took a deep breath and hastened away. A little hard work never hurt anyone, that's what Arthur believed. He spied Cud sidling toward him, seeking attention, and he escaped into an elevator.

⚖

He took lunch in the Law Courts Inn, joining a couple of judges of long acquaintance, Ken Singh and Bertha Rudweiler, both of whom felt he'd overreached with his sniping at Kroop.

"Lay off him, Arthur," said Rudweiler, an ill-tempered appeal judge better known to the bar as Rottweiler. "He's being feted tonight. He retires this summer, let him go in peace."

"Yeah, why antagonize the old bugger?" Singh said.

"Because I need an enemy. I can't get keyed up for a case unless I'm tussling with someone. Abigail Hitchins isn't even putting up a front of opposing me."

"Bending over backward with her legs spread, the way I heard it," said Singh, then yelped as Rudweiler stabbed him in the ankle with the point of her shoe.

"I suspect Abigail is waiting in the weeds for Florenza LeGrand," Arthur said.

"She must have a shitty case against you," Singh said.

"Meantime, we are racing to get the chief to the Governor General's soiree on Monday."

"I worry he'll have a cardiac first," said Rudweiler. "He was carrying on about you and Abigail ganging up on him.

Profane language." The censorious justice went on to talk about her current appeal, the Ruby Morgan case.

Arthur listened with discomfort to her complaints about the "mutinous lot of brigands" who were the defence crew, finished his sandwich, excused himself, and headed outside for a pipe and a couple of calls, the first to Dr. Alison Epstein, to tell her he'd talked to Pomeroy last night.

"What was your impression?" she asked.

"He wasn't entirely unresponsive. He has maintained his slashing wit. But conspiracies abound, and he seems to be lost between this world and a fictional one of his creation."

"That's perceptive, Mr. Beauchamp, but there may be more to the puzzle than that. I may not have mentioned some strange language he used when he was on cocaine: 'They're after me,' he said. 'I know too much. I know who killed the judges.' Paranoid utterances maybe. He said all the clues were in his manuscript."

"Does he remember anything of a visit with Flo LeGrand last month?"

"He says not. He may be withholding. Or some major event or disclosure may have caused a memory block."

He next tried Margaret, who must be peppier now that the NDP vote was collapsing. She'd turned off her cell but left him a message. "I have just heard the noon news, Arthur." He was taken aback by the cool, clipped tone of her rebuke over his repartee with Professor Chandra, his quip about election day not coming too soon for him. The phrase was "flip, impolitic, and implied a lack of support." Arthur was hurt – no such innuendos were intended.

She should be *pleased* he was dragging the Conservatives through the mud – he'd lowered himself, engaged in the grimy game of politics (for her!) with his blunt hints that Whynet-Moir bought his judgeship. The press had gobbled it up.

He was dolefully packing his pipe on the steps when he heard voices from below, by a fountain around which reporters had convened. "Yeah, right now it's a work-in-progress, but I'm hoping it'll hit the shelves for Christmas."

Arthur hurried down the steps, saw the poet in his poncho by a cement railing, behind a bouquet of microphones, holding a sheaf of verses.

A reporter asked, "What's its title?"

"*The Day the Hall Burned Down*. My publisher already sent me the cover copy. 'Laden with subterranean meaning and subtle subtext mined from the coal-pits of painful memory.' I'm also working on a memoir about this case, called *Scapegoat* . . ."

Arthur yelled, "Cut!" and broke up this impromptu, leading Cud away. "Damn it, you're not on a book promotion tour."

"Give a starving artist a break, Arturo, a big publisher wants my story; I got to strike while the anvil is hot."

"The only poem you ought to be interested in right now is 'Reading Gaol.'"

"How's it go?"

"'Pale anguish keeps the heavy gate, and the warder is Despair.'"

"Nice groove. Hey, what was all the fuss about this 'matter of great urgency?'"

"All will be revealed." Arthur wasn't about to tell him yet about April Wu's subterfuge for fear he'd put it on the street. He led him past his cheering section, past a young couple holding a banner, "Poetic Injustice," and back into the building.

"So how's it looking, are we beating back the forces of reaction? The only honest witness for the last two days was a lowly wage-earner, the waitress; the others must've been told their eyes would be gouged out if they saw anything. So what do you think, compadre, what does the big picture look like?"

"The prosecution has drawn the curtain on the literary evening. The next stage will be police evidence, then forensics. The big-ticket items, Astrid Leich and Florenza LeGrand, are being saved for the end. Then you testify. Maybe. Depending on what they say. I'll want to confer with you about that."

Cud's fan base had decreased by one: no sign of Felicity Jones. But he was not wanting for admirers — a pair of rose-lipped cherubim were on the courtroom terrace offering thin volumes for his willing pen.

Within was Wentworth, unpacking his briefcase. "Loobie had beans all to add to his double-murder theory. I don't think it hangs together. The good news is, when I mentioned Carlos, he gave me this."

A photocopy from the *Province*, November 1992. "Teenaged Heiress Jailed in Mexico." It began: "Wealthy heiress Florenza LeGrand, 17, was arrested on drug charges yesterday near Guadalajara, Mexico, eight months after she disappeared from her Vancouver home."

She'd been picked up by federal police at a farmhouse she shared with a "known" drug dealer, Carlos Espinoza, twenty-four. Charles Loobie, settling into the press table, bestowed on Arthur a wide smile that sought forgiveness for past sins.

Wentworth pointed to a paragraph mentioning Carlos's record of three arrests, two escapes, a reputation as a dashing cavalier. He'd obviously had no difficulty slipping past Canadian immigration. Presumably he was benefiting from some manner of cover-up by the LeGrand family. The likely engineer of that was Shawn Hamilton, still on the counsel bench, with his trademark deadpan look with its touch of misery, as if life had dealt him a hard hand.

Time to strategize must wait; court was in session and a young officer was testifying, in the stolid manner taught in the policing academies, as to her "attendance" at the scene of "an apparent collision between a vehicle and a tree." Constable Gaynor and her partner "responded to a call issued at 3:15 hours" and arrived just as an ambulance pulled in.

About twenty neighbours were milling around an Aston Martin and a badly wounded cypress.

Swerving tire marks scarred a driveway and described an S-shape on a lawn, allowing Constable Gaynor to conclude the brakes had been applied "in a forceful manner." The impact crushed the right front fender and bent the passenger door. The sole occupant was fully dressed and shod but minus poncho, and was snoring behind an air bag. When aroused, he appeared to be intoxicated, and assistance was required to place him in the patrol car.

"I had conversations with several neighbours, and consequently proceeded on foot approximately two hundred metres to an address at 2 Lighthouse Lane, where I found the driveway gate open and one of three garage doors open as well. I was about to radio the major crimes unit for instructions when a motor vehicle braked in front of me with emergency equipment on."

That was Detective Sergeant Henry Chekoff, unaccountably late in responding to the 911 call from Astrid Leich. More emergency vehicles, crime scene personnel. Gaynor's account of the ensuing melee prompted images of a travelling carnival setting up at Lighthouse Lane. Two 911 calls four minutes apart, Chekoff slow to bring order from chaos, uniformed and forensics officers meandering up and down the street, getting in one another's way.

Chekoff sent Gaynor back to the accident scene to help officers loop quarantine bunting around trees and fence posts. "The accused was transferred to a department vehicle, at which point I observed a Breathalyzer test being administered, after which he was taken away."

"Your witness," Abigail said.

"And do you know the result of that Breathalyzer test?" Arthur asked.

"Point two four, I believe."

"Enough to bring an elephant to its knees, do you agree?"

"I couldn't say, sir."

"Intoxication at that level would manifest itself how?"

"Slowed reaction time, slurred speech, lack of coordination, impaired judgment."

"Exactly. According to your telling, Mr. Brown couldn't even walk unaided."

"I would say he had difficulty, yes."

"Double vision, nausea, tremors, memory loss, those are also indicia?"

"He'd be grossly impaired, sir."

Given that Cud had found his way into the garage and taken the Aston Martin for a two-hundred-metre joyride, Arthur didn't see much profit in portraying him as too immobilized to perform the basic tasks of murder. But it didn't hurt to draw from Gaynor that Cud, when asked to produce his licence, dropped it, lost his footing while bending to retrieve it, toppled onto his face in the grass, and vomited.

Her partner added little. He'd patted the accused down, given him the customary warning, accompanied him to the police station. There, a further Breathalyzer was administered – point two three. Cud was booked and shown to a cell.

Arthur asked if Cud's belongings were catalogued, and the officer checked his notes. "Wallet with eight dollars, sixty-three cents in pocket change, six Tylenol tablets, three Cuban cigars, one peace medallion, one half-smoked marijuana cigarette, and I think they removed his ring."

"He was wearing a ring at the time?"

"I'm not sure. I don't remember seeing it earlier."

"Please describe it."

"Gold or imitation gold, with a big oval stone, kind of yellowish-orange."

"An opal."

"Could be."

Arthur nudged Wentworth to write all this down – he seemed inordinately fatigued. There was Vogel in the back, the old farmer bamboozled by Clearihue. Arthur didn't know how to build that defence, a murder to abort a judgment. Clearihue lived a twenty-minute walk from Whynet-Moir, so there was opportunity and motive but not much more.

Detective Sergeant Chekoff took the oath. Bull-like, with a razor-resisting muzzle, a suit that hadn't known pressing for a week. An old-style cop from the ranks, not a bad fellow, though an exemplar of the Peter Principle and out of his depth here.

Roused from bed by his dispatcher shortly after 3:00 a.m., he'd "jumped" into his car and "raced off" to 2 Lighthouse Lane. Given that Gaynor easily beat him there, this effort to imply he leaped buildings with a single bound seemed suspect – maybe he'd got lost or stopped for a coffee and doughnut. Two more detectives arrived on his heels and were directed to Astrid Leich's home. Then came the forensics unit, another ambulance, two more patrol cars, sirens howling, neighbours congregating.

In the LeGrand manse the windows remained dark, only a few exterior lights burning. While officers fanned out along the deck and directed beams onto the rocky shore, Chekoff buzzed the front door. Twice. Three times. Then he was summoned to an area of the deck where a metal chair lay on its side. Officers were gaping down at a "human form, male, partially clad in a dressing gown."

At this point Abigail began to thrust exhibits at Chekoff: pictures of the house exterior, the yard, the decks, the fallen chair, the sprawled body thirty feet below, shots of intrepid climbers lugging up the corpse on a stretcher. House plans, a landscape architect's drawings, diagrams showing distances, elevations.

The fingerprint people went inch by inch over the railing and fallen chair but found nothing to place Cudworth near the critical area. Towels were seized from around the pool, as well as a bottle of Hennessy VSOP, nearly empty. Cud's prints were lifted from the bottle and the door. No clothing strewn about, though Cud claimed he and Flo had stripped by the pool.

Chekoff made another fruitless effort to arouse someone, knocking and yelling, "Police!" Probably because he knew these were the diggings of local nobility, he'd shied away from radioing for a search warrant or attempting forced entry. Instead, he posted two guards on the grounds until morning.

Unfortunately, Chekoff's only instructions to the constables, both rookies, were to forbid anyone leaving the house, and before he showed up again at 8:00 a.m. they'd let the maid and gardener in and given fawning admittance to Florenza's father, Donat J. LeGrand, as well as an entire medical-legal entourage. Chekoff and his crime scene team were guided to a bedroom doorway where "I observed Ms. LeGrand in bed, apparently ill, and under treatment by a doctor and a nurse." He did not venture in.

He was then led to a drawing room and introduced to "a lawyer named Shawn Hamilton, whom I identify as sitting right over there." Shawn nodded, unsmiling. "As a result of that conversation, I did not make further inquiries of Ms. LeGrand, but I produced a search warrant and told them I intended to enforce same."

That search turned up nothing but Cud's cigar butt, overlooked by the maid, who had already done the living room, dining room, and tidied up what the caterers hadn't. Assuming her employers were still abed, she hadn't entered the main bedroom. The gardener was also on duty, raking leaves.

Chekoff looked uneasy as he related this fiasco, especially with Kroop muttering under his breath. Arthur could read his lips: "Nincompoop." He caught the forewoman's eye and couldn't help smiling – but he felt sorry for Chekoff.

The sergeant next made inquiries of the Haitian maid, Philomène Rossignol, who escorted him to her suite. The bed had been tidily made and its linen washed. She'd set aside a backpack and male toiletries for whoever was the rightful claimant.

The judge ordered a break, and Arthur nudged Wentworth, who was staring at the protruding bottom of a junior prosecutor bending over the counsel table. "Wentworth."

"Oh, sorry,"

"I'll want a transcript of Leich's 911 call. And ask Abigail to produce the maid for cross-examination. Rashid too, while we're at it. I'll want you to interview them first."

Arthur went out to the gallery to check his messages. Nothing from Margaret. It still smarted that she'd chastised him, but when he thought back, yes, he could see how his jests about her campaign, about Ottawa, might have smacked of smirking faithlessness.

Nicholas Braid had called. "I guess you're not there. A couple of locals are out in the barn, they told me you hired them to build a pedestal for that monstrosity in there. A Mr. Stonewell and some fellow he calls Dog, they assured me they have permission to use the Fargo to haul the cement. Nicky vouched for them, so I gave them the keys, hope you don't mind."

Arthur uttered a profane lamentation; the Fates had it in for him. He dragged himself back to court 67, looking for Wentworth. A junior prosecutor, buxom and freckle-faced, had him in close encounter, trapped against the jury railing. Finally, he moved back to his station, flushed.

Arthur said, "Well?"

"She said yes."

"Who said yes to what?"

He stammered. "Oh, um, Abigail, she'll produce the maid and Rashid."

Chekoff stepped back into the box, smoothed his rumpled suit, and described his wanderings around the grounds with a photographer, illustrating the tour with photos. Exhibits P-33 through P-39 showed views of Leich's balcony from the vantage of the fallen chair, an unobstructed distance of sixty metres.

They next went to the other side of the little nipple of an inlet, to 5 Lighthouse Lane, Leich's house, where photos were snapped in the opposite direction. "I had a conversation with Ms. Leich following which I escorted her to headquarters. There she attended a lineup of eight men as depicted in Exhibit 54, in which the accused is shown wearing a placard with number six. I instructed Ms. Leich to write down the number of any person she'd seen from her balcony at approximately three a.m." And of course she wrote down number six.

"That's the man," she'd said – hearsay, but Arthur didn't object, didn't want the jury thinking he was hiding an awkward truth.

He rose to cross-examine, wondering why the jury seemed distracted – they were watching Felicity Jones return in a pout. She retook her seat between Cud and Mrs. Brown, quickly withdrew her hand when Cud tried to press it.

"Let's try to understand this, sergeant – after you discovered the body you made no attempt to enter the premises?"

"Okay, I called the chief and he spoke to some other people, I don't know who, and he called back to tell me to button down the place and post guards until the daylight hours."

"The night before, responding to Ms. Leich's call, you arrived well after my client ran the car into the tree."

"I had to do some checking, see who lived at 2 Lighthouse Lane."

"Prominent people – is that why the investigation was put on hold?"

"From what I could determine, there was no one at home, and it looked like it could have been . . ." Hesitation.

"Suicide?"

"Well, it had some of the earmarks."

"Suggesting that Ms. Leich didn't see what she claimed to see."

"We were keeping all options open." Sullenly.

"In your search of the house, did you find any copies of Mr. Brown's poetry books? *Liquor Balls, Karmageddon*."

Chekoff pondered. "Can't say we did."

"Not in the maid's room either?"

"I have no note of that."

Shawn was writing his own note. Arthur wondered if he'd gone so far as to remove evidence. He played with a thought that Shawn might be representing not just Flo LeGrand but, more surreptitiously, friends in Ottawa, friends who wanted things hushed up.

"Odd to think that my client, even intoxicated, would drive off and leave behind his belongings – unless, if he was doing any thinking at all, he intended to come back. Did that thought strike you?"

That, in retrospect seemed a foolish question, and Arthur got the answer he deserved. "Maybe he had a reason to wanna get out of there fast."

"As I understand it, Ms. LeGrand was under instructions not to talk to you."

"That's about it, counsellor."

"Does the name Carlos Espinoza mean anything to you?"

"Can't say it does."

Again Shawn was writing, an indication Arthur was on the right track. "Are you aware that fourteen years ago Ms. LeGrand had a lover in Mexico by that name?"

"I may have heard something about that."

"And what did you hear?"

"Mr. Beauchamp, we're not interested in scuttlebutt."

"But I daresay, milord, we are interested in knowing who killed Rafael Whynet-Moir."

"What the sergeant may have heard is of absolutely no

probative value. I will not have this court used as a forum for backhanded attacks on reputation."

"Nor should the court erect a shield against relevant inquiries that involve reputation."

"Mr. Beauchamp, your lack of deference to this court has not gone unnoticed."

Arthur had the old fellow going, and he was thinking of adding fuel, but Abigail was now trying to enter the fray. "Milord, if I may . . ."

"You may not. I do not need to hear from you. The question is entirely unseemly and is disallowed. It's four o'clock, we'll adjourn." He swept out, slammed the chambers door. Arthur felt badly about putting the fellow in a sour mood when he was soon about to enjoy accolades with his rubber chicken.

As the courtroom buzz settled, Arthur turned to see a familiar but unexpected presence. Provincial Judge J. Dalgleish Ebbe, who, after he'd been passed over for elevation to the Supreme Court, had foul-mouthed Whynet-Moir in a cocktail lounge. Arthur riffled through his papers for the 2006 Law Society complaint, reread Ebbe's claim that His Lordship and his spouse were major contributors to the Conservative Party, and that Whynet-Moir bribed the justice minister, the late Hon. Jack Boynton, to get the appointment.

Ebbe didn't, or wouldn't, look at Arthur as he joined the exit queue. Odd that he'd take time out from sentencing vandals, brawlers, shoplifters and other minor miscreants to come here. His curiosity must have been piqued by Arthur's broad hints about hanky-panky in high places.

Schultz's comment came back: *Can't blame him for being bitter.*

24

THE OWL AND THE HOOKER

"*Thirty days in the lockup will cure you of your insolence. Mr. Chance, you will have to carry on for the defence as best you can. Hmf, hmf.*" Wentworth rose with a scornful smile. "*With pleasure, milord . . .*"

The reverie was shattered by a whining power saw, carpenters below, working overtime, it was after five o'clock. Wentworth had stopped in there, saw three neckless long-haired heavyweights setting up the sound system for tomorrow's grand opening of the Gastown Riot, heavy metal with Blood'n'Guts.

His stomach was growling; that lunchtime chowder hadn't much staying power. With Loobie's steak sandwich and his three whiskies and tip, $48.27. This newshound was a leech.

He rubbed his eyes, tried to focus on his to-do list. Newly added to it: Judge J. Dalgleish Ebbe. What was *his* interest in this case? Maybe he was just waiting like a vulture for the boss to give Kroop a heart attack so he'd get shortlisted again for the high court. "And get me all you can on Boynton," the taskmaster commanded after court recessed, "misdoings, misappropriations, skimming from expense allowances – every politician leaves a trail. Google him, or whatever one does."

He awoke his computer, returned to the transcript of the Naught inquest, just couriered; he was at page 30 of 280.

There was no one to share the burden, no one to replace the beautiful Oriental spy, he had to do all the filing. He sighed, took a deep breath. He will bend, won't break.

This evening's mission: debrief Minette Lefleur – they're to meet a couple of hours from now. He skipped to page ninety-three, her testimony. It didn't amount to much; she saw nothing, heard nothing, knew nothing, but was devastated that such an awful thing had happened to this well-respected client of her licensed massage business.

The other key witness was Joe Johal, Honest Joe, the Chevrolet-Pontiac dealer, who encountered Naught on the houseboat ramp. "Evening, judge," he'd said as they passed in the night. Naught looked unsteady, Johal had picked up a strong smell of alcohol. Counsel at the inquest made something of Honest Joe having lost a breach of contract before Naught, but no one could pin anything on him.

The receptionist had stuck a few Post-it notes to his phone, calls to be returned. Haley, half an hour ago, saying she was free after court on Friday and delighted to accept his offer for a cocktail in lieu of the dry-cleaning bill. He hoped she wouldn't expect dinner as well, payday wasn't until the end of the month. She seemed totally forgiving, but there was something about her – he couldn't pin it down – that made him uncomfortable. An earthiness, a forwardness. Close up, she smelled of jasmine.

"Mr. Jobson," read another Post-it, "will be at this number until 5:30." He racked his brain. Right, Clearihue's lawyer at the Vogel trial. Wentworth had left him a message.

Jobson picked up right away. "Mr. Chance? Glad we could catch up to each other. I take it you're acting for Mr. Vogel?"

"Well, yes, I am."

"That's a relief, I was afraid he'd be without counsel." That sounded sincere, but Wentworth was on guard. "I have instructions to talk." Wentworth blinked. That was code for a settlement offer. "We'd like to close the book on this thing now that Mr. Clearihue has passed on."

Wentworth almost dropped the phone. "He *what?*"

"The Clearihue family hasn't issued any statements, so it wasn't generally known that he'd been in a coma since the accident."

Wentworth confessed he was in the dark. The accident, Jobson said, occurred while Clearihue was checking out some timber properties in the Borneo rain forest. Sadly, he wasn't wearing a helmet when a falling mahogany tree clipped his skull.

Jobson wasn't one to hedge about, he was offering to rescind the entire deal, return the title to Vogel. Each side to pay their own costs.

Wentworth said he'd get back to him. He was too dazed to work this out right now, but he guessed Clearihue's estate didn't want the expense of a new trial, especially since they'd lost their main witness.

"We'll hear from you then, Mr. Chance."

"Fine, um, just a sec. Exactly when was this accident?"

"Let me check . . . Yes, just over four months ago, the first weekend of October."

Cross Clearcut Todd off the list. Wentworth chucked the eight-hundred-page transcript; it hit the floor with a satisfying whump.

⚖

The boss seemed to take it in stride. "Felled by a tree, you say? Poor fellow, a taste of Ceres's revenge. 'In solemn lays, exalt your rural queen's immortal praise.'"

"That's Virgil."

"Very good."

They were bent into the wind-driven rain, walking to the parking lot. "You used that line in the Northwest Produce conspiracy."

"I did?"

Wentworth didn't want to seem smug, but he knew more about the boss than the boss did. He was enjoying a little uptick in his spirits. Magically, thanks to a mahogany tree, he'd just become a hero to Vogel and his three beautiful granddaughters.

He sought Arthur's advice about the settlement. "Hold out for thirty thousand in costs in lieu of punitive damages. That will amply pay your bill." Thirty thousand! Wentworth wouldn't have the gall to dicker that high, he wasn't skilled in the art. The partners were always on him about his low billings.

They climbed into the Chrysler, Wentworth at the wheel. It wasn't until Arthur directed him toward West Shaughnessy that he mustered courage to ask exactly where they were going.

"To see my oldest and most valued client."

"Faloon. The Owl."

"You know that too."

They passed by grand gated properties hidden by tall cedar hedges; the people around here had the kind of money you don't need to show off. Arthur pointed to a driveway, and after he announced himself at the intercom, the gate swung open to receive them. The house looked like a replica of a small English castle, block and stone, with towers.

As he parked under cover by the entranceway, a short, swarthy man came out, arms spread wide, a face-cracking grin. Faloon. Wentworth had read about him; he used to be the world number three jewel thief. They'd never got him for his last caper, in Cannes, a rumoured fortune in uncut African diamonds.

He gave Arthur a bear hug and Wentworth a vigorous handshake. "Your headman here must've got me off a hundred times."

"Well, actually thirteen wins and two losses, but it's the record for most acquittals for a single client."

"What's this guy, your personal encyclopedia?" Faloon led them through a palatial entrance hall into a parlour about ten times bigger than Wentworth's flat, done in an Arabic style, colourful rugs and carpets, patterned floor cushions, settees, ottomans.

"Claudette's in the ballroom with her tango class, but she left some appetizers." Cheese, grapes, sliced oranges, pita bread, miniature sausages, a feast. Wentworth was famished.

"Mr. Beauchamp don't partake, but I got beer, wine, or hard, or I got jake, regular or decapitated." Wentworth took the regular to help him stay awake. "Put some of them canapés away, Stretch, you look like you been working eighth oar on a slave ship."

Wentworth silently concurred. He sat a hand's reach from the tray, willing himself not to descend on it like a wolf. Arthur sat with a grunt of comfort on a plump settee. "I have a small favour to ask."

"Already done."

"I am keen to secure a certain item of jewellery, to wit, an opal ring likely hidden by an insane lawyer in a second-floor suite of Hollyburn Hall in West Vancouver."

"Don't know the joint."

"Haute bourgeoisie hospice for junkies. Overstaffed, but they don't lock the doors."

"I can do it in my sleep."

"You might check for any non-prescription drugs while you're at it. In recompense, I can offer a one-third reduction in my next fee."

"You're not gonna see the Owl professionally again. I ain't into free trade no more, I've given up the game. This time I mean it."

"I'm sure you do."

⚖

After dropping Arthur off for dinner at his club, Wentworth found his way to Fishermen's Wharf, on the docks of False Creek. The rain had lessened, so he wandered around the slips for a while, early for his appointment with Minette.

Several years ago, when he'd beat her first case, she'd offered him a treat – which of course he declined, though it prompted many torrid imaginings. They'd carried on as friends in a non–sexually threatening way. She still used him, the odd bylaw complaint, a threatened nuisance action by neighbours. After Naught's death, the police tried to shut her down, but Wentworth got her business licence back. She actually did know how to massage, had a bodywork certificate, but her sideline was more lucrative, with maybe three dozen regulars, well-to-do professionals, business persons.

Here was her boathouse, two storeys on a sturdy, timbered raft, sandwiched between a sloop and a yawl. This was the gangplank on which Naught had bumped into Johal.

Minette swept out to greet him in style, a cocktail dress, dark eye shadow and hot red lips, prepped for work – they liked to watch her undress, she'd told him. She pecked him on the cheek. "Still a virgin, honey?"

He didn't want to admit that for all practical purposes he was, though technically not if you count a few strained episodes with his landlord's tough-talking daughter, who used to barge into his room. That was two years ago, before she joined Officers Training. Then there was his teenage sweetheart, she'd finally let him do it, after about his fiftieth try, in the back seat of her dad's Impala. That led, a few days later, to a bizarre quarrel; she claimed she'd been saving her virginity for someone special. No wonder sex scares the pants off him. It's become a neurotic thing.

Minette led him to the second floor, a stylish boudoir with Matisse and Modigliani nudes, a massage table for those who wanted to pretend that's what they came for, vials of scented oil, sex toys, an array of quality condoms, a bed turned up.

"Poor baby, you look beat, what's up?"

"I'm under siege. You been following this murder trial, the poet guy?"

"Yeah, I read on the Net he's being railroaded."

"Well, guess who's acting for him?"

"Arthur Beauchamp."

News of Wentworth's critical role had yet to make it into cyberspace. "I'm his indispensable assistant."

She seemed impressed, and this encouraged him to talk about the case. He found himself getting wound up, pouring out the details, the ins and outs, evidence, witnesses, suspects, his back-breaking load.

She interrupted. "Take your shirt off."

Wentworth froze. "Why?"

"Lay down on the table over there. I'm going to give you a massage."

He did as directed, felt uncomfortable as he climbed on the massage table, exposed, scrawny. He was afraid he'd get a hard-on, but he didn't, and her hands felt good, very good, he could feel the tension melt. She went at him in silence for twenty minutes, and when he sat up he felt better. Maybe all he needed now was sleep.

As he pulled on his shirt, he got to the point: he was exploring a theory someone wanted to kill both Whynet-Moir and Darrel Naught. When he asked for a rundown of what happened at about midnight of August 18, she turned silent, went to a tall window, drew open the curtain. Wentworth went behind her, stared over her shoulder at lights glinting on the undulating inlet, a forest of masts, the glow of downtown towers. There, distant but in clear view, was the spot where Naught went over, at the end of the floating dock, just below a metal ramp to the shore.

"I usually open the curtains when I'm alone. I like to look out."

"It's pretty, I don't blame you."

"I said at the inquest that Darrel didn't show up for his midnight appointment. That was true. I also said I didn't see him that night. That wasn't true. This is between you and me, Wentworth, huh?"

"We're bound to silence. Me and Mr. Beauchamp."

She leaned on the windowsill. "Joe Johal took an extra ten minutes, but he left a good tip. I closed the door after him, but I didn't see him bump into Darrel. I had no idea they knew each other."

"When did Judge Naught make his appointment?"

"That night, around nine, he called from some bar or restaurant. He'd do that when he got lonely. Guy needed a wife. Anyway, I was at this window, and he hadn't shown up, and I assumed he'd cancelled. And then I saw . . . I don't want to get nailed for perjury, okay?"

"Don't worry."

"Darrel – I only saw the back of his head – was walking away, weaving a little, probably drunk; he was never sober when he came to see me. He stopped and clung to a pier, then continued on to where the floating dock meets the ramp. He was leaning over like he might throw up, but I don't know if he was sick or what. And then I saw a guy come down the ramp, average height or a little taller, in a suit, I think. And then I saw a flash, like on a camera, only I didn't see a camera. And Darrel straightened up, kind of flailed out at the guy, like he was blinded, and this dude pushes him back, not hard, but more than a nudge, enough to set him off balance, and he went into the water."

She shivered. Wentworth sensed her relief, she was getting rid of this, unburdening. She eased into a chair he held for her, but stayed fixed on the view. "He didn't come up. Not once. And the guy, I don't know what he was thinking, he looked around I guess to see if anyone was watching. And he went back up to shore."

"Did he have a car?"

"Not that I saw. He walked up to Creekside Drive. I was standing there frozen."

"Could it have been Johal?"

"Not likely, unless he'd lost fifty pounds."

"He was in suit?"

"Now I'm not sure. But he was wearing a tie. And suspenders, I think."

That had Wentworth blinking. Suspenders? They weren't much in fashion outside the legal profession. Arthur Beauchamp, Q.C., fancied them for court. Brovak always wore them, Pomeroy often. Silent Shawn too. He remembered Cudworth's mocking self-portrait: *The hick in the red braces.* That's what he'd worn at Whynet-Moir's.

"Overcoat?"

"No."

"What colour shirt?"

"I couldn't tell."

"Beard, moustache, glasses, hairstyle, hair colour?"

"I couldn't tell the colour, not black, the light there plays tricks. Definitely not bald. No beard, I don't know about a 'stache or specs — it's more than a hundred metres away."

Wentworth watched a couple descend the ramp. He could make out a short man and a tall woman, but not their features. Jackets of no discernible colour.

"Sorry, baby, I have a client in ten minutes." She bussed him at the door. "You don't look like you're getting enough, Wentworth."

"I'm working on it."

"She hot? Need any lessons?"

"I'll figure it out."

In the car, Wentworth censored a brief erotic moment, then brought out his notepad. Poor Judge Naught. A senseless homicide? Some psycho in a suit who happened to be wandering by? Or a stalker who'd finally found his chance? That flash of light didn't make sense, unless it was a camera.

Then a thought popped into his head: maybe the perp was a photojournalist who spotted Naught hanging around Minette's houseboat, hoped to catch him consorting with a hooker. Or he'd followed him from the law courts, followed him all evening.

Loobie. Loobie the leech. Scandal-digging Charles Loobie . . .

25

FOWL PLAY

After guiltily overeating – a rib roast with extra trimmings – Arthur settled into an appropriately overstuffed chair in the club lounge, earning nods of non-recognition from the pair of old fixtures next to him. He wondered whether he'd be like them in his dotage, fustian and discursive. Old School Tie drank old-fashioneds. The Goatee was more with the times, a thin computer open across his knees.

"Imperial Oil class B bonds up twenty-one points."

"And people whine there's a fuel shortage."

"Plenty more down there. Just have to get at it."

"Not enough freeways is the problem. My driver took half an hour to get here."

Arthur pawed through his briefcase, found his cellphone, drew Margaret away from a session with her campaign team.

"How are you faring, Arthur? I hope you're not loading up on calories; I worry."

He hedged: "Only overdid it once. Suffered a fuel shortage. You're well?"

"I'm probably exhausted, but I won't feel it until after Tuesday. We're having a problem over some unauthorized e-mails accusing O'Malley of cruel and unusual punishment at his chicken factory. It's been popping up on screens all over. And he's still making oblique references about how my hubby is acting for you-know-who. How's *that* going?"

"Over the hump, I think. Two main witnesses to come. If they don't do me severe damage, I may be able to raise enough reasonable doubt to keep Cud off the stand." He feared what Abigail might do in cross; the Badger, too, might go after Cud, transferring the ire he holds for Arthur. But he expected Kroop would not be in his usual troll-like temper tomorrow, after being lauded, applauded, and lied to at tonight's bar dinner.

"Eric Schultz wants to talk to you."

The turncoat Tory. Arthur doubted he was a good influence on Margaret; he played by the old rules.

"Ah, Eric, how goes the campaign?"

"Tight, very tight. NDP's done, but we're still a few points behind O'Malley. Problem is we've got three parties courting the environmental vote, and O'Malley's cornered the rest, the global warming deniers. Outspending us ten to one."

"Dalgleish Ebbe popped into court today."

"Still sore about being passed over for Whynet-Moir, hopes you'll be his instrument of vengeance, that's my take. Might be an idea to talk to him; he and Whynet-Moir were in law school together, he may be able to confirm rumours Raffy had a few same-sex dalliances in his college days."

"How would that be relevant?" Arthur wanted to say he'd left his shovel on the farm.

"Just a thought. Not here to tell you how to run your trial, but we could bridge the gap if you keep hammering away at the payola issue. Polling tells us it's a growing factor. The latest: a reliable blog with Ottawa sources says an audit of Jack Boynton's books will show he and Whynet-Moir were up to their eyeballs. Rumours of a numbered account in the Bahamas."

Arthur wondered if some crafty campaigner was feeding the blogs with that sort of tattle. This brave new form of communication had potential for villainy. "I'd hesitate at this point, Eric, to make accusations based on rumours. It would be a terrible thing if we're proven wrong."

"Of course. I understand. Tricky business, politics. Mind you, one can't defame the dead, and you're in a libel-proof venue anyway. Not saying something you don't know. Wouldn't dream of suggesting anything against your client's best interests. Getting Brown acquitted, that's the main thing, it'll go a long way to muzzle O'Malley and his insinuations. Best of luck, Arthur."

Arthur couldn't get rid of a sour taste as he slid the phone into his pocket.

"Here's a scurrilous election ad." The Goatee, at his laptop. "Calls our man a dirty rotten chicken plucker."

"They'll stop at nothing."

⚖

Arthur went to bed early, but a bout of indigestion made for a night of phantoms. Dreams fuelled by his distaste for politics. A mini-nightmare in which a man dressed as a chicken asked him to accept a judgeship. And this truth-based oddity: he was cross-examining Astrid Leich, with Kroop running his usual interference – but it was a film set, cameras on cranes and dollies, and he was an actor playing a lawyer. On the director's stool, with a clipboard, was Brian Pomeroy. The dream awoke him.

His fretful night stayed with him as he read a newspaper piece about those chicken plucker e-mails from some renegade geek. Though they carried no virus, they'd riled computer users. The Green Party had denounced their author but was still getting the blunt of the blame, accused of sleaze, of being anti-business.

He perked up over coffee with Wentworth in his firm's lounge, with its lovely view of the North Shore's snowy peaks – a brighter space than Pomeroy's office, with its patrolling pigeons and views of junkies, bums, and tourists.

Arthur was a little confounded to learn Naught had met his end not by mischance but by a relatively polite form of homicide, a push into the drink by a faceless nondescript in, unusually, suspenders. Arthur himself was an aficionado of braces, as he preferred to call them, and typically so was Cudworth Brown. Not that he otherwise fit Ms. Lefleur's description – Arthur couldn't conjure an image of the proletarian poet in dress shirt and tie.

"That wasn't a gun flash Ms. Lefleur saw?"

"She didn't hear any noise. My guess is a camera. Um, I hope you won't think this is way too bizarre, but I'm going to nominate another candidate for bad guy. Charles Loobie."

Arthur didn't scoff as Wentworth made his case, in fact was piqued at the hypothesis that the sleaze-seeking scribe had been lurking around the False Creek docks. Indeed, there was something almost compelling about throwing into the mix a fellow who insisted on calling him Artie. All those efforts at misdirection, putting them off the scent. His unfounded speculations about Naught: *Maybe he had some corrupt dealings with Whynet-Moir . . . maybe Raffy personally rubbed him out.*

In support of his case, Wentworth cited Loobie's presence at the press table as Ruby Morgan and his cohorts were sent up the river – seven hours before the judge sank like a stone into the saltchuck. Add to that: Loobie knew Naught was being investigated for frequenting, as Loobie put it, "high-end pros like Minette Lefleur."

"I don't think I've ever seen him in suspenders, though," Wentworth said.

"I'm almost sure I have." Loobie was wearing a belt these days, but Arthur dug into memory and came up with an old snapshot of the pot-bellied reporter snapping his braces in the El Beau Room, a parody of Arthur beginning cross-examination.

A murder motive seemed entirely lacking, but according to Ms. Lefleur, there'd been a brief shoving match. Homicide without intent may not be murder, even in second degree, but could well attract a manslaughter conviction.

It seemed a long leap to connect Loobie with Whynet-Moir's murder, but they speculated awhile about the possibility. A judge about whom floated rumours of corruption, newly married to a woman of wild reputation, a poet with a similarly loose history invited to a staid gathering – these were the spicy ingredients that might entice this maestro of yellow journalism to sneak onto private property. A confrontation, a push, presto.

Arthur put the matter to rest for now, asked about the late justice minister, whether Wentworth had found any skeletons in Boynton's closet.

"It's pretty bad."

"How bad?"

"Twenty years happily married, adopted three refugee orphans, active in legal programs for the poor . . ."

"My God."

"There's worse: various charities, Christian Aid Society, the Darfur Hope Mission, honorary chair of the Children's Literacy Foundation . . ."

"Enough!" Surely the ex-justice minister could not be such an unblemished saint. Maybe Wentworth hadn't got past the protective layers of political boosterism.

On the desk, freshly couriered, was a recorded disk of Astrid Leich's 911 call. Wentworth slipped it into his computer.

"*Hello, 911, hello, are you 911? I just saw a horrible thing, terrible, terrible, I think I've just witnessed a cold-blooded murder!*" Dramatic, yet not histrionic. The call came in at 3:11 a.m., according to the transcript.

There followed a quick question period: name, address, identity of victim, where, when, how. "*Do not hang up, one moment.*" A pause for a relay to police dispatch. Then:

"*He was standing on a chair in a dressing gown, and he was . . . he was . . . oh, it was horrible . . . awful!*"

"*Please be calm, Ms. Leich. Police are on their way. Are you talking about your neighbour?*"

"Yes, Rafael . . . he's a judge. A judge! Another judge has been murdered, oh, my heart, and I'm the only witness!"

"*Have you locked your doors?*"

"Yes, but I'm terribly frightened."

"*The police will be there within seconds. Now tell me again what you saw.*"

"A man came over and pushed him right over the railing of his deck, just like that. And I heard him scream, and . . . and then there was a crunch and then just silence, and I don't know where the man went, he disappeared somewhere."

Arthur wasn't blind to her talent as a stage performer. Yet this frantic account of death cry and crunching bones seemed natural, unrehearsed. No hint of inebriation, no mental confusion, no dissembling. When asked if she might recognize him again, she said, "*I believe I would, yes, I believe I would.*" A troubling eagerness.

The dispatcher kept her on the line with a questionnaire, personal statistics – Leich almost balked when asked her age, but who would deny her a touch of vanity? She was seventy-three, hardly ancient, Arthur wasn't far behind. Marital status? "*Long and happily divorced, young lady.*" Occupation? "*Semi-retired professional actress.*" Still available for roles, it would seem.

Reception said Faloon was in the waiting room. He was whisked in, his round, owlish face lit by a beaming smile. "A slice of pie, took me two minutes. First thing I did was check his pants, hanging on a chair. The item of interest was in a little zipper pocket of his wallet, in this here scrunched-up wad of paper."

A torn corner of a newspaper. Arthur shook the ring free. It fell with a comfortable plop on the reception countertop, gold, inset with an oval opal, a restive stone, yellow, orange, red. *The power must not be used for evil.* Arthur had trouble believing Pomeroy forgot it was in his wallet; it would have made a bulge.

"Find any drugs?"

"He was clean."

"My gratitude is unbounded."

Faloon clapped Wentworth on the back. "Whattaya think, Stretch, Mr. Beauchamp got this in the bag? He ain't lost a murder yet, right?"

"Three losses, but fifty-four wins, if you count the ones on appeal. Eleven were reduced to manslaughter, and there were four mistrials."

Arthur rewrapped the ring in the newsprint, handed it to Wentworth with advice not to lose it on penalty of ending his legal career in ignominy and disgrace.

⚖

Arthur stood there puzzling, wondering why the Chrysler wasn't in its allotted space. He'd left it in the lot an hour ago, after leaving his club. Was he losing his grip? Wentworth seemed to think so.

"You sure you didn't, like, sort of forget . . . I mean, given how preoccupied . . ."

"Damn it, Wentworth, my mind hasn't turned to sludge. Right here. Stall Eighteen."

"Um, did you leave the keys in it?"

"I have them right here!" Jingling them.

They wandered about, found no sign of a 1970 Chrysler New Yorker, and finally made inquiries of a grease-stippled young man changing a tire. "You sure that car was yours, because the towtruck driver said it hadn't been paid for, and he had some kinda seizure order."

"Stoney," Arthur snarled.

It took only a few minutes to flag a taxi, Arthur muttering imprecations all the way to the law courts. *Wondering about my jitney. Just checking, no reason to be concerned.*

He wasn't able to put the matter aside until they found themselves alone with Hank Chekoff in an elevator. Arthur was gruff in his greeting, and the sergeant went on the defensive.

"Give me a break, counsellor, enough with the boot marks all over my ass. Even my wife's laughing at me. This ain't the VPD; I got limited resources in West Van."

"Nothing against you, Hank, you're doing just fine."

Though forbidden to discuss his evidence until his cross-examination ended, Chekoff did just that. "I had nothing to do with this April dame, you got to believe that. I didn't see her reports. Ask Florenza's old man about her when he shows up – I served a summons on him last night, by the way, after I finally got past the butler and the bodyguard."

"Was Shawn Hamilton there?"

"Always." As the elevator slowed for level six, he said quickly, "All I ask is go easy, counsellor. As a favour I ran Carlos Espinoza's name last night. That's a hint." As they walked out into the hallway, he added, "By the way, Abigail Hitchins ain't feeling too good. Something about bad food at a restaurant."

That diagnosis was confirmed when Arthur found the ashen-faced prosecutor standing by the railing outside court 67, looking as if she might lose her breakfast. She was being attended by her courtier, who was mopping her brow. Haley, the girl Wentworth seemed keen on.

"Salmonella in the rubber chicken," said Abigail hoarsely.

"Why are you even here? We must adjourn and get you home to bed."

"No. Can't show weakness. Kroop will lynch me if he misses his date with destiny. I'm waiting for legally prescribed narcotics to kick in."

Ire at Stoney faded in the face of his learned friend's distress. "The main course was chicken?" He supposed it would be too much to hope the supplier was Chip O'Malley.

"No, almost. *Canard à l'orange.* Rubber duck."

"Your tainted bird, I would imagine, was shared by others?"

"I don't know who." She put a hand to her stomach, fought off a minor tremor.

"I think we should call it a day."

"Never surrender. I'll see how far I can go."

"Who do we have?"

"Florenza's maid. Then Rashid. Donat LeGrand is in the building, with counsel."

"Silent Shawn?"

"No, bigger."

Arthur had no chance to ask who; she went off quickly to the ladies' room.

A reconciliation of sorts was underway between Cud and Felicity, who was holding his hand as they took their seats. Irma Brown hadn't joined them today. Shawn Hamilton was at his usual station, tapping out a message on a Blackberry. And at the press table, newly nominated suspect Charles Loobie was grinning, as if at some private feat of cunning.

Abigail walked into court tightly, a cosmetics-enhanced complexion, a grim smile. Chekoff shambled into the witness box with a look at Arthur, seeking clemency. The jury took their places — no sour faces there except, oddly, from Tom Altieri, who was frowning rather severely at his former brother steelworker.

Arthur told Wentworth to take a break, pull the maid and the guard from the witness room, and sit them down to take their statements. As Wentworth gathered his papers, Kroop shambled in, his pallor battleship grey, a pained and ravaged look that clearly marked him as another luckless duck victim. Wentworth fumbled pen and notepad onto the floor as he stared at the judge as if at an apparition. He bowed and hurriedly left.

"Good morning, milord. Though I regret having missed last evening's grand banquet, may I add my own heartfelt applause to the many well-deserved tributes that I'm sure flowed as abundantly as the food and wine."

Kroop, knowing Arthur was digging at him, said something undecipherable and slid down in his chair, only his head and shoulders in view. A touch of red by his anthracite eyes, other colours too, a hint of olive green. He was a warrior though, a lion, proud, contemptuous of weakness. Arthur will see how long he lasts.

"Sergeant, let's see if we can pick up where we abruptly left off. I had asked you about a gentleman named Carlos Espinoza. You weren't sure if the name rang a bell. Have you given that any further thought?"

Chekoff glanced at Kroop, who had vetoed this line of inquiry yesterday. But the Badger seemed preoccupied with deeper concerns. "Yes, I ran that name through the system, and there's a match with a Mexican resident who has a record involving drugs."

"And I take it the system disclosed that back in 1992 he was the paramour of Ms. Florenza LeGrand?"

"In that year, a certain Carlos Espinoza and a certain Florenza LeGrand were jointly arrested in Mexico for drug trafficking."

Kroop seemed in no mood to joust this morning, so Arthur pressed ahead. "And the outcome?"

"The record isn't clear what happened to him, but we're checking on it. Ms. LeGrand was held for two weeks, then deported back to Canada."

"And what would you say if I suggested Mr. Espinoza was seen in Ms. LeGrand's company only last year?"

"Not much, because I don't know that."

"Assuming he was, indeed that he was her house guest, how would you suppose he entered Canada?"

"Illegally."

"Mr. Beauchamp!" Agony in Kroop's voice. "Assumptions, speculation, hearsay! This is a court of law, not a gossip mill."

That took a lot out of him, and he subsided, breathing heavily, tight as if holding back belches or farts.

Arthur felt a little sorry for him, sorrier for Abigail, who was holding her head with both hands. He changed tack. "Sergeant, it's fair to say, is it not, that Rafael Whynet-Moir was not the only local judge who died suspiciously, or at least mysteriously, last year?"

"Fair to say."

"In the course of your meticulous investigations, did you consider whether these deaths were in any way connected?"

"I didn't see how."

"What about Justice Warren Naught, who drowned off a dock last August 18, at Fishermen's Wharf?"

"Well, that's out of my jurisdiction, I don't know much about it except what I've been told."

Arthur was tempted to ask the ultimate hearsay question – *What were you told?* – to test Kroop, to see if he had any fight left, but it didn't seem cricket to take advantage of his suffering. It would be unjust to trigger an audible gas eruption – which, from the intense look in his eyes, seemed impending.

To give Wentworth more time in the witness room, he backtracked to the higher priority matter of Carlos Espinoza, directing Chekoff's attention to the news clipping from 1992 relating the dashing dealer's history of arrests and escapes. When he sought to file the story as an exhibit, Kroop gave no sign of response except for a slight bulging of eyes and tightening of face muscles.

"You're looking into whether Carlos Espinoza was recently in Canada?"

"Well, I can check with immigration, if you like."

"I'd appreciate that. Thank you."

Arthur sat and looked around for Abigail, but she'd obviously bolted for the loo. Haley looked anxious, seeming not up to the task of standing in. "Well?" Kroop said, irritated at the delay. "Well?"

Well was obviously what His Lordship was not, for he suddenly stood, holding his stomach, and sped to his chambers, emitting a clenched squeak from behind as he hurtled inside and slammed the door.

A spell of awkward silence, not even a titter from the bemused gallery. Cud Brown, out of the loop again, gestured to Arthur: something weird's happening, man, visit me, explain. Haley joined Arthur and asked, "What do we do?"

"I suggest, my dear, that we give thanks that we missed out on the canard à l'orange."

A few minutes passed, some jurors fidgeting; others, more attuned to the fact that judge and prosecutor were in extremis, suppressing ungracious joviality. Charles Loobie caught Arthur's eye, winked. It was hard to see him as a murderer, but if one accepts the wit and wisdom of the noted author Pomeroy, the perp is always the one you least suspect.

Arthur scanned the gallery for familiar faces. J. Dalgleish Ebbe had taken another day off to pursue his intense interest in this case. Presumably he had time off to compose judgments, and was playing hooky from that task.

The clerk took a call, then addressed the room. "His Lordship has advised that circumstances have arisen requiring us to recess until two p.m."

All to the good, Arthur decided. It would give him a chance to get on top of things – the case had been moving too swiftly, the witness list expanding. And there was the matter of Donat LeGrand's subterfuge to deal with, the hiring of April Wu, the adage-spouting private eye. LeGrand was somewhere on the grounds, along with his counsel. A big name, Abigail said.

He turned to Shawn Hamilton. "Take me to your leader."

Though still in his gown, Arthur followed him outside, toward Robson Square, past its skating rink, where young couples were gracefully swirling, and across the street into the

lobby of a boutique hotel. Shawn's only words en route were
to confirm he'd been at Kroop's jamboree. "I had the salmon."

"Good choice." Appropriate, given he was on retainer to
federal Fisheries. Arthur's own firm, Tragger, Inglis, had
handled their prosecutions until the Conservatives began
rewarding their friends.

Shawn led him into an elegant penthouse suite. Donat
LeGrand was standing by an ersatz fireplace, gas-powered and
brightly flickering. He acknowledged Arthur with a nod but
made no move to greet him, perhaps appalled on seeing
Arthur black-robed, like the angel of death. The tycoon was
tall, a thick thatch of greying hair, amply jowelled and
girthed. A dejected look.

More welcoming was the cherubic silver-haired gentleman rising from behind a tray of pancakes and eggs to his
full height of five foot six and extending not just a hand but
both arms in loving embrace. Gib Davidson, Q.C., the most
courteous and benign lawyer in the ranks of the bar. Such
qualities disarmed all who opposed him while his weapon of
choice, a polite stiletto, made them cautious. "King Arthur,
the ground shakes whereon he walks." He backed off a step,
examining him. "Where have you been hiding, in a health
club? My God, the years have treated you well."

"More true of you than me, Gib. How a man keeps such
robust health when he never stops eating is beyond me. But
who else do we have aiding in this cabal?" Not that he
needed to ask: the Kowloon Mata Hari herself, April Fan
Wu, perched delicately on a lounger. "Ah, so you didn't flee
the country, my dear?"

"Once on a tiger's back, it is hard to alight, Mr. Beauchamp."

He couldn't help but smile.

"Let's hope the tiger will have less bite after he hears me
out," said Gib, "Then he will either make a meal of the lovely
Ms. Wu or offer clemency. Would any of you mind if Arthur
and I have several minutes?"

At the door, LeGrand finally took Arthur's hand, saying, "My pleasure, sir, and I'm deeply sorry," then led April and Shawn out.

Gib took a plate of wafers and blue cheese and a bowl of almonds to a couch, sat it on his lap, kicked off his shoes, rested his feet on a glass-topped table, and patted the seat beside him. Arthur took it.

"Nice cut, *très distingué*, as Roberto might say. Still using him? That's his British Ambassador, isn't it? There's coffee, sodas. Anything? Almonds?"

"Lost my appetite after seeing the casualty list from Kroop's banquet."

"Damn, I'm glad I missed that. There's a rumour someone tried to poison the old bugger."

"A gross canard. Okay, Gib, what is the game we're playing here?"

"Face the music."

"Play a few bars."

He took a breath. "In the mid-1970s, Donat LeGrand was negotiating port fees for lucrative routes from Vancouver to the Far East, and he spent a lot of time in exotic places. One was Bangkok. That's where Florenza LeGrand was conceived of the loins of Donat and his . . . lover? Concubine? Call girl? Who knows."

This music, if not the food of love, was food for scandal, an explosive one. Gib nodded, as if in response to Arthur's astonishment.

"He didn't abandon her. Give credit to Thesalie too, Donat's wife. She forgave – not because of possible stigma, but from her good heart. Lovely, decent woman. Shy. I didn't feel she should be stressed by coming here; hope you agree."

Arthur nodded. Gib had a subtle way of extorting agreement.

"Mrs. LeGrand consented to her husband bringing the young woman to Canada, on maternity leave, as it were.

Given an apartment, an allowance, sent to a well-endowed clinic to have her child, then quietly returned to a comfortable job with LeGrand's Bangkok office. Meanwhile baby Flo was adopted by both LeGrands. No papers exist to prove she's his bastard child. Thesalie LeGrand was barren, poor thing – and they spoiled their sole heir. Let her go wild. And she grew up believing, despite the golden skin and the Orient in her eyes, that she was conceived in their bed."

"I have a feeling I'd rather not be hearing this. And made to feel responsible if it comes crashing down."

"Devastating for Mrs. LeGrand especially. Such a gracious lady. And despite his sins, Donat, too, has shown nobility, wouldn't you say?"

"What are you trying to sell?"

"First, let me plead the case of other suspects. I don't know what Silent Shawn knows – he won't tell even me – but Donat LeGrand says he personally engineered the hiring of April Wu. Shawn was just a mail drop."

"And Ms. Wu was planted in my office to find out if we knew anything about Flo's provenance."

"Ah, still the old silver fox. Nothing lost upstairs but a little off the top." Munching contentedly on almonds. "Yes, indeed, that clever young beauty was hired to find out whether you'd uncovered a shameful thirty-three-year-old secret. And now you know it. It took some effort to persuade my clients that Arthur Ramsgate Beauchamp would be the last person in the world, the *last* person, to inflict pain on such an upstanding, charitable couple. Training programs for the destitute in the Third World, that's where his major contributions go, seventy million at last count. The cheese is a delightful Cambozola. Give it a go."

Arthur dutifully nibbled. "The story going the rounds is he was also charitable to the less deserving."

Gib grinned. "Right. Whynet-Moir. Two million dollars in July of 2006 upon his promise to marry Florenza. With an expectation of two million more after the vows. Cash. All under a pretense of anonymity, the funds sent to a Bahamian bank. More almonds?"

"No thanks."

"Reform her, that was the idea. Marry her off to the handsome, cultured, top-ranked lawyer high on the short list for a judgeship. Under whose steady, nurturing hand, Flo would finally blossom from twenty years of painful adolescence into womanhood and take on her intended role as a priestess of high society."

"July 2006, you said?"

"Two months before Raffy got the nod from the justice minister." He drew a sheet from a briefcase. "Donat's sworn affidavit. It will attest that he had no knowledge the money was to be used to buy a judgeship." Before offering it to Arthur, he said, "In trade for this, all we ask is that you not break confidence over Florenza's maternal origins. Deal?"

"Deal."

26

THE MAID, THE MAJOR, AND THE MEXICAN

"*Here he comes,*" *someone said. Then a hush as Chief Inspector Chance stepped into the circle. The room had been cleared of all but sheriffs, lawyers, and court staff. The death grimace on Kroop's face, the risus sardonicus, the pungent smell of curry provided all the proof he needed. Strychnine. Who here had motive . . . ?*

Wentworth jumped as the door opened. A sheriff peered into this cramped, dark interview room. "You wanted to see Mr. Vogel?" Who was standing there in a tractor cap, chewing on a toothpick, looking sour, as if expecting the worst. Stealing up behind him, Philomène Rossignol, not looking too anxious to resume her interview. Wide-eyed, elflike, barely past her teens, she'd been so nervous with him she looked like she might pee her pants, which is maybe why she rushed away to the washroom.

He asked her to wait, sat the old rancher down, told him he had news, good news.

Vogel didn't show any reaction as Wentworth, blushing at his own exaggerations, explained how he'd entered into protracted negotiations after learning Clearihue had been felled. Played hardball, refused to settle for partial victory. With a modest shrug, he explained that Clearihue's counsel had finally thrown in the towel. He was a bit disgusted with himself, but he'd watched how top guns like John Brovak enhanced their fees. "I'm going to try to get something extra for the insult too."

Nothing from Vogel. For a long time. Finally came the dawn. "He got his nut clobbered, Clearihue?"

"I'm afraid so."

"All them years going to church are paying off. You mean I won? You saved my ranch?"

"The whole megalith."

"Well, I'll be darned. Mr. Chance, soon as I set eyes on you, I knew you was a fighter. You're the champ. Now I guess I got to pay a fancy bill, and that's fair. But when you get something for that there insult, you buy yourself a ticket to Hundred Mile House and come on up and spend the weekend at Vogel Ranch. We'll put on a celebration like you never believed, Joy and Penny and Lucy and me and you."

Wentworth tried not to stammer. "Paperwork, there'll be paperwork. I'll call you when it's done."

He ushered Vogel to the door, not finding it easy to suppress visions of grateful cherry-cheeked granddaughters snuggling him around a fire. Life looked better, he sensed a turning point, improving prospects. Look at the way Haley has been coming on to him, earthy, jasmine-smelling Haley who liked to brush her breasts against him.

Philomène entered the room tentatively, a frightened fawn. She must have had anxiety bred into her in Haiti, fear and distrust of authority, of lawyers – Wentworth didn't know how to make her relax. Her English was maybe okay for household chores, but so far the session had been hard work.

What he'd learned so far was she'd arrived for work shortly after seven on Sunday, October 14, after spending the night with her boyfriend. She identified herself to the constables on duty but was unsure why they were there, thought at first there might have been a break-in. Or a rowdy party, because in her suite, she found men's toiletries strewn about, the bed in disarray, her stuffed animals tossed on the floor beside a mystery backpack. Without really thinking, she wiped everything down, gathered used linen, towels, washcloths, and later threw them in the wash.

She'd found nothing of Florenza's, no handbag, brush, comb, lipstick, underthings. Still, Wentworth assumed that the lovemaking had progressed from steam room to bed, given all the disorder. No bottles full or empty. No copies, signed or otherwise, of *Liquor Balls* or *Karmageddon*. She trashed some cigarette butts that were in a soap dish, a couple on the floor.

It wasn't until she started in on the main house that she realized Donat LeGrand and his medical-legal advisers had set up camp there, but no one stopped her, and she just carried on cleaning until Chekoff showed up.

"Okay, Philomène, try to relax and let's finish this." Wentworth tried to warm her up with a smile, but that didn't seem to work. "I want to ask you about a man named Carlos Espinoza."

Had she met him, heard of him? No, monsieur. A helpless look. He asked her to recall January 9, a Wednesday, six weeks ago – when Brian had paid a visit to Château LeGrand.

"That day, I do not work. All that week."

Why? Because Florenza had given her that week off. Which seemed too coincidental.

He learned that Donat, not Florenza, had asked Philomène to stay on after Whynet-Moir's death. She didn't have a whole lot of work: Flo became a recluse, cut all ties – no more dinner parties, no social occasions at all, no visitors unless you count father, mother, Silent Shawn, and the occasional pizza delivery person.

"Did she have *any* visitors?"

"I think she has like to be alone with her computer or TV or books, magazines. She swim, maybe, sometimes, and drink a lot."

Wentworth dug the opal ring from his briefcase.

"Recognize this?"

"It belong Madam LeGrand, her favourite ring."

On his way to fetch Rashid from the witness room, he checked around for the boss. No sign of him. Down below, in the great hall, he could see Cud coming in after finishing a cigarette, his girlfriend, the wannabe poet, hanging on his arm.

He found a clutch of court staff gossiping by the locked courtroom door. Prognoses for the chief varied. He's up and raring to go, said one deputy. Still leaning over a toilet bowl, said another. He'd irately sent a doctor packing, the clerk confided.

The witness room was much grander than the cramped interview room, and ten times as comfy as Wentworth's flat. Soft chairs, waxed tables, reading lamps, magazines, tiled bathroom. But its population was totally depleted, except for Rashid. Astrid Leich had been excused until tomorrow.

He sat and opened his briefcase, drew out his pad as Rashid, neatly dressed, straight-backed, sat defensively, hands flat on the table, as if steeling himself for a form of light torture. Bengali, eight years in Canada. "Retired major, sir, third division, India Army, sir." Each *sir* exploded like a pistol shot.

He and Heathcliff the dog had been doing the day shift at the gate since mid-October, a four-month tour, noon to eight, defending against the curious and the prying press. "The usual riff-raff, sir."

Florenza had rarely left her luxurious prison, though he'd heard from the night guard she'd been whisked away occasionally by taxi or limo service, but never for long, never past midnight.

When Wentworth dropped Carlos's name, he cleared his throat. "I am under orders, sir."

"Excuse me? What orders?"

"I could lose my job, sir."

"Rashid, you are under subpoena, you have no choice."

"I understand, sir, but my instructions are clear."

"Exactly who instructed you?"

"The lady of the house. Mrs. LeGrand."

"Well, I'm countermanding them. She's a civilian. I am an officer of the court."

That seemed to work because after a few moments he took a deep breath and said, "Yes, sir."

Wentworth finally drew from him that a gentleman of pleasant manners and fine taste in dress, whose first language was Spanish, was Florenza's house guest for a week shortly after New Year's.

"Carlos Espinoza – that might have been his name?"

"We were not formally introduced. I heard him addressed as Carlos."

And he was there January 9, at the time of a sneak visit by a man who fit Pomeroy's description – especially the twitching and the glinting eyes. But the account was both confusing and questionable.

"He gave madam his card and telephoned London to confirm he was a British tabloid reporter. Oh, it was quite a scene, even the neighbour came out to watch."

"Ms. Leich?"

"From her balcony. The famous actress herself."

As best Wentworth could make out, this occurred about where Whynet-Moir had gone over the railing. Pomeroy's cellphone was seized. Carlos disappeared into the house. But then things settled down – Rashid didn't hear much conversation, but ultimately Flo invited the man inside. "I was disappointed that she would grant an interview to this riff-raff, sir,"

Then, several minutes later, Carlos hurried out, waving off Rashid when he offered to take his bags. "He said, 'You've never seen me, amigo.' A taxi came for him."

Soon after, Flo told him to return to his post at the gate. Brian stayed in the house another hour.

"What do you suppose they were doing?"

"I am not able to answer that, sir."

⚖

Wentworth found the gallery outside court 67 deserted except for a lone reporter at her cellphone and Felicity and Cud on a settee, she scribbling and he glowering, arms folded. "I'm outside, doing a burn, I come back, and everyone's AWOL. If there was a bomb threat, nobody told me. I think I got a right to know what's going on."

Wentworth didn't admit he was equally in the dark, and sidled up behind the newswoman. ". . . adjourned for the day, according to the clerk of the court. Also stricken is the chief prosecutor, Abigail Hitchins, who was seated with Chief Justice Kroop at the head table, along with two appeal judges, both of whom have also taken ill . . ."

Cud grunted, "Gotta hear it on the fucking radio news. I'm tired of being ignored."

Wentworth asked, "You seen Mr. Beauchamp?"

"Who's he? Oh, I remember, my *mouthpiece.* Who promised to go balls out to get me off."

"Where's your mum?"

"She had to get back to her waitress job. We managed to scrounge up a bus ticket."

Wentworth assumed there'd been a scene; three's a crowd. "Why don't you and Felicity go have lunch. Then come to the office, and I'll start prepping you for the stand."

"Is *melancholy* spelled with a *c* or a *k*?" Felicity asked.

Arthur wasn't in the barristers' lounge, but here was Haley, by herself, almost as if she was waiting for him, bright and eager, "Hey, looks like we've got some free time."

"I wish."

"Oh, come on. What about that drink? Maybe over lunch?"

Did he dare charge the firm? He was already over his monthly spending allowance. "Uh, sure, why not. By the way, where's Arthur?"

"Oh, he said to tell you he was splitting for Garibaldi by float plane, he'll be back in the morning." Tomorrow, Friday, the trial's most crucial day. A mini-holiday, as if he didn't have a care in the world.

She boldly took his arm as they crossed the street to the El Beau Room, packed with lawyers refuelling for the afternoon or making loud, insincere noises about the food-poisoned judges and their rotten luck. John Brovak was with his co-counsel for Morgan and Twenty-one Others, all getting into the juice, jabbering and laughing. Loobie was there too, mooching off them.

Haley started to come on like gangbusters after her second $9.50 Mai Tai, leaning close, squeezing his hand, posting a little air kiss before forking the breaded trout filet ($19.75) into her mouth and hinting she was available "all afternoon," for what she didn't say, but he could guess. She was seated across from him, so footsies à la Florenza weren't on the menu. He felt an unbearable tingling in his groin, wondered about condoms, about whether he should drop some loonies into the washroom dispensing machine.

Meanwhile, he sipped his lager, making it stretch, and made nervous small talk. "Looks like the trial will spill over to next week. So much for the chief getting his Order of Canada on Monday."

"Yeff," she said, masticating her pan-fried potatoes.

"Let's see, we have the guard and the maid tomorrow, and then the two star witnesses. Maybe Donat LeGrand too, I don't know what Mr. Beauchamp wants to do with him. He's under subpoena, he's supposed to be in court, but I haven't seen him."

"Your guy going to take the stand?"

"That's up in the air." He wasn't going to give anything away. "The summing up to the jury, that's another half day. Mr. Beauchamp usually likes to go on for about an hour, he averages out at just over sixty-eight minutes. The judge's charge, that's another couple of hours."

"I'm pooped. Abigail really keeps you running."

Wentworth hadn't noticed her doing any running. "How is she?"

"Pulling through. She'll be back in action tomorrow. Let's not talk about it, we'll go off our food." There seemed no prospect of that, she was looking at the dessert menu. "We should go for a walk after; it's stopped raining. Hey, we could go by my new digs, I'm up on the nineteenth, great pocket view of English Bay."

Gazing upon her plump, freckled flesh, Wentworth was just about ready to put off his interview with Cud in favour of a hot and sweaty payoff for this expensive lunch. But now John Brovak swaggered over with his whisky soda, straddled a chair backwards, close to Haley, and called for drinks all around.

"Join me in a toast to Madam Justice Rottweiler, whose absence from the appellate bench due to last night's swanky fowl has given us a day to recuperate from her savage mauling." He was typically loud and windy after too many drinks. "She's been ambulanced to St. Paul's. We can only pray for a lengthy recovery. How's the Badger?"

"Still barricaded in his chambers," Wentworth said.

"Guy's got a constitution of carbonized steel. He'll be the last man standing." The waiter placed another lager, another Mai Tai, and another Scotch on the table. "Everything on my tab, Samson."

Wentworth now realized he should have gone for the eight-ounce tenderloin instead of a salad, maybe he'll make amends with the honey-almond pie.

"And who is this stunning creature? Can't be your sister, she's too good-looking."

Haley introduced herself before Wentworth had a chance. "I'm *so* pleased to meet you, John. I've heard *so* much about you."

"Nothing good, I hope."

"All bad."

What were they doing, flirting? On Wentworth's watch?

"Hey, kid, I met Arthur in the locker room." Brovak always called him kid, it was demeaning. "He said to give you this."

A manila envelope with a three-paragraph affidavit sworn by Donat LeGrand. Wentworth reviewed it, hoping he wasn't showing his astonishment. Two healthy donations to a secret account, Whynet-Moir's, to which, presumably, the saintly Jack Boynton had access. He excused himself, found a quiet alcove, dialed Arthur's number.

His grandson Nick answered. "I'll call him, he's out on the dock, we're getting ready for a fishing trip." Wentworth pondered his boss's audacity: a humungous trial and he takes time off to fish.

Arthur came on. "Wentworth, I meant to call, got bogged down with a little crisis here."

Wentworth didn't ask, suspected a ruse – he was struggling with a little loss of faith in the boss. He briefed him on his interviews with the maid and guard, Arthur listening politely but with a hint of restiveness. "Yes . . . yes, well, that sounds excellent."

"What am I supposed to do with LeGrand's affidavit?"

"Ah, yes, the affidavit. You might fax me a copy while I ponder how to handle the matter."

"How the heck did you get hold of it?"

"It's a payoff for releasing LeGrand from his subpoena and keeping silent about certain family difficulties. Enough said for now."

Wentworth had to be satisfied with that. "Okay, what's the fax number?"

"I'm not sure, I think it comes through Margaret's computer . . . Never mind, I'll phone you from the general store – I'm stopping there to pick up my mail, you can fax it there." Shouting: "I'm on my way, check to see if the silver spinner's in the bait box. Oh, Wentworth, one more thing. Do another run-through with Cudworth, that'll give you something to do with all this lag time."

"I've already set that up."

"Good, good, you're right on the ball. Get the full version this time, he's had long enough to think about it. If it sounds halfway credible we might go with it. But he's a loose cannon, he could sink his own ship." Shouting again: "Make sure the reserve tank is full!" Back on the line: "Sorry, Wentworth, things are a little hectic right now. Some important, ah, family business."

Like the business of fishing? Wentworth sought assurances that Arthur would return on time tomorrow, then ruefully disconnected. The boss must figure the trial's in the bag – doesn't he worry about Astrid Leich? Maybe if you've won 83.5 per cent of your trials, you stop giving a hoot.

He returned to the table to find Brovak making a big deal of signing the chit, rising, helping Haley on with her coat. "Oh, Wentworth," she said, "we were just going for a little stroll. Why don't you join us?"

Wentworth read the insincerity of that invitation, and his heart sank.

"Yeah, kid, why don't you come along?" Brovak said. "Unless you got too much to do."

"I'm overwhelmed, but thanks for the thought." That little sardonic edge was as much as he could muster. As they slipped away, he stood there dazed, jilted at the altar, helpless, foolish, cuckolded, and he stumbled off to the bar and ordered a rye and ginger, amended that to a double. He pictured Haley waddling into court a couple of decades from now, a victim of overeating, spreading hips, ponderous breasts.

I've heard so much about you. What a sleaze. Brovak too, they don't call him the Animal for nothing. Thinks he's God's gift. No taste in women.

He gulped his drink, made a face. "Same again." He knew better than to seek solace in drink, even a couple made him spinny, his stomach queasy, but he needed courage, however false, to get through this abysmal day.

As he fumbled for his wallet, a man drew beside him, stilled his arm, threw some bills on the table. "My treat, young fellow." Judge Ebbe, J. Dalgleish Ebbe, maybe a little liquored up himself with his flushed complexion and the way he slipped climbing on the stool. "Delighted to stand a drink for counsel doing such a meritorious murder." He leaned close. "Scum. The deceased, in my respectful opinion, was scum."

Wentworth thanked him for the treat, but felt contrary, the alcohol making him ornery. "You have any hard facts on that, Judge?"

"Aside from the fact that the dearly departed and the equally late and unlamented Jack Boynton were undoubtedly locked in an unholy embrace, no. The more notorious fact is that they were as corrupt as untreated sewage."

"Whynet-Moir's death had something to do with corruption?"

"Indubitably."

"There's a lot of people with motive."

"One should not be surprised."

Wentworth might not have probed further, but the rye had combined with the gall of feeling dumped. He tossed back his drink, shocked himself by saying, "Would you be surprised if your name came up, sir?"

Ebbe jerked back. "What are you suggesting?"

"Well, your animust . . . animosity to Raffy is pretty well known."

Ebbe reared back. "I *beg* your pardon."

Wow, he was taking major affront. But Wentworth was in too deep to pull back. "Well, ah, we wouldn't want to make any wrong accusations in court, Judge, so if we knew where you were on October 13 . . ."

"Why, you impertinent prick!"

Heads turned. The bartender was advancing. Wentworth slid off his stool, focused on the nearest exit, found his way outside, took several deep breaths, and tried to walk it off along the harbour to Gastown.

⚖

Inspector Chance looked down at the stiff with a world-weary smile. Many had motives to lace the chief's buttermilk with strychnine, but only one had a cold killer's heart. "In your insane lust for a high court judgeship, Judge Ebbe, you have been thwarted again. Take him away . . ."

Screaming guitars from below sliced through his throbbing head like an executioner's blade. Blood'n'Guts in rehearsal for tonight's opening. He'd looked in on them, unshaven brutes in black leather. Even the pigeons were fleeing, seeking sanctuary across the street on the hoardings of the Olympics 2010 renewal project.

How was he going to survive the upcoming hours with his balky client? Cudworth was on his way, he'd called five minutes ago, complaining, where the fuck had Wentworth been, he must've called ten times. Leaning over the Burrard Inlet seawall was where he'd been, hoping someone might come along and nudge him over. To join what was left of his stomach.

He should pack up, go home to Fort Nelson, open a traffic ticket practice, escape from this firm with its sweatshop pay and bullying prima donna partners. It had seemed so magical when he signed on to article here, the baddest, boldest criminal law firm in town.

He checked his e-mails. The first message: "Chip O'Malley is a clucking chicken plucker." A photo of fat, immobile birds in tight cages. Electoral spam, infiltrating in-boxes, maybe even address books. Crudely adolescent, one rhyme short of obscenity. He'd heard these were going out all through the province, mostly to well-to-do businessmen, lawyers, other professionals.

His bottle of Zap jiggled with the vibrations from the Gastown Riot, an incessant bass beat like someone was pounding his chest with a hammer. The entire office resounded.

Oh-oh, an e-mail from Brian Pomeroy. "Private and Confidential" in the subject line, then: "Another judge will die." Why was Wentworth the undeserving recipient of this information? He had an image of Brian hunched over his keyboard bug-eyed on withdrawal drugs, plotting his next death. He shook his head, refusing to be drawn into Pomeroy's unreal world.

Here was an e-mail from Jobson, Clearihue's lawyer, an attachment setting out the terms of their offer. Wentworth looked over it, but didn't have the resilience to respond to it now.

A screech of guitar as he answered the intercom line. "I'm going to have a breakdown, do something, for Christ's sake!" The receptionist was near the stairwell, got the brunt of the noise. He should serve a writ for noise nuisance, an injunction, but how would he find time? "Mr. Beauchamp's on the line."

"Afternoon, Wentworth. I'm at the store and ready for your fax . . . Could you turn down your radio?"

"It's a heavy metal band downstairs." He had to shout. "How's the, ah, crisis?"

"Can't talk about it on the phone. Nothing for you to worry about. I'll call you this evening to give you my arrival time."

Wentworth wrote down the number, the general store on Garibaldi, then banged out a cover letter, scanned LeGrand's one-page affidavit, faxed both pages. The receptionist buzzed him to tell him she's had it, she's out of here. Also, Mr. Brown had arrived.

Wentworth looked numbly up as Cud entered, pulling off his poncho, impatient and sour. "You think you got some time for me, counsellor?"

Wentworth rose wearily, led him to a chair. Cud's sour beer breath threatened to induce another bout of nausea.

Another howl from below. "Shit, I'm gonna pop a drum," Cud said. Now a yowling, amplified voice over squawking guitars. Cud propelled himself up. "What kind of ape-fest is going on down there?"

He strode out before Wentworth could warn him that those guys *were* apes. He dialed Jobson, might as well get it done.

The lawyer sounded cheery. "Got my note? What do you say we wrap it up and put this sucker to bed?"

Wentworth was tempted to let it go at that, forget the $30,000 insult Arthur wanted him to push for. But this guy seemed anxious. He took a deep breath, tried to sound on top of things, assertive: Vogel had shelled out heavily for his first lawyer, Vogel's case was unassailable, victory was assured should they go to court, with taxable costs and punitive and aggravated damages. Throw in $40,000, save half a million.

In background, he could hear shouts from downstairs. Drums and electric guitars were stilled.

"No can do. I'm rather disappointed, Mr. Chance, we've been overly generous."

A curse-enhanced tirade from Cud. Somehow this emboldened Wentworth. "I look forward to going to trial then, Mr. Jobson."

No immediate response. From below, scuffling, more shouts.

Finally, curtly: "I'll get back to my people. But I doubt . . . Maybe we can sweeten it a little, ten or twelve."

"I'm sorry, Mr. Jobson, but my principal very strongly advised me not to take less."

"Your principal?"

"Arthur Beauchamp has taken an interest in the case."

Another long silence, punctuated by a crash in the Gastown Riot, more scuffling, a twang of strings. "I might be able to recommend, say, fifteen, twenty."

"Can't see our client accepting that, after all he's been through . . . but, what the hell, maybe we can split it down the middle. Thirty."

"I'll get back to you, Mr. Chance." Sullen, but Wentworth knew he had it in the bag. The hell with Haley, he'll surround himself with grateful granddaughters. Joy and Penny and Lucy.

A wild clanging of cymbals and a fierce ripping sound, possibly a boot going through a bass drum. Then golden silence.

Cud strolled back in, sweating heavily, brushing himself off. A wide red welt on his cheekbone, the collar torn on his grey flannel shirt, and an obviously skewed back. He sat, working his shoulder muscles. "Okay, Woolworth, where were we?"

27

JUST THE FAX, MA'AM

Arthur whipped Wentworth's fax from the machine before Abraham Makepeace had a chance to study it and was punished with a sour, offended look. He covered the two pages with his arm as the postmaster passed him a box. "Here's some books you must've ordered, and this here's an open letter from the Liberal candidate, most of the rest is bills and flyers and stuff. Be careful of this one, says you're eligible to win a million dollars, could be one of those lottery scams."

As Makepeace grudgingly doled out the mail, Arthur found himself squeezed against the counter by Nelson Forbish, peering over his shoulder. "Nelson, you're squashing me."

"Well, I can't see, you've got your elbow right on the last paragraph." His heft caused Arthur to give way, and before he could retrieve the fax, Nelson's camera flashed on it. "Is this for real? Whew. It's the smoking gun, you got them on the run. Four million, is that what he paid the judge? Who's this from?"

The cover page had fluttered to the floor, and Nelson went down on his knees to photograph it too.

"Blast it, Nelson, give me that camera, this is not for public consumption." He swiped at the camera, but Nelson clutched it to his chest.

"Maybe you heard of freedom of the press, Mr. Beauchamp? It's right there in our Charter of Rights, at the top of the page."

This was as close as Nelson ever got to sarcasm. He was still on his knees, struggling to rise.

Arthur stooped to pick up the page. "I'm warning you, Nelson, this is a very delicate matter."

"I got my story." He gripped the counter, pulled himself up with a groan. "Now you made me hurt my back." Before Arthur could protest further, he squeezed through the doorway, out to his ATV.

A minor calamity, because his next edition wasn't due for a week. At any rate, the LeGrand camp obviously expected the matter to go public, though in a carefully engineered way, not on the front page of the Garibaldi *Island Bleat*.

A crisis of far greater moment was brewing, a possible electoral disaster, and that is what had whisked Arthur to Garibaldi on this baleful Thursday. A tip from the cops, more particularly from Ernst Pound, by way of the constable's best friend, the fire marshal, as confided to the marshal's best friend, Reverend Al Noggins, who'd called *his* best friend, Arthur, just before noon.

The tip: RCMP investigators would be arriving on today's late ferry to interview a certain party thought responsible for the anti–chicken farmer spam that had invaded computers province-wide. That unnamed party resided on Potters Road, near its dead end – which was Blunder Bay.

Nick is helping with Margaret's campaign, handling the computer traffic or something. Nicholas Senior had spoken proudly, with no idea how his son was helping. The family computer wiz, brighter than anyone knew, off on a wild, illicit tangent. Arthur had felt a trembling, like a coming earthquake about to pull down the Beauchamp household and the entire Blake campaign.

In near-panic, he'd phoned Nicholas: he and his son were to lay low, speak to no one, Arthur was chartering a flight. He'd met them at his dock an hour later, Nicholas pale with worry, Nick distraught, fighting tears. They went fishing, or at least made a pretense of it, an hour of quiet, intense confession and confabulation.

Arthur had been dropped off at Hopeless Bay, he planned to walk home, to work out how to deal with the investigators. Was spamming illegal? Surely not. But maybe they found some criminal charge. Mischief. They'd want to examine Nick's laptop, maybe the phone records.

An alluring scent wafted from the lounge, addictive, fearsome. The house special, *café à la rhum*. A drink, a drink, my kingdom for a drink . . .

Arthur paid for some groceries, threw them in the pack with his mail. He knew he wouldn't be able to escape without passing a few moments with the locals, hungry to hear about the trial, the inside story, an exclusive. They wanted to believe in Cud, wanted assurances he'd been railroaded to protect powerful interests.

All in the lounge were wearing "Free Cud" buttons except for Stuffy Stankiewiczs, a contrarian heavy-equipment operator with a long-simmering grudge against the hero poet. Truculent when he had a few glasses, and he'd had more than a few.

"I ain't got nothing against you, Arthur," he said. "I know you got no use for Cud after what went on between him and your wife." He rose dramatically, paused at the doorway. "Jumping people's old ladies, that's his modus opera-andy, it's obvious the judge caught him boffing his wife, and Cud croaked him." He threw open the door, nearly tripped over his feet on his way down to his truck.

Arthur felt smothered by the heavy, shuffling silence. Finally someone said, "He don't count for spit, that assoholic."

"Hey, remember how Cud broke Stuffy's jaw outside the old Brig tavern?"

"He wasn't the transgressor, Stuffy was the transgressor, came at him with a tire iron."

"Shut him up for a while."

"Good old Cud."

As they prattled on about that scrap, the calumny about Cuddles and Margaret was buried as if never spoken. Arthur strove to maintain an unflustered façade, but his face muscles were tight. *After what went on between him and your wife.*

⚖

Arthur slung his pack on and headed morosely down Eastshore Road, still feeling humiliated by that ugly slur from Stankiewiczs. Forget it, he wasn't going to let it hobble him from mounting a zealous defence for Cudworth. That's not how lawyers must think.

He watched waves curl and flip on a roiling sea, a front quickly moving in, a light sprinkle of snow from the darkening sky. He'll have to drain the water lines. He'll phone Syd-Air, make sure their Friday schedule is in effect. "Can't leave Wentworth in the lurch," he mumbled. "Sounded a little harassed on the phone."

Here came Ernst Pound in his RCMP van, stopping, rolling down his window, an anxious look. "I've been sent to fetch you, Mr. Beauchamp. A couple of members from the telecom unit are outside your house with a search warrant. I told them given your prominent status they better not just walk in."

Arthur climbed in beside him, feeling a little unstuck. The investigators had got in earlier than expected, he hadn't yet armed himself for their coming, hadn't devised a strategy, a way of delaying things.

"I better give you a little heads-up, which I wouldn't except I'm pulling for Margaret and I don't want to see her chances hurt. Seems someone hacked into the Conservative Party address book, got their list of possible donors, big wheels, businessmen, accountants and doctors and law firms and the like, and that chicken plucker spam is coming from your house."

Arthur tried to collect his thoughts – they had a warrant, there was little wriggle room, they're not likely to buy any bluff.

As they pulled into his driveway, he craned to see if the *Blunderer* was tied up. No, just Icarus plummeting into the surf, a telling, dark metaphor. Stoney and Dog had actually finished a promised job, setting Icarus into a pedestal of lumpy cement at the tideline.

Then he saw the boat a couple of hundred metres out, putting into the bay. Nick gathering up rod and tackle, his dad at the stern, disappearing below, returning with binoculars.

Snow was falling harder, lightly coating a green sedan in the driveway. Two plainclothes officers, a young man and woman, rose shivering from the porch. The house was unlocked, they might have just walked in. It was a sign they were courteous, respectful.

Not umbrage but courtesy, even affability, was the right tool. Take a lesson from Whynet-Moir – *such a lovely host* – and brazen it out with charm. A broad smile and firm hand-shake extracted their names, Eloise and Matthew, corporals both, learned in the computer sciences, newly recruited to the telecom unit.

Before they could produce the warrant, Arthur said, "Please come inside, you look chilled to the marrow. Ernst, you as well, you can help set a warm fire."

"Naw, I got to run, Mr. Beauchamp, sure as shooting there's gonna be all sorts of problems with bald tires in the snow." He hurried off.

Arthur opened the door wide – nothing to hide here, folks – and ushered the two corporals into the parlour, then excused himself for the kitchen. "Would a hot cocoa go down well?" he called. "Though if you prefer, coffee or tea."

"Please don't go to any bother," Eloise called back. He imagined them scanning the room, seeking tools of the culprit's trade. The simmering of the kettle made it hard to hear their talk, but it seemed innocuous: the weather, concern over the ferry cancelling its run.

He looked outside – the boat was nudging the dock. But here was Lavinia at the window, calling: "Is freeze coming, you want I run taps like last time?"

Arthur slid the window up a few inches, spoke in a low, tight voice: "Tell Nick the chicken plucker police are here."

"Chicken . . ."

"Plucker. Go, right now. Tell them to stay clear." He didn't want them trooping in, unready, Nick blurting out something inculpatory.

Returning with three steaming mugs on a tray, he found Matthew crouched before the fire, enjoying the manly pursuit of blowing on lit tinder, while Eloise stared out at the clouds racing in. Being stuck on a storm-tossed rock in the Salish Sea seemed not a fancy they cared to entertain.

The fire took but was slow to warm the parlour, always the coldest room in the house, lacking baseboard heaters. Eloise, after hesitating, as if unsure if regulations allowed it, accepted Arthur's gift of a floppy sweater, draped it over her shoulders. "Front's coming in fast," he said. "Minus ten tonight, I heard. Last winter the power went out for nine days straight."

They silently sipped their cocoa. Through a window he could see Lavinia and the Nicks hurrying toward the woofer house.

"Now let's see if I can help you folks. Ernst mentioned something about the Internet. I'm totally bereft of computer skills, I'm afraid, so you'll have to fill me in."

Matthew explained they were acting on a complaint about political junk messages. Records of the Internet host had been obtained by warrant and the alleged offender traced to Blunder Bay. A charge under the Elections Act of unauthorized political advertising was under review, as was one of mischief involving theft and misuse of telephonic data.

Arthur had never heard of the latter offence, but doubtless it existed, buried in sub-paragraphs of subsections somewhere, and equally doubtless it would be full of holes. But the preferring of any charge would be damage enough.

"And who is the complainant?"

They looked at each other, and both spoke at once: they weren't authorized to say.

"A political organization maybe?" Chip O'Malley's campaign team, for instance. These officers must be aware that they were in the home of his opponent but seemed to regard the matter as too delicate to raise, and they remained mute, merely showed him the warrant.

Arthur studied it. A loophole! The warrant permitted a search of only Arthur's house, not the woofer house. "Oops, looks like you folks have a little problem. The phone line written down here, that's for the neighbouring dwelling, where we pasture our woofers. Young folk from overseas, constantly coming and going, Japan, New Zealand, Finland, all over the map. Well, looks like this warrant has to be amended. Bit of a nuisance, reckon it means another trip back and forth on that old tub of a ferry, if they don't cancel."

Eloise grinned as if to tell him she was seeing through his crafty spiel. "Well, let's see," she said, "next boat doesn't go till four-thirty, I reckon." Mimicking his folksy mannerism. "Guess we have a little time to sit around and jaw with you folks." She sipped her mug of cocoa, smiling, watching out the window as the Nicks jogged up the woofer driveway. Stow the bullshit, she was saying.

Arthur raised his hands in mock surrender, took a deep breath: "Okay, let's go about this another way. See that boy out there? That's my grandson, he's fourteen. Computers are his passion – as I'm sure they were for both of you at his age. My wife, as you obviously know, is a candidate in next week's federal byelection. She knew nothing about this, nor did I. Nick went tearing off on a secret frolic for which he meant no harm. He doesn't even live here but in Australia with his mother, my daughter, and he's on the cusp of returning there from an extended summer vacation. He's already missed school opening."

They nodded without expression. "What he did was out of affection for my wife, not malice. Maybe out of a rebellious spirit, but we were all rebellious at that age, weren't we? I don't have to tell you he can't be brought before the adult courts or that your mischief charge will be embarrassingly difficult to prove. I don't have to tell you that the Charter of Rights permits – indeed exalts – free political speech, and I don't have to tell you that the RCMP won't want to find itself in the inglorious position of seeming to take sides in an election campaign."

A blast of wind rattled the windows. The snow came in whirling gusts, no longer melting but caking the roofs of outbuildings, driveways, vehicles. The two officers were staring at each other again, neither daring to be the first to speak. Finally, Matthew said, "Wow, look at that snow. Guess there'll be a lot of cars scrambling to get off the island."

Eloise nodded, handed back the sweater, and rose to lead her partner to the door. "We'd better not miss that old tub of a ferry." For Arthur, a little wink, like a kiss.

⚖

It was an hour later, after lines had been drained and animals sheltered, that Arthur came into Nick's room and caught him teary-eyed on the bed, issuing directives to his humming computer.

"Everything erased?" Arthur sat down with him, propping himself up with a pillow.

"I'm doing a deep dig, cleaning out the register."

His dad had already talked to him, severe but sincere. Arthur suspected he was suppressing pride in his boy. And in truth it was quite a feat, despite the close call. One could only pray that the repercussions to Margaret's campaign would dissipate.

"Other officers might have mindlessly followed through. We were lucky."

"I'm sorry. I've been so stupid."

"You're too bright for your own good. That's a blessing, you'll need to scramble to pick up a few weeks of school."

Nick wiped an eye, shut down his computer. "It wasn't real hard to hack in to them. It was sort of an experiment, figuring out how spammers beat the system. I hate spam."

"Well, you'll never want for a job in cyberspace. Looking forward to getting back?"

"Yeah, but I like it here. I didn't at first. I guess I've been a real headache."

"We'll always welcome you back."

A smile came out of nowhere. "Lavinia told me the chicken fuckers were here."

⚖

All day, Arthur had fought off calling Margaret, not wanting to alarm her, to tell her about Nick's escapade – it would be too distracting, could put her off her game in the campaign's critical final days. But he decided to touch base after hearing on the news that the latest poll had her only a whisker behind O'Malley, two points.

He caught her canvassing in Porcupine Bog, so hoarse as to be barely audible.

"Arthur, I'd like you to come to the last all-candidates." On Saltspring Island, Saturday afternoon, half past one.

"I thought I made you nervous."

"I'm beyond nervous." He barely made out the next phrase: "I need you."

That caused a welling of feelings that for some foolish reason he couldn't translate into words. She *needed* him. The political recluse had been elevated several feet above the level of excess baggage. "Of course I'll be there."

He told her he'd stopped by the school, the advance poll, and marked a big fat X for a soon-to-be-sitting member of the House of Commons. He wanted to discuss the LeGrand affidavit with her, but she was being greeted by a voter. He shouted: "On to Ottawa." If it comes to pass, he'll tough it out, an act of love.

She had passed the phone to Eric Schultz. "Christ, I'm freezing out here. How is it your way?"

"We're battening down."

"This blow could help. Our vote's firm, we'll pull out ninety-five per cent. Socialist hotbed here in Porky Bog, but they're looking over our merchandise, they may be ready to board the bus. O'Malley is holding at thirty-five, Blake thirty-three, the rest fighting for scraps. That spam attack bled a lot of vote away, probably enough to . . ."

"The bleeding has stopped."

"How did you hear?"

"There was a police investigation, Eric. Someone filed an official complaint."

"Never thought they'd carry through. I bitched, I hollered. Find some kind of charge, I said, shut down that operation."

Arthur was speechless.

"You still there, Arthur?"

It was Schultz's turn to be at a loss when Arthur filled him in. Finally: "I don't know what to say."

"I didn't tell Margaret."

"Best that we do. Don't want her boobytrapped by some clever reporter." Soft profanities, he was flustered. "Any chance this will get a proper burial?"

"I'm hoping so, but it's probably all over Garibaldi."

"Christ."

"That's the bad news."

"There's better?"

"Eric, I'll ask you to deliberate long and carefully on this, but we now have a strong intimation of a corrupt payment to the office of the late justice minister."

His recital of LeGrand's affidavit produced a long whistle. "That clinches it. Keep this under your hat – it'll come out in Question Period tomorrow that the administrator of Boynton's estate has uncovered an account worth four million and change, untouched, that would normally devolve to his survivors. What's the best way to handle this? Tomorrow's Friday, a bad media day. Just before the election is best, Monday. Has to be released carefully, shouldn't come from us."

"It may be too late already." Arthur told him how he'd lost a free speech debate with Nelson Forbish. He got a laugh, Schultz in a spirited mood now.

"Better tell Mr. Forbish to keep mum."

"Not to worry, the *Bleat* comes out mid-week." Nelson had been known to put out special editions, single pages emblazoned "Extra!" but this weather promised to thwart such a plan.

⚖

The storm accelerated into the evening, yet another blizzard on the mild Pacific coast, weather patterns changing, hotter summers, capricious winters. Outside, the sound of a tree cracking under the weight, a leaner, an electric pop as a breaker snapped. Lights out.

Arthur fumbled his way to the candle bin, arrayed several on the dining room table, threw more logs on the fire. The Nicks and the woofers were out in that whirling snow, by the brick barbecue, preparing to grill steaks. They seemed content, in parkas and toques, laughing in the dusky light, tossing snowballs.

The phone lines were still open, so Arthur dialed Wentworth, who must be worried his general will be trapped here, Napoleon on the isle of Elba.

"I'm afraid we may be forced into a slight change of plan, Wentworth."

Just silence but for the sound of a gulp.

"Not sure I'll be able to fly in early tomorrow, the weather may not permit. I'll try for the ferry."

"That doesn't get here till noon."

"Right, so I'm going to ask you to cross-examine the maid and the guard. I think you're ready for that, and I can't comprehend how I could do a better job. Anyway, Kroop may need another day to settle his insides. If not, find a way to spin things out until I get there. I'm sure you'll do a rip-snorting job."

"Two witnesses aren't going to fill the morning."

"Oh, raise some argument or other, something that will get the old boy going. If nothing else works, feign illness."

"I *am* ill."

"I have complete faith in you, Wentworth. You've done admirably. Admirably."

"Are you sure, Arthur, because . . ."

"Any problems, I'm always right by the phone."

Arthur made tea and sat down with Virgil's great and ancient tome, and began to read aloud by the flickering light. "It is sweet to let the mind bend on occasion."

But he kept wandering back to his trial, fussing over it, even though there wasn't much he could do to ready himself for the final, vital witnesses.

One can't rehearse for Florenza LeGrand; it would be like rehearsing for the unknown. He wondered about her, her hints of narcissism, sociopathy. Did this daughter of a Thai concubine suspect her provenance? Was that at the root of her rebellion, a suppressed fury at her father's lies? A rebellion intensified by an artfully arranged marriage to a possessive dilettante? And thus a hick from the sticks became a murder weapon. But Arthur didn't want to believe Cud was a murderer . . . Or did he?

He was nagged by ignoble suspicions that none of his battery of suspects was guilty, that Cud actually did do the deed, recklessly, drunkenly, or deliberately, propelled by base motive, lust, greed, twisted notions of honour and deliverance. *Help me escape.* Had he answered Florenza's call while nearly senseless with drink?

And Astrid Leich, well, she'll probably identify Cud, and Arthur will have to loosen the clasps and buckles of her finger-pointing confidence. Such cross-examinations are best done raw, but he should devise tactics for Kroop, who will break all records for churlishness as the trial drags on through Monday, as he misses his day of glory.

Arthur hadn't told Wentworth that April Fan Wu was still in town, that he'd granted her absolution as part of his deal with Gib Davidson, but these matters were too tricky to be canvassed by phone. As was the matter of loosely wrapped Brian Pomeroy, from whom getting information was like prying bricks from a wall. What will the jury make of his outlandish visit to the LeGrand estate? They'll likely decide he was bonkers, the right conclusion.

Let it go. Seek solace in the *Aeneid.* The night had come, and weary in every land, men's bodies took the boon of blissful sleep . . . Soon he nodded off.

⚖

He awoke at daybreak, aroused by a winter wren fluttering about the bedroom, clawing at the window. He opened it wide to a blast of frigid air, and while waiting for the disoriented intruder to make its break, he jumped back into bed and worked at a turbulent dream set in a Roman arena. Familiar faces everywhere: LeGrand, Ebbe, Silent Shawn, and many more, a cast of thousands, all waiting for the lions to be loosed on Cud Brown. Arthur was disoriented – was this the right court, was he defending that frightened gladiator? Too late, a toga-swaddled jury roared their verdict. *Vae victis!*

Woe to the vanquished! Then the roaring faded, and there was only the clicking of a keyboard, a madman in the throes of creation . . .

The power was still out, so the day's toilette included longjohns, ski socks, and a bulky country sweater. Downstairs, the Nicks were by a crackling fire. He thought to warm himself there but realized they were discussing family issues, so he pulled on his boots. Odd that twitchy-nosed Pamela had not joined her fiancé here – maybe they weren't as serious about each other as Nicholas claimed. Arthur hadn't mentioned the filched Fargo, not wanting them to feel badly about having been conned out of it.

It remained very cold, but the wind had relented, and snow abated under a sullen sky. The pond would soon support a hockey team. A path of sorts had been tramped toward the woofer house, where he found Lavinia at a battery-powered radio, listening to the forecast: an Arctic front had settled in, a few more freezing nights expected. He called Syd-Air – they were vague about whether they'd be flying at all today. Wentworth was off-line, but Arthur left a message saying not to expect him early. The young man knew what to do.

The nine o'clock news came on. Power outages, traffic tie-ups, accidents. But then, from "our political bureau," came this: "Questions are being raised in Ottawa about an apparent gift of four million dollars from shipping magnate Donat LeGrand to the late Justice Rafael Whynet-Moir." Embellishing this account were references to the timing of payments, half down and half after Florenza's betrothal, an equivalent sum showing up – after Raffy was named to the bench – in Jack Boynton's Nassau account.

And who broke this story? Why, the editor of the Garibaldi *Island Bleat*, of course, who, determined to earn his pound of glory, had e-mailed his photos of the fax to multiple news agencies.

What set Arthur worrying was that Wentworth was mentioned as its sender. "Mr. Chance could not be reached for comment." No mention of senior counsel, though no doubt Charles Loobie and his cronies made efforts and drew blanks. Well, it's out, the entire bribery scandal, and the chips will fall where they may. Many of these will fall on Arthur, who now must bear the brunt of Kroop's wrath – the defence has contaminated radio-listening jurors.

He was about to ring Wentworth again, but here was a bald-tired flatbed sliding and slipping up the driveway, weighted down for traction with a rusting engine block, a snowmobile, a beat-up generator, and Dog. Arthur almost slipped on an icy patch as he rushed out to collar the defalcator.

"Heard you was here, and came right over," Stoney said, directing Dog to lug the generator off the truck. "Let there be light. A special service for my most valued client."

Arthur folded his arms, glared, waiting for him to come up with an improbable excuse for the missing Fargo: *I'm trying to solve a little drive-train problem.* Or possibly: *I traded her in for this here spiffy snowmobile.* Most likely: *She's now officially an off-road vehicle. She went off the road and down Hemlock Hollow.*

Stoney had the brass to turn toward sea-bound Icarus, saluting it. "What think you, bwana, of this magnificent display of local art? You oughta thank Dog too; he lugged umpteen bags of cement down there, hammered up the forms when the tide was almost up to his nuts."

"Thank you, Dog," Arthur said. "I know you're not consciously involved in this caper with the Fargo."

From the cab of the truck, a strong smell of reefer, accounting for the slowness of Stoney's reaction: "Now, this here generator rents out at only . . . Caper? Fargo? Am I being accused of something here?"

"Your act of being vastly affronted doesn't wash with me, Stoney. I want my truck."

"I am hurt, deeply hurt." He ploughed off to the garage, cleared a snowdrift from the door, managed to wedge it open. There was the yellow Fargo, gleaming, it had been washed.

"You mean *this* Fargo? The one I borrowed once to haul in the cement? The one me and Dog spent an hour washing?"

It was only later, when Arthur realized he'd forgot to challenge Stoney over the chattel-mortgaged Chrysler, that he rued having let him soak him for the generator.

28

A TRAGEDY OF JUSTICE

Wentworth held fast to one of the westbound lanes on Sixth Avenue, the tires of his Outback 310 spitting slush on his pants and boots. He was cold, his patched sheepskin jacket bringing little comfort, his feet and ankles sopping. Mindless of the traffic he'd backed up, he was finally forced into six inches of snow by an impatient driver. He stopped, wiped his goggles. Don't be a traffic fatality on this day of all days.

His dreams of glory were to be tested by a live audience this morning. Wentworth Chance gets his turn to show his mettle in swordplay with the chief justice – assuming he's good to go today. If he's still ill, another recess, giving the boss time to get back and ruin Wentworth's debut. But when weighed, his dreams were jokes, he was terrified of Kroop, terrified of screwing up – Arthur had *better* make it back, if not for Philomène and Rashid, then for Astrid Leich, next on deck. How long could he spin things out for?

What was he supposed to do with the LeGrand affidavit? Why had the boss cancelled LeGrand's subpoena? Also bugging him was that he blew yesterday's interview with Cudworth, who'd been a jerk, thinking he was wily, but just slippery, proposing unlikely scripts, none saleable. "I'll chew on it, give you a fresh draft in la *mañana*," he'd said as he walked to the door with a crooked back. "I got to get some painkiller."

The sidewalk had been cleared the next few blocks, so he risked a ticket, darting around pedestrians all the way to the Cambie Bridge, across it, then downhill to Gastown.

A sign behind the bicycle rack read, "The Gastown Riot is closed until further notice." A window cracked and taped. Inside, a custodian cleaning up, a guitar with a broken fretboard leaning against a broken chair, a bashed-in drum. Wentworth had worked in the office till ten last night, undisturbed. He'd even been able to take a nap, despite his fearful anticipation of this day.

The staff hadn't arrived yet, but Brovak was in the library, looking up law – a chore so rare that Wentworth gaped. Brovak was dressed in black, as if in mourning. The room smelled of stale cigar smoke, a stogie in the ashtray.

"Hey, kid, what happens to an appeal when one of the judges is rendered combat ineffective?"

"Like what, sick?"

"Bertha Rudweiler has gone to a better world. Acute salmonellosis complicated by choking on her upwardly mobile stomach contents."

"Oh, my God." Wentworth sat, feeling shaken, queasy. *Another judge will die.* Wentworth had read somewhere that mentally ill persons were often prescient. He shuddered. Another unnatural death of a judge unloved by the criminal bar. If the canard à l'orange had been poisoned, John Brovak was a likely suspect . . .

"I've still got two live ones on the panel."

"They'll have to start over. Section 13, Appeal Court Act."

"Dearie me, that'll take a year to set up. Now my poor lads must be released on bail. I hear the Badger is off the endangered list, kid. Watch he doesn't take you off at the knees; you're high on his hit list. Hey, that Haley, man, she wouldn't stop. Great view from her suite when you come up for air."

Brovak rose, groaned, reached for his stogie — he was having trouble moving, it looked like a severe hangover. When he lit up Wentworth began to hiccup.

The receptionist peaked in, with the mail and newspapers. "Wentworth, you've had several calls from the media."

"Later, I've got a zillion things." Hic.

"Maybe you want to look at this."

She left him the *Province*, with its loud, accusatory question: "Multi-million Bribe for Judgeship?" A subhead: "Parliament in Uproar." One photo depicted LeGrand's affidavit, another the cover page, legibly signed by one Wentworth Chance. The hiccupping accelerated. The enterprising editor of the Garibaldi newsweekly quoted Arthur as saying, "This is a very delicate matter."

He pulled a bottle of Zap from his pack, drank slowly. Ten seconds later, another hiccup.

Brovak yawned, limped to his sofa. "Put up the don't disturb; I need an hour's kip. When are you going to bring in some bread, kid? Pomeroy's five-star hospice is draining the general account, and I'm up to the knuckle with spousal payments." He closed his eyes.

Wentworth mentioned the Vogel receivable of $30,000.

"Maybe it's time to reconsider that raise you promised five years ago."

"We'll have a partners' meeting over it. Augie's winging in from Thailand today. Max won't be long behind."

"He's in Europe for the next three months."

"I'm on your side, kid, count on me." He rolled over, tucked a cushion beneath his head.

⚖

"One at a time, please. Yes, you, in the grey fedora." "Mr. Chance, can you tell us how you were able to trace the suspect?" "Pecker tracks, gentlemen. Next?" "Sedgwick, New York Post. Does it

bother you, sir, that you worked in the same office with this pervert?"
"It would be wrong for me to let personal feelings . . ."

The picture shattered as Wentworth, his hiccups coming like clockwork, pedalled around Nelson Street to the law courts entrance, where a pack of reporters was waiting. Maybe they won't recognize him in helmet and goggles, he'll try to slip past them. And he did, sneaking into the entrance hall. But then: "Yo, Wentworth." Charles Loobie.

"Pressed for time, Charles."

"One question: what's going to be your strategy when Kroop goes berserk?"

"Do I look worried?" Hic. When he was tense, like now, they sometimes went on for hours. Something about an over-sensitive glottis, a doctor had told him.

"I got a remedy for those," Loobie said.

"Tried them all."

"Stand on your head for two minutes sipping soda water through a straw . . ."

"Got to run." Wentworth had a remedy for Loobie. Imprisonment. Where was he on October 13? In the lounge he took some water down slowly. Thirty seconds passed. Hic.

In the locker room, he removed his wet trousers, borrowed an ill-fitting pair from the firm's locker. Pomeroy's; he recognized the gaily coloured suspenders. After robing, he made his way to gallery six, where a dozen firstcomers were lined up outside court 67 to stake claims on prime seats. The witness-room door was ajar, and he could see Abigail with Astrid Leich, who was saying, "Oh, yes, I'm quite certain . . ." Abigail, looking queasy, closed the door on him.

Haley was in an interview room with Florenza LeGrand, who was wearing tons of eye shadow, wrapped cellophane-tight in something she hadn't bought at Dress Mart. Gold locket, an emerald ring where once there'd been an opal. She was ignoring Haley, reading a glossy. Silent Shawn was in a corner chair, his thumbs hooked into his braces. "We're busy," he said.

Flo studied Wentworth's ill-fitting robes, looked down at where his pant cuffs ended above his ankles. "Cute outfit, Wentworth." She knew his name! She rose languidly, as if stoned, pulled her Gitanes from her bag, slung on her coat, and brushed past him, too close for comfort. He smelled something earthy, spicy, exotic.

Shawn rose with a groan and followed his client. "Bye-bye," Haley said icily, and turned to Wentworth, making like she was holding a pistol on him. "Kroop's back." She aimed, squeezed the trigger.

"I hope Brovak warned you about the diagnosis."

"What do you mean?"

"Scabies venerealis. Antibiotics don't help." Hic.

"I've got a remedy for those. Stick your head in a bucket of ice water and hold your breath for fifteen minutes."

He walked off. The perfect line would come too late, after he replayed the scene, recasting himself as master of the pointed barb. He could see Florenza below, leaving. She almost bumped into Cud and Felicity coming in. It looked like he said something to her as she paused to light up. She smiled, waved, floated down the street. Shawn watched through the glass, coatless, unwilling to test the weather outside.

Felicity, obviously in one of her pouts, overtook Cud at the top of the stairs, went straight to Wentworth. "He called her 'Goddess.' It was totally not cool, and embarrassing."

Cud shrugged from his poncho. "'Keep them guessing, Goddess,' that's what I said. A message. I'm saying, Hey, baby, we're in this together, let's pull together."

"She gave me this smirk."

"I'm sorry, but that lady and I share a little past, one hot night on the same wavelength; she reads me, I read her. Where's Arthur?"

"He asked me to handle a few minor witnesses until he gets here."

"No way, man, we hold everything off until he shows. You don't have the experience, Woodward."

"Oh, you are *so* insulting," Felicity said, and turned to Wentworth. "He doesn't mean that, honestly."

"No offence, but Arthur's the guy I personally hired. I'm wondering if he ain't taking this case serious enough. Maybe he's decided it's a duck shoot, he doesn't want the jury thinking he has to bust his ass over it. That how you see it?"

Wentworth answered with a hiccup, a stray one. They were letting up.

"I use a tablespoon of Alka-Seltzer with honey," said Felicity, who'd morphed into a better humour. "Oh, you should've been with us last night, Mr. Chance, when the power went out. Cud had to do a reading by candlelight in the Cinco de Mayo Bar and Grill. It was, like, transcendental."

"I had the place rocking." Cud took Wentworth's arm and drew him away. "Let's try this on for size. When I hear Raffy scream, I jump out of bed, rush outside in time to see the perp run across the lawn, through the rose bushes, or whatever they've got, and over the wall. But I catch a look at him, and he resembles me, same brawny build, which is why Astrid picked me out in the lineup, right? The Mexican guy, Carlos, what's his complexion, could he pass?"

Wentworth showed him a picture he'd copied from the Net last night, Carlos Espinoza handcuffed to a Mexican cop, both of them grinning at the camera. Bronze-skinned, thin-waisted, an unbent, aquiline nose, jet black hair. Cud's hair was light, almost sand-coloured.

Cud frowned over the picture, disappointed. "Well, there were only a few outdoor lights. That neighbourhood snoop, how was she gonna see details? Let me continue. I figure I'll jump in a car and follow him. And I zoom out in the Aston Martin just in time to see him running down the street. And

I . . . maybe I slip on a wet patch – did it rain that night? – or if that doesn't work, I swerve to avoid a cat or dog . . . and bang, I hit that tree. Think it's got legs?"

Wentworth made no effort to respond. "Look invisible. Astrid Leich is in the far witness room."

A girl came by with a copy of *Karmageddon*. "It's for my mom's birthday." Cud didn't look so invisible signing books and CDs.

Abigail exited the witness room, took Wentworth aside, grimacing, slugging from a bottle of Mylanta. "I'm not going to let the chief know my pain. Bertha Rudweiler's death has confirmed for him the essential weakness of women. What's up with Arthur?"

"Riding in at high noon. I'm the whipping boy for the morning."

"Maybe you shouldn't have sent that fax to an open mailbox."

It would be easy to blame the boss, to claim he was acting under orders. But Wentworth Chance wasn't made of custard filling, he won't squeal even if they apply electrodes.

"There's a chance we won't go ahead out of respect for her ladyship. The chief wants to see us in chambers."

"When?"

"Now."

Hardly anyone got invited to Wilbur Kroop's sanctum; why was junior counsel being so honoured? Maybe he wanted to take his shots at Wentworth out of view of the jury. That's fair. He'll stand tall, die bravely. "Give me liberty or give me death."

"What the hell are you talking about?" Abigail was looking oddly at him.

"Um, nothing. Okay, let's go."

Haley was not among the invited; Wentworth took satisfaction from that, giving her a pitying smile as he walked by. She won't have the pleasure of seeing Wentworth get slapped around.

The thirty-inch TV in the chief's room seemed totally out of place, as did the library of DVDs. Otherwise it was right out of Dickens, gloomy and cluttered, wall-to-wall books and musty law reports. Old English masters on the wall. A small-wattage bulb under a flower-patterned lampshade. A yellow pool under a lit brass desk lamp, spotlighting a gnarled, hairy hand signing papers with a fountain pen. A hulklike form on a high-backed throne. His gown and vest were on a hook, and he was in shirtsleeves. Yellow suspenders. Smiling . . .

"Miss Hitchins. Mr. Chance. Very kind of you to join me. Please sit. That chair is more comfortable than it looks, Mr. Chance."

Wentworth took it, feeling discombobulated. He had trouble drawing his eyes from a desk photo of a steely-eyed young man in a 1950s haircut, beside him, a smiling woman, Kroop's late wife. She'd died in an accident forty years ago. He'd never remarried.

"A sad day, milord," Abigail said. "Madam Justice Rudweiler was a powerful voice on the appellate bench. I know you had enormous respect for her."

"And for a very good reason. She regularly upheld my rulings. Hmf, hmf." He didn't seem to be mourning that much. "Bertha had little time for modernist ideas that divorce laws from ancient authority. Old-fashioned, you might call her, but her breed is fast disappearing."

If he was baiting Abigail, the ultimate modernist, she wasn't rising to it. Wentworth dared throw in his two-bits' worth, a mindless bit about Rudweiler's reputation for hewing to principle.

"Well said, young man." Wentworth sneaked a look at Abigail, who seemed equally amazed at this display of bon-homie. "But where is my friend Arthur Beauchamp? Are we to expect he'll be wandering by at some point?"

Wentworth sought to leave the impression Arthur had been called away briefly on vital matters. He didn't mention fishing.

"Normally, of course, we would adjourn to mourn the passing of our sister Rudweiler, but that would be unfair to our jury, given all the interruptions they've endured. You're up to it, Miss Hitchins?"

"Raring to go, milord."

"Whom do you have left? Obviously the deceased's spouse, and Miss Leich – whose Hedda Gabler, by the way, was among the finest I've seen – and did I hear there may be two others?"

Abigail said she'd added the maid and guard to her list.

"Surely they won't take long."

"The Crown's case could be wrapped up by day's end."

"And you, Mr. Chance? How long do you anticipate the defence will take?"

Wentworth was bold: "Well, sir, if the Crown's case doesn't shape up by the end of the day, I'm sure you'll hear Mr. Beauchamp move for a directed verdict. Otherwise I can't honestly say what he plans to do. It depends on those two main witnesses."

"Then it's best we press ahead. But I propose – and I'll hear you on it – a slight digression from the usual timetable. I have in mind that we plough ahead this week until all the Crown witnesses are in. That means sitting tomorrow, Saturday. Defer our weekend by a day, with Sunday and Monday free. Happily, that would allow me to attend to my state duties in the nation's capital. Then we can all be back here on Tuesday. Does that seem practicable?"

Tuesday, election day. Wentworth strived to frame a complaint. Words didn't come.

"I see no alarms being raised, hear no howls of protest. Excellent." He rose. "Thank you, both of you; you've been most considerate. Now shall we all return to the tasks at hand?"

Wentworth walked out in a daze. Ebenezer Kroop had been visited by the Ghost of Judgments Past, or maybe by Bertha Rottweiler, and had evolved into a repentant, kindly human.

Judge Ebbe was again in the gallery, giving him the evil eye, still smarting from Wentworth's insinuation of guilt. Sitting behind him was another familiar face . . . He jumped, startled, recognizing her, a ghost from his own recent past . . . was that really April Fan Wu? Shouldn't she be in Hong Kong? Wait . . . sitting beside her was an even scarier visitation, Brian Pomeroy, looking totally cleaned up. The nicotine-stained moustache was history. Blue suit, blue silk tie, tailored off-white shirt. The blank stare said he was not at any advanced stage of recovery.

As Wentworth bore down upon them, April looked up from a clipboard, smiled her ultra-cool smile. "Either your legs have grown or you're wearing someone else's trousers."

"They're mine," Pomeroy said. "Did you find the ring? Check the pockets."

"Why are *either* of you here?"

"The info feed into Hollyburn Hall is zero," Brian said. He held a pad of lined paper, a sharpened pencil. "We're getting close to the final chapter. I don't trust the court reporter."

Wentworth had to check his own sanity. Okay, he was in court 67, all normal, sheriffs, clerk, prosecutors, Silent Shawn, the jury filing in.

"April, why aren't you in Hong Kong?"

"I renewed my visa."

"She's come back for the climax, Wentworth."

"I have taken him out on a day pass," April said.

"Order in court!"

Wentworth got a frustrated out-of-the-loop look from Cud as he returned to his battle station. Cud had a dread of Pomeroy – nobody warned him a madman was defending him for murder, that was his refrain. Wentworth hoped April could keep the senior partner under control; he might erupt, pull some crazy act.

Abigail stood to call the next witness, but Kroop stilled her with a raised hand. "Before we proceed, Madam Prosecutor, there is a matter I wish to discuss with the jury." He scanned them with his dark, cavernous eyes. The union organizer, Altieri, was looking distrustfully at Cud for some reason.

"One would have to be blind and deaf," Kroop said, "not to be aware that on a matter entirely unrelated to this trial, the media have, regrettably, mentioned the deceased in connection with an alleged financial transaction. None of that is admissible in this court, and will play no part in your deliberations. I hope I make myself clear."

Heads nodded. Everyone on that jury had heard about the four-million-dollar bribe.

Now the chief's bulk shifted as he turned to Wentworth, who was suddenly impaled by his eyes, intense like the eyes of a cat stalking a rat.

"It would appear that Mr. Chance here, the seemingly unassuming gentleman at the end of the counsel table, let slip to the press a document they eagerly seized upon for their headlines. In doing so, Mr. Chance, you demonstrated wanton disregard for the high ethical standards of the legal profession."

Wentworth was frozen, partway out of his chair, hands raised as if to ward off a blow, his face a map of shock and consternation.

"Properly I should call upon you to show cause why you should not be cited for contempt, Mr. Chance. Were we not so severely pressed for time, I would have no hesitation doing so. I do, however, intend to report the matter to Law Society with a recommendation for your suspension."

Wentworth finally made it to a standing position, the blood rushing from his face.

"Sit down. The matter is closed."

He almost fainted into his seat. He could barely hear Kroop addressing the jury, the tone courteous now, confiding, as he apologized for disturbing their weekend plans. Wentworth turned, looked around for support; it wasn't coming from impassive Silent Shawn. Judge Ebbe was grinning.

He felt the creeping edge of panic. Why had he just stood there and let the sadist humiliate him in front of everyone, in front of the press, accusing him of deliberately leaking that document? Arthur would have waded into him.

"Asshole." Wentworth heard it, and probably so did most spectators, but the obscenity didn't travel well to the bench. The chief perked up his ears, though, and as he searched the gallery, he scowled on seeing Pomeroy in the back row, the jeering expression.

Wentworth held his breath. He could tell Kroop was itching to confront Pomeroy, flail him into admitting he'd uttered a slur. He looked at the wall clock, then Pomeroy, then again at the clock. "Call your next witness, Madam Prosecutor."

29

FOWL MURDER

Arthur was pleased with himself, he'd survived the power outage, braved the frigid weather, conquered the Salish Sea, and he was going to make it to court in time. A generous endowment had coaxed Stoney to truck him to the ten-fifteen ferry, and now he was in a taxi, speeding by the lush farmlands of Tsawwassen and Ladner. Tomorrow was Saturday, he'd have the weekend to reinvigorate himself for the finale, his jury speech. He'd have to dig deep to find pity for Wilbur Kroop, whose illness had set the schedule askew, and who must now abandon hope of schmoozing with the Governor General on Monday.

Nonetheless, it would be a hectic weekend. With the election only a few days hence, he'll not enjoy much ease, nor will he be kicking back with his old cronies Ovid, Milton, and Bach. He must *not* miss the candidates faceoff on Saltspring tomorrow afternoon. Also, Lavinia was returning to Estonia in a few days, so Blunder Bay has to wish her bon voyage. Poor Nick will be desolate, but he's leaving too and will share top billing at the farewell party.

This weekend will also see the Garibaldi winter season's major cultural event, the official unveiling of Hamish McCoy's act of penance, the supposed Venus. As seen from the aft deck of the ferry, her body was still hidden in sheeting, but there was a promise of beauty above, a pair of gracefully curved wings, taut as the wings of a braking goose.

Arthur was eager to catch an update on his trial on the noon newscast, but felt it impolite to intrude on the East Indian raga his driver was listening to. One could only hope that young Wentworth got through the morning without mishap.

Presently, an hour or so from now, he must face Astrid Leich. *I think I've just witnessed a cold-blooded murder!* Emphatic enough except for the *I think. That's the man,* she cried as she pointed to the sixth of a male octet. Too vain to admit to uncertainty, had she made a lucky guess? Had a bent cop bent her ear with a hint that the killer had a bent nose? Surely she'd have needed more than corrective lenses to make out the contours of a nasal organ from sixty yards.

Abigail's claim that this eyewitness hasn't been contaminated by press coverage will have to be tested. And if she fails to identify Cud, the defence could glide to a soft landing. Barring a ringer from Florenza LeGrand, there'd be nothing for a jury to chew. *Ex nihilo nihil fit.* From nothing, nothing can be made. The verdict could be in before quitting time today.

He sat back, enjoying the melodious interplay of sitars and lutes and reeds.

⚖

At the law courts, he crossed paths with John Brovak, shrugging into his Harley-Davidson jacket. "Another black day, Arturo, for those who dare sit in judgment of Morgan and Twenty-one Others. A perilous profession, the judiciary. I weep." He hurried off.

Thus was Arthur informed of Bertha Rudweiler's death, especially disturbing news given she'd been in fair fettle during lunch on Tuesday. Cud benefited from her death — or at least its morbid byproduct: her poisoning would add to the common bruit that some loosely hinged loser with a grudge against the courts was serially killing judges.

Given that both justices Naught and Rudweiler had died in combat with the Ruby Morgan defenders, one might want to cross-reference those dozen lawyers with the attendees at Kroop's banquet. Arthur supposed it was scientifically possible to taint a fowl with salmonella – doubtless the recipe could be found, as with so many other barbarities, on the Internet.

Alone among the several lawyers in the barristers' lounge was Wentworth Chance, staring out a window, arms folded. Oblivious, gone. Arthur let him be – Abigail was wiggling a finger at him, and he joined her at the coffee counter. "He's been standing there for the last twenty minutes," she said. "Comatose."

"How did he do?"

"Not brilliant, but he managed to fill the morning. Wrung his two witnesses dry. The chief was going, 'Do we have to hear how he rose through the ranks of the Indian army?' 'Do we really need to know all the names of Ms. Rossignol's stuffed animals?'"

"Did Rashid put Carlos at the scene of the crime?"

"Yeah, but eight weeks later. So he was her live-in lover for seven days in January, where do you go with it? What confuses me is the droll scene around the Limey paparazzo. Flo lets this jerk into the house for a two-hour exclusive – I don't get it."

It seemed she hadn't guessed who this mystery man was. Arthur continued without a beat. "The ring went in?"

"Exhibit 46."

"Philomène identified it?"

"Sure, but why don't you ask him?" Wentworth, mesmerized by a wall of office windows across the street.

"He tends to get inside his head. I'm not sure what he does in there. Equations, maybe."

"It's shell-shock, Arthur. Kroop shat all over him. Not just cruel and unusual. Sadistic."

Arthur's jaw dropped as she described the scene, a public drawing and quartering. He excoriated himself, he shouldn't have left the lad in the sandbox with the neighbourhood bully.

This was payback for Wentworth's role in the Gilbert Gilbert trial. Arthur's fury would have to be controlled, he didn't want Kroop taking revenge by denying a motion to dismiss.

"By the way, Bry Pomeroy popped in for a while this morning. With some woman — his nurse?"

"How odd."

"We were all holding our breath. And get ready for this. We're sitting tomorrow so Kroop can free up Monday."

Arthur almost spewed his coffee. "Tomorrow? Saturday! I have plans!"

"Softly, softly. He intends to sit until all the testimony is in, but maybe we can wrap it up early."

"Do I understand you may not oppose a motion for a directed verdict?"

"Depending how it goes today."

"Abigail, you have been most evenhanded during these proceedings. More decent to me than I deserve, frankly."

"Well, there's a reason for that." She pinched his cheek. "I'm secretly in love with you."

"Give me this boon, Abigail, don't allow Leich a look at the lineup photo until she's had a chance to pick my man out in court."

"For you, Arthur."

He'd like to believe Abigail was motivated by affection for the old fogey, but of course that wasn't it. The prize fish she hoped to catch was Flo LeGrand, and if Cuddles got swept up in her net like some helpless guppy, too bad for him. Doubtless, she ached to pull in this wealthy, predacious playgirl, an embarrassment to the feminist movement.

He confronted Wentworth, blocking his view out the window. No immediate sign of recognition until he sighed. "Where were you?"

Since the answer was obviously known, Arthur took that as accusatory — why weren't you there in my time of need? "Let's call it a chicken-plucking emergency, I'll explain later."

"I should have become an archaeologist. That was my second choice."

"Abigail said you did splendidly. As to Kroop, you'll just have to shrug it off; if he's not rewarded appropriately in the afterlife, we'll know there's no God. I assume the police and media are scurrying about looking for a British tabloid reporter."

"I left it at that. I didn't drag Brian into it, I worried he'd go off half-cocked. He was in the gallery with April Wu. I was pretty confused about that. They've gone somewhere for lunch."

"Did you take note of his mental state?"

"He still thinks this trial is some kind of novel."

Arthur felt he'd be a step up if he could solve Pomeroy's whodunit, if he could pin the tail on the right donkey, the right perp. He had a sense the key to the mystery lay hidden in the messy tangle of Pomeroy's synapses – something had happened during that two-hour tête-à-tête with Florenza LeGrand, something other than an exchange of pleasantries. Had she told him who the perp was?

And what role was the unpredictable Lady of the Proverbs playing? If she wasn't still on Donat LeGrand's payroll, had she gone off on some fancy of her own? Was she serving as ward to Brian out of sympathy, affection, or simple curiosity? She was an enigma. Arthur was troubled by her in ways he couldn't define.

In the locker room, he ran a comb through his British Ambassador, shrugged into his robes. As he slipped outside for a quick puff, Felicity Jones burst past him and down the street, tears streaming. This grand exit looked more permanent than the last, her face set with unforgiving stubbornness.

On his way up to level six he detoured past his pestering client, who was on a landing thronged by chirruping nubile Cudaholics. One of them was giving him a back rub. Cud's latest creative effort, as related by Wentworth – his heroic leap into the Aston Martin to catch a killer – has persuaded Arthur he would be a fool to put him on the stand. There, Cud could be cross-examined about his two prior assaults – leaving it open to the jury to conclude he was prone to violent acts.

Wentworth was waiting near the door to court 67, anxious, jittery, apparently not much perked up by the pep talk Arthur had just given him. Several young lawyers were laughing at the bon mots of Judge Ebbe, in good spirits, back here to enjoy the savaging of Raffy and Boynton, the savaging of the dead. Wentworth had cheerlessly described their contretemps in the El Beau Room. Very snappish fellow, this judge, he had a history of angry outbursts.

Almost inevitably, here was Charles Loobie with his "Hey, Artie, I got something for you." Arthur's suspicions about this overly helpful reporter were renewed each time he played prompter to the defence, keeping him prominently on the short list. Arthur listened patiently. This one was about a long-ago sexual conquest by Cud, the teenaged daughter of the president of Steelworkers Local 305 in Edmonton. There'd been a small scandal around that, and Cud had taken a powder from town.

"You want to worry about that union guy, he's been looking fish-eyed at your client." Tom Altieri.

If this rumour was true, the client had again been hoisted by his unregulated sex drive – the last thing Arthur needed was an unsympathetic juror.

As Cud came striding toward him, Arthur hurried his junior inside the court but couldn't get distance. A tug at his gown, the dreaded importuning voice. "I don't get it, my life's on the line, and my counsel takes a bunk? Leaving me defended by a gawk who gets beat up by the presiding fascist despot. I need protection from this judge, man, he even looks like Hermann Goering. On top of everything, Felicity has a fit because I get tied up with my reading public."

Arthur directed him to a seat near the back where short-sighted Astrid Leich might not quickly spot him, placing him between an older woman and a man in a leather jacket whom Arthur knew to be a plain-clothes officer. There were always a curious few of these here, cops killing time, under subpoena for other trials. The room also attracted its share of law students, mostly women, but enough men to give Leich pause. Several lawyers from the aborted Morgan appeal were sharing the counsel bench with Silent Shawn. Sergeant Chekoff was in the back row, beside two reserved seats.

Moving in to claim them were cleancut Brian Pomeroy and his keeper, April Fan Wu, sliding past Chekoff, trying not to step on his shoes. They picked up their markers, a hat and a scarf, and sat. Pomeroy looked medicated, not much emotion showing, but he caught Arthur's eye, a form of recognition. Arthur didn't want him here, a time bomb in the back row. Kroop could be the one to light the fuse.

Several jurors gave Arthur smiles of relief that he hadn't abandoned ship. There was an air of expectancy – all the circumstantial evidence was in, and the trial was moving toward its defining moment, the eyewitnesses, the stars.

"Order in court!"

Enter the bullying martinet, lumbering onto the bench, glowering at Arthur, as if daring him to give him a bad time today. Kroop located Cudworth, squinted at Pomeroy, and then, for some reason, fixed for a moment on Judge Ebbe.

All eyes turned to Astrid Leich, pausing at the door, sizing up the audience, then regally walking up the aisle. Seventy-three but hiding those years well, a reasonable facsimile of the slender belle Arthur recalled from the Playhouse Theatre. Modern fluffy hairdo, a little darker than it ought to be, an ersatz rose at her left shoulder. No glasses, presumably contacts.

Kroop seemed instantly under her spell. "I hope that chair is comfortable for you, madam. Mr. Sheriff, bring her a fresh glass of water." She smiled her appreciation.

Abigail led her through a personal history: forty-year stage career, divorced a decade ago but left in comfort by her spouse, a financier. Long-time homeowner at 5 Lighthouse Lane. Chair of the North Shore Arts Council. No dramatic flourishes. Increasingly warm smiles for the judge, eye contact with several jurors.

She had spent the afternoon of Saturday, October 12, at a show of an artist friend's seascapes, returned home before nine o'clock, ate, made tea, and was about to settle in with a rented movie when she was reminded, by the lights and activity across the inlet, that her neighbours were holding a fundraiser for the Literary Trust.

She'd been a guest at similar arts events, and on learning her neighbours planned to host one had left a phone message commending them. "I had read that three writers of note would be present, but I'd heard only of Professor Chandra and Ms. Tinkerson. The name Cudworth Brown meant nothing."

Arthur managed to resist the impulse of turning to see how Cud was taking this.

"Living alone these many years has made me a curious old woman, I suppose – my other excuse is that it was a lovely fall evening – so I took my tea out to the balcony. Their outdoor lights were on, but I was a little embarrassed to be seen, so I didn't turn on mine."

Abigail asked how well she knew Whynet-Moir and Florenza.

"Well enough to shout occasional greetings across the water. I'd met Florenza through her parents – before they passed the property on to her and Rafael. That was a year and a half ago; 2 Lighthouse Lane was their wedding gift. Flo and Rafael have been over for tea, and I've attended a couple of their dinner parties."

"And what view of 2 Lighthouse Lane do you have from your balcony?"

"I can see about, oh, a hundred feet of the upper cedar deck and the adjoining living quarters – not inside, the curtains are usually drawn. Evergreens block their front entrance and the entire rear of the house, but there's a gap between their driveway and the parking area."

"What about their garage?"

"It's obscured. You can just see the roof."

"And where is that garage in relation to the deck?"

"It's about a hundred feet behind it, on higher ground."

"Tell us what you observed on the deck."

"It looked like dinner had concluded. I saw a caterer bustling about replacing ashtrays. Florenza was smoking – she loves those smelly Gitanes – with a gentleman in blue jeans and suspenders – I believe they were red – over a denim shirt. Shaggy light brown hair, over the collar. Some kind of chain around his neck, with what looked like a medallion. I could only suppose this was the poet, Mr. Cudworth Brown, and that was soon confirmed – though I shouldn't get ahead of myself."

Arthur listened with morbid fascination. The clarity of her phrasing, her management of details, her disarming frankness: all indicators of the truthful informant. An impressive witness. He had expected she'd be . . . flightier.

"How well could you see this man in the suspenders?"

"Well, from over a hundred and fifty feet away . . . I must confess I'm quite astigmatic, but I'd had my eyeglasses renewed just two months earlier."

"And you were wearing them?"

"Yes, I'd taken my contacts out. I could see him well enough."

This was neatly blunting Arthur's main line of attack. He may have to remodel his cross-examination.

"Describe this man."

"Average height, fairly broad in the chest, an open face, handsome, good lines. A little rugged, I thought."

"His age?"

"Mid-forties."

She didn't mention the nose. Its slight warp at the crown must not have registered.

"Had you ever seen him before?"

"I very much doubt it."

"Or since?"

"I've had no cause to. I've been instructed many times by Detective Sergeant Chekoff not to contaminate my evidence by looking at newspapers and newsreels."

"Good for you, madam," Kroop said, reinforcing her as a witness of vast probity.

"Could you hear any conversation?"

"No, they were speaking softly, they were quite close together. I had no trouble hearing Rafael when he came out to fetch them. He said, 'Ah, here you are, Cudworth.'"

"Then what happened?"

"The three of them went back in. So did I. Olivier was prodding me, my poor old tomcat – I'd forgot to feed him and give him his medicine."

Wentworth Chance's reaction to this appallingly sweet witness was to fidget like a monkey with fleas. Arthur nudged him in the ribs. In contrast, the chief justice was placid, his eyes calflike, soft with adoration. The sight of Pomeroy writing furiously in the back row caused Arthur a spectral, preternatural twinge, an odd sense he was a character in a book. An echo from his dreams.

"After putting away my tea things, I plugged in the movie – *Vertigo*, with Jimmy Stewart and Kim Novak."

"To my mind, one of Hitchcock's best," said Kroop, surprising Arthur, who hadn't imagined him as a film devotee.

"I'd only just settled in front of the set – maybe twenty minutes had passed – when I saw several headlights, so I went out again. The guests were leaving, and Rafael and Florenza were seeing them off. I had a clear view of the man in the braces – he was smoking a cigar near the stairs to . . . I guess their pool, but it's walled in, I can't see it from my house . . . Oh, you'll think I'm a terrible snoop." The jurors smiled. So did Arthur; she practically owned the courtroom.

"How was he dressed?"

"The same, denim shirt and dark trousers, medallion, work boots. One of the braces had come loose, and he tugged it back up."

"About what time was this?"

"Oh, maybe ten o'clock. And I went back to my movie, and . . . well, quite honestly, I fell asleep in front of the set."

"I've done that myself, madam." Bonding with her.

The jury's attention shifted, a stirring at the door: Felicity Jones, looking sullen with loss of pride. An overly considerate deputy found her an empty seat, far enough from Cuddles to reduce, though not eliminate, the risk of a rattle-brained scene that would help Leich pick him out.

Meanwhile, Arthur had lost the thread of her evidence. As he picked it up, she was upstairs, asleep in her four-poster bed.

"And did something awake you?"

"I often doze in fits and starts, it's something to do with age, I'm told." A smile for one of the older women on the jury, who nodded sympathetically. "I'm not sure what it was, the noise, but it was like something slamming shut, a shutter or a door, an unusual sound in the small hours. So I put on my glasses and dressing gown and went out."

"To the upstairs balcony you described, off the bedroom."

"Yes."

"And what did you see?"

"Nothing at first, everything was quite dark, but when my eyes adjusted, I saw something very odd. A few night lamps were on at 2 Lighthouse, and in their glow I saw him standing on a chair. Rafael, Judge Whynet-Moir. He was in a dressing gown. I couldn't see what he was looking at, an area back of his house, I think."

"He was upright?" ·

"Yes, as if craning to see someone or something. He didn't look all that steady, and I was worried for him."

"Then what happened?"

"Then a man came . . . almost out of nowhere, running along the deck, and as he reached Rafael, he just gave him a shove, with both hands, like this . . ." She pushed her hands forward and slightly upward, forcefully. "It sent him right off the chair and . . . oh, it was horrible, I'm sorry . . ."

"Shall we take a break, Miss Leich?" Kroop said.

A tissue to her eyes, a brave smile, a sip of water. "No, I'll be fine. It's, well, I've had nightmares, but I was told this could be . . . an appropriate way to purge them."

Told by a therapist? Arthur stood to lose, not gain, if he made an issue of that. He ought not to whale away at this entirely too bright and engaging witness. After she identifies Cud Brown, as assuredly she will, he must beg the jury to believe she made an honest mistake.

With the pained look of one forcing down bitter medicine, Leich composed a graphic scene of Raffy spilling head-first over the railing, a strangled, phlegm-thick wail, a sickening thud. When she went silent, Arthur could almost hear the slapping of the waves on those bloodied rocks.

"I think you're over the worst of it, Ms. Leich," Abigail said, solicitous but obviously pleased, entertaining thoughts of pulling it off, a surprise win for the Crown. "And what about the attacker? What did he do?"

"Well, he stumbled against the railing and knocked the chair over. But he steadied himself, and he didn't look over the railing, didn't look down there, and . . . he ran to the staircase and down to the pool area. I called the police."

"Describe the attacker."

"Well, I would say he was the same man I saw earlier. Whom Rafael addressed as Cudworth."

"Thank you, but describe his appearance."

"Well, same build, hair, blue jeans . . . I couldn't see their colour, to be honest, but they looked like the same pants, the shirt too, the shirttail was out. When he hurried off, he passed right under one of the night lights, and I could make out his face. It was the same person. His suspenders had come loose, they were just dangling there, and he was holding up his pants as he went down the stairs."

Intimate detailing that added telling verisimilitude. Arthur shook his head, as if to clear it. Why was he buying all of this so readily? He was lapping from her cat dish, nearly as captivated as Wilbur Kroop. She may have rehearsed this disarming manner, spent hours, days, weeks in front of the mirror. A final turn under the spotlights for her last great role, witness for the prosecution.

"I am looking at the clock, Madam Prosecutor." It was well past the afternoon break.

"Almost done, my lord. Ms. Leich, I would now ask you to look about the courtroom and tell us if you can see the man who propelled Mr. Justice Rafael Whynet-Moir to his death." Spoken with brio, Abigail feeling her oats.

Leich looked first at the prisoner's dock, as if expecting the accused to materialize there. She next checked out the defence table, quickly rejecting Wentworth as a possibility. She studied the dozen barristers in front of the bar, and fixed for a long moment on Silent Shawn Hamilton – so long that Shawn shifted uneasily. She looked at the jurors, as if half-expecting the culprit to have been set among them. Then the press table. Loobie bowed his head, scribbled a note, looking splendidly guilty.

"Ms. Leich, are you wearing your contacts?" Abigail was showing impatience.

"Yes. I'm not sure where I'm supposed to look."

"The whole courtroom."

"Oh, I see." She began scanning it, front to back. A telltale squint.

"Madam, please feel free to step down from the witness stand and move about the courtroom." Kroop gallantly spreading a cloak over the puddle of her confusion. "You may simply point to the man you have described."

Leich stepped from the witness stand, hesitant, as if she'd been tossed a last-minute script, an unrehearsed scene. She again looked at Silent Shawn, and Arthur saw a likely reason why: his jacket was askew, a few inches of a blue suspender showing.

Leich went about her tour slowly and with great deliberation, aisle by aisle, row by row, face by face, ignoring women – except one husky lass keeping her pants up with wide brown braces.

All the men, even the aged, short, and overweight, earned a few moments of scrutiny, occasionally longer, seven or eight seconds for Dalgleish Ebbe. No braces showing, his suit buttoned tight.

The room was as silent as interstellar space. And then, ominously, a smothered hiccup at Arthur's ear.

"Your pipe," came Wentworth's muffled plaint. "Must be in your pocket." His face taut, his eyes bulging with the effort to stifle the next one.

Arthur whispered: "Get them under control or you're fired."

Wentworth's face began to turn purple as Arthur redirected his attention to Leich, who had progressed to the third last row, Cud's row. Arthur's view was from an awkward angle but he was careful not to stand – that might tell Leich she was getting warm.

People shifted to give Leich room as she worked slowly past them and finally confronted Cud. He boldly met her gaze, expressionless. She tarried, stared, a breathless time.

Arthur worried that Wentworth might explode, though he emitted not a peep. But there came a sound from the gallery, a whimper, Felicity Jones daubing her eyes with a handkerchief.

Arthur fought to suppress fury, this silly girl had signalled that Leich was not just getting warm but hot. But she didn't look Felicity's way, stayed with Cud. A slight nod of affirmation, as if she'd decided to tuck that one away.

Her pace accelerated down the penultimate row, mostly young Cuddites, no one qualifying for the medal round. In the final row, she stopped short on seeing Hank Chekoff, a kind of doubletake. The apparent message: Where have I seen this man before? "Oh, you!" she said, as she recognized the detective who, for the last four months, had been all but living with her.

Pomeroy was to Chekoff's right, playing along, it would seem, being sensible and not acting out some wild paranoid delusion. But instead of meeting Leich's eye, he was looking straight ahead. At Arthur, in fact. Looking at him with his trademark sardonic smile. He was letting Arthur know this was his book, his plot.

The witness stepped in front of Pomeroy, hampering Arthur's view, but he could see April taking in the silent byplay, and was startled to see her go wide-eyed as Leich turned to the bench and said, "This is the man."

Pomeroy's smile had evaporated somewhere along the line, and he seemed in some kind of trance, mesmerized by the index finger pointing at him, with its manicured red nail.

Several silent seconds followed. April put a hand to her mouth, hiding a smile, a gesture that triggered a solution for Arthur that came with lovely clarity. Leich had assumed Chekoff had purposefully put himself next to the accused, to guard him perhaps, to prevent escape – or simply as a signal to pick the fellow on his right.

Though Brian had cleaned up his appearance, shaved off his moustache, he must have been imprinted in her memory from when she'd spied upon his extraordinary foray to Château LeGrand. A remake of an earlier scene, the same setting but in daylight, without a climactic death.

Abigail looked woebegone. "You are pointing to the man in the blue suit beside Sergeant Chekoff?"

"Yes, that's him." Confidently said, but she must have twigged from the tension in the room that something was amiss.

From behind Arthur, an undefined rumbling that resolved into the shape of words. "For the record . . ." Kroop cleared his throat. "For the record, the witness has identified Mr. Brian Pomeroy, a barrister known to this court . . ." His voice slowly rose to a terrible roar. "And who shouldn't have been here in the first place!" Kroop slammed his desk book shut. "We'll take the break!"

30

ON HER MAJESTY'S SERVICE

A traffic jam, reporters, and other smokers forming a flying wedge at the door, pushing past the health nuts, everyone on their feet but Wentworth. He tried to boost himself up, but his knees weren't obeying. He twisted around, saw another frozen, seated figure, Hank Chekoff, alone, deserted, no colleagues to comfort a brother with his head on the block.

Pomeroy had been among the first wave out the door, April sailing along behind him, clutching his arm. Cudworth wasn't far behind. Arthur wandered out, the remaining spectators opening a path for him, some of them bowing, like vassals of the king.

Get them under control or you're fired. Somehow, this low, ferocious command had jolted Wentworth's breathing apparatus, forcing open his recalcitrant glottis. He couldn't remember a more fearsome threat since his mom dragged him to church and the pastor damned masturbators to suffer the eternal fires of hell. As a weird fallout he felt cured of his malady. He should go out with the smokers and test that thesis.

The prosecutors were sheltering Astrid Leich, who looked distraught, apologizing or explaining herself. Wentworth felt badly for her, she'd been upfront, self-effacing. She'd almost settled on Cud before happening on Pomeroy, who'd been sitting wrist to wrist with Chekoff, as if cuffed. Shifty-eyed, not meeting her gaze.

Haley sauntered over with fake nonchalance. "She wants to say she made a mistake."

"It's obvious she made a mistake. Why does she have to say it?"

"She'd like a second chance."

"Mr. Beauchamp won't let himself be sandbagged like that, not in a blue moon."

"Abigail just wanted to know."

He excused himself, ran off to warn the boss about this attempt to plug the dike. In the great hall, he met Cud Brown parading about with Felicity, playing the vindicated martyr to the two dozen satellites swept up in his orbit. "Who do we sue, Woodward? The cops, the Attorney General, the provincial government? Seven figures, pal, we're not going lower."

April was looking out the glass door, keeping an eye on Pomeroy, who had two cigarettes going, one in each hand. The boss was with him, listening patiently to a harangue.

"April, who the heck are you working for?"

"Brian has rehired me."

"Brian isn't doing any hiring. Brian is delusional. Have you told him who you really are?"

"A retired and hopelessly inadequate private detective. I am applying for immigrant status and have secured a work permit." As the door slid open, she touched his arm. "By the way, Wentworth, I'm not homosexual. That was a cover. Can that be our secret?"

Wentworth almost tripped as he wrong-footed his way outside. Brian, butting one of his cigarettes, raised his arm to steady him, talking all the while. "It's not supposed to end this way, Arthur. My readers will feel cheated. What have we got? An attention whore whose comeback bombed."

The still air was dense with smoke. No hint of a hiccup. A miracle.

. "Arthur doesn't get it, Wentworth, he doesn't know the genre. We've left out the twist that comes out of nowhere. Just before the end."

"Good point, Brian. Arthur, I've got to talk to you about some shenanigans they're trying to pull."

He pulled him away, looked back at April and her crafty smile. What was her game? What was she trying to get out of him?

Arthur puffed his pipe as Wentworth griped that Leich had been coached into doing a repairs. The boss nodded, blew a perfect smoke ring. "Well, poor Abigail has a job to do. To be fair to her, she has let me run amok. *A fronte praecipitium a tergo lupi.*"

"Meaning?"

"She's between a rock and a hard place. Literally, a precipice in front, wolves behind. She can't be seen to roll over completely, Wentworth, we can't deny her a bit of patch work. In any event, our moonstruck chief justice will be unmoved by a plea that Ms. Leich not be shown the lineup photo, and there's ample law to support him in that."

"You're not even going to object?"

"Vir prudens non contra ventum mingit."

Wentworth gave him another blank look.

"A wise man does not urinate against the wind."

Leich seemed embarrassed on resuming the stand, couldn't look at Kroop, even though he was doggy-eyed with sympathy. But she turned on a stiff-upper-lip smile while the lineup photo was circulated to the jury. She didn't study hers for long. "Number six. I made a mistake earlier."

"And do you see that man in the courtroom?"

She was explicit: third row from the back, eighth seat to the left, in the brown cardigan with leather elbow patches.

"For the record," said Abigail, "identifying the accused."

"No more questions."

Leich heaved herself up with great relief and left the box. She looked like she was about to make a complete getaway until Kroop hesitantly called her back. "I'm sorry, madam, but there is the little matter of cross-examination." He was looking darkly at Arthur, sending a message that he'd better go easy on her or else.

Arthur slowly rose, and all through the room you could feel the tension rising with him. This was going to be the cross-examination of a lifetime.

"I have no questions."

⚖

Wentworth pedalled the long way around, looping by the southern belly of the West End, taking time to ponder why Arthur hadn't cross-examined, a letdown, like air hissing from a balloon. The boss hadn't wanted Leich to embellish her revised version. But choosing not to object to the lineup photo — couldn't that boomerang?

And then there was the weird thing with the chief justice, how he mooned over Astrid Leich, thanked her with even more applesauce than usual — she'd bravely come forward, she'd done her best under stressful circumstances. Wentworth, who hadn't got over his mauling by the chief, wanted to throw up.

Leich had stuck around a while in the gallery, but couldn't have been too impressed with her admirer, watching him tussle with the boss. Kroop insisted on recessing halfway through the afternoon and starting fresh on Saturday with Flo LeGrand. That made Arthur livid; he'd made urgent plans for Saturday. His best line: "May I congratulate Your Lordship for having been cured of your obsession with running this trial as if it were the Olympic hundred-metre dash."

"This court is adjourned," said the chief.

"He wants to rush me, wants me ill-prepared," Arthur had complained as they left the courts. "He correctly has assumed

I'd planned to be with Margaret for her debate tomorrow. Damn him to hell. When is his turn?"

For what? His turn to die? Arthur didn't expand, though he did explain why he'd been called away to Garibaldi. Then he went off to the quiet of his club to prepare for Florenza LeGrand.

His bike secured, Wentworth took a moment to read the notice on the door of the former Gastown Riot. "God Loves You. Welcome to the Leap of Faith Prayer Centre." Opening this weekend, that was fast. "Rev up your spirits with Pastor Blythe at our grand opening on the coming Lord's Day."

Wentworth tried to look on the bright side. At least these guys won't drive everybody nuts with amplified heavy metal. The broken window had been replaced. A couple of people hanging bunting on walls, setting up chairs. One of them spotted him, opened the door. "Are you sick, brother?"

"No, I'm fine, I bicycle every day."

He fled to the elevator. Upstairs, at the front desk, April Fan Wu was filling in for the receptionist, who'd gone on stress leave. A group of Ruby Morgan's backers, his financial team, were waiting for Brovak, valises at their feet. Wentworth recognized all but one, a pink, shiny, bumlike face, a neatly trimmed beard, a suit of the latest cut. Maybe he was security, the guy with the gun.

April rattled him with her sultry look, a pucker of smiling lips. He didn't have a clue why she seemed to be hustling him. There was nothing she could get from him. The lesbian thing had been a cover, okay, but why was that "our secret?" Maybe she didn't want the Animal to know she was straight. Or that other womanizer, Pomeroy.

He bent toward her. "What did you do with Brian?" As she slipped off her headset he smelled something nice, like apple blossoms.

"I took him to his psychiatrist's office. I expect she drove him to his treatment centre."

"Did you talk to her?"

"We had a few private moments. She's afraid he may be bottoming out. That may cause him to snap back to reality. Or he could go under."

"What's that mean?"

"Destroy himself. Apparently, writing is the only thing that keeps him from giving in to dangerous impulses. That is why I'm doing this." She gestured at her monitor. "Brian's manuscript. He's been dictating it to disk." Wentworth twisted around to read the line just transcribed: "It is time, dear reader, before we close our list, to meet our final suspect . . ." In his descent, Brian had turned to flowery prose – in the manner of that writer he favoured, Widgeon.

Brovak walked in, hung up his helmet and his Harley jacket, ignoring his clients. "Augustina checked in yet?"

"Ms. Sage is in her office," April said.

"About fucking time. I'm exhausted from running this show alone." Alone? Had Wentworth turned invisible?

Brovak looked over the several faces uplifted in inquiry. "Bail has been set, gentlemen. Five hundred kilos for Señor Morgan, smaller change for the peons. Please proceed to my office so we may discuss my own financial needs."

He sent them down the hall with their valises, grinned at Wentworth, as if to say, This is how it's done, kid. He gave April a head-shaking appraisal before following them. "What a waste."

The bumface stayed in his chair, unsmiling, flipping through *New Yorker* cartoons. Wentworth said, "Excuse me, are you here to see someone?"

"I was hoping to catch Mr. Beauchamp."

"He won't be in today. Can I help?"

"Yes, well . . . You must be Mr. Chance? Can we talk?"

"About what exactly?"

He rose, extended a perspiring palm. "Thomas Drew. Tom to my friends. Her Majesty's Service." He produced a card embossed with the Canadian crest. Office of the Prime Minister. Just his name, no title. "I may have some useful information." Close to his ear: "About someone you may wish to add to your list of suspects."

Wentworth blinked. This was too eerie. *It is time to meet our final suspect.*

He deposited Tom Drew in his cramped office (incorrect feng shui, according to April, poorly designed). He held his curiosity in check long enough to pop across the hall to greet Augustina Sage, who was sipping herbal tea and going through her backlog in a dreamy, desultory way. A touch of grey in that curly mat of hair. Still pretty in her forties, thinner, cut off from the world at her Buddhist retreat – yet another effort to figure out why she was prone to self-destructive relationships.

"I don't want to hear about Brian's problems, Wentworth. I don't want to discuss him at all. I don't want to hear about dead judges, either, and I don't want to hear about your lurid trial."

"Okay, well, welcome back."

"I have achieved a level of holiness that I intend to main-tain as long as I can, despite knowing it will all go to shit after five days in this madhouse. At which point I will com-pletely fall apart, join a lonely hearts club, and try to get laid."

"Good luck."

"Bless you. Peace." A bowed head, a Buddhist salute, palms pressed together.

Tom Drew was standing by a window, examining the fire escape, as if calculating a means of escape.

"So, Mr. Drew, what exactly do you do for the prime minister?"

"Let's say I look after certain security issues."

Wentworth could smell his sweat. He didn't think a high-level cop should sweat. "You've come from Ottawa to tell us something?"

"I thought we might share some information."

"Don't expect many answers from me." Wentworth was emboldened by the man's nervousness.

Drew sat, contemplated, then bluntly asked. "Who do you think murdered Rafael Whynet-Moir?"

"Who do *you* think?"

"Can I have your undertaking that this is off the record, Mr. Chance?"

An undertaking – a very solemn matter for a lawyer. How would Arthur respond? Wentworth decided to play along. "Okay, but I have to share this with Mr. Beauchamp."

"Understood. Whynet-Moir served as Jack Boynton's parliamentary aide some years ago."

"We know that."

"Yes, and in return for a judgeship, he paid a substantial bribe to Jack Boynton. No question. Can we put that to rest?"

"Okay."

"Our information is that an intermediary was involved. Have you considered that?"

Wentworth nodded.

"And have you considered that this party might have a motive for murder, to cover up his corrupt role?"

Wentworth was chafing at the way this Tom Drew was giving information under the guise of interrogating him. "Okay, I assume we're talking about some bureaucrat?"

"I'm afraid that's not the case. In fact : . . well, I may as well tell you that our investigation has been seriously compromised by such rumours."

"Compromised in what way?"

Drew cleared his throat. "Frankly it would help us get to the bottom of this if, ah, certain persons refrained from making allegations that the go-between was in government service."

"Certain persons like Mr. Beauchamp?" Drew winced, as if in affirmation. "Who was the go-between?"

"Perhaps the deal was brokered by a certain solicitor – have you considered that? Someone not unknown to the LeGrand family?"

Again, this clumsy interrogative phrasing. Wentworth waited him out.

"There may be evidence to suggest this solicitor accepted a substantial broker's fee. Do you have any idea whom I might be referring to?"

Wentworth wondered if Tom was secretly recording this. "You tell me."

"Maybe a lawyer representing a member of the LeGrand family?" The list had just been narrowed to Silent Shawn Hamilton. "Would you care to guess the amount of the fee?"

"Well, no, I'd like you to tell me."

"Would you be surprised if it's in the high six figures?"

"How high?"

"Three quarters of a million has been mentioned."

"By whom?"

"We are acting on information, Mr. Chance."

"From whom?"

"A person of high repute in the, ah, court system. I can say no more."

Judge Dalgleish Ebbe? That would add a touch of plausibility, but it didn't make Wentworth any less skeptical.

"Can you see, Mr. Chance, why this lawyer might want to do away with Judge Whynet-Moir?"

"Are you a cop?"

"Let's say I'm close to important people, for whom I handle sensitive issues." He began to talk rapidly, heightened colour showing in his round pink face. "Let us hypothesize that after Jack Boynton died of a stroke, Whynet-Moir was the only person who knew of the go-between. Let us assume Whynet-Moir was under suspicion and that we were about to question him. His obvious tactic would have been to deflect blame by denouncing the intermediary. And . . . you can figure out the rest."

This stank. Who in high places was he protecting?

Drew rose. "I'm afraid that's all I'm permitted to say. I have to catch a plane. Pleasure to meet you." Once again he proffered a damp, soft hand, then departed.

Wentworth figured he'd heard a lot of bullshit. In which case, maybe he'd just met someone involved in the murder.

31

FEMME FATALE

Arthur lowered himself with a comfortable grunt into his preferred chair, a wingback facing away from the bar's distracting offerings. After a week at the Confederation Club, he'd finally staked a claim to this chair, a claim recognized by members and enforced by staff.

The maître d'hotel, who liked to fuss over him, set out linen, cutlery, and his regular welcome basket: tea, menu, and newspapers. "The garden salad and the lamb stew, please, Manfred." That should satisfy Margaret, the rich food critic, when she cross-examined him tonight from . . . where will she be? Moose Hills, Mosquito Flats, Mud Creek, maybe one of those logging camps where they heckle her.

"The trial goes well, sir?"

"Ups and downs." He wasn't in the mood for small talk, preferred to wallow in his resentment at Kroop, the Grinch who stole Saturday. "I need you," Margaret had said. "I'll be there," he'd assured her.

But maybe Florenza LeGrand won't fill the day. Maybe she'll be mute on the stand, be cited for contempt, the trial aborted. Maybe she'll claim to have been asleep or passed out, a witness to nothing. But the more he thought about it, the more unlikely that seemed. Had she been insensible, Silent Shawn would not have issued a gag order.

From somewhere, tinnily, came a familiar Bach fugue. When

those bars repeated, he realized it was his cellphone, and he went salvaging in the wilderness of his cluttered briefcase.

Wentworth, with an excited, disjointed account of an off-the-record dialogue with a "spook from Ottawa," keen on fingering Shawn Hamilton. Arthur made him start from the top, coherently.

"I did a search on Thomas Drew; he's a real person, some kind of political aide to the Prime Minister. Some pooh-bahs in Ottawa want to shut you up, or misdirect you."

"In such a brazen way?" Dispatching a trained monkey on a five-hour flight to snitch on Silent Shawn Hamilton – even on the murky playing fields of political connivance, that seemed extreme. "Maybe they do have the goods on Shawn."

"Oh, God, I read him completely wrong."

"Wentworth, I'm just speculating."

"I blew it. I have to think through this again. I actually thought Drew might be the perp." His high, cracking voice.

"Calm down."

"Sorry."

Arthur fretted through his lamb stew about this political hack's bizarre visit – especially outlandish given that Margaret was running neck and neck with the chicken-plucking candidate for Drew's party. Reluctantly, he phoned the Green campaign office to compare notes with Eric Schultz, who knew the backroom boys of Ottawa.

Schultz was in session with his finance team but took the call, orating in his burp-gun manner. "Bad news is that we're skint, Arthur, in deep hock. O'Malley's got money to burn. TV attack ads. We're naive, we're environmental scaremongers. The good news is we've evened up, it's decimal points either way. But they're holding on to their core vote; it's like chipping away at a brick wall. All depends on the all-candidates. And your trial, of course, they're still making hay about Blake being up a tree with Brown. Innuendo, guilt by association."

That's why Arthur had been reluctant to call him, the pressure, the constant nagging about the trial, its political implications.

Schultz had some background on Drew: ex-Alberta oil patch overseer, long-time soldier in the election trenches, rewarded with a job in the PM's office, generally regarded as useless. "What did he have to say?"

"It was off the record, Eric. We gave an undertaking."

Schultz grumbled at that, passed the phone to Margaret, who sounded tense and weary. "I've lost fifteen pounds, nothing fits. It's like an episode of *Survivor*. Three more days."

"And then we celebrate."

"Then we sleep."

"Darling, about tomorrow, I have some distressing –"

"It's okay, Arthur. It was on the news. I'm fuming at that judge."

"I made you a promise."

"You're absolved."

"I feel wretched."

"Oh, nonsense. I'll see you at home on Sunday. I'm taking a day of rest, if you can call it that. There may be some press following me around. We'll have to do Reverend Al's service, that's a given. A few teas and klatches. Oh, and I guess there's that party for Lavinia and Nick. Well, we'll just have to find some time together."

She carried on stoutly like that, determined to let Arthur off the hook, refusing to hear regrets or apology. So he let the matter be and entertained her with tales of the trial, the muff by Leich, the star-struck judge, Cud with his swaggering demands for financial redress. But he was depressed on disconnecting, burdened with a sense he'd failed her.

A trio of codgers, armed with martinis, sat down to watch the news. "Tellie, old boy." Manfred clicked on the TV and turned up the volume to aid the hard of hearing.

"Bangladesh is going under again," one said.

"What?"

"Bangladesh." Shouting over the newscaster. "A thousand homes washed away."

"Global warming."

"No way to stop it. Head for higher ground."

"Here's that poet character. Screwed the judge's new bride in the hot tub."

"Don LeGrand's daughter."

"Bit of a whore, they say."

"Bad seed. Happens in the best families."

Footage of Cud flashing a victory salute at the camera. Here was Astrid Leich avoiding microphones. Here was the British Ambassador himself, walking from the law courts, looking fat, Wentworth at his shoulder like a pilot fish. He couldn't hear the announcer over the shouted commentary.

"What?"

"Hanky-panky!"

"Hank who?"

"Bought himself a judgeship!"

Brian Pomeroy appeared on screen, staring bleakly from a taxi window, sylphlike April giving the driver directions.

"Wouldn't kick *her* out of bed. Who's in the car?"

"Lawyer who flipped out."

A rerun of the famous scene of Pomeroy galloping down Nelson Street, his gown flapping in the rain like a loose sail. Arthur must banish him from the courtroom, he's a menace, Polyphemus reincarnated. *Cyclops! Cruel one! who didst not fear to eat the strangers sheltered by thy roof.*

⚖

It had forgotten to rain today, so Arthur took a brisk morning walk to Gastown, down Hastings and Water Streets, enjoying the sweet, damp smell of coming spring. He'd already seen snowdrops. Crocuses soon, then daffodils in vast bounty. Skunk cabbage blossoming in the swales. He must get back to garden and greenhouse, there's much to do. Spring comes two months later in Ottawa . . .

Outside the Leap of Faith Prayer Centre a scrawny man bleated a greeting. "Hallelujah, brother!"

"Yes, indeed, hallelujah." Arthur didn't accept his tract but read the posted announcement. Sadly, he will miss Pastor Blythe's revving up on Sunday.

Upstairs, at reception, he was greeted by the seraphic smile of April Fan Wu, whose continuing role in this *spectaculum* confused him. Arthur had recently fired her for spying; why ought she be trusted now? Her sponsors, the LeGrands, had obviously pulled strings with immigration, and no one seemed concerned that the office madman had rehired her. Wentworth had explained they were short-staffed, insisted she was "on our side." The artful young lady seemed to have beguiled him.

"I can't deny I'm a little astonished to see you back, April, but welcome."

"I am sorry I deceived you. I had always dreamed of immigrating to Canada, and I took stupid risks. I'm really not such a shady person, Mr. Beauchamp, and I'll prove my loyalty." She shook his hand with a penitent smile, then added, enigmatically, "There are many paths to the top of the mountain, but the view is always the same."

Arthur would have to work at that one. "I understand you've been babysitting Brian. For some reason he seems accepting of that. I do not want him in court today."

"It's the last place he wants to be. Ms. Leich's evidence has convinced him he's the target of a conspiracy. 'They're setting me up to take the rap,' is how he put it." She pressed a key combination and a printer expelled several pages. "His latest chapter."

Arthur idly browsed through this farrago of comment and fiction, part novel, part a Pomeroyesque stream of consciousness, with quotes from Hector Widgeon's witless, dreary prose.

"'The tardy entrance of your final suspect must not be seen as an afterthought, idly tossed off. Even the dullest of readers should exclaim Eureka! as they realize they ought to have paid more attention to the boring parts.' That's low, you smarmy bastard, pay attention to your own boring parts. Help me through this, April. Are you there? I'm enslaved to him and his cookie-cutter recipes."

A faultless transcription of an unexpected bit of self-awareness. April gave him an odd smile, knowing and sharing. Again, that sense of her peering into his soul. Others had fallen victim to her; Arthur must not.

Wentworth emerged with two heavy book bags, tried to herd Arthur down to a waiting taxi. Arthur held back for a moment, flipped the pages, came upon this narrative: "Florenza had heard of the cagey old dog defending Cuddles. Little did Beauchamp know how well she'd prepared for him . . ."

Another twinge. That sense of unreality, of being Brian's invention.

As they settled in the taxi, Arthur asked, "Did you remember the letters?"

"What letters? Oh." Wentworth went into his briefcase, produced a file folder with about a dozen hand-written or typed letters on white paper, lined paper, airmail paper. "I had to ransack my bottom dresser drawer. A lot of these are from my mom, some are from a girlfriend I had once. A few from a dating bureau I belonged to."

Arthur sat in silence, pondering. *There are many paths to the top of the mountain, but the view is always the same.* April's aphorism bugged him. The view, the solution, was obvious if one made the effort to see it?

On entering the great hall, he watched steely-eyed as Cud held court on the stairs, Socrates-like, dispensing wisdom. His bandwagon was growing, former doubters climbing on board. He'd become the adored teddy bear of the West Coast arts scene, his evenings spent drinking beer, slapping palms, and signing books and CDs at the Western Front and other hip venues.

Felicity drifted around the fringe of this ecstatic mob, notebook out, and bore down on Arthur. "Help. Help. What rhymes with ardent?"

"Retardant."

Cud was carrying on about how the oligarchy stifled dissent by crushing the artists. Arthur beckoned him, sliced his throat with a forefinger.

"The masses are hungry, counsellor, I got to feed them."

"Not another peep for the duration of this trial."

Cud looked peeved. "It's about over, ain't it?"

"It ain't. Cud, please tell me how you managed to offend the entire Edmonton Local 305 of the Steelworkers Union."

"Uh, what's that about?"

"Juror number two, Tom Altieri, knows about your escapade with an underaged girl —"

"Under . . . She was a woman. All of seventeen."

"You might start looking a little less triumphant and more concerned." He strode off to the robing room. *The view is always the same . . .* There are many ways to defend Cud Brown, but the outcome is always the same. There are many ways to win, but the effort isn't worth it.

Arthur's temper rose when the clerk told him the trial would be delayed while staff ran a video feed into the adjoining empty courtroom. The weekend had brought the crowds out: murder, wealth, sex, and politics — cheaper than the movies. He leaned over the railing, gazed down at the scurrying figures six floors below. *There are many paths to the top of the mountain . . .* He was stumped. Damn that woman.

Coming up the stairs was Dalgleish Ebbe, back for another fix of *Regina v. Brown*. Here was a chance to buttonhole him, spell out Tom Drew's insinuations, ask about his alleged role as informer. But as Arthur worked his way toward the stairs, he lost the judge in the swarming citizenry.

The witness room door opened to cast out Abigail, affording a view within of black-stockinged legs, crossed, a dainty sandal dangling from a toe. Shawn Hamilton shut the door, but not before Arthur saw a puff of smoke, the illegal burn of a cigarette.

Abigail took Arthur's arm, walked with him. Arthur enjoyed the camaraderie between them, wasn't sure why he deserved her respect. But feminists tended to react to him that way. Non-threatening A.R. Beauchamp.

"Florenza has something to hide, and I want it out of her. Give her your famous third degree, and I'll pick up the pieces."

"If it were only that easy."

"It's a hard one, isn't it, Arthur?"

She knew the peril he faced. Ask the wrong question, get the wrong answer, and counsel implicates his own client. *Help me escape. We'll just have to find some way to get rid of him.* He dares not quote those pithy lines.

As the jurors sat, Tom Altieri, whose robust and persuasive tongue could be a potent force in the jury room, fixed on Cud, now in the second row with Felicity, and flared his nostrils as if reacting to a repugnant odour. In compensation, Arthur won a smile from foreperson Jane Glass. He couldn't pinpoint where he'd had a tête-à-tête with this retired classicist, a reception after some do or other, but he recalled, embarrassingly, that she'd corrected his Latin.

Silent Shawn's deadpan look mutated briefly into one of wincing discomfort when Judge Ebbe, unable to find a seat in the gallery, settled beside him on the counsel bench. No words were spoken, but the brittle chemistry was palpable.

Kroop welcomed the jury to this unusual Saturday session, assuring them they'd have the rest of the day off after hearing one witness. "Depending on counsel, of course." The innuendo: any grant of early freedom depended on the windy cross-examiner for the defence.

"Call Florenza LeGrand," Abigail said, looking sideways at Arthur. They were in this together.

Enter Donat LeGrand's misbegotten child, costumed as femme fatale: a stylish mid-thigh black dress, a cream V-necked top exposing a dagger of flesh between her breasts. As she went by counsel table, she gave Arthur a quick sizing-up. *Florenza had heard of the cagey old dog defending Cuddles.*

When asked to take the oath, she addressed the judge. "I'd like to make a statement. I am here against my wishes. I want to bury all of this. It can only hurt my family and friends, who have already been dragged through the mud."

Kroop's benign expression slowly transformed into something more familiar. "Madam, in this forum we do not offer witnesses a choice to stand mute. I shall take severe measures if you do so."

She glanced at Silent Shawn. He gave her nothing, not a twitch. Back to the judge. "Severe measures?"

"The appropriate order, madam, would be to hold you in the Women's Correctional Facility until you expunge your contempt."

"How long could that be?"

"Life."

That was a stretch – in more ways than one – but Arthur kept silent. Kroop was showing uncommon patience; a less prominent witness would have been harangued mercilessly.

Abigail rose to intercede. "Let's see how far we get, Ms. LeGrand. We can discuss this further when we touch on areas that bother you."

A subtly attractive offer that had Florenza biting her lip, as if wrestling with an image of herself as a dowdy elder in prison brown. "Heavy," she muttered, then looked up. "I'll go as far as I can."

Abigail warmed her up slowly, taking her through innocuous personal information, age, family, education, abode, some scattered work experience – light sinecures with her father's shipping business and, until her marriage, manager of a chic dress shop the LeGrands owned. Though Abigail carefully avoided her wilder escapades, the jury must have seen a spoiled woman of leisure.

She'd met Whynet-Moir on a Danube cruise in the early summer of 2006. The coincidences of shared home town and shared acquaintances led to a romance quickly consummated and an extended holiday. Vienna, Salzburg, Florence, the erudite lawyer wooing her with his learning in history and the arts.

They flew home together and were regularly seen, in the better social milieus, as the couple to watch. In early September 2006, Raffy won his ticket to the Supreme Court and they married within the month. Among the lavish gifts: joint title to 2 Lighthouse Lane.

All this was narrated in a casual, idiomatic way, as if in her living room. Arthur read much between the lines. Clearly the courtship had the near-fanatic approval of Donat and Thesalie LeGrand, an opportunity to get their naughty girl out of their hair. Let someone else rescue her if she got busted again.

Coddling Florenza, Abigail drew her through their twelve months of marriage, an unremarkable time, he spending long days mastering his new trade, she managing the house. "Believe me, it was a full-time job." A juror made a face, the young restaurant hostess, who doubtless earned the minimum wage plus tips.

"How were you and Rafael getting along?"

"Copacetic."

"What do you mean?"

"Well, we just carried on. Like any married couple."

"Can you expand on that?"

She went silent, and Arthur thought she was about to balk, but she nodded, decision made, and there came a surge of words. "Okay, if I have to get into it . . . How do I put it?

The bloom went off, the thrill was gone, the power went out. I kind of woke up one day and realized we weren't made for each other. Raffy wasn't . . . maybe adventurous is the word. I'm sorry, but people are built in different ways, I guess."

Amazingly garrulous for one recently tight-lipped. Some drugs do that. She was probably on something prescribed, one of those wonder relaxants that don't slow one's thoughts.

"Did the bloom fade for him as well?"

"I'm not sure if he ever bloomed in the first place. I think it was all artifice." She took a deep breath. "Okay, I may as well say it. I'm totally persuaded he married me for my money. I was an object, I was bickered over, the dowry was half of Lighthouse Lane and four million to take care of the justice minister. I knew zero about that. Now it's all over the media."

An electric moment, a loud buzz in the room that jerked Kroop from his reverie. He sputtered, "What? What? This is out of bounds. I have ruled on that very firmly." With a frown at Wentworth, whom he'd pistol-whipped for the same sin only yesterday.

"It goes to her state of mind," Abigail said.

"State of mind? She says she knew zero about it." Kroop looked wounded, astonished that she would defy him. He looked about for help. "Mr. Beauchamp."

Arthur rose with a magnanimous smile. "I move that her mention of the four-million-dollar bribe be stricken from the record."

"Motion accepted. The jury will disabuse their minds of anything they have heard about the subject of . . ." He stalled, unable to find the right phrase.

"Bribes, milord," Arthur said. "The subject of bribes."

"Okay, let's go back to last October." Abigail was anxious to keep her unexpectedly frank witness chugging along. "You and Rafael were preparing to host a literary dinner. How did that come about?"

"It was Raffy's idea, he liked his soirees and dinner parties, liked to fringe about in the arts scene. I don't mean to put him down, he knew lots. Especially literature. He was working off and on at a book, something about intrigue in the Florentine dynasty."

Arthur might have expected that, a dilettantish littérateur, more interested in being between book covers than bed covers. For this, a burden others shared, forgiveness was owed.

"Did you play any role in preparing for this dinner?"

"Not really. When I first looked at the guest list I thought it would be tedious. Until I learned Cudworth Brown had been pencilled in."

"Why did that make a difference?"

"I'd heard him on Co-op Radio a few months earlier. I was out for a drive, surfing the FM band, and this poet was being interviewed and giving readings. I actually pulled over to listen. I was getting a kind of high from him, he had this totally radical attitude, he wasn't delivering the usual crap."

Kroop's eyes widened but he didn't chastise. Arthur was astonished not so much by the loose language but by the drift of her evidence, the way she bulled ahead, unstoppable. "I had a sense of liberation from him, he was where I wanted to be. The whole thing felt kind of life-changing. And I went out and bought his books and his CD. They spoke to me of freedom, of living a life without regret."

A nice turn of phrase, but life-changing? Arthur had never quite seen Cud in that light, Christ-like, with powers to transform and heal. He resisted the urge to glance back and see how he was taking this. Soon it would be time for Felicity to march out again.

"Tell us how you spent Saturday, October 13."

"I just tried to keep out of everybody's way. We had staff buzzing about, caterers all afternoon, and Raffy was totally involved, directing the show. I spent some time in the exercise room, took a drive, did some shopping, got back maybe an hour before the guests so I had time to change." Pausing to catch her breath. Arthur listened, rapt.

"Cudworth was the first to arrive, and when I came down, Rafael had already seen him in. He went out to greet more guests . . . oh, before that, he told me to change the seating cards, he didn't want to be near Cudworth. That was fine with me; I put him on my right. Then I saw Cudworth out on the deck, having a smoke, and I joined him."

"And what transpired?"

"Well, I was ready for him. I had his two books. I let him know how meaningful I found his work, and was about to ask him to sign the books when I thought it would be better to ask him to wait. He didn't really know me yet." A fair paraphrasing of Cudversion. So far, a credible witness with far more to say than anyone expected.

Abigail took her through the dinner talk, Cud in top form, playing up the hard, lonely life of the under-recognized poet. If Florenza recognized the pitch for what it was, a fund-raiser for Cuddlybear, she didn't say. "He told me about grow-ing up in a mining town, being taunted for his literary ambitions, learning to fight by standing up to bullies. He'd hitched across Canada, worked on high steel, sent all his money home to his impoverished parents. He'd had a ter-rible accident with his back, and found his way to his lonely little island, destitute. Only the poetry saved him from suicide. I was riveted, he'd lived a life of pain but a life without compromise."

This was Cud at his bullshitting best, he'd used the thoughts-of-suicide line to seduce a score of Garibaldi maidens. The lazy libertine wasn't capable of suicide. Flo con-tinued to impress as credible, if naive, but Arthur had picked up unnatural intrusions in her relaxed, idiomatic speech, the clever phrases, *a life without regret . . . without compromise.* Was Silent Shawn also a wannabe author, a writer of scripts?

"Tell us about your end of the conversation."

"There wasn't much. He asked if I was happy. I told him I could be happier. No, that's not what I said, I told him I was living a lie. I told him his poetry had awakened something in me."

"During this, was anything else going on between you?"

"I'm not going to downplay it. I couldn't keep my hands off him."

It started with a nudging of knees, a touching of hands. There was audible heavy breathing in court as those hands grew bolder, he going under her dress, her fingers finding their way slowly, unerringly, to Cud's so-called private parts. The intimate details repelled Arthur.

The adventure with the opal ring provided comic relief, a release of erotic tension that helped pacify the several jurors shifting in discomfort.

"I wanted him. That's all I can say. When I think about it now, I feel badly. I'd had too much to drink . . . But that's not it. With Raffy it wasn't . . . it wasn't happening, Cud seemed so different, so opposite, so alive, a beautiful, lustful savage. He was worried Rafael would notice we were playing around, but I'd reached the point I didn't care. I was going to have this man. I'm sorry if that seems abrupt and immature. I was horny and infatuated and a little loaded, and I wasn't thinking about consequences."

She looked at Cud. Arthur swivelled around, saw his puzzled face. Cud's attitude toward their antics had been cynical, he'd believed she'd merely wanted a sex slave for the night. Now he was hearing about infatuation. Felicity looked frozen.

Florenza didn't say much about her exchanges with Cud on the patio, didn't mention asking him to sign the two poetry books. *Never regret. New love blooms as the old lies dying.* The jury could well have read something ominous in those inscriptions.

As to his reading of "Up Your Little Red Rosie," Flo thought it hilarious. "I got it, but I don't think anyone else did, the way he was sticking it to all the stuffed shirts. I remember him smiling at me, like it was our secret joke." She looked at Cud again, who engineered a wan grin.

It was nearing morning break, but no one asked for a break, certainly not Abigail, whose allegedly reluctant witness was sailing along. Arthur was getting antsy, this was definitely liable to spill over to the afternoon.

The other guests gone, the caterers looked after, Flo went upstairs to her husband, already in bed, exhausted from his day and with a slight heartburn. A glass of warm milk and a swig of stomach medicine settled him down, and by the time Flo had removed her makeup he was asleep. Again, this fairly accorded with Cud's version, though in his she'd sounded sinister: *I gave him something to help him sleep.* She bypassed a salient line: *We'll just have to find some way to get rid of him.* Which the jury might have presumed was in jest. Maybe not.

She and Cud met by the pool as planned, took a diversion into the steam room. After a few moments of play, they abandoned the last vestiges of civilized reserve – that's how Arthur saw it. His sense of morals was offended by this hormonally unbalanced pair.

Her account was expurgated but raw enough. They'd been near climax when a cool gust signalled Raffy's presence. He sorrowfully reminded Flo of the time, just after one. Urged her to come to bed. Made complaint about her wantonness, ever so timidly, then left.

"And what did you and Mr. Brown do then?"

"We showered and gathered our clothes."

"Did you and he have anything to say at that point?"

"Not that I can remember."

"Morning break," Kroop said. "Ten minutes."

EBBE AND FLO

Wentworth tried to rise, he needed to walk off the erotic tension, but the boss gripped his elbow with his big farm-toughened hand and pulled him down hard. "What do you make of her?"

Wentworth thought of saying, "Hot stuff," but that didn't seem analytical enough. "She's pretty direct. Mostly telling the truth, except I didn't hear 'Help me escape.'"

"What should we deduce from that?"

"That she doesn't want to implicate her and Cudworth." That seemed obvious, the more Wentworth thought about it.

"You think that's where she's heading?"

"Looks that way."

"A well-crafted piece of testimony." They both turned to look at Silent Shawn's backside as he led his client out for her mid-morning Gitane. "Never trust a sociopath."

Wentworth wasn't sure which of them he was referring to.

The nearest washroom had a lineup, so he went a flight down, past Felicity sulking on a step, Cud loudly imploring her. "It's only you, baby; that was just a oncer, she was suffering terminal lackanookie."

A lavatory on a lower gallery was uninhabited except for one guy at the end urinal. Concentrating on his aim, Wentworth didn't recognize Judge Ebbe until he looked up.

"We meet again," Ebbe said.

Wentworth didn't know what to say, he had trouble peeing.

"Sorry I erupted the other day." Another pause, then a tight laugh. "October 13. I was at home writing a thirty-page judgment. My wife remembers having to drag me to bed."

Ebbe zipped, went off to wash his hands. Wentworth struggled for something neutral to say. "So what do you think Ms. LeGrand is up to, Judge?"

"Covering for Hamilton."

When Shawn Hamilton retook his seat beside Ebbe, still not acknowledging him, he looked a little bilious. Wentworth had seen Flo shrug him off as they got off the elevator. He wondered what that was all about.

Now, as she took the witness chair, she seemed composed, crossing her legs, displaying, vain about her beauty. Not like April, who was accepting of it, serene, confident. He wondered if he'd misread April's signals, that little air kiss as he left for court. Maybe she got a kick out of seeing him twitch and blush. Last night, he'd pretended she was his pillow. He mustn't get distracted from this trial.

Abruptly, not waiting for Abigail, Flo said, "I forgot something." Reaching into her bag. "Before he did his reading, I asked him to sign these." Out came Cud's two books. Abigail moved quickly to retrieve them, opened the covers.

"It's on the title page," Flo said.

Abigail offered the books to Arthur, who waved her off. "For the record," said Abigail, "the first book, *Liquor Balls*, will be Exhibit 47, *Karmageddon*, 48. The former bears the inscription 'Never regret,' and the latter, 'New love blooms as the old lies dying.'" No mention that she'd practically dictated those inscriptions.

Abigail asked how much she'd had to drink.

"A martini and four or five glasses of wine. I wasn't really smashed, but I was feeling it. I may have had one last thimble of cognac with Cudworth, but after that I stopped drinking."

Cud had polished off the rest of the Hennessy, the empty was by the pool. Wentworth felt queasy thinking of the alcoholic intake, he couldn't imagine how Cud could even stand up, let alone make it up the stairs to his quarters. But that's where they went, nakedly clutching their clothes.

They didn't bother to turn out the lights, went at it as soon as they hit the bed. "I'd never felt such hunger, it was like we couldn't get enough of each other. We were oblivious to the world." This was right out of a Harlequin. It was like a lot of her evidence, overstated.

"How long did this lovemaking go on?"

"I can't even remember. I didn't want it to end. I was smitten."

Wentworth was having a little trouble accepting the smitten bit. Horny, for sure. He understood horny.

At some point, booze and exertion had got to Cud, and he either passed out or fell asleep. Flo disentangled from him to go to the washroom. From her second-floor window she saw the eerie sight, a hundred feet away, of her husband's head and torso sticking out just above the eaves of the living room. She jumped up, made out that he was on a chair. "I was spooked, I kind of freaked."

"And what did you do?"

A silence, Flo musing. "I don't want to answer that question."

Kroop scowled. "Miss LeGrand, we are not playing a parlour game, which you can withdraw from at your leisure. This is a *court!*"

"I was told I could object."

"And you have done so, and what you say cannot be used against you. But you must say it. I will not hesitate to hold you in contempt."

"I don't want to implicate anyone."

"Very well, Miss LeGrand, I call upon you to show cause why you should not be cited for contempt."

Another long moment, as her face kind of puffed up, tears coming. "I said . . . I awoke Cudworth, I said, 'That bastard!

He's spying!' Oh, God, I'm sorry, Cudworth, I'm so sorry. Forgive me."

A rush of tears, real or make-believe Wentworth couldn't tell, but she talked through them. "He pulled on his clothes and rushed out, I pleaded with him, I grabbed him, tried to stop him, but he pushed past me. He was drunk, I can't imagine he knew what he was doing, it was like a nightmare, maybe *he* was having a nightmare, and then he was out on the deck, and I saw . . . I saw him push Rafael off balance, down over the railing."

She got all this out loud and clear somehow, despite the liberal use of tissues from a handy packet in her bag. She blew into one, wiped, bowed her head till it was just above her knees, and continued crying. "I'm so sorry, Cudworth."

Arthur shifted about to face her and with huge audacity, and with a voice reaching into every corner of the room, said, "Nobody's buying it, Ms. LeGrand."

Kroop went livid. "Counsel will hold his tongue!" He simmered awhile, got under control, then turned to Flo, a different face, solicitous. "Madam, it would not be fair to add to your distress by continuing now. We'll take the lunch break early, so you can repair yourself, and resume at one-thirty."

The court emptied fast, but Wentworth was stuck to his seat, waiting for some pronouncement from beside him, a word of assurance, a snort of derision, anything. But Arthur was staring at the wall clock, running his thumbs up and down under his braces.

Finally, he said, "I'll want you to phone my wife. I can't handle it."

"No problem." Wentworth was anxious for him, he looked tired. He wasn't sure nobody was buying Florenza's story; some of those jurors looked like they were ready to write her a cheque.

"Are we going to put Cud on the stand?"

"I'd rather cut off my left arm." A drawn-out groan. "You have two days to prepare him." He rose. "I need time alone to think." As he walked off, he sighed and said, "There are many paths to the top of the mountain, but the view is always the same."

⚖

Sinking into a soft chair in the barristers' lounge, Wentworth fiddled with his phone as he worked through what to say to Margaret Blake. He didn't want to tell her the trial had taken a nasty turn, that Arthur had suddenly turned old in front of him. The case was taking a toll, her campaign compounding it.

"I should never have encouraged him to defend that arrogant clown," Margaret said. "What was I thinking?"

"Not to worry, Ms. Blake, he's rounding into top form."

"Where is he now?"

"Well, he went out for a walk."

"I hope he's bundled up, it's very cold."

"He needed time to plan his cross-examination."

"Florenza LeGrand? How is she coming across?"

He may as well tell her, she'll hear anyway. "She set up Cud as the fall guy. We kind of anticipated it, so we're ready. Yep, totally under control. Oh, and Mr. Beauchamp told me to wish you well, he knows you'll do great this afternoon. That goes for me too."

"Give him a hug for me."

On his way to Taco Takeout, his preferred inexpensive eatery, Wentworth tried and failed to conceive of himself hugging the boss. He wished there was some way to buoy him up; he felt sad for the great man, the pressure he was under. It would be tragic to end his career with a loss, a black blot on the archives.

He worried Arthur might falter in cross, wouldn't be able to crack that snake – she'd really pulled the rug out from them, and this had suddenly become a very sticky case. Her evidence accorded pretty much with Cud's, so there wasn't that much working space for cross-examination, no room to contradict her. The boss was handcuffed, didn't dare accuse her of egging on Cud to help her escape a life with boring Whynet-Moir.

I don't want to implicate anyone. Said with a straight face just before she caved in and tearfully grassed on her lustful savage. Silent Shawn had probably come up with that one, it was brilliant. And she'd been good. She, not Leich, wins the drama critics' prize.

He'd expected Cud to come bounding up to the counsel table at the break, demanding the lying slut be charged with perjury, ordering Arthur to carve her to pieces. But he'd wandered out in a daze, abandoning Felicity, abandoning his followers, looking like a man in need of strong drink. What rhymes with disaster?

Tomorrow he'll spend some quality time with Cud, who had better come up with a straight story this time. Wentworth should check to see how Pomeroy has written it.

He wondered where Arthur's walk was taking him. Somewhere in the West End, or English Bay, the deserted beaches of winter. Maybe he was taking one of those paths to the top of the mountain.

He slipped onto a stool, ordered the meatless taco and a side of refries, $7.35 plus tip. Taco Takeout discouraged dining in, but they had counter seating, a polyglot place, skins of many colours but mostly Latino. That cool dude in a suit kind of looked like Carlos. Drawn back to the scene of the crime, to claim his mistress and her fortune.

The Mexican lunged, but Wentworth caught his wrist, twisting until the knife dropped, piercing the taco with a twang. "Who paid you? Silent Shawn?" Carlos winced with pain. Wentworth twisted harder.

"I tell you, amigo, I tell you. Some hombre from Ottawa, I don know hees name."

"Describe him."

"Beard, round face like back of ass."

⚖

When court resumed, Cud and Felicity were back together, seated in the third row. Cud must have been to a tavern, he smelled beery. He continued to avoid his lawyers, which was abnormal. Arthur wasn't any more communicative, he'd returned to court sombre and thoughtful.

Flo looked composed enough, but she'd repaired the damage with too much mascara and eye shadow, like a punk rocker. Wentworth found it odd that her parents weren't here to support her.

"Witness, you're still under oath," Kroop said.

"As if that mattered," Arthur murmured. Good, the boss was getting himself pumped, booting up for his cross.

Abigail had a few more questions, she wanted to nail down Flo's evidence. Were the windows of the maid's room curtained? No. Were they open? No. How well could she see the action? Well enough, she had a good view from higher up, it happened near one of the night lamps. How did the accused make his approach? From behind. Show us Cud's pushing motion. Palms out, arms extended, contact made with Whynet-Moir's buttocks. Describe how he fell. A leg got caught on the railing and he went down headfirst.

Abigail brought out these specifics methodically, Flo unemotional in her responses, detached. As if she was resigned to the disagreeable task of putting Cud behind bars.

"What did you do next?"

"I don't know, I was in a total fugue state. Scared, confused." She picked up the pace, in a hurry to get to the end. "I was gathering up my clothes. I heard the garage doors open, and I looked out and the Aston Martin was roaring out of there. I didn't see the crash, but I heard it. I ran to the house. I was terrified. I didn't know what to do. I went up to the bedroom, half-convinced I'd been hallucinating, but he wasn't there, Rafael wasn't there."

She was starting to blink tears again. Abigail must have decided not to push her any more, she had what she needed. "Your witness."

Wentworth was displeased when Arthur didn't snap his suspenders like usual when about to pitch into a lying witness. You could see it on his face, he wasn't confident, he was distracted. Wentworth didn't want to see a repeat of the bingo hall massacre in 1984, a limp cross, a rare loser.

Arthur liked to stand near the jury when he worked, to fraternize, but he took his time getting there, pausing to throw his first question: "So you didn't know about the four-million-dollar gift to the groom from your father?"

"You're already on thin ice, Mr. Beauchamp." Kroop wasn't wasting any time getting on him, which was good, would stoke the fires.

"I have no intention of mentioning the bribe, milord." Touché. Kroop deserved it. Wentworth will never forgive him for that mortifying dressing down. "Is that right, Ms. LeGrand? 'I knew zero about that,' you said."

"Until I read it in the newspaper a couple of days ago."

"So it was a deep, dark secret. You didn't know how the money was spent."

"That's right." Looking right at him; Shawn had told her to do that, look confident, convinced.

"And of course you didn't know how this dowry, as you call it, came into being, or who helped engineer it."

"No."

"How long have you known your counsel, Mr. Hamilton?"

She seemed taken aback by this shift. "Several years." She looked for help from Shawn, but he only glowered at Arthur.

"You're looking at the tall gentleman in the blue suit on the counsel bench, Shawn Hamilton. He'd acted for your family on several matters?"

"Solicitor-client privilege, Mr. Beauchamp. Beware."

Arthur ignored Kroop's backseat driving. "And they'd retained him on your behalf over several scrapes you got into, yes?"

"I had a hit-and-run a few years ago. There were no injuries."

"A two-thousand-dollar fine and six-month driving suspension."

"That's correct."

"And he acted for you on a charge of assaulting a sales clerk."

"I was acquitted of that."

"Mr. Beauchamp, I will not allow you to establish bad character by eliciting a record of acquittals."

"If her bad character hasn't been established by now, it never will."

Kroop didn't fire back, he was distracted by activity at the door, Judge Ebbe returning late, taking up his spot beside Shawn Hamilton.

"Let us now talk about October 13, but please spare us more details of your intemperate romp with Mr. Brown." Arthur was nestled in beside the jury now, next to the forewoman, Professor Glass. "We have the two of you in the maid's bed. While rising to use the toilet, you claim to have seen your husband watching from outside."

"It was degrading. He was like a peeping tom."

"A peeping tom prefers to stay hidden. He was looking right at you as you stood upright in your nakedness."

"He wasn't making any bones about it."

"And he didn't withdraw, didn't get off the chair, didn't budge. He remained there, you'll have us believe, as the clock ticked away, just watching. You claim you awoke Mr. Brown with shouts and expletives. Now surely in the stillness of the night, your cries carried to your husband."

Hesitation. "I didn't say I was shouting. I was arguing with Cud, trying to push him back to bed."

"And what was he saying?"

"Nothing. He just had this determined look."

"Your husband would have seen Mr. Brown rising and dressing and going outside, yes? And still he didn't stir from his perch."

"Yes, but Cudworth would have disappeared from his view. The stairs go down the other side."

"Let's time this. You have Mr. Brown dragging himself drunkenly from bed, drunkenly looking for his clothes, drunkenly pulling on his pants – that must have been a test – and all the time, you were protesting, pleading, pushing, pulling. Without hindrance, a sober man would have used up two or three minutes. Agreed?"

"I have no experience dressing as a man." She could counterpunch. Point for her. "He did this in an awful hurry."

"In a *hurry*, madam?"

"He scrambled right out of there."

"Oh, no doubt he scrambled. First if all, he scrambled for his underwear, yes?"

"His shorts? I guess so."

"Yes, he was wearing those shorts on his arrest. And where in the room did he find them?"

"I can't remember. I think they were under the bed."

"So he looked all over, then found them under the bed."

"I suppose so."

"And his other clothes had been flung all over the room, yes?"

"Okay."

"And he had to scramble around for them too. Then what – he scrambled out of there in his bare feet?"

"Well, no, he puts his socks and boots on."

"Oh, I see, he was in such an awful hurry, he pulled on socks and boots?"

"I don't know what was in his mind."

"Surely madam, what was in his mind was to grab all his clothes and get the hell out of there."

No response. Kroop let the profanity pass, he seemed engrossed in this exchange. The boss was in a groove.

"And then he must drunkenly tromp down the stairs in his boots, making all manner of noise, and find his way around the house in the near darkness. Two more minutes, maybe three. And somehow after this amazing journey he arrives unobserved behind your husband's lookout. Is that what you'd have us believe?"

"That's what I believe."

"Madam, I don't accept it, the jury doesn't accept it, and I'm sure you don't either."

This was boomed out, and Florenza sat back. Arthur was way off base with that last blast, but Kroop was being unusually patient.

"During this entire interval, you claim to have been watching through the window?"

"Yes."

"Watching your husband as he was staring at you naked at the window, is that what we are to believe?"

"You have to understand, Mr. Beauchamp, I was in an absolute daze. I was in shock. I couldn't move." A shrug. "Maybe you had to be there." Give her another half a point, but the boss was well ahead.

"You made no attempt to warn him."

"Yes, because I didn't think he was going to come to any harm. At the worst, I thought Cudworth would yell at him, maybe, or just talk to him. I wasn't expecting him to do anything like this, even as drunk as he was. I wasn't expecting anything. I was just frozen there."

"Frozen. And for the entire time apparently heedless of the call of nature that got you out of bed."

She had no good answer to that, no memory of going to the can. She was looking increasingly uncomfortable as Arthur continued to work at her in his gently mocking way, throwing in asides about his more logical theory that Cud was awakened not by her but by a scream outside. And that it prompted him to get dressed and hightail it out of there. Kroop admonished him from giving evidence, but mildly. Wentworth suspected the judge wasn't exactly buying Florenza either.

Arthur got out of her that she threw her dress in the wash that night. She couldn't explain why. She was frozen, a mantra that by now verged on the foolish.

Was there a telephone in the maid's room? Yes. Arthur found it beyond comprehension that she didn't immediately call the police, her parents, a friend, anyone. He greeted with head-scratching confusion her attempts to explain why she hid in the wine cellar while Hank Chekoff hammered on the door. She was frozen, she wasn't thinking, she just hoped they'd go away.

When she did decide to call someone, it was Shawn Hamilton. "There were still policemen outside, I could hear them talking, and I took the phone into a little closed-off guest bedroom and called his home number."

"This was at what time?"

"About five."

"Five a.m. Two hours after Rafael fell to his death. You seem to have been frozen for a peculiarly long time, Ms. LeGrand. Did you consume any alcohol during this hiatus?"

"I'd quit hours ago. I was pretty sobered up."

"Any sedatives, pills, drugs, anything that might have aided this frozen state?"

"I smoked a number. Marijuana."

"And what effect did this number have on you?"

"Cooled me out a bit. That's when I phoned Shawn."

"Not your father."

"He wouldn't have answered."

"And you got your lawyer out of bed?"

"Don't answer that question. Mr. Beauchamp, I've warned you once. Solicitor-client privilege."

Arthur smiled up at Kroop like they were sharing a joke. The chief reddened a little when it dawned this was a silly issue. He harrumphed and said, "Carry on."

"And what did you do as a result of talking to Mr. Hamilton?"

"He told me to stay put. I just lay down in the darkness and waited."

Shawn, Donat, and their entourage – an extra lawyer, a doctor, two nurses – showed up forty minutes later, and the sickbed scenario was set up, which sounded pretty fishy, like a cover-up. "So at about seven a.m., when Sergeant Chekoff and his team showed up, you were in bed suddenly very sick, is that it?"

"I *was* sick. I was in very bad shape."

"You'd stopped drinking many hours ago. What were you sick with?"

"I don't know. Worry. I just did what I was told to. I didn't say anything, I didn't argue. It wasn't my idea."

"Whose was it?"

"Shawn's."

Kroop threw up his hands. "Solicitor-client privilege!"

"Privilege does not adhere to deceitful schemes, milord. This young lady has been dancing to tunes of her puppeteer for the last five months."

Arthur's tactic of lobbing the occasional curveball at Shawn Hamilton finally paid off. He was on his feet, red-faced, in a rare fury. "Milord, I must be allowed the right to object."

This deflected Kroop from his original target, and he erupted. "You have no business before this court! Sit down!"

Arthur continued unflustered. "Sick with worry, then, is that it? Worry about what? Your unloved husband's consignment to the afterlife? The perils facing your drug-dealing lover? Or your own skin?"

"All of those, Mr. Beauchamp. For one thing, I was worried I could be wrongly suspected. No one told me Astrid

Leich had seen it. And yes, I was upset at my husband's death, you'd have to have the soul of a slug not to be. And yes . . ." Drawing a great breath. "Yes, I was afraid for Cud Brown, tremendously afraid. I couldn't believe he'd done this, he was in terrible trouble." Overdramatized, only one point.

"Poor Cud. The man you were smitten with. Smitten, you said."

"Something very deep happened between us."

"Love at first sight, is that what we have here?"

"Call it that if you like. Call it infatuation."

"How remarkable. And it carries on to this day?"

"I continue to have strong feelings for him, I can't deny that." A glance at Cud, but it didn't hold, and she dropped her eyes. Cud was a blank, you had no idea what he was thinking. Felicity was gripping his hand, asserting her right of possession.

"And while he was on bail, did you seek him out to express those feelings?"

"No."

"No phone calls? No love notes?"

"I have been acting on advice, Mr. Beauchamp."

Arthur looked long and hard at Shawn. "Yes, I can imagine."

Hamilton had retreated behind his wooden mask, but Wentworth saw rancour in his eyes. Ebbe, though, was enjoying this.

"I believe it's generally known, Ms. LeGrand, that in your youthful years you had a habit of running away from home." Another quick shift, deflecting her from the prepared script.

"A few times. You had to know my situation . . . I don't want to get into it."

"Once to join a cult in Oregon, from which you were rescued and deprogrammed. *Deprogrammed*, madam." Getting lots of juice from that word, letting the jury know she was susceptible to fantastical beliefs.

"The media made a lot out of a simple religious experience."

"Another time, you ran off to Mexico."

"I was seventeen, Mr. Beauchamp. I was restless, immature, and all the other illnesses of youth." A good answer, she'd quickly adjusted to this new line of attack. Point for her.

"While in Mexico, on a farm near Guadalajara, you were arrested on serious drug charges."

"I was arrested as an accessory, but I wasn't really, I was just . . . there."

"Just there? A shed full of pot, cocaine triple-wrapped in feed sacks, ecstasy from a lab in Mexico City. Visitors coming by, smugglers with money. And you only stood by and watched?" A tone of utter disbelief, but she stuck to her story that she played no role.

Kroop asked where this was going, and Arthur urged patience. Carlos Espinoza, Carlos the Mexican, that's where this was going. For six months she'd cohabited with Carlos at this drug depot, which was run so lackadaisically that Wentworth wondered how they expected not to get busted. Maybe they weren't paying the *Federales* enough. The LeGrands more than made up for that, probably to someone high up. Flo was deported after two weeks in the cooler.

Arthur showed her a photo of Carlos, the one where he was handcuffed to a grinning cop. "A dashing buccaneer, a cunning risk taker, two escapes to his credit. Handsome fellow. One could see why you were so drawn to him."

"Well, I was. He was the first man I loved."

"First love. And what happened to this admirable chap?"

"He took the whole blame. He exonerated me, everyone else. He paid for it, did five years."

"And did you correspond during that time?" He turned to Wentworth, who made a show of pulling a file folder from his brief case. Flo darted an anxious look at Shawn as Arthur put his glasses on and picked through the various folded letters. This was a decisive moment: could Florenza be seduced into believing some of her prison letters had been intercepted? Mexican jails were notorious for undelivered mail.

"Yes, we wrote letters, I sent him money."

The boss had got a foot in the door. "Of course you did. And you talked on the phone." He was studying a printed page, not a long-distance telephone record but a list of recipes for making healthy soups and stews from Wentworth's doting mother.

"Yes, we spoke on the phone." Another look at her deadpan lawyer. Not a flicker from him, maybe because Ebbe was scrutinizing him.

"And you flew down and visited him in the jail."

A gamble, but it paid off. "Yes, as I'm sure you know."

"Time and time again in your letters you expressed your undying love for each other." Flipping through pages.

"I'm sure we did."

Arthur adjusted his glasses, pretended to read. "'Our love is rapturous.'" He looked up over his glasses. "That fairly sums it up, madam?"

"I probably wrote something like that."

"And you planned to meet after his release."

"That's right."

"And in fact you did get together."

"Yes, we did." Softened up now.

Arthur took another leap. "Quite a few times."

"A few times."

"Where?"

"Here and there. I did a lot of travelling. So did he. Mexico. Honduras. We met in Paris one time."

She wasn't sure how much Arthur knew and didn't want to risk being seen a liar, that's what Wentworth intuited. So she even admitted to recent liaisons in the States, L.A., San Francisco, Aspen. A few weeks here, a couple of days there, long weekends, posh hotels, beaches, ski hills, financed mostly by Flo, but occasionally by Carlos when he was flush. She made no bones about his trade, drugs; he loved the danger, the freedom. "He wasn't interested in my money, that was rare among the men I'd known." Even the dumbest juror had to see this was not just some sporadic affair, Arthur had opened up a lot of territory thanks to Wentworth's possessive, letter-writing mom.

"He wasn't interested in your money, but you did send him money." Looking at another sheet of paper, a series of figures, Wentworth's budget for 2005, he'd ended up $800 in the hole.

"I sent money."

"How much all told?"

"Over the years, a few hundred thousand."

"More than that." A confident smile. "What was the last payment?"

"I can't remember. It was cash."

"Oh, you handed it to him. Where was that?"

"Seattle." She'd lost eye contact with Arthur by now. Losing points big time.

"Ah, closer to home. When?"

She looked at the ceiling, found no answer there, then said, "That would be August, year before last."

"A little break from your boring husband-to-be, was that it?"

"We weren't engaged yet. I told Carlos I was seeing Rafael, I told him I wasn't, you know, going to be . . . able to carry on with him."

"And how long were you in Seattle with him?"

"A few days."

"Separate bedrooms?"

"We shared a hotel suite. I was a free woman. I wasn't shackled to anyone." Getting back her pluck. "We knew it couldn't go on. He had a different life, a rebel life. I was in the mood for something different."

"So you paid him off, is that what we're to believe?"

"I gave him . . . maybe three hundred."

"Thousand."

"Yes."

"And you mutually agreed not to continue your fifteen-year affair?"

"We did."

"But you did see him again, during your marriage, after you'd decided you'd had enough of it."

"No, we didn't, we didn't write, didn't talk on the phone until . . . after Rafael died. I contacted him during the Christmas holidays, I was lonely."

Wentworth suspected she was covering her ass – if they'd conspired to do in Raffy, they've have planned it out. But Arthur couldn't budge her, she must have felt on safe ground.

Arthur took one of his little detours. "Earlier that year, you decided this marriage was not for you. The bloom had gone, you said."

"That's true, I can't lie about that."

"I don't know why not, madam, it seems second nature." Kroop let this zinger pass, maybe he was running out of gas. "So you must have been contemplating a divorce."

"Well, no, I . . . I didn't have grounds."

"You didn't have grounds for an amicable divorce? Surely they aren't hard to come by. Incompatibility."

"I'd lose millions . . ." A quick look at Silent Shawn, she'd gone off script.

Arthur leaped into the lurch. "Millions. Hundreds of millions. A good lawyer could get a settlement of half your fortune, your shares in your father's shipping empire, the mansion on Lighthouse Lane. But a dead man, Ms. LeGrand, can inherit only the grave."

A long spell of quiet. "The thought never struck me, Mr. Beauchamp." Weak. Five-point loss.

Arthur made what hay he could over Carlos's stay at 2 Lighthouse in January, but Flo had anticipated this. Yes, his visit was clandestine, he'd entered Canada illegally, that's why she'd dismissed the maid for the week and sworn Rashid to secrecy. She wasn't abashed over admitting they resumed their roles as bed partners.

"So while still claiming to hold the torch for my client, you were sleeping with your long-time lover, your true lover."

"I'm not a nun, Mr. Beauchamp."

"No one in this courtroom will disagree. Love at first sight with Cud Brown, you said, an intense, almost religious experience. In truth, he's been set up to take the rap so you can ride merrily off into the sunset with the only man you've ever truly loved." Topped off with his trademark vibrato. Wentworth shivered. Beauchamp was back. "Madam, I put it to you that you and Carlos Espinoza conspired to murder your husband."

"No way."

"In the early morning hours of October 14, he came out from hiding, saw opportunity beckoning, and obeyed your murderous summons." The raised finger of accusation. This was the climax.

But not the one Wentworth expected. Flo took a gulp of air and shouted: "That is absolute, unadulterated bullshit! What I said in this court is exactly what I said to Cudworth's ex-lawyer last month. Ask him! Ask Mr. Pomeroy!"

Arthur darted a look at Wentworth, like he needed help all of a sudden. This had come out of nowhere.

"Excuse me, madam," Kroop said, "exactly when did you speak to Mr. Pomeroy?"

"Last month. He sneaked onto the grounds past Rashid –"

Arthur cut in desperately. "Yes, Ms. LeGrand, we've heard all about that from other witnesses."

"But not this business about Pomeroy," Kroop said. "I'd understood there was an altercation with a British news reporter. Are we now to discover this was Pomeroy? Your predecessor in this defence?"

"Milord, I am in cross-examination."

"Yes, of course, and that will continue. But first I think the jury wants to know what Mr. Pomeroy was doing there, what this conversation was all about."

The jury looked confused, Cud looked lost, Abigail astonished, then a little betrayed – Arthur hadn't been up front with her. Silent Shawn was unperturbed. Maybe that was a smile.

"I would be pleased to be allowed the traditional courtesy of cross-examining uninterrupted."

Abigail said, "I support your Lordship." Smiling at Arthur, enjoying his discomfiture.

"About time, Miss Hitchins, you've been sitting there like a lump. Objection is dismissed." Kroop swivelled to Flo, gave her a sly, searching look. At last he'd caught the detested Pomeroy up to some hanky-panky. "He sneaked onto the grounds, you say? We heard something about a news reporter, so forgive us –" A sweep of his hand to take in the jury, "– if we are confused."

Arthur made a show of sitting, leaning back, his hands clasped behind his head, giving the judge the floor. Wentworth wasn't fooled by this nonchalant act. *Ask Mr. Pomeroy.* That had a dreadful ring to it. Major points for Flo LeGrand.

"Rashid thought he was one of the reporters who parked out front like they owned the street. Yeah, there was this whole scene with the dog and Rashid and Carlos. Then Mr. Pomeroy, Brian Pomeroy, gave me his card, and I checked with his office, and sure enough he was Cud Brown's lawyer. Frankly, he looked a little smashed, he wasn't making a lot of sense, but I realized I needed to talk to him . . . Shall I just go on?"

"Indeed, do."

"I took him inside. Carlos decided to skedaddle, things were getting a little extreme, he wasn't legal. Anyway, I had this strange conversation with Brian Pomeroy. He talked about his ex-wife a lot. And about some kind of book he was writing, a creative non-fiction mystery, he called it, something like that. I couldn't make head or tail of it, I was actually wondering what kind of lawyer poor Cud had hired."

"This is pure hearsay," Wentworth whispered.

"Keep smiling."

"Anyway, he finally asked me if I'd seen Rafael get killed, and I told him, told him everything I said here in court. I told him because he was Cud's lawyer, I was trying to help, I wanted him to know the worst. I knew I wasn't supposed to blab away, but it was a relief to let it out. And as I got to the end, where Cud does this terrible thing, he began acting really strange, paranoid, he wanted me to keep my voice down, the police were listening, the thought police. I asked him what was going to happen to Cud, and he told me he hadn't got to that part of the book yet. Oh, yeah, he asked if we could do some coke. I said, I don't think so, and then he left."

She shrugged, as if to say, that's it. Kroop looked at Arthur. "Do you have anything arising from that?"

Arthur rose wearily. "You had a supply of cocaine?"

"Yes."

"And you were snorting cocaine earlier with your boyfriend?"

"Carlos, yes."

"How much?"

"Several lines."

"Meaning what? Ten, fifteen, twenty?"

"I didn't keep count."

"No more questions."

"Trial is adjourned till Tuesday, nine-thirty a.m."

⚖

As Wentworth slouched past the Leap of Faith Prayer Centre, he was accosted with, "Are you in need of help, brother?"

A lot, a hell of a lot.

33

THE REAL MCCOY

Arthur was in a strange, elaborate house, looking for a way out, but all the doors led to more doors, like a maze, then ultimately to a bedroom where Florenza and Shawn were drinking champagne and laughing at his nakedness. "It's not supposed to end this way," said a familiar voice. Then he was transported to the top of Mount Norbert, lost again, fog rolling in, the view not the same.

He didn't know what woke him from this dismal dream, maybe the distant shouts. "Lug the camera up here!" "Can we get her feeding the goats?"

He dragged himself upright. A hazy day, mists in the fields. A TV van in the driveway, Margaret leading its crew to the goat corral. Nelson Forbish of the *Bleat* was also out there with his camera. Should she get elected, this is what it will be like for the foreseeable hereafter. She'll be the poster girl of the Green set, media everywhere, like wolves circling, seeking weakness, seeking scandal. *It's not supposed to end this way.* The end of privacy.

But Ottawa may be receding from the future. It had been on the radio last night, how she was sabotaged by the chicken-plucker issue during question period, an O'Malley stooge accusing her of being the source of those e-mails. She'd answered truthfully: a youthful escapade by her husband's grandson, unbeknownst to all others. This was met by her opponents with scathing disbelief and by the press with damaging headlines.

Their reunion last night was sad and strained. They gave comfort to each other, but neither felt like making love. "I couldn't not answer," she said. "I couldn't lie. That could only come back to haunt me." Arthur insisted she'd done the right thing, tried to be cheery, but had to hide his despondency – he should have been there. He felt renewed sympathy for Gilbert Gilbert, failed assassin of the Badger.

"Watch out! That's Polly, she can kick!" Arthur had the window open now, could see the camera operator stumbling backwards. A warm day, springlike weather, not a snowball left of last week's snow. The melt had brought crocuses, delicately offering themselves to the sun, violet and yellow. The *Blunderer* was not at the dock, meaning Nicholas had taken his son out fishing, hoping to hide the computer ace from the media.

Arthur had returned to Blunder Bay to find Nicholas fretting about how to handle his son's apparent initiation into the mysteries of the erotic. He'd discovered Nick's iPod, three days lost, in the barn, along with a well-used condom – proof positive, in his view, he'd been seduced by the Estonian temptress.

"He's only fourteen, for God's sake, how am I going to explain this to Deborah?"

Arthur suspected it was somehow sexist of him not to be grossly offended by this apparent tryst, but the condom was evidence that reassured as well as blamed. Still, he was relieved this hadn't happened on his watch.

Nicholas had silently returned the iPod but hadn't confronted Nick, and wanted advice on how to do so. Arthur merely said there was no point in spoiling the farewell party tonight. He wasn't the person to ask for advice, anyway, he'd been a late bloomer, his deflowering at twenty-three a predictor of a lifetime as a sexual non-starter.

He must get up, get out, take advantage of this clement weather. But he couldn't stand, he was paralyzed by feelings of incompetence and failure.

He didn't want to believe Florenza had bested him, but his cross-examination had ended with a crash, its climax snuffed out like a candle, all his hard work in ruins as she entertained with the strange tale of Pomeroy's visit. A credible tale, possibly because it was true. Tough to refute in any event, despite the cocaine.

Yes, he'd made severe dents in her evidence, but the jury expected more, expected the famed barrister to thrash her. They watch too many TV shows, these modern jurors, they demand naked exposure on the witness stand, wails of confession and contrition. He'd been distracted, of course, distressed that he'd been forced to abandon Margaret in her most important hour, but that was no excuse – he was a professional, damn it.

Afterwards, he hadn't been able to look Wentworth in the eye. "You were terrific," he'd said, almost dutifully.

Blame it on Pomeroy . . .

"Big smile." That was Nelson, capturing Margaret, feeding alfalfa to a kid. "Now I want you looking really sad."

"Why?"

"In case you lose."

Arthur finally rose when he saw the television crew packing it up. A quarter to eight; he would have a couple of hours of peace before the obligatory appearance at Sunday service.

But when he came down fifteen minutes later, showered, shaved, and dressed to go out, he found the Garibaldi news anchor still here, at the kitchen table, wolfing down a plate of scrambled eggs and sausages, his chair creaking under his weight. After swallowing, Nelson said accusingly, "Your trial is taking me very close to deadline. I have to prepare two different front pages. 'Local Poet Gets Off' or 'Local Poet Gets Life.' I'm going to need comments to fit each of those eventualities."

The potential for typographical blunders was extreme. "Not now, Nelson."

Forbish wiped his lips on a napkin and rose, fondling his camera. "Then maybe a couple of pictures. One smiling, one sad."

Margaret came in, a little ruffled, shedding her jacket. "God, Polly got him right in the scrotum. Arthur, I put your breakfast in the oven to stay warm . . . Oh, Nelson, I didn't see you."

That seemed virtually impossible. Nelson apologized profusely, adding, "I came in because I was cold, I figured you made me something to eat like usual. Sure was good, tastes like more." When encouragement was not forthcoming, he added, "Can't stay, sorry, I got to put the *Bleat* to bed."

⚖

Never one to mix religion and politics, Reverend Al eschewed religion altogether today, except for some obscure opening passage from *Isaiah*, opting to give his sixty parishioners, five journalists, and the Conservative Party spy a spirited speech about the need for electoral ethics. The spy was a "smart-ass college student," to quote Margaret, like a leech on her for the last week, appointed by O'Malley's team to listen, report back, and sometimes heckle.

They had staff assigned to attack her on call-in shows. Others did midnight forays to steal her posters. A high-powered agency wrote their attack ads. Ottawa had chipped in, millions for a fisheries research station, a Tourism Canada office. All to shore up their thin lead in Parliament amid rumours a few backbenchers were revolting over the bribe scandal. Well, the whole process was revolting. The doughty woman sitting hip to hip with him was a rarity in this vile trade. As the birth mother of Gwendolyn Park, she'd already done more for her country unelected than most of those 308 squabbling Members of Parliament.

And now she's being attacked for being honest, for frankly admitting Blunder Bay was the source of electoral spam.

Arthur would have taken tomorrow off to campaign had the trial been less demanding. He must give thought to his summing-up to the jury, though he was usually at his best extempore. More importantly, there was work to do tomorrow with Cudworth Brown. Wentworth was to meet with him at noon, he'll have to extract an account that doesn't beggar belief.

Arthur was loath to put the loudmouth on the stand, but juries can be capricious when they think there's a case to meet. A verdict of manslaughter would be no victory at all, given the Badger's predilection for giving the statutory max, in this case, life. Knocking off a judge would merit nothing less. Besides, it would teach that impertinent Beauchamp a lesson.

Outside, post-sermon, it was, "Do it again, Ms. Blake, kind of turn to the camera." She shook hands again with Reverend Al as Arthur stood by with an insipid smile.

Margaret had to stay for the women's tea, then stop at the Evergreen Estates neighbourhood yard sale, so Arthur planned to hike home, with a stop at the general store. But here was another photographer following him to his truck, where he'd packed a change into country clothes. The fellow had the decency to quit his pursuit when Arthur went behind his cab to remove his pants. This was not how Arthur wanted to live.

He chose a shortcut to Centre Road, across the cemetery – where he feared he might be residing soon, done in by the stress, the close election, the beastly trial. The graveyard was well kept by volunteers, with its flowerbeds and sculpted hedges. Spikes of daffodils poking through the earth, spring coming an inch nearer every year with global warming. Not much to be done about that. As inevitable as the ultimate dying of the sun, thereby putting into perspective the infinitesimal matter of an alleged poet and his alleged crime.

Cud had reacted strangely to Florenza's testimony, as if confounded, sitting up suddenly as if he'd had a flash, a revelation. Arthur could see him on the witness stand, arrogant and coarse, offending jurors, easy meat for cross. Yet it would be a daredevil's gamble not to let them hear his proclamations of innocence.

The Shewfelts had finally rescued Santa and his reindeer from their roof, Christmas was officially over. Expect another pagan display at Easter, a monster bunny rabbit. Smoke was curling from Stoney's chimney, so he must be up, though it was only noon. "I'll try to come by to look at that dock." This obscure message may have been garbled in translation, given the flustered state of Nicholas, its recipient.

Kurt Zoller's aluminum twelve-seat water taxi was tied up at the store dock, but the only land vehicles around were Makepeace's old delivery truck and Emily LeMay's motorcycle. Unusually for a Sunday, a sparse congregation in the coffee salon: Emily, plus a city freelancer taping an interview with Kurt Zoller, and Gomer Goulet weaving his way from the counter with a fresh-poured rum. "Arthur, we gotta have a heart-to-heart. I heard in the news Cud's in shit, we gotta save him. I'm begging you, from the bottom of my heart."

Arthur veered away from him, past Zoller, who was into one of his circumlocutions. "The way I see it, Garibaldi is a big winner with all this publicity over a sensational murder trial featuring local celebrities, one of who has just walked in – good afternoon, Arthur – who nobody seems to remember I personally defeated his wife in the last trustee election."

The young freelancer looked bored. She must have assumed Zoller was an interesting oddball with his buckled-on yellow fluorescent life jacket.

Virgin oil, five green peppers, sliced almonds; Arthur had written it down this time. "Where is everybody?" Arthur asked Makepeace as he tallied his purchases.

"Ferry dock. Hamish is just about to unveil his *Goddess of Love*. You must have forgot."

He had. The ceremony was scheduled for the arrival of the Sunday inter-island ferry, a popular tourist run.

The freelancer, thwarted in her search for local colour, started packing up.

"Wait, I haven't got around to the event that's going to put Garibaldi on everyone's lips." Zoller launched into a spiel about McCoy's statue.

Makepeace chimed in: "He's gonna get the church ladies all churned up if he shows naked boobs."

"When it's art, it's morally acceptable," Zoller proclaimed, "as long as they're regular breasts. Normal, not exaggerated, like, ah . . ." He stalled on seeing Emily's venomous look.

"Like what, Mr. Art Expert?"

"Abnormal."

"Like your two inches?"

Zoller turned petulant. "I don't get a darn lick of gratification for all the sweat, blood, and tears I volunteer." He checked his watch. "We don't want to be late." He jumped to his feet, urging his interviewer up too. "Stop the presses, all aboard, this is your lead story. I modestly admit to having a role in it."

"What was your role, Mr. Zoller?" the journalist asked.

"If Hamish hadn't been busted . . . forget it."

In his zeal to earn kudos, Zoller had practically admitted his invidious role as fink, widely suspected and, to Hamish McCoy, undoubted.

Arthur followed them out to Zoller's boat, not wanting to miss this. He helped with the lines as Zoller, ever safety-conscious, strapped on a seat belt. Arthur hopped on, but here came Gomer Goulet, tottering down the planks with his mug of rum, crying, "Wait for me!" Arthur helped him aboard.

The reporter was up with Zoller, so Arthur had to take one of the bolted plastic seats, with Gomer breathing alcohol fumes right behind him. "Tell me he didn't do it, Arthur. We still love him anyway, don't we? 'Cause he did it out of love. Love, Arthur, thass what makes the world go round."

The *Queen of Prince George* was cruising into Ferryboat Bay as they barrelled around a sharp point, almost grazing the buoy. Zoller was heading for the public dock beyond the ferry slip, and he went full throttle past the ship's stern.

Arthur was holding on, jolted by the turbulent wake. Though he was standing, Gomer Goulet astonished Arthur by keeping his balance, his legs working mechanically, like pistons, with every rise and fall of the deck. A lifetime as a crab fisher must have adapted him, Poseidon-like, to deal with the seas. "Cud loves her, Arthur, and she loves *him*. Thass a fact! Give them their happiness, for God's sake!"

When the salt spray cleared from the window, Arthur could see three dozen vehicles in the ferry lineup, as many foot passengers and cyclists. All eyes were trained on Ferryboat Knoll, two upswept wings above scaffolding draped with tarps. Hamish McCoy was scurrying about, untying ropes. The Lions Club hot dog wagon was busy. The Highland Pipers were squeezing out "Scotland the Brave." Two news vans. The railings of the *Prince George*'s outer decks were crammed with the curious.

Zoller decided they weren't going to get a better view on land, so he idled and they sat in the cove. The freelancer deserted Zoller, who'd been talking non-stop, and shifted to the back. "I can't make head or tail of what he's saying, Mr. Beauchamp. What's this all about?"

But now the tarps were falling, people were cheering . . .

And there it stood. Arthur had trouble at first discerning the artist's intent. Sweeping curves, a snakelike creature with a great round belly and two knobby bare feet and a curling rat's tail. No, not a snake, that was its serpentine neck, sprouting from between the wings in a graceful arc downwards, past dwarfish male sexual organs, a rat's head seeking entrance into the anal cavity below. The creature was painted bright fluorescent canary yellow, and a similarly coloured life jacket was draped over its upper neck. McCoy had combined the motifs of snake, rat, and canary.

The pipers stopped playing, a final squeal, as from a frightened, yowling cat. A hush. Then Gomer. "Forgive him, Kurt. Oh, God, forgive him. Hamish is our pal, he *loves* you."

Zoller wasn't buying that. The water taxi jolted forward, made crunching contact with the dock, splintered a kayak, and sank a rowboat, whereupon the skipper bounded from his cabin and raced down the planks to shore.

Arthur tied the craft up and made sure all systems were off, then led the survivors along the rickety boardwalk to the ferry slip. Arthur had left his cellphone at the house, so the freelancer lent him hers before racing on ahead for her local colour.

He connected with Margaret in her truck. "I thought I'd take a quick spin out to Ferryboat Bay," she said. "All the media are there."

"Turn back! You don't want to be seen anywhere near here." Parents were sheltering their children from the sight.

It took Arthur a few moments to explain, then a few more while Margaret reversed into a driveway and turned for home. She warned him not to tarry, the barbecue was about to begin.

He hastened to the off-ramp to hitch a ride, waited for foot passengers and cyclists to disembark. Laughter from above, then yelling, Zoller's full-tongued recriminations. Then, closer to his ear, a voice that caused as much surprise as dread. "That's the bleeding edge, man, art as it should be, raw and real."

Cuddles himself, *lupus in fabula*, the wolf in the tale, once again proving his talent for being in the wrong place at the wrong time. The wrong place was walking off a ferry on Garibaldi Island. The right place was Wentworth's office, where he was to have shown up two hours ago.

He was staring up at the *Goddess of Love*. "McCoy's got balls of steel. I feel like a poem coming on."

He continued to extol this masterwork as he led Arthur to a little bench behind the Winnebagel, then said, "I had a brainstorm, too heavy for your apprentice to handle, I need to talk to the top dog." Arthur lit his pipe, waited with foreboding.

"Florenza, man. I didn't know what to make of her at first, but then I realized, hey, this lady sounds totally up front, she's not slagging me off like I expected. It's like I got like a pact with her. If she's got nothing to hide, maybe I should follow suit; it's the honourable thing."

"What do you mean she's got nothing to hide?"

"Hey, she admitted it in front of everybody, she's still carrying the torch and it's burning bright."

"Your ears must have been plugged when she named you as a murderer." Plugged by ego-wax.

"I heard it loud and clear. That's just it, maybe she honestly said what she saw."

Arthur blew out a spume of smoke. This had the earmarks of a horror story, not the way the author wrote it. The hollering above ceased as Constable Pound's van pulled up, emergency equipment on. If Arthur was asked to defend an obscenity charge, he would hide in bed, feign a crippling ailment.

"I'm going to give you the goods, counsellor. Trouble is, I don't remember nothing. Not from the point I passed out in bed with her. Not until I woke up doing the Technicolor yawn with cops all around. So I must have got out of bed like she said, got dressed, gone down those stairs. I was out of it, a zombie. She said maybe I was having a nightmare. I could've been sleepwalking, man. She told me she wanted to be free of him, so maybe I was acting on a kind of post-hypnotic suggestion. That's got to be a medical defence, right, Arthur? I've got amnesia, so you can argue I was in a trauma because of what went on, battle fatigue, what do you call it, post-traumatic stress . . ."

He'd built up a head of stream but finally trailed off.

"Florenza is a psychopath, Cud, much cleverer than you. As clear proof of that she has set you up as the fall guy, and you are more the fool for acting the role."

"Jesus. You think that's it?" He looked hurt, incredulous.

"You are to get back on this ferry and go directly to Wentworth's office. I will try as best I can to explain matters to him. I will see you Tuesday in court."

He walked up Ferryboat Road, his thumb out, but by now the traffic had disappeared up the road. He turned to see Cud shuffling sadly back to the *Queen of Prince George*.

Then he realized he'd almost walked off with the borrowed cellphone. Before returning it, he called Wentworth, who, as expected, was flustered and breathless, worried Cud had gone on the lam. Arthur's instructions were brief. "Find some way to tell him we won't be putting him on the stand."

The view is always the same from behind prison walls.

Arthur ended up walking home, having dallied long enough to see law and order prevail. Pound had ordered the tarps rehung and might have contemplated arresting McCoy, but the crime of obscenity wasn't in his area of competence, so he went off to seek instructions.

⚖

As he trudged into his driveway, not too late, he felt relief that Cud was out of the game, a wild card he didn't have to deal to the jury. That meant more time with Margaret's campaign; he'd been a useless appendage. Tomorrow he will go door to door with her in Cobble Hill or Honeymoon Bay or Ladysmith or wherever her agenda takes her.

This evening he'll put the trial out of his mind, there will be barbecued lamb chops, good cheer, fond farewells. Lavinia was leaving Monday, Nick the next day. Invitations to

Blunder Bay's fetes were highly prized, but the list had been restricted to old friends and neighbours, many who'd already arrived. The two Nicks and the Japanese woofers were at the outdoor brick barbecue, from which sizzling smells were coming. Young Nick was looking sad, his father hawk-eyed. But Lavinia was up in the milking shed with Margaret, chores had to be done.

And here, predictably, came Stoney's flatbed, Dog in the back guarding the beer. They waved at Arthur and the guests, pretending they hadn't planned to crash the party. *I'll try to come by to look at that dock.* That's where they went, with hammers, nails, crowbars, and a chain saw. Arthur was fleet of foot to join them.

"You should have called us earlier, eh, someone could've broke his neck tripping on this plank." Wasting no time, Stoney positioned himself, grunted, levered out a resisting, screeching nail. Many of these boards did need replacing, a task Arthur had set for himself; he'd even piled some fresh-milled wood behind the barn.

"How odd, Stoney, that I don't remember engaging your services."

"That's totally natural, you got a lot on your plate. Thought we'd use them uncured planks you got behind the barn, that way we don't have to charge too much additional for materials. So leave the grunt work to me and Dog and go back and enjoy your fiesta. C'mon, Dog, let's hop to it." He cracked open a beer.

Margaret was watching from the goat corral. She shrugged, surrendering to the inevitable.

"I don't suppose you'd care to join us?"

"Naw, we set our minds to do this."

"The invitation's open." Arthur started walking away.

"Well, okay, if you insist."

Though the house was available for those wishing to take their plates inside, most guests enjoyed the softness of the springlike evening, their bottoms warmed by a roaring pit fire. Nick was squatting by it, contemplative. No iPod, no laptop – he'd hidden that away after his sorry episode with spam. Lavinia stayed far away from him, looking guilty.

There was food enough, even with Stoney and Dog, who, *mirabile dictu*, were on good behaviour. Gossip, election, and weather were the preferred topics, everyone laying off Arthur, as if picking up from his body language that the trial was a forbidden topic.

He conversed little and listened less, proving himself not to be as attentive and amiable a host as the late Justice Whynet-Moir, whose spectre visited, his look of shock and horror as he began his headlong flight. Arthur imagined him getting a flashing glimpse of the last man to see him alive, prayed he hadn't seen a broken nose and red suspenders.

Arthur had become increasingly bothered by his little chat with Cud, who had almost seemed close to confessing, in his guarded what-if way, who'd seemed ready to believe Florenza had bent him to her will by witchcraft.

Stealing a car, one can understand that, the Aston Martin was a temptation too compelling – Cud was always borrowing vehicles on the island. And yes, he had a small record for assaults – barroom scuffles, avenged insults and the like. But propelling someone to his certain death, a man who had caused him no great offence – that seemed not in his makeup. It was hard to accept that Flo's urgent *help me escape* turned him into an obedient automaton.

Fortunately, Florenza's bowdlerized edition lacked those three damning words, and with Cud on the sidelines, the jury wouldn't hear them. Yet Arthur worried they might read between the lines and conclude she was an accessory to murder, the prompter.

Nicholas had got tipsy from a guest's homemade hooch, was becoming voluble. "I like it here, makes you feel one with the earth. Milked a goat, what an experience." They settled onto porch chairs. "Guess you're wondering where Pamela is. She was going to come over, but . . . I guess she's not hip to the country life. Things aren't going well between her and me, Arthur, she's kind of . . . I hate to say it . . . stick-in-the-mud." He laughed. "That's what Deborah used to call me."

With truth, sadly.

"Nick thinks I was doing a lot better with Deborah, he never cottoned on to Pamela. I phoned Deb this afternoon. Woke her at three o'clock tomorrow morning, but she was okay about it. She said I should let the matter be, the thing with Nick and that . . . Baltic floozy. Too traumatic, she said, he'd forever resent me. She's a teacher, I guess she knows these things. Plus Nick is devastated over pulling that stunt with the e-mails. Too complicated for me." He called. "Nick, come here, join us."

He was coming up the steps, a slouch, a backwards-facing cap, a bottle of pop.

"You better run off to bed," Nicholas said. "Early ferry to Vancouver tomorrow."

"Yeah. I have to get something first." He went within, re-appeared in a few moments with his laptop, took a deep breath, shuffled over to Lavinia, and presented it to her. A parting gift. She balked at first; he insisted. She seemed about to kiss him on the cheek, but he whirled about, raced back to the porch, paused there.

To Arthur: "I'm sorry I messed things up for Margaret."

"Can't be undone," Arthur said. "Don't let it oppress you."

"I'll try. Guess I won't see you for a while, Grandpa. Kind of hard to say goodbye." He choked. "I love you." He raced inside.

After the guests left, Arthur did tai chi on the grass. It had been a long time since he'd performed these graceful move-ments, and he felt the tension melt from him, leaving only melancholy from Nick's sweet parting words. Afterwards, he wandered along the beach. "Ladies and gentlemen of the jury," he began, "hallowed in our law is the concept of reasonable doubt . . ."

34

YEAR OF THE RAT

Finally, an off-day for Wentworth, and after a lie-in during which he replayed, critiqued, and catalogued the boss's duel with Florenza, he set out for the office on his Outback. It was a warm day in the winter's dying, but he was blue. Arthur had started off brilliantly, but struggled at the end, like a great opera singer who could no longer reach the high notes. Where was the Pavarotti of the legendary sixties, of the late eighties, the golden decade after he went off the sauce?

An even deeper concern: where was this trial was going? The jury wouldn't hear from Cud. No defence evidence at all. Florenza LeGrand will have got the last word. She hadn't been shy about being seen as spoiled and loose, and in fact was so candid about it she gained credibility. Arthur will have to pull it together for his speech.

It was mid-morning as he dismounted. He was confounded to find Brian Pomeroy arguing with the scrawny born-again outside the Leap of Faith Prayer Centre.

"Find refuge in the arms of Jesus."

"Sorry, I'm an idolater."

"Come home, my friend, come into the lap of Jesus."

"That's my graven image." He gestured at Gassy Jack, pigeon excreta dripping over his eyes. "Who are these people, Wentworth, why have they been allowed to defile our neighbourhood?"

How did he know Wentworth was here? His back was to

him. A madman's sixth sense, or he'd seen Wentworth reflected in the plate glass.

"Let Jesus enter your heart."

"Can he cure the insane? That's my problem, pal, I'm an escapee from a nut house." Brian grabbed Wentworth's elbow, pulled him toward the door. "I'm not supposed to leave without an escort." He looked quickly about. "I want you to keep an eye out for the Facilitator."

In the elevator, he asked, "Are you like the rest of them, Wentworth, do you think I'm crazy?"

"You don't seem so bad right now."

"I am free of him."

"Who?"

"Hector Widgeon. I finished it." He waggled a CD at Wentworth. "Needs an edit, that's all." His other hand held Widgeon's how-to book, from which he recited in a machinelike voice: "'The editing process. Now you may touch and fondle every word and phrase, enjoying the fruits of your sweat.' Sounds like fucking."

"How does your book end?"

"Widgeon did it. He kept a list of judges."

The regular receptionist was at her desk, but they found April Wu at a cubicle near Pomeroy's office. "I've made eight appointments for you this week, Wentworth. Business is rolling in." For the lawyer who leaked the affidavit – that was the sum total of his fame from this trial.

Pomeroy handed her the disk. "I have to get back. Caroline's coming. Where are the pages you did?"

"On your desk, Brian."

"Caroline's coming," he repeated. "This afternoon." He wandered off to the office.

"He seems better," April said. "You cut yourself." It tingled where she touched Wentworth's chin. She wasn't wearing a bra today; you could see the breathtaking bumps of her nipples under that loose top.

"How was your weekend?" he asked.

"Lonely."

What was her scheme?

Pomeroy roared from his office, slamming his door. "Pigeons! They're flying and shitting all over my office!" He was terror-struck.

He was definitely not better. April was on the phone, dialing for an ambulance maybe, or Hollyburn Hall.

"Pigeons! Call the exterminator! I have pigeons!"

He was frantic and loud, his arms flailing. A crowd gathered, Brovak, Augustina, secretaries, frightened clients. "They've come, they've finally come!"

"Who let Pomeroy out?" Brovak yelled. "Anyone got a fucking straitjacket?" He pinned Pomeroy's arms.

April opened the office door. "See, Brian, there's . . ."

Pigeons. That's what Wentworth saw from behind her, pigeons *were* flying and shitting all over. Three of them. A window was partly raised, and Wentworth threw it all the way up, and it took a while to shoo the birds out. The receptionist confessed. "I'm sorry, it was so stuffy in here."

"When one opens a window visitors will come," April said, out of breath, her breasts dancing with the rise and fall of her chest, causing Wentworth weakness.

Pomeroy was finally enticed back in. He stared down at his neat ring-bound manuscript. *Kill All the Judges*, a wet, white turd leaking down the side.

⚖

Cud came in at noon with a cheese and salami hero, crumpled the wrapper, and scored a three-pointer into the waste basket. "I'm going to open my heart, Woodward. Here's the real deal." He took a chomp out of his sandwich.

Wentworth wasn't holding out much hope for the real deal.

"She wasn't there." Talking with his mouth full.

"What?"

"Florenza. She wasn't there when I woke up. She wasn't in the maid's bedroom. This is going to be a little embarrassing." Putting aside his sandwich, patting his pockets. "Do citizens have civil rights here or is the no-smoking bylaw taken seriously?"

Wentworth didn't want to cramp his style. He gave him a saucer, opened the fire escape window. He could take it now. Hadn't had a bout of hiccups for three days.

"I'm sort of half-asleep, and I reach out my arm for her, and she's not there, nowhere, and I'm awake now and I hear this blood-curdling scream, followed by a thump. I'm still real hammered, okay, and I'm not sure if I'm hearing things, but that scream sounded like Whynet-Moir, like shrill. I jump up and I don't see nothing at first, then there's this guy, like this shadowy figure running down the stairs to the pool until he's out of view. Don't ask me for any description, maybe he had suspenders, I was too pie-eyed to get a lasting impression."

Wentworth made notes. He had his barriers up, but this had the ring of truth.

"By this time I was halfway into my clothes, man, I was out the door pulling on my pants. I was spooked, even my short hairs were standing up. I must have grabbed my sock and boots, I don't remember putting them on. The thing is, man, I panicked, I turned yellow. I have to admit it."

Wentworth could see it, his famous machismo deserting him, a humiliation. Real men don't turn chicken and flap off in panic.

"I admit my reaction was totally out of nature for me. Maybe I can shade it a bit in court because the guy left before I had a chance to pull myself together."

"He left."

"Yeah, I heard like a door slamming, a car door, and an engine, so he must've took off. But now I'm looking at another possible calamity. I instinctively knew some bad thing had happened, an axe murder, Christ knows, and I'm a person of interest, man, I'm the logical suspect. I'm not saying these were all coherent thoughts, it was like my subconscious was taking over, a flight impulse, whatever. I don't remember getting into the Aston, I don't remember none of that, I'd gone off the air."

Cud had cried wolf so often that Wentworth couldn't tell if he was being bamboozled. Rubbed to a fine polish, could this account sway the jury? "I have to tell you, Cud, that Mr. Beauchamp thinks you're better off not taking the stand. There are a number of reasons for this —"

Cud coughed out smoke, put up a halt sign, coughed again. "Whoa. Say what? Hey, it's *my* turn. The jury heard from all the liars, when do they hear some truth? That dame set me up real good, I half-believed her bullshit myself until sober second thought kicked in. I finally spill out my heart, and now you guys want to gag me?"

Wentworth began a lecture about the presumption of innocence and how a defendant doesn't have to prove innocence, doesn't have to prove anything, but he could tell Cud wasn't listening.

"Hey, man, I can't go through life with people suspecting I done it because I didn't deny it on oath. I got fans out there, people who believe in me. No way, I got to go over your head on this one. Where's Arthur?"

Hustling votes in the rhubarbs, last Wentworth heard. He called his cell, his home, without response. He ushered Cud to the door. "Stay by your phone."

⚖

"You must try to forget me, I am wedded to the law." But she'd already slipped her top over her head. He was helpless. There would be no escape . . .

His phone twittered. He fumbled for it. His palms were sweaty, and the phone slid onto his takeout tortilla. "April? I mean, hello, Wentworth Chance here."

A gruff male voice. "You know where I can get ahold of your boss, counsellor?" Hank Chekoff, out of the blue. Wentworth was on alert.

"Mainstreeting in the Cowichan Valley, I believe, and he's not taking calls. What's up?"

"I guess I better talk to you. This is serious." He suggested his favourite doughnut shop, a Tim Hortons in the Park Royal Mall. That was a haul, all the way to West Vancouver, but Chekoff couldn't make it over the bridge, he had a heavy day at the office. So Wentworth put on his helmet and pedalled off to the SeaBus.

As the boat planed across placid Burrard Inlet, he sat at the stern watching the spires shrink while fussing on the phone, trying in vain to locate Arthur. He was taut with apprehension, he couldn't tell if Chekoff had good news or bad. Maybe Silent Shawn has confessed. Maybe Shiny Shoes has resurfaced as a suspect. Some crushing blow to the defence? The perp list had shrunk, the defence couldn't afford to lose any more. Carlos was still a solid prospect, but Ebbe, Silent Shawn, Loobie, the Ottawa hit man, all were connected by the slimmest of threads.

At the North Shore terminal, he jumped back on his bike and lit out for the mall, weaving his way through tied-up traffic. A call to April to say he'd be late getting back. "I'll be here," she said.

Chekoff was at a table in the back, behind a newspaper. Coffee and a puffy doughnut shiny with glaze. Wentworth didn't go to the counter, instead pulled a bottle of Zap from his pack.

Chekoff put down the sports section "Watch the game last night? 'Nucks are on a roll."

As Wentworth tilted his Zap, a woman came over, the manager, he guessed. "Sir, can I ask if you bought that here?"

"Take a powder," said Chekoff, lifting his lapel, showing his badge. She backpedalled away. "Okay, you get a head start on this. This here disclosure should come through the prosecutors, but they're all up at Whistler. This sucks, what I got to tell you, believe me. Watching this trial unfold, I figured Cud for a square guy, a typical working-class Joe but with talent. Faults, yeah, maybe a few too many beers on a Saturday night, punches some guy's lights out, that's normal. I had actually bet on Carlos for perp, pinned my hopes on him in fact, the fucking sleazebag."

He attacked his doughnut. Wentworth was holding his breath, waiting for the crippling blow.

"DEA had eyes on him last fall, an undercover sting in L.A. Carlos had a nice business going there for a while, but he went off the radar somewhere around New Year's. That's when he showed up here, I guess, for a week of fun and frolic at Lighthouse Lane. The border's a sieve, illegals pour across it, hell, he could've strolled over and back ten times."

Wentworth let out his breath, slumped. "Where was he on October 13, Hank?" End the suspense, damn it.

Chekoff set a portable DVD player on the table. Fuzzy figures, a restaurant. Coming into focus, a table of five men in casual open-necked gear, and there was Carlos Espinoza, laughing at some joke. Voices couldn't be made out, too much restaurant clatter.

"Saturday, October 13. The Palm, it's where the shitheads to the stars gather, lawyers, agents, managers, connections, dope suppliers. Takedown is today, right as we're talking; it'll be all over the TV. But they ain't going to nick Carlos. Last trace we had, he was in Colombia."

"You just learned this?"

"Yeah, they held on to it until the last minute. Didn't want their case to be compromised, is the way they put it. They're Americans. They're secretive. They don't tell us shit."

⚖

Wentworth was back on the SeaBus, staring forlornly out at the downtown edifices shining gold against the lowering sun.

He'd taken a long run to Lighthouse Lane. What had he expected to see there? Shawn Hamilton's car? A pickup full of potted plants, that's all he saw, the gardener unloading them, a gnarly old guy, not a perp, not Lady Chatterley's lover.

Who was left? Cudworth Brown was who they had left. Cudworth Brown, who'd been jacking them around. Who didn't deserve the sweat put into his case, who didn't deserve Arthur Beauchamp. Maybe what he deserved was twenty to life.

Still no response from Arthur to increasingly urgent calls. Meanwhile, a DEA agent was on his way from Los Angeles to give evidence. This case was starting to look like a big fat loser. Is this how Wentworth's hero will end his career, with a thud? Wentworth Chance, archivist and co-counsel, may have to commit hara-kiri as a gesture of loyalty.

Dodging rush hour traffic, he finally pulled up in front of the Leap of Faith Centre, a sandwich board proclaiming this was "Happy Hour with Pastor Blythe." The cherry-cheeked proselytizer was on a platform with a mike, revving up two dozen wretches waiting for their soup. Wentworth slipped past their barker. "Have you given up hope, my friend?"

Everyone had fled the office but April, supposedly lonely April, braless in tight skirt and loosely hanging top. The kind they just pull over their heads, no zippers, just a little tie in front.

She looked up from a page of Brian's composition. "Was he having an affair with his secretary?"

"Roseanne, yeah. But his marriage was already kaput." When he told her of the latest disaster, she smiled in sympathy and said, "Fortune seldom repeats, troubles never occur alone." Then she asked him out to dinner to celebrate the year of the rat.

He quivered as she took his arm, leading him down crowded Pender, Chinatown, its glitter and neon, the tourist restaurants and souvenir shops. He was thrilled by her closeness, the scent of her, of apple blossoms, but he felt awkward, still unsure of her intentions. She'd insisted on buying, wouldn't go halfers, a modern woman. What did she want in return?

She took him down a street of gingerbread houses and tidy narrow yards, one of them lit by a beckoning strand of yellow lights leading to a back entrance. "It's not legally zoned but has good feng shui." A mom-and-pop operation, Wentworth guessed, known to the favoured few. "I live three doors down." Pointing to a two-storey frame house. "Basement suite. Even better feng shui. Maybe you will come over after for a glass of wine?"

"Maybe . . . I mean yes, of course. I guess they don't serve wine here." A dumb comment, but he couldn't think what else to say. It wasn't like his heroic dreams, where he always had the right line. Did she actually ask him over for a glass of wine? Somehow he was going to blow it tonight, he was convinced.

"My landlord bottles his own Merlot, very pleasant, but potent."

That's how he'll blow it, he'll get drunk, throw up on her rug.

He followed her into a funky small salon, jade plants, a blackboard with chalked Chinese offerings. He listened politely to the sing-song Cantonese of mom and pop and April, but felt out of place, disoriented, as if catapulted into some bizarre fantasy, with possibilities dangerous and erotic, a place beyond imagining, beyond where daydreams dare to go.

He wasn't sure what he was ordering, number two, something called ginger noodles. He was tongue-tied, grateful she carried the conversation, listened in a haze as she spoke of her long-held dream of fleeing the crowded East for Canada, where there was air to breathe. How she'd nearly botched this dream. How she was terrified she'd be deported after she spilled the truth to Arthur. How grateful she'd been when forgiven. Grateful to Wentworth, for taking her side.

That was true, he'd worked at it, entreated Brovak, pitched Arthur hard. Was that was this was about, was she paying off a debt? He worked clumsily with chopsticks, twirling his noodles. Finally, after a long, searching look at her, he asked, "What's the catch?"

"What do you mean, Wentworth?"

"I mean why me? You seem interested in me. I don't get it."

"That's what I like about you. You don't get it. You're not aware of what an attractive man you are. I've known many lawyers. I've not worked with many I liked. Most are full of themselves. You're quite the opposite. So I want to celebrate with you. The year of the rat. It's my birth sign."

"The rat. That doesn't sound awfully auspicious."

She explained that the rat was much admired in the Asian zodiac. Those born under it were seekers of new adventures. She seemed delighted to learn Wentworth was born in the year of the dragon – they were profoundly compatible. "The dragon has a powerful spirit and bravely faces challenge."

He began talking then, slowly at first, not sure why he was opening up, maybe to dispel her notion he wasn't full of himself, telling of growing up in a small town, his Pentecostal mom and self-flagellating father, rueful anecdotes of his social awkwardness and failed romances that, to his surprise, brought smiles and gentle laughter. He was entertaining her! He was amusing! He pressed on, confessed to his silly daydreams, his wonky obsession with the law, his fears he'd never rise to the upper tiers of counsel.

"You will rise. You are a dragon."

She held the door for him. "It is small but cozy."

If there existed such a condition as erotic panic, Wentworth was its victim, trembling in her doorway, under a wind chime, taking in the feng shui. Clean and uncluttered, framed epigrams in Chinese characters, a squat stone Buddha in the corner. A glimpsed corner of a bed behind a door.

April caught him staring at it. "We believe the bedroom door must not face the soles of the feet. Please relax, Wentworth, you are making me nervous."

For a few minutes, an eternal few, he stood about helplessly as jacket and coat were hung, lights lowered, stereo turned on, something electronic, Philip Glass. Somehow he found himself transported to her kitchenette, where she poured the Merlot. "To the year of the rat," she said.

They raised their glasses, and as he sipped from his, she rose on her toes and kissed him lightly on the cheek. A spasm of wine-spill terror, her skirt turning orange, the evening brutally ended. He set his glass down shakily, his cheek tingling with the soft touch of her lips. He felt faint, he was going to blow this, he was going to blow this. No! He was a dragon . . .

He took her in his arms, feeling fire if not breathing it, giddy with scent of her, the feel of her slender, supple body, her mouth opening to his, the electrifying sensation of her hot, searching tongue . . .

Her phone rang. "I'm not home," she said huskily, but they waited until it stopped, still clenched, breathless, the moment altered.

Then silently she led him to the bedroom, and he found himself standing by the foot of the bed that must not face the door. April set down the wine bottle, and they came together again, she on her toes, pulling him to her mouth, pressing against him. Through fogged glasses he made out a white, loose breast, her top askew.

A different ring, chimes, his cellphone. From his jacket, the other room. He tensed, but she still clasped him hard. The phone sounded twice, thrice, four times. April looked shocked as he pulled away.

"Oh, God, I have to *answer*!" Because it would be Arthur getting back to him. At a royally horribly inopportune time. He raced for his phone.

Not Arthur. Dr. Oswald Schlegg from Hollyburn Hall. "Sorry to be a bother, Mr. Chance, but Ms. Wu wasn't by her phone."

"What's the damn *problem*?" His voice cracking with frustration.

"We have a little spot of worry here. It seems Mr. Pomeroy tried to hang himself with a bathrobe cord."

⚖

The cab curled along the causeway that slices like a scimitar through Stanley Park, its lone passenger slumped in the back in torment – not because of Pomeroy, who had apparently botched the job, not because of acute pre-coitus interruptus, though that was bad enough, but because of fate's cruelty, his own bad chi.

Wentworth had not only entertained the woman of his dreams with anecdotes of his romantic fuck-ups, he'd brought the show live to her bedroom. After assuring Schlegg he was on his way, he'd thought of ignoring Pomeroy's plight for, say, the next half hour. But how could he and expect to live with himself?

He'd found himself stammering. But she'd smiled, even laughed at the absurdity of their fate, and kissed him again as she straightened her garments. "It's okay, Wentworth. As my grandmother used to say, find happiness once, and the next time is always better." She'd offered to come with him, but he dissuaded her, he might have to stay the night there.

As for Pomeroy, his neck got stretched a bit, Schlegg said, that was all. He'd got his foot tangled in the chair he was standing on, and a steward heard the racket. Wentworth guessed the poorly executed effort had been triggered by

Caroline's visit. He was wired to her, despite his history of marital negligence.

The skies had begun to open as they pulled off the highway, into the rain shadow of Hollyburn Mountain. Schlegg hurried out to greet him with one of the custodians. "Bertram here was right on the job, fortunately. We're always checking – the doors have no locks, we try to anticipate this sort of thing. I hadn't realized he was that depressed." He led the way into a foyer, speaking softly: "We don't like to bruit these things about, Mr. Chance. It gets some of our guests upset. Some are hardly coping as it is."

Wentworth couldn't believe that was proper practice, suicide attempts must be reported. The Facilitator. Wentworth could see why he repulsed Brian.

"Brian's okay?"

"Little the worse. He was gagging, some neck bruising, strain to the muscles. A bathrobe cord wouldn't have been my choice for this kind of folly, too loose. One doubts whether he expected to succeed at it."

"You shot him up?"

"He's about ready for another." Checking his watch. "Lately, he had been unusually quiet in relating to me – a quite fractious fellow normally. We observed nothing untoward about his wife's visit, no outbursts or screaming fits, but I overheard her talking about a year's sabbatical in Ireland. He seemed rather flattened afterwards."

"You should have anticipated this," Wentworth said, peeved.

Schlegg sourly led them past tables of drug-deadened patients playing cards or backgammon, past a fireplace and conversation pit, up the stairs.

Brian was in his pyjamas, prone, snoring lightly. He wasn't strapped down or anything, but a muscular warder was in a chair beside him.

Wentworth put a hand to his brow, warm, slightly damp. Then he moved to a couch, kicked off his shoes. "Okay, everyone please leave, I can handle him. I'll be staying the night." In his view, it would be healthier for Brian to open his eyes on someone he could trust.

"He'll need his medication . . ."

"Just leave him be."

"One every two hours." Schlegg left a zip-lock bag with four big ugly tablets and led his crew out. Behind the couch were shelves, cluttered with floppies and CDs, crime novels, reference books, psychiatric texts. Several bound transcripts of the Gilbert Gilbert trial, all the schizophrenia evidence Wentworth had slaved over. He opened an Inspector Grodgins mystery, marked up, red-lined, pages marred by doodles and crude critiques. *Crap. Bullshit. Learn to fucking write.* He felt a bulge under his cushion, pulled out a pack of Craven A.

He sighed. This is how it will be, a night on a couch in a junkie wellness centre instead of a bed with good feng shui, and meanwhile there's Cud Brown to deal with, who insists on taking the stand in an act of self-immolation. And Chekoff with his DEA witness. And, mostly, Arthur, the boss, who knows nothing of any of this. He drew out his phone.

Success, finally. "Ah, Wentworth, I've been meaning to return your calls."

He was in a B & B in some village called Tumwat, near a First Nations reserve where he'd spent the day hashing over old times with the chief. He had to tell Wentworth all this, his enjoyable time. "Charley Jumping Deer, an old AA comrade from the less-than-halcyon days of yore. He's a respected elder, he'll bring in 90 per cent of the vote around here."

Arthur's manner turned far more sober when Wentworth described his own less-than-halcyon day. "Carlos was in Los Angeles?"

"Yeah. Jeez, I'm sorry."

A very long pause. "Well, we'll just have to work around it."

"What about Cudworth?"

"He will hang himself with his own tongue."

"What if he insists?"

"Then I walk out!" A beat. "Forgive me. I'll see you in the morning."

Oh, boy, he was pissed. Wentworth hadn't mentioned Pomeroy, and a powerful sense told him not to. "Right. Tomorrow. Um, well, have a good night." He clicked off, sunk into himself, depressed, the bearer of bad news.

"You lost Carlos, eh?"

Wentworth jumped.

"You should've stocked up with more suspects, they have dwindled to a precious few." Brian rose a little, had trouble clearing his throat, winced as he touched his neck.

Wentworth got up, poured him a glass of water. Weird how he just woke up like that. As if he hadn't really been sleeping. "How was *your* day?"

Pomeroy drank, coughed, cleared his airway. "In your traditional parlour room mystery, Miss Marple picks out the stableboy from a host of household staff. Your suspects, however, have sneaked off like thieves in the night before you even got started on the last chapter. You've done it all backwards."

"Are you aware you tried to hang yourself a little while ago?"

"I changed my mind. This is your lesson for the day. 'When you have excluded the impossible, whatever remains, however improbable, must be the truth.'"

"Widgeon?"

"He's been written out of the script. Get with it. Conan Doyle's most famous line." A coughing fit. "Get me a cigarette."

⚖

Wentworth arrived at the courts bleary, bedraggled, still bugged by his romantic megaflop, and in a total funk. He'd slept badly, waking when he sensed Brian wandering to the balcony for a smoke, then turning the television on, a dumb movie, followed by a cooking show and the 6:00 a.m. news. Headline item: film industry prominents swept up in drug conspiracy.

Whatever remains, however improbable, must be the truth . . . Cudworth remains. He was at his usual station in the great hall, but with a smaller corps of the usual clinging groupies – there'd been desertions, telling proof of Florenza's persuasiveness. Cud was ignoring Felicity, staring dully at nothing, looking not a little hung over. Wentworth had called him last night to pass on the boss's confirmation: Cud would not be starring in his own show.

He hurried to the barristers' quarters. On top of everything, he was late, his taxi had got trapped in the Lions Gate squeeze. No sign of Arthur in the commotion of lawyers in the gowning room. One of them called out to him: "A twenty-spot for manslaughter must be sounding pretty good right now, hey, Chance?" He didn't parry, wasn't in a mood to try.

On tier six, the usual milling crowd, the daytime soap fans now outnumbering Cud's diminishing army. Shawn and Ebbe eyeing each other warily, at pistol-duelling distance. Loobie avoiding him; maybe he'd run out of blind alleys to send them down. Wentworth played with the thought of confronting him, accusing him. Sure, right, make an utter fool of himself.

The court was locked, but a deputy let him in, and there was Arthur, conferring with Abigail, Chekoff, and a suit, presumably the DEA guy. Arthur didn't look happy but didn't look down. Didn't look anything. He had to be masking pain.

He finally took his seat, told Wentworth the defence had no option but to admit as a fact that on the evening October 13, 2007, Carlos Espinoza was closing a deal on a quarter kilo of coke in a Hollywood restaurant – otherwise the U.S. agent would be called, and more made of the matter than necessary.

Wentworth still hadn't mentioned Pomeroy's clumsy suicide effort, it could throw the boss off balance in his most important hour. The deputy opened the room, and as it filled, the jury came in. They didn't look ready to decide anything, seemed restless, unsatisfied, itching to hear the other side. That's how Wentworth read them, but maybe they'd had bad Mondays.

The chief justice, however, was in rare high spirits, more bounce to his entry now that he was on the country's highest honour roll, straighter of back, chin up, a smiling nod of recognition to his underlings at counsel table.

Abigail read out the admission of fact about Carlos's whereabouts on October 13, jurors frowning, digesting this unexpected blow to the defence. *We'll just have to work around it.* Wentworth hoped Arthur had a plan for doing that.

"That is all the evidence for the Crown."

"Thank you. Done expeditiously, commendable job. I will hear from Mr. Beauchamp."

"Well, milord, given that one could probably drive a tank through the holes in the prosecution's case, we elect to call no evidence."

That didn't come close to spoiling Kroop's hearty start to the day. "Save the rhetoric for the final speech, Mr. Beauchamp." Adding with a puckish smile, "I'm going to have to watch you today. Hmf, hmf." This didn't bode well. Whenever Kroop had a good day, Arthur had a bad one.

"Madam prosecutor, you have the floor."

Abigail assembled a few notes, warmed up the jury with a few remarks about their vital, historic role, then reeled off a fluid summary of evidence, concise, organized, straightforward, even-handed. Wentworth hadn't expected much less, but she was terrific, especially the way she anticipated the defence.

"Mr. Beauchamp will urge you to disbelieve Ms. LeGrand, but you will have examined her words and manner closely, and, yes, you will conclude she's lived a life of too much ease. You may have found her naive, saucy, irreverent, even sinful – shamelessly sinful. But she offered herself to you without disguise. Blunt, forthright, and with unembarrassed honesty. How easily she could have held back the truth, pretended she saw nothing, shielded from harm the man for whom she'd proclaimed her love."

As she patched up some of the holes Arthur poked in Flo's evidence, a few heads nodded in the jury box. Abigail's hopes to lasso Florenza had been dashed, but she was determined to leave court with at least one scalp. You couldn't blame her; no barrister worth her salt wouldn't covet victory over mighty Beauchamp.

Abigail didn't waste any time crowing over how the Carlos theory blew up on the defence, and dismissed the political cover-up angle as remote and fanciful. Despite her learned friend's valiant attempts, none of his "shadowy suspects" had ever taken form.

As to Astrid Leich: "You will recall how coherently her evidence flowed until . . . well, she had difficulty at the end, but who under the demanding gaze of judge and counsel and jury might not have faltered? Think of the pressure that good, decent woman was under in this tense, crowded courtroom." Leich had made a little slip, a forgivable lapse, soon corrected.

"Bear closely in mind that the man she first pointed to, Brian Pomeroy, the defendant's former lawyer, is the very man she saw at 2 Lighthouse Lane only six weeks ago. They are of similar age, and not dissimilar in body proportion, and from fifty metres not vastly dissimilar in features – close enough in hair colour, facial structure, broad foreheads, strong chins."

Wentworth felt she was making a lot of hay with this. Their noses, he wanted to shout. Look at their noses. Tom Altieri was studying Cud, maybe buying into this, or wanting to. Strong-chinned Cud was slouched there, hungover, brooding.

"The telling fact, and it's beyond contradiction, is that the accused fled the scene in a stolen car. Why? What would

414 William Deverell

possess an innocent man to rush off in such blind haste? Who runs but the guilty? The cowardly, maybe, but Mr. Brown has demonstrated himself to be anything but that."

Wentworth didn't dare another peek at Cud, but this, above all, must have hurt. *The thing is, man, I panicked, I turned yellow.* Maybe the truth, finally, the unmanly truth. Too late.

"He was intoxicated but obviously not blind drunk. He found the key to the Aston Martin, he drove it from the garage, he made it halfway down the street. Was he sober enough to form the intent to kill? That is the question. Drunkenness is no excuse for homicide but does permit a verdict of manslaughter. And you may be of a mind to consider that verdict."

So that's where she was going, not for the throat, no, a high-minded approach, offering a comfortable middle way, tempting the jury with easy compromise. But the jury would not be told that the judge held free rein in sentencing, with life imprisonment the max. Juries aren't allowed to consider such things.

She ended on a strong note, about how the jury should be proud of themselves for taking part in this great, hallowed, democratic process of the common law.

Eight and a half out of ten.

The boss seemed in no hurry to leave court during the break, instead hung about the prosecutors' table, offering Abigail a bouquet of compliments, earning a little hug. As Wentworth headed morosely for the door, Haley joined him. "He's *so* courteous, even in defeat." He merely nodded. "Oh, stop being such a grump, Wentworth."

"Sorry, it's the tension."

"I know how to relieve that."

He was totally uninterested. *Find happiness once, and the next time is always better.* April hadn't written him off. That was the one bright spot of his day.

Cud and Felicity joined him on the terrace. "Okay, that's the crucifixion; I'm ready for the resurrection." He hugged

Felicity. "Rhymes with erection, baby. The jury don't know the real me, Woodward, that's what Arthur's got to work on."

⚖

The boss opened casually, with his standard courtroom jokes, tested over the decades, jury relaxants, he calls them. Then some banter about how, with farm chores stacking up, his wife campaigning, he'd felt bound to take this trial on short notice, and now knew why the first lawyer had a break-down. Laughter.

He schooled them on the basics, burden of proof, rea-sonable doubt, the presumption of innocence that remains with the accused through every moment of the trial. A great baritone tremolo as he concluded with a quote from Canada's highest court: "'If the presumption of innocence is the golden thread of criminal justice, then proof beyond a rea-sonable doubt is the silver, and these two threads are forever intertwined in the fabric of criminal law.'"

Then he made a show of abandoning a folio of notes on the table – I don't need these, was the message – and strolled toward the jury to talk from the heart. It was the old Beauchamp, the master, one of his best, maybe just a step below the McHugh case, the rogue chiropractor.

He made what hay he could over the scandal – Whynet-Moir and the justice minister – telling the jury they must be mindful that someone may have desperately wished to stop Whynet-Moir's mouth, to hush up "what we now know has become an explosive political scandal."

That got Kroop into it. "You're in danger of transgress-ing, Mr. Beauchamp."

The judge remained obsessive about refusing to hear the word *bribe*, stubbornly holding onto his early, ill-thought-out ruling. That didn't deter Arthur, who hammered away at the possibilities: a hired assassin, or someone with a grudge against Whynet-Moir, or someone whose freedom or reputation was at stake, someone who brokered the multi-million-dollar payout — this with a fierce look at Shawn Hamilton, who remained poker-faced under the jury's gaze.

Arthur deftly handled Astrid Leich, reminding the jury of her confident fingering of Brian Pomeroy. *This is the man.* Said twice, emphatically. Having made a completely wrong identification of Brian Pomeroy — "Mr. Brown's former *lawyer*, for goodness sake" — how could her second choice be relied on even in the remotest degree? "Especially after, during a break, my flustered friends for the Crown persuaded her to attempt a last-minute patch job as a means of saving face."

Blaming it not on the sweet soul who erred but on the prosecutors, implying they leaned on her hard. Pretty crafty. Nudged the line, but you do what you have to in a tight case.

"Let us dispel any notion that the issue of manslaughter is of any consequence whatsoever. You can't get there, my friends, without being satisfied to a moral certainty and beyond any reasonable doubt — that, as His Lordship will tell you, is the unswerving rule that must guide you — that my client was the assailant."

He moved down the aisle, a fatherly hand on Cud's shoulder. "Cudworth Brown, who runs the recycling depot on Garibaldi Island, a blunt-talking working man with a bad back, raised in a hardrock mining town, a former steelworker, active in his union, who gave every cent he earned to support his impoverished parents, a poet who writes of love and truth and beauty — often intemperate in manner, yes, as poets often are, lustful, yes, and easily led. But where's the crime in that? Cudworth Brown had done harm to no man or woman. And then one day —" striding back to the jury, voice rising, "— he was chosen to be a victim of a diabolical scheme, seduced into a spiderweb of deceit and trickery. A web woven by the black widow of 2 Lighthouse Lane."

Wentworth felt a shiver wiggle up his spine, the room silent but for an errant cough.

"And who was her aide-de-camp? Her true lover, her only true lover, handsome, dashing Carlos Espinoza. You've seen his photo – compare him with this rough-hewn fellow in the third row, with his slightly off-kilter nose: an honest, plain mug to be sure, but it hasn't won him any beauty pageants."

This drew smiles from the jury, particularly from the Steelworkers guy, who obviously liked the way Arthur was portraying Cud as a good old-fashioned union guy with human faults.

"But, you say, Carlos was caught on police video two thousand miles away from the intended murder. Of course he was! Because this was his carefully crafted alibi. Florenza's real lover is no fool – no, Carlos took pains to be seen in a most public place, a popular Hollywood restaurant, on the night he knew Judge Whynet-Moir would die."

He smiled upon the prosecution table. "Come now, Ms. Hitchins, surely you don't expect the jury to believe that Carlos, with all his criminal connections, would do the deed himself. Nervous Carlos, who fled from his mistress's side when a lawyer came sniffing about – no, he doesn't dirty his hands with the foul business of murder, not when there's a wealthy heiress to pay the shot. What's a few hundred thousand dollars when it can buy the services of the finest assassin the Colombian mafia can offer? Thus saving her from the complications of an ugly, contested divorce and a costly award that would deplete her fortune.

"Who was this hired hit man? We may never know. Why would the police care to put in a lot of extra work when they had an easier target, someone so handy, so nearby? Tunnel vision, ladies and gentlemen, a known occupational hazard that besets our otherwise dedicated constabulary."

Hank Chekoff was taking it okay, he was basically onside. The boss was getting away with murder, building a compelling structure with zero evidence, strands pulled from the air. And the jury was listening.

"When was the scheme hatched? We can't be sure, but its details must have clicked together a few days before the fundraising dinner, when Florenza learned Cud Brown had been sent in as a late substitute. The same self-taught poet she'd heard on the radio, with his backwoods philosophies. A loquacious rebel, but a man of no great complication, unsophisticated in the ways of high society. Yes, the perfect dupe had just become available, a sap to take the rap."

It made sense to set up the client as more dull-witted than he actually was, but Wentworth worried Arthur was putting the blocks to Cud too hard, relishing it too much. He feared to look behind him, hoped Cud was masking his reaction to these slurs.

Arthur spent the next while picking apart and scoffing at Flo's testimony. The charade that she was infatuated with Cud. "She would have you believe the love carried on even while she sought to nail his hide to the wall of this courtroom. She could have said she saw nothing, that's what a woman in love might say, but not such an honourable woman as Florenza LeGrand."

She knew Raffy would be jealous, that he'd be unable to sleep, might wander about in despair, might even spy on his faithless wife – even as the lurking killer waited his chance. And just in case a witness – a neighbour, say – heard something, maybe the slamming of the door to the maid's bedroom, wouldn't it be clever to dress the assassin in the gear the stooge usually wore – "Like this," Arthur said, displaying the cover of Cud's CD, open-necked shirt, medallion, red suspenders.

Nice spin on troubling eyewitness evidence. Wentworth wished he'd come up with it.

A peroration about the risk of convicting the innocent, a softly worded plea that they deliver a verdict that would not haunt their dreams, an evocation of a sombre scene of clanging prison doors and freedom's loss, a verse from "The Ballad of Reading Gaol": "The vilest deeds like poison weeds bloom well in prison-air; It is only what is good in man that wastes and withers there."

Finally, the golden thread again, burden of proof, reasonable doubt. "*Ubi dubium ibi libertas!*" he concluded. "Where there is doubt, there is freedom."

Professor Glass, the forewoman, nodded with approval.

35

CRUCIFICTION

Under a benign noonday sun, Arthur sat with a pizza slice by the Robson Square waterfall, thankful to be alone for a while, a chance to clear his head, relax his weary lungs, his weary soul. An hour of solace from a trial whose difficulties had accelerated exponentially day by day. Never had he known a case turn so inexorably, so unforgivingly, so quickly, from a walk in the park to a stumble at the edge of a cliff.

He was kicking himself for having got into this with such shallow preparation. Three months wouldn't have been adequate. He'd been egged into it, seduced into it, tricked into it. To defend whom? Cudworth Brown, to whom he owed nothing, who made a pass at his wife, who played charades with the lawyers. A monkey with a buzz saw, too much to answer for had he taken the stand, he'd have been ripped apart by Abigail. But was Arthur just making excuses for keeping Cud from testifying?

Arthur hadn't read acquittal on the jurors' faces. Only uncertainty. They'd been responsive enough, it was clear they liked him, but did they like his client? Arthur shouldn't have mocked and demeaned him, that was a mistake, he'd let his antipathy show.

Otherwise a good speech, though not worth the nine point six Wentworth awarded. Arthur wished his gushing junior would stop stargazing and come into his own – he had the right stuff deep down. God knows Arthur would have blown this trial ten ways to Sunday had Wentworth not been around to back and fill.

He played with his cellphone but was hesitant to call Margaret. She'd be visiting polling stations, pumping up her scrutineers. Tragically, he saw no chance he'd be at her side when the results came in. Polls close at 8:00 p.m. Kroop will take two hours with his charge. The jury will be deliberating this evening.

Here was Wentworth jogging toward him, breathless. "I won't bug you, I know you want to be alone, but you got away before I could tell you about Brian. I hadn't wanted to burden you earlier."

Arthur listened with concern to the story of Brian's attempted foray into the afterlife.

"A poorly planned job, you think?"

"Yeah, a custodian was just outside his door."

"Then maybe it was well planned. How did Brian sound to you?"

"I don't know. Crazy but sly. Oblique, you know the way he gets. Still talking about the trial as if it's a book."

"The view is always the same," Arthur muttered. "See if you can reach Caroline; it would be useful to hear her observations. And make sure Dr. Epstein knows about this." Wentworth made a note.

"I don't want you spacing out when Kroop gives jury directions. We are at the point in this sorry trial where we have to anticipate grounds of appeal."

⚖️

Much of the effect that Arthur's speech had on the jury was buried in the rubble of Kroop's rambling charge, a mind-deadening recital of seven days of evidence embellished with legal lectures. But not weighted, surprisingly, toward the prosecution. A fair and ample direction on reasonable doubt, a slightly incredulous inflection in his voice when he recounted Florenza's evidence.

Kroop sent the jury out and asked, "Do counsel have any exceptions?"

Arthur suggested His Lordship might wish to devote a few more words to the cover-up in the high councils of the Conservative government. The latter was for the press, an aid to Margaret's campaign if it made the supper news.

Kroop demurred with a smile. Nothing was getting to him today. Arthur had wearied from the battle, and he supposed Kroop had too, and they'd settled into a grudging truce that suggested Arthur had been forgiven for the worst of his sins and insults.

Word was sent to the jury to begin deliberations. To satisfy Arthur's morbid curiosity, he'd asked April to run off a copy of Pomeroy's manuscript, his true-crime fantasy or whatever he called it. He took it to the barristers' lounge to kill time until dinner.

⚖

"Didn't happen in my day, these school shootings."

"There used to be discipline."

"Too much TV."

"Kids today, they're lazy. Manfred, old boy, can you switch to the local news?"

Arthur was hiding behind the codgers, in his little cove, working his way through a chef's salad, determined to get his strength up for his reception on Garibaldi, a chilly one if he returned ignobly from his quest: the averted eyes, the throat clearings, the commiserative mumbles. "Well, you tried."

Here was Margaret in high definition, poking her ballot in the slot. Cut to a quickie interview outside the polling place. "I'm exhausted. I'm hopeful. The choice is in the people's hands."

The same routine for the other main candidates, followed

by an unfunny sidebar, a costumed independent running for the Clown Party. Arthur dialed Margaret's cell, left a message. "'The choice is in the people's hands.' A splendid example of iambic pentameter. As in, 'Love's gentle spring doth always fresh remain.' As mine remains for you."

Disconnecting, he muttered, "How corny, Beauchamp," then looked up to find himself staring into the penetrating silver eyes of Caroline Pomeroy.

"Corny? Not at all. Lovely, in fact, Arthur. How blessed Margaret is to have a partner who quotes from *Venus and Adonis* instead of *Inspector Grodgins's Last Case.*" She pulled up a chair. "Are women actually allowed in here?" A mocking look about, a sardonic smile – how twinned she was with her ex-husband, her duelling counterpart.

"The bill of rights says so, but you wouldn't know it. The ladies get frozen out."

The habitués had checked her out with reproving looks, squirms of discomfort. Even Manfred looked haughty and displeased as he took her order for a whisky sour.

"The last bastion of male hegemony. I'm surprised at you, Arthur."

"Ah, well, old habitats die hard. They leave you alone here. If it helps, I put eight women on the jury."

"How magnanimous of you."

The trial, the by-election, the travails of a divorced mother of three – these topics canvassed, she said, "Shall we move on to the main topic of this evening's symposium? The headless horseman of Hollyburn. What would cause him to fake a stab at suicide? Lord knows. We talked of the children, of course, and I told him – and I almost grieve to say it – that they deeply miss him." A moment to muse. "As do I, in an aberrant way. 'I, the Masochist,' it's the title of one of my stories."

"I especially enjoyed your portraits from the barrens of academia. You got my note?"

"Yes, and thank you. I spoke to him about my taking
Gabriela, Amelia, and Frank to Ireland. Not as a dig or taunt –
I actually encouraged him to visit. Trinity College, Dublin.
Wilde, Shaw, Joyce, Yeats. A shrine. Never mind. That didn't
set him off. He said, yes, he'd like to visit."

"He sounds to have been unusually . . . together."

"Oh, there was much of the same unintelligible galli-
maufry I'd heard on the phone. Otherwise, he was desperately trying to be on his best behaviour. I suppose he feels
there's some . . ." She shrugged.

"Hope? Is there?"

"Hope? Not till he has a lobotomy." She snapped back her
drink. "Loneliness is easier, chicken soup for the fucking soul.
Though I have to admit he does scintillate against the
dullsville of the professoriate."

A glistening in her eyes caused Arthur discomfort.
"Manfred, I think we have an empty glass here."

Manfred did his duty with a snotty lack of enthusiasm.
"I'll bet you hate being called Man Friday," Caroline said.

"A fake suicide, you said."

"I did twenty years' hard time with Bry; I used to know
when he was lying or faking, but now maybe it's *all* lies and
fakery. Yes, he had a breakdown, yes, he got wired on toot,
and yeah, his shrink probably nailed it with her acute substance-induced delusional whatever. As illustrated by that literary grotesquery he's been potting about with."

"A fair description. I've been reading it."

"If he's been off cocaine for nearly two weeks, why is he
still crackers?"

"They say it takes time."

"Maybe. Or it's all a game."

"He frequently mentioned you when I saw him. He said
you got sucked in. Everything happened because of you."

"He got junked up and went crazy because of me?
Endearing. If you see him again, don't let him show you his

Cuban photos. I humoured him. Beaches, babes, 1960 Plymouths, Habana Vieja, boring, boring. When he went out for a smoke, I dug back further on his hard drive and saw pictures of his rat hole in the Ritz, with its seedy street views. He'd been taking snaps of his so-called followers, one of them the pizza delivery guy. Another was a bongo player. Portraits of the weird. Some cluck in a suit who looked like he'd just vomited off a dock."

Arthur checked his watch. "I suspect my jury are returning from dinner. I should get back to the courts."

"I'll drive you."

⚖

Looking down over the great hall, checking his watch obsessively, Arthur was having one of his rare addiction attacks. Caroline's whisky sours had been the visual trigger, and memories had given it muscle, memories of tense hours, tense nights, waiting for juries, the antidote for nail-biting a mug of whisky or a tall gin. But tonight his only solace, if you could call it that, was *Kill All the Judges*, which he'd ploughed through to its confusing ending. Some flashes of wit. Bizarrely entertaining. Unpublishable.

It was exactly two minutes to eight. He expected the chief would call time out around nine. Attendance was down, only diehards remained, just a handful of Cud loyalists. Only two reporters left. Silent Shawn had not returned from dinner break. Wentworth had gone off somewhere to pace and fret, having picked up that the boss didn't want to be bothered right now.

Here was Dalgleish Ebbe, giving up for the evening, leaving. The judge, who'd avoided Arthur all through the trial, seemed uncertain whether to respond to his beckoning finger. But then he joined him.

"I'm curious, Dalgleish, at your devotion to this case."

"Ah, but I'm your devoted fan, Arthur. Always a treat to see you in action. Brilliant speech, by the way."

"Thank you. A couple of holes have been opened up on the superior court benches. I presume your name is being considered."

"Having been left at the altar multitudinous times, I'm beyond any reasonable expectation."

"Nonsense, an erudite fellow like you is wasted on the lower court." Arthur dug into his briefcase. "Of course, you may not want this to fall into the wrong hands." Passing him the fax from the Law Society's Discipline Committee.

Ebbe gaped at it, his critique of Raffy: "Someone would be doing a blow for justice if he'd drop him down a well."

"Fuck me," said the erudite judge.

"Good luck," Arthur said, then sidled over to a headset-equipped radio reporter. It was eight o'clock. The polls had closed in Cowichan and the Islands.

"Any results yet?"

"I promise to let you know, Mr. Beauchamp."

Ten minutes later, she called him over. "One poll out of 160. Mosquito Flats. O'Malley thirteen, Blake eleven, the Clown two."

He retreated to his reserved space by the concrete railing. There hadn't been a whisper from Kroop's chambers. The old boy was probably taking a nap. Cud was walking in circles down below. The looks he'd been giving Arthur reflected felt insult and betrayal. His neighbour, his compadre, the famed barrister who was supposed to have walked away with this one, had slammed him, shamed him.

He approached the newswoman again. "Coming in now," she said. "Twelve polls heard from, Conservatives 1,008, Green 875, NDP 610, no one else close." Arthur went off to fret. The NDP was holding, bad news. But these must be the mining and lumber camps, small polls quickly counted.

He wondered whether the jury was stuck on something. Some point he might have made clearer. Some argument inadequately put. They weren't buying Arthur's bold assurances about driving a tank through the holes of the Crown's case.

His fingers curled around his phone. Don't call her. Too early.

"Blake 2,558, O'Malley 2,549," the obliging reporter announced.

"Splendid! Hurrah!"

But by nine o'clock, she'd slipped behind. Conservatives 7,518, Green 7,498. Everyone else had fallen from the race.

Before long, Kroop called the jurors in, explained with yawning unction that he didn't want to overwork them after an already long day, and sent them off to a comfortable downtown hostelry.

"What now?" Wentworth asked in the gowning room.

"You go home and get a good night's sleep."

Outside, he waited until Wentworth pedalled off, then hailed a cab.

"West Vancouver, please. Hollyburn Hall."

⚖

They crawled, only one lane open to the bridge, Arthur restive, fidgety, finally digging out his phone. Margaret wasn't picking up, and there seemed no hope of reaching campaign headquarters. He could imagine them, all wired on caffeine, Margaret trying to keep calm amid the tempest around her.

On his tenth try, he finally connected, to a background of whoops and groans, cheers and lamentations. Margaret could barely be heard. "Vocal chords gone. Fingernails too." He didn't realize she'd passed the phone on until his undying expressions of love were interrupted by a male voice. "Oh, you're just saying that."

Arthur asked the voice for the results of poll eighty-nine, Tumwat First Nations reserve. Green forty-one, Tories nine; Arthur had pulled it in. The amiable young volunteer stayed on the phone until the taxi pulled into the driveway of Hollyburn Hall. With three polls uncounted, at a quarter to ten, Margaret had a sixteen-vote edge.

In the main hall, some kind of break-into-groups session was underway, four clusters of patients nodding and murmuring. In one of the circles, a man was sobbing. Elsewhere, a wail. "Everyone hates me!"

Not partaking was Brian Pomeroy, who was in the well of the conversation pit, in repartee with Dr. Schlegg. Arthur made his way toward them, around the crackling fireplace, past a vocalizing groupie: "Don't give me that bullshit."

Brian was lecturing the balding, bearded Facilitator. "Damn right I was trying to send out a message. I was at the end of my rope. Save me, I was screaming, save me from group therapy. I did one, no more. *Everyone* had a story that would drive you to suicide. Stop ragging me, doc, I ain't facilitatable. Bring me an exorcist."

Brian did a double take as he looked up and saw Arthur, on his haunches at the rim of the pit. "Jesus. Don't scare me like that."

Schlegg rose. "No more smoking in the room, my friend, or the privilege may be denied altogether."

"Fank you, please delete yourself, I have an important guest."

"Always a pleasure, Mr. Beauchamp. Please remember the time, we rise early here." He departed, clapped his hands, and the four circles broke up, though one of the group leaders remained clinched in a hug with a tearful male patient.

"Crybaby," Brian said. "If he was a man, he'd kill himself."

Arthur descended into the snake pit. "Everyone but me seems to dismiss your aborted suicide as a rather empty gesture. Given that you have spurned all medical aid around here, one could hardly call it an attention-seeking device. I see it as a scream of despair."

Reflections from the fire played on Brian's face as he twisted away to listen to Schlegg, on a dais. "Good, excellent. So let's have the group leaders up here for final feedback."

"Let's have our own session, Brian." He took Brian's elbow, helped him up.

"Right." He shook himself vigorously, like a wet dog, as if to shed unwelcome feelings. "How's your version of the trial working out, Arthur? Has it ended yet?"

"The jury is out. How has yours ended?"

They paused at the stoop of the stairs. "Widgeon shot Inspector Grodgins and Constable Marchmont, then he hanged himself out of guilt over having made a fool of me. The literary allusion is subtly entertaining – the death of Widgeon symbolizes the death of this novel. Even my disordered mind could tell, in the course of editing it, that no sane man could have written this. I have failed. Thus, the scream of despair."

Crazy but sly, said Wentworth. Cleverly oblique.

His room was neat, the bed made, the only disarray a dirty ashtray and a spilled carton of Craven A on the desk. Brian slid open the sliding balcony door, took the ashtray outside. His trash can was full of manuscript. The DSM-V of the American Psychiatric Association was open beside the computer, a line in boldface, "Psychotic Disorder Not Otherwise Specified."

Arthur joined him outside, drew out his Peterson bent. "'I know too much.'" Arthur repeated the phrase, it was playful, had a double edge. "That's not my line; it's yours, as quoted to me by Dr. Alison Epstein. You told her you knew who did it. You said the clues were all in your manuscript. What I find interesting about that manuscript, other than its lack of such clues, is that however flawed, with all its jumps and starts, it seems not the output of an insane mind. You were able to express insanity more effectively *off* the page."

Brian made no response, pulled on a sweater. It was a cool night, but the rain was holding off. Arthur itched to turn on Brian's radio, suppressed his election-result anxiety.

"I have read enough mysteries to know that an implied contract exists between the writer and his reader. The writer provides clues as his part of the bargain; they may be clever but must be sufficient. What's the point of a whodunit if even the cleverest puzzle-solver gives up because the author has broken the contract?"

He thrust an index finger at Brian's forehead. "The clues were in here, not in the book. You couldn't avoid it, could you? The scattering of clues."

Brian chain-lit a second cigarette. "What clues?"

Arthur gestured at the psychiatric texts, the thick pile of *Regina v. Gilbert* transcripts. "The bulk of those dozen volumes consist of eight shrinks testifying for Crown and defence. Research material for your book, I first thought. But then I realized the transcripts might be an excellent aid to constructing an airtight insanity defence. Just in case."

"In case of what?"

"A glitch, a witness. Anything that might lead them to you." Arthur blew two perfect smoke rings. "The twist that comes out of nowhere."

Brian's face was undergoing a metamorphosis, caving in, the crooked smile fading, the spark of combat dulling in his eyes. Arthur set down his pipe. "You showed Caroline some photos from Cuba. May I see your photo library?"

Brian took a deep drag, looked up in sad contemplation at the black slopes of Hollyburn, the black sky. Then he butted out and led Arthur to his computer.

The photos were grouped four to a frame. A street salsa band in Havana, old-timers playing dominoes, Hemingway's hotel room. "Let's go back to the start," Arthur said.

Brian slid a bar to the top of the screen. Summertime. The three adopted children, raven-haired and beautiful, playing on a beach. "Pre-divorce," Brian said. "I used to get them weekends."

There were three dozen more such shots, all date-marked July 21, 2007. Brian was showing emotion as the photos rolled up the screen, phlegm in his throat. "I forgot about these. God. Look at Amelia. She'll be a ballet dancer."

The next grouping showed several lawyers in a Karaoke bar, a Friday night near the end of the marathon Morgan trial. Brian's defence cronies, a duet miming on a stage, Brovak with an air guitar. Then nothing until a series of shots from an open car window, out of focus, possibly of Brian's former house. Yes, there was Caroline sitting on the steps with one of the girls.

Brian caught him glancing at the radio. "You want to hear the results? Last time I turned it on they were head to head."

"Scroll down to August 18."

"What's August 18?"

"The day Morgan and Twenty-one Others went down. Stop there, please, Brian."

The same picture Caroline had spotted. The cluck in the suit did indeed look as if he'd just vomited off a dock. He was startled by the flash, a dribble coming from his chin. It was not one of Mr. Justice Darrel Naught's more noble portraits, though there was little in the jurist's bland, pasty, oysterlike face worth memorializing.

After a few moments of absorbing this picture: "Are you my lawyer, Arthur?"

"No, Brian, I am your disappointed and lamenting friend."

"It's not anywhere close to cut and dried."

"Perhaps. I know he pushed at you first. There was a witness, though from a distance too far to make you out, except for the suit and suspenders."

Brian retreated outside, lit another cigarette, still staring at the monitor, the ghoulish, soon-to-die Darrel Naught.

"I can't believe you simply forgot taking the picture. The writer within remembered the rules, the genre's demand for the final telling clue."

"I need to explain. Not friend to friend, Arthur. Client to lawyer."

Proof of a mind well repaired. For Arthur's part, he didn't wish to carry the burden of being a compellable witness.

"On this condition. You will accept my advice. Advice only. I don't do trials any more."

"Like what advice? To give myself up?"

"I will simply ask you to make the decision that justice and honour require. And give me no more garbage."

Arthur zipped his jacket, retrieved his pipe from the balcony ashtray, and sat down on a padded plastic chair to listen to a halting history of a soul-devouring effort to save a broken marriage, tearful episodes with Caroline, with the children, bouts with booze and drugs as Brian buckled under the stress of the interminable Morgan trial. A final post-sentencing carousal with fellow counsel, a wake for jailed clients.

He'd found himself driving alone, hungry, his preferred restaurants booked on a Friday night, finally finding a table at Moishe's Steak and Chops, and there, across the room, smiling to himself but otherwise absorbed in his lamb tenderloin, sat Justice Darrel Naught.

For no pressing reason – curiosity, a lark – Brian followed him from Moishe's, saw him enter a parking lot, got in his own car, pursued him over Granville Bridge to Creekside Drive, the False Creek docks. Brian parked on Creekside, hurried to the wharves in time to see Naught making his way to a boat-house known to his firm, Ms. Lefleur its faithful client. Here was food for vengeance, and Brian raced back to the car for his digital camera.

In the few minutes it took him to drunkenly paw through the mess in his car, he missed the awkward moment between Naught and Joe Johal, then was disappointed to find Naught retreating the way he'd come. Brian hurried down the ramp nonetheless, determined to take a photo to pass among the bar, showing Naught on a naughty midnight ramble. If he hurried, he might at least be rewarded with a record of His Lordship throwing up into the saltchuck.

But Naught had straightened up in time to see the camera flash. He swung an arm at Brian, clipped him on the shoulder.

Brian pushed back, abrupt, heedless, and the judge tripped on a coil of rope, went backwards into the water.

"He didn't come up. I panicked. I split." Brian retreated inside, sat on his bed with a rasping sigh of relief. "It's out. Maybe I can finally get rid of it."

"Haunts you, I imagine."

"It wasn't homicide."

"Your flight makes it seem so." He returned inside, his pursuit not done.

"Have you ever killed anyone, Arthur?"

"No, but I imagine it comes easier the second time."

Brian was expressionless, all but his eyes, which held tightly to Arthur's.

"Poor Astrid, needlessly embarrassed. Had she stuck to her guns she might have saved herself from the ridicule that has branded her a false witness to murder."

Brian slumped, his shoulders heaving – with grief, Arthur thought, but it was laughter, morbid and soft. Brian shook his head. "And everyone said I was clueless. I say, Holmes, what else have you got there? Lay it out. 'Whatever remains, however improbable, must be the truth.'"

"Your continued insistence that the two murders were connected. Darrel Naught and Whynet-Moir, you said, were connected in an unusual way. 'You have to dig deep for this one,' you said. A teaser from the author within. Well, there's no obvious nexus between those deaths, no common motive, no shady relationship between the two men. The modus was similar, but that's not what you meant. *You* were the connection."

Brian lay back on the bed in crucifix position.

"Found in your bottom desk drawer by the estimable Ms. Wu was a crumpled page from the *Georgia Strait*, October 11 last year, two days before Raffy's charity dinner. An article with your ex-wife's beaming countenance, a Q and A interview. A note that she'd be dining Saturday night at the manse of a man you abhor among all others, Rafael Whynet-Moir, who you believe slagged you in court, who sundered your marriage, and who, in your coloured view, was openly flirting with Caroline."

Brian broke the silence, still splayed on the bed. "Is this how it should be written? The alleged perp, who for the last month, post-divorce, had been in a disgusting, drunken stupor, wasn't aware that the author of *Sour Memories* had been swapped for Cud Brown and switched to a soiree in West Point Grey."

"That interview piece was found scrunched up into a little ball, as if waiting to be found. Screaming to be found. Here I am, another clue. Outwit me, reader, dare guess before the final chapter that the assailant is none other than the author himself."

Brian snorted, half laughter, half grunt of appreciation. "That's the twist, Arthur." He sat up, looked hard at him, as if assessing him, measuring the extent of his disapproval, his disgust, his capacity for forgiveness. "Thank God you're not a priest, Arthur, you'd be imploring me to turn myself in and praying for my soul. No, I'm in safer hands with Arthur Beauchamp than with the Almighty. The law extends no privilege of silence to the confessional. But confession seals every lawyer's lips."

Arthur understood then that Brian needed catharsis, was consumed by a need to share a searing, gut-clenching secret that had driven him beyond nervous breakdown, beyond the borders of sanity. An irresistible need to escape reality had led to addiction, to cocaine-induced delirium. Now, finally, safely, he could expel the demons.

Brian gained his feet once again, checked the hallway, kicked a slipper under the door as a wedge. He again began to pace, to the balcony and back, smoking, defying house rules. "Okay, here is how it should have been written. The revelatory final chapter. Beset by jealousy, unable to sleep, Pomeroy paced and smoked and drank through the night. If indeed the judge and the ex were balling each other – such were the twisted thought processes of this pizzled perp – the divorce decree must be quashed and the judge suspended from office until inquiries are complete."

He was performing, like the old Pomeroy, loquacious, amorally sardonic. "Armed with his faithful camera, he pulls up a few houses from 2 Lighthouse Lane in his Toyota Tercel. It is nigh on three o'clock as he vaults the stone wall, steals to the back of the house. His initial investigative process will involve checking for Caroline's car. Is it on the street? No. In the driveway? No. Perhaps in the garage. But something was confusing about this scene, lights were on behind the house – that would be the maid's room, of course – and someone in a dressing gown was carrying a chair to the deck railing and boosting himself up onto it." He had two ciga-rettes on the go now, a pace of a pack an hour.

"Pomeroy scrambles across the lawn for a better view. It's the gaseous, oleaginous smarmaholic himself, staring over the gutters. So what we have here are the perp and the peep. Two tragedians in grand Shakespearian style, equally inflamed by jealousy. Pomeroy's alcohol-addled sensory system picks up that something dirty is going on, something evil. What has this monster done with Caroline? A yell: 'That dirty fucker is spying!' Sounds like Caroline, could be.

"Then bingo, the perp snaps, everything goes haywire, love, anger, jealousy, hatred, it all boils up until there's no reason left, just mindlessness." He was breathing hard, his eyes locked with Arthur's, imploring him to return with a fair and favourable verdict.

"Was it just a reflex action, Brian? Or were you bolder now, less afraid of detection – after all, you'd got clean away with the first one, there hadn't been a whisper of suspicion. Second time, easy, they say."

Brian walked stiffly out to the balcony railing, stared down at the rock-strewn slope below. "I went mad, Arthur, I did go mad." There was such a tremor of insistence to these words that Arthur, who had been playing with the buttons on the radio, felt uneasy. He joined Brian at the railing. Close enough to restrain any dangerous, despairing final gesture.

Who could deny him a true moment of madness? It wouldn't be right to abandon him to hopelessness. "Undoubtedly temporary insanity is there. It could be strongly argued. Gib Davidson, I'd suggest, for that."

Brian picked up a remote, turned the radio on, the volume up. Music. Commercials. The news on the half-hour. "Canada tonight chose its first Green Member of Parliament, but only by the slightest of margins. With all polls counted, Margaret Blake leads by twenty-seven votes . . ."

"Thank you, Brian, turn it off."

He did so. "Give her my love."

Several silent minutes. A plinking of rain. Arthur didn't know where Brian's thoughts were, but he was with Margaret, delighted for her, vastly relieved.

Brian cried out. "I didn't plan for Whynet-Moir to die! Christ, I came armed with a camera!"

"Take any pictures that night?"

"No."

"Well, take one tomorrow. Of Cud Brown, as he's being shackled and led to the wagon. Give some thought, as you wave him a fond farewell, as to how you eagerly undertook his defence, then sabotaged it. That's the real twist, Brian."

⚖

"How do you plead?" Kroop asked Arthur, who was bound and gagged on the witness stand. "My client has the right to remain silent," said Pomeroy, who was working rapidly at a keyboard. Despite his mightiest efforts, Arthur couldn't shout, not a squeak. The scene morphed to a suite in the Confederation Club, a telephone ringing. "I can't talk!" he yelled, finally coming awake.

It was Margaret, but she couldn't talk either. Or barely. He heard, "Beat the plucker by a whisker."

"I am bursting with pride."

"Not counting my chickens. Recount ordered."

"You'll win. Ah, you'll be the belle of the ball in Ottawa. I can hardly wait. The nation's capital, its beating heart."

"Bullshit artist."

He would join her at Blunder Bay at trial's end. Now comes the task of finding caretakers for the farm for the several months that Parliament sits. In the meantime, while he waits for the jury, he will do some library time, bone up on the recount process.

⚖

That's where Wentworth found him a couple of hours later, reading precedents. A ballot must be rejected if it identifies the voter. An X consists of any two crossed lines, a swastika qualifies, not a circle.

"The sheriff says they're talking a lot. No loud arguing. At the Gilbert Gilbert trial, we had this army drill major who tied the jury up for five days."

"Has Pomeroy showed up?"

"Yes. He's sitting down the hall. Isn't saying much. Said you spoke with him last night."

"We had a tête-à-tête." Nothing else could be said. It was a monumental task, holding his terrible secrets. Already they had inspired a bad dream.

He'd left Hollyburn last night only after receiving Brian's promise to attend court. There'd been a few final questions. Brian denied that Florenza ever told him she saw Cud do an act of murder. Instead, she teased him. "Darling, he kind of looked like you."

Why had she lied so blatantly to the jury when she hadn't needed to? Silent Shawn, of course – he'd not trusted her account of a stranger rushing at Raffy; it sounded incriminating, a scheme between her and Carlos, the hit-man scenario. Blame Cud Brown, he'd counselled, assuring her it was the safer course.

Not much more was said between confessor and priest last night. It was understood that Brian must make the right decision, the decent, moral one. Understood by Arthur, at least. Whatever remained of Brian's humanity and nobility would be sorely tested if the jury convicted a man guilty of many things – including an unregulated sex drive and the writing of bad poetry – but not murder.

Wentworth was looking pensive, and Arthur was feeling sorry for having been curt. He must speak to the young man's associates about granting him a partnership, long overdue. "You've done stellar work throughout, young man . . . Wentworth?" Far, far away this time.

He came to. "Sorry, what?"

"This case could not have been won without you at my side. If the jury remains out tonight, I intend to reserve the finest table . . ."

"I can't, not tonight. I . . . I have a date."

"April?"

"Yes, yes! How did you know?"

"The old man isn't as tuned out as you think. Picked up the vibes."

"God, I almost blew it with her. I hope I'm not in love."

"Ah, well, given that wondrous possibility, it will be my pleasure to invite you both for dinner and quietly disappear."

Here came the sheriff, huffing and puffing toward them, trying to keep his voice down in the silence of the library. "They're ready, Mr. Beauchamp."

Eleven-thirty, one would have thought they'd have waited until after Her Majesty bought lunch.

It didn't take the courtroom long to fill, lawyers flooding in, the case's faithful followers swarming in from God knows where, like bees to the hive. Cud's groupie base had been decimated further, their hero an anxious, hunched-over, pale imitation of the cocky maverick of yore. He'd been placed in the prisoner's dock for the verdict, Felicity behind him, tissue at her flooding eyes.

Pomeroy was in the back row, staring at his hands.

No surly faces as the jurors filed in, even Altieri seemed at ease with his conscience. Arthur made eye contact with Professor Glass. A barely perceptible smile. Arthur relaxed.

The clerk stood, slowly intoned the options: murder, man-slaughter, innocence.

"Not guilty," said the forewoman.

Kroop nodded, seeming not dissatisfied. "So say you all?" All stood in confirmation.

"The accused is discharged."

Cud couldn't seem to move, then started to back up, stumbled, nearly fell. He was taking great gulps of air, the free air he'd thought he might never breathe again. He began to weep.

Felicity, as if turned off by this show of unmanliness, slipped his grasping, comfort-seeking arms, ran to Arthur, hugged him, and then, to his utter embarrassment, mounted him, her legs curled around his like pincers. "Thank you, thank you," she repeated.

Looking over her shoulder, Arthur saw Brian numbly staring at this scene. He dared one look at Arthur, then joined the crush for the door.

A few minutes later, standing with Abigail at the terrace railing, Arthur watched as Brian, in raincoat now, slouched toward the exit, alone but for the spectre of the guilt that must stalk him for all his days. He turned again, looked up at the man who must forever hold his secret.

"What's with him?" Abigail asked.

"I wish I could say."

Brian whirled, and raced outside. He began to run, darting through traffic, his raincoat flapping in the wind. He ran and ran . . .

© Ken Woroner

WILLIAM DEVERELL's acclaimed first novel, *Needles,* which drew on his experiences as a criminal lawyer, won the $50,000 Seal Award. Since then he has published thirteen further novels, including *Trial of Passion*, for which he won the prestigious Hammett Prize for literary excellence in crime writing and Canada's Arthur Ellis Award for best crime novel. He won the Arthur Ellis Best Novel Award again in 2006 for *April Fool*. He is creator of the CBC series *Street Legal*, a founder of the B.C. Civil Liberties Association, and has twice been chair of the Writers' Union of Canada. He winters in Costa Rica and spends his summers on Pender Island in B.C.

Please visit his website at www.deverell.com.